Christmas
Baby

Christmas Baby

Judy
DUARTE

Joanna
SIMS

Linda
WARREN

Published in Great Britain 2014
by Mills & Boon, an imprint of Harlequin (UK) Limited,
Eton House, 18-24 Paradise Road, Richmond, Surrey, TW9 1SR

CHRISTMAS BABY © 2014 Harlequin Books S.A.

A Baby Under the Tree © 2011 Judy Duarte
A Baby For Christmas © 2012 Joanna H. Spielvogel
Her Christmas Hero © 2010 Linda Warren

ISBN: 978-0-263-25043-5

011-1014

Harlequin (UK) Limited's policy is to use papers that are natural, renewable and recyclable products and made from wood grown in sustainable forests.The logging and manufacturing processes conform to the legalenvironmental regulations of the country of origin.

Printed and bound in Spain
by Blackprint CPI, Barcelona

A Baby Under the Tree

JUDY DUARTE

Judy Duarte always knew there was a book inside her, but since English was her least favourite subject in school, she never considered herself a writer. An avid reader who enjoys a happy ending, Judy couldn't shake the dream of creating a book of her own.

Her dream became a reality in 2002, when Mills & Boon released her first book, *Cowboy Courage*. Since then she has published more than twenty novels. Her stories have touched the hearts of readers around the world. And in July of 2005 Judy won a prestigious Readers' Choice Award for *The Rich Man's Son*.

Judy makes her home near the beach in Southern California. When she's not cooped up in her writing cave, she's spending time with her somewhat enormous but delightfully close family.

Chapter One

As Jillian Wilkes entered El Jardin, an upscale bar in downtown Houston, she couldn't decide whether this was the most therapeutic move she'd ever made—or the craziest.

After all, how many thirty-year-old women celebrated the day their divorce was final when they'd gone from princess to pauper in a matter of months?

Not many, she supposed, unless they, too, had been humiliated by their wealthy husband's serial infidelity.

Eight years ago, marrying Thomas Wilkes had been a fairy-tale dream come true, but the split, which had created quite a stir in the highest social circles, had been a nightmare.

Now that the worst was behind her, she planned to treat herself to one last bit of fine dining and some much-needed pampering at a good spa before retreating to the real world in which she'd been born and raised.

So after leaving her lawyer's office, she'd checked in for the weekend at a nice but affordable hotel, then took a short walk to one of the newest and classiest bars in town. There she intended to raise a glass to salute her new life. No more grieving the past for her. Instead, she would embrace whatever changes the future would bring.

Now, as Jillian scanned the interior, with its white plaster walls adorned with lush, colorful hanging plants and an old-world-style fountain in the center of the room, she was glad she'd come.

She spotted an empty table at the back of the room, near a stone fireplace that had a gas flame roasting artificial logs. After crossing the Spanish-tiled floor, she pulled out a chair, took a seat and placed her black Coach purse at her feet.

For a moment, she considered her decision to make a good-riddance toast to Thomas Wilkes. Another woman might have just gone home to lick her wounds, but Jillian couldn't do that. Thanks to an ironclad prenuptial agreement—and the fact that all of the properties in which they'd ever lived during their marriage had been owned by the Wilkes family trust—Jillian didn't have a home to go to. But she'd remedy that on Monday, when she would find a modest, one-bedroom apartment near the university where she would start graduate school in the summer.

It was a good game plan, she decided, and one deserving a proper kickoff. She was a free woman. So out with the old, and in with the new.

As if on cue, a waiter stopped by the table and set a sterling silver bowl of mixed nuts in front of her. "Can I get you something to drink?"

"Yes, I'd like a split of the best champagne you have."

He nodded, then left to get her order. Minutes later, he returned with a crystal flute, a silver bucket of ice and a small bottle of Cristal.

The sound of the popping cork gave Jillian an unexpected lift.

"Shall I?" the waiter asked.

"Yes, please."

When he'd poured the proper amount, Jillian lifted her flute, taking a moment to watch the bubbles rise to the surface. Then she tapped the crystal glass against the bottle, setting off an elegant sound that promised better days ahead.

As she leaned back in her chair and took a sip of champagne, she surveyed the rest of the happy-hour crowd.

A forty-something man sat to her right, drinking something that appeared to be Scotch. She surmised he was a businessman because of the gray suit he was wearing—or rather, make that *had been* wearing. The jacket, which he'd probably hung on the back of his chair, had slipped to the floor.

When he glanced up, his eyes red and glassy, his tie loosened to the point of being sloppy, she realized he'd had a few drinks too many.

As their gazes met, he smiled and lifted his glass. "Hey, there, pretty lady. How 'bout I buy you a drink?"

She looked away, letting her body language tell him that she wasn't the least bit interested in having a barroom buddy.

Maybe coming here hadn't been such a great idea, after all. She probably ought to pay her tab and head back to the hotel, where she could kick back, order room service and watch a pay-per-view movie.

That sounded a lot better than avoiding glances from an amorous drunk.

But before she could motion for the waiter, she spotted a dark-haired cowboy seated at a table near a potted palm tree, a worn Stetson resting on the chair beside him, his long denim-clad legs stretched out, revealing scuffed boots. His hair, which was in need of a trim, was a bit mussed, as though he'd run his hands through it a time or two.

Funny, but she hadn't noticed him before, which was odd. She wasn't sure how she could have missed seeing someone so intriguing, so out of place.

Who was he? And why had he chosen to stop off at El Jardin for a drink? Maybe it was the relaxed pose of his lean body and the way he gripped the longneck bottle, but it seemed to her that he'd be more comfortable in a sports bar or honky-tonk.

She had no idea how long she'd been studying him—longer than was polite, to be sure. So when he glanced up and noticed her interest in him, her cheeks flushed. She should have turned away, embarrassed to have been caught gawking at him, but the intensity of his gaze—the heat of it—nearly knocked the breath and the good sense right out of her.

Unprepared for the visual connection or for her reaction to it, she finally broke eye contact by reaching into the silver bowl of nuts.

Three almonds and several sips of champagne later, she found herself turning her head once again—and catching him looking at her as though he'd never stopped.

A surge of sexual awareness shot through her, which didn't make a bit of sense.

How in the world could her first post-divorce interest in another man be directed at a *cowboy?* Goodness, Jillian had to be the only woman in Houston who didn't even like country music.

She tried to chalk it up to curiosity. Or to the fact that he couldn't be any less like her ex than if she'd joined an online dating service and specifically ordered someone brand-new.

When she turned her head and saw him still studying her intently, she realized that the interest was mutual. She might have been married for the past eight years, but she still remembered the kind of eye contact that went on between a man and woman who were attracted to each other.

Not that the cowboy was flirting with her. Or that she'd even flirt back.

If she were a free spirit, she might have asked him to join her. But that was even crazier than sitting here drinking expensive champagne by herself and ogling a handsome, dark-haired stranger—and a cowboy to boot.

Okay, this was *so* not like her. She was going to have to motion for the waiter, ask for her bill and then head back to the hotel.

Yet she couldn't seem to move. Instead she continued to wonder who the cowboy was and what brought him to El Jardin.

Maybe he was waiting for someone—a woman, most likely.

He lifted his longneck bottle and took a swig, then glanced toward the doorway as though he really was expecting someone to join him.

Jillian certainly hoped so. Because if he wasn't, if he was unattached, if he came over to her table...

She wasn't sure what she'd do.

Shane Hollister couldn't take his eyes off the classy blonde who sat all alone, practically begging for a guy to mosey on up and ask if she'd like some company.

She'd caught him looking at her on several occasions, too. And each time, he'd been tempted to toss her a smile. But he'd kept a straight face, since the last thing he needed today was for her to get the wrong idea and send a drink his way.

Or worse yet, invite him to join her.

Not that he wouldn't be sorely tempted. After all, she was attractive—the kind of woman some men—especially the insecure and weak type—might put on a pedestal.

Shane usually avoided women like her. Those classy beauties were high maintenance and a lot more trouble than a common man wanted to deal with, especially today.

He glanced again at the entrance, a habit he'd acquired during his years as a detective with the Houston Police Department.

His waitress, a dark-haired woman in her early thirties, offered him a smile and nodded toward his nearly empty bottle. "Can I get you another beer?"

"Sure."

Again, his gaze was drawn to the blonde drinking champagne.

Maybe she was waiting for someone. Cristal, even a split, was a pricey order for someone to consume alone.

Of course, by the looks of that fancy handbag she carried and the clothes she was wearing, he had a feeling that price was the last thing she considered when making a purchase. Even her hair and makeup appeared to have been styled and applied by professionals.

In fact, everything about her implied grace and class, from a sizable pair of diamond earrings, to the trendy, rainbow-colored jacket she wore over a black top and slacks, all of which had to be designer wear.

But even with the bling or the extra effort she'd put into her wardrobe, hair and makeup, he had a feeling she'd look just as stunning in worn cotton and faded denim.

The cocktail waitress was more his type, though— more down-to-earth and approachable. That is, if he wanted to hook up with a woman instead of heading over to his brother's house for his nephew's birthday party late this afternoon.

If truth be told, though, he wasn't all that eager to face the squealing kids, with sticky hands and chocolate on their faces. Not that he didn't love them, but ever since he'd lost his son, it had torn him up to be around children.

And that was why he'd decided to have a beer before facing the Hollister clan today.

Of course, he didn't usually frequent fancy places like El Jardin, but he'd had some papers to sign at the escrow office down the street and decided to stop here, since it wasn't likely he'd be offered anything stronger than a soda when he arrived at Jack's house.

Ever since Joey's death, Shane's big, extended family—none of whom had been teetotalers—had cut way back on alcohol consumption, at least whenever Shane was around.

Okay, so he'd gone over the deep end for a while and they'd thought his drinking had become problematic. He doubted any of his siblings would have handled the grief any differently than he had back then. Besides, he'd taken control of his life again.

He glanced at his wristwatch. He probably ought to call back the cocktail waitress and cancel his order. Yet for some reason, he turned back to the sophisticated blonde who was spending a lot more time studying the elegant flute in her hand than drinking from it—when she wasn't looking his way.

There was something going on between the two of them, and whatever it was held a bit of a promise, at least for the here and now.

If Shane hadn't already agreed, albeit reluctantly, that he'd make a showing at little Billy's birthday party, he might flash her a smile and come up with some clever way to strike up a conversation—something that didn't sound like a worn-out pickup line.

As it was, he'd better leave well enough alone. He was more cowboy than cop these days, and she didn't seem to be the kind of woman who would find either very appealing.

Still, he continued to glance across the room for what he swore would be the very last time.

She wore a lonely expression on that pretty, heart-shaped face. Her frown and the crease in her brow suggested she carried a few burdens herself.

Was she running from her own demons, too?

Or was she just thinking about another lonely Friday night?

Before he could even attempt his best guess, a guy seated near her table got to his feet, swaying a bit before starting toward her.

Shane's protective nature sparked, and he sat upright in his seat, listening as the guy spoke loud enough for the whole room to hear.

"Hey, come on, honey. Don't you want some company?"

The blonde stiffened and said something to the guy. Shane couldn't hear her words, but he suspected they'd been something short and to the point.

On the other hand, her body language spoke volumes, and only an idiot—or a drunk—would ignore it.

Sure enough, the snockered fool pulled out the chair next to hers and took a seat, clearly ignoring her verbal response, as well as all the outward signs of her disinterest.

Shane expected her to put the jerk in his place, but she looked to the right and left, as if searching for the waiter. What she needed was a bouncer, although Shane doubted a place like El Jardin had to use the services of one very often.

Did he dare try to come to her rescue?

Oh, what the hell.

He got to his feet, grabbed his hat—leaving his beer

behind—and sauntered to the pretty blonde's table, determined not to make a scene.

"Hi, honey," he said. "I'm sorry I was late. Did you have to wait long?"

"I...uh..." She searched his eyes as if trying to figure out what he was doing, where he was going.

He reached out his hand to her, and she studied it for a moment, not understanding what he was trying to do—and that was to avoid causing a scene that was sure to draw unnecessary attention to her. But she seemed to catch on, because she took his hand and allowed him to draw her to her feet.

"I didn't think my meeting would take so long," he said.

"I understand. I knew you'd come as soon as you could get away."

Shane brushed a kiss on her cheek, then turned to the drunk. "Excuse me, but that's my seat."

"I..." The drunk furrowed his brow, then got to his feet. "Well, hell. She should've said something."

Shane narrowed his eyes. "She *did*. But maybe you didn't hear her."

"Yeah, well, maybe you shouldn't leave a woman like her waiting. It makes people think she's free for the taking."

Shane's right hand itched to make a fist, but the guy wasn't going to remember any of this tomorrow. And El Jardin wasn't the kind of place that lent itself to barroom brawls.

"Speaking of free for the taking," Shane said, "I'm going to give you some good advice."

"What's that?"

"It's time to call it a day."

As the waiter who'd been working this side of the

bar approached, he asked the blonde, "Is there a problem here?"

She looked at Shane, who nodded at the drunk. "This gentleman is going to need a cab."

Within seconds, the manager of the bar entered the picture, and the drunken businessman was escorted away.

"Thank you," the blonde told Shane. "I wasn't sure what to do about him without making a scene."

"No problem."

"They should have quit serving him a long time ago," she added.

"You're right. And your waiter is getting an earful from his boss as we speak."

"What makes you say that?"

"By the look the manager shot at him when he realized how drunk that guy was."

"I didn't notice that."

He shrugged. "I'm observant by nature."

"Well, I'm glad you stepped in when you did."

"Me, too."

Now what? he wondered.

Well, he'd gone this far, so why not?

He glanced at the empty chair across from her. "Is that seat taken?"

It was a lame line, he supposed, but it was the best he could come up with at the moment.

"No, it's not. Would you like to join me?"

Well, how about that? He'd made it to first base. Before pulling out the chair, he extended his hand in greeting. "My name is Shane Hollister."

"Jillian Wilkes." As their palms met and her fingers slipped around his, a warm thrill shimmied up his arm and sent his senses reeling.

He had to force himself to release her hand, and as he did so, they each took a seat.

As much as he hated pickup lines and all the small talk that went into meeting someone for the first time, he realized there wasn't any way around it.

"So what brings you to El Jardin?" he asked.

"I came for a glass of champagne." She smiled, as though that made perfect sense, but the detective who still lived somewhere deep within found that hard to believe.

She must have read the question in his gaze, because her demeanor grew shy and uneasy.

Why? he wondered, more curious about her than ever. What was her story? Why would a woman like her be in a sophisticated bar all by herself?

Shane glanced at the nearly full bottle. "Are you celebrating a birthday or something?"

"Actually, yes. My divorce is final today."

He nodded, as though that was a perfectly good reason to drink alone. Heck, he'd downed nearly a bottle of whiskey after his.

Jillian didn't appear to be tying one on, though. He hadn't seen her take more than an occasional sip. It must be some kind of mock celebration, which suggested the breakup hadn't been her idea.

If not, what kind of man let a woman like her slip through his fingers? Or was there more to Jillian Wilkes than just a pretty face and graceful style?

Was she a spendthrift? Or someone who didn't appreciate a man's family or his job?

Shane could relate to that, but he wasn't planning to talk about his past, let alone think about it. So he turned the conversation back to her. "How long were you married?"

"Nearly eight years."

"Kids?"

A shadow darkened those sea-blue eyes. "No."

Had they split for that reason? Some people wanted children; others didn't.

He regretted his curiosity, yet couldn't shake the raging interest. "Something tells me you're only putting on a happy face."

She twisted a silky strand of hair in a nervous fashion. "I'll be okay. *Really.* And to be honest, I'm looking forward to the changes my new life will bring."

"Was the divorce your idea?" Shane didn't know why it mattered. But it did.

"I had higher expectations from the marriage than he did." She shrugged, then said, "I believe that promises should be kept, that marriages are meant to last and that people in love need to honor and protect each other from heartbreak, not dish it out."

The guy must have screwed around on her. If so, he was a fool. Or so it seemed. "He left you for someone else?"

"A lot of somebodies." She lifted her glass, took a sip.

He watched the movements in her throat as she swallowed, amazed at how something so simple, so basic, could practically mesmerize him and send his blood humming through his veins.

She leaned forward. "And what about you, Shane?"

What about *him?*

He wasn't about to spill his guts. Still, her self-disclosure was a little refreshing, and he found himself admitting, "I *was* married, but not anymore."

"Do you mind if I ask why not?"

Yeah, he minded. He'd rather keep things focused on her and on why she was here. On the soft sound of her voice, the stunning blue of her eyes, the graceful way she sat before a glass of champagne and hardly took a drink.

But he supposed it wouldn't hurt to be honest.

"My ex-wife didn't like my job," he admitted.

She'd also resented his family. But he kept part of the equation to himself.

"What do you do for a living?" Jillian asked.

He hesitated before answering. "I'm a ranch hand on a little spread about two hours from here. But when I was married, I had a job that kept me away from home a lot."

He'd also had a competent—and beautiful—female partner who'd managed to gain the respect of the entire precinct, and a wife who'd been jealous of the time they'd spent together, even though it had always been work-related. But there really wasn't any reason to go into that.

"My husband," she began, "or rather, my *ex*-husband, traveled on business, too. But I hadn't bargained on his infidelity while he was on the road, and I refused to forgive him for it."

Something in her eyes, in the gentle tone of her voice, convinced him she was being honest.

Again, his conscience rose up, suggesting he unload his whole story on her. But what was the use? He knew nothing would amount from this...whatever *this* was. A mere conversation, he supposed. A pleasant diversion for two battered ships passing on a lonely night.

It was too early to predict anything more. And with him living and working two hours away in Brighton Valley... Well, there wasn't much chance of *this* becoming anything else.

She leaned forward. "Can I ask you a question?"

"Sure, go ahead." But Shane couldn't guarantee an answer.

"Do all men cheat?" Those brilliant tropical-blue eyes nailed him to the back of his seat. "Did *you?*"

The raw emotion bursting from her question—both of them, actually—took him aback, but he was glad he could be open and honest with her, at least about that. "I suppose a lot of men are tempted, and some give in to it. But I didn't."

He'd been brought up in the church and had been an altar boy, which didn't necessarily mean anything. But more important, his parents had been happily married for nearly forty years. Divorce had never seemed like an option to him. And neither had lying to or cheating on a spouse.

"I'm glad to hear that." She slid him a pretty, relief-filled smile, as if he were some kind of hero.

A man could get used to having a woman look at him like that. And while Shane had never really thought of himself as particularly heroic, even when he'd been one of Houston's finest, it was nice to be appreciated for the values he did have.

"I don't suppose you'd like to join me for dinner," she said.

Her suggestion, which was more than a little tempting, knocked him off kilter, especially since he had other plans.

He didn't need to look at his watch again to know that it was time for him to head across town to Jack's house for that party. Nor did it take much for him to envision a houseful of kids on sugar highs.

But that kind of scene didn't bother him too much. What really got to him, what shook him to the core, was the sight of an infant nursing at its mother's breast or a toddler bouncing on daddy's knee.

He loved his nieces and nephews—even the babies. He really *did.* It's just that whenever he was around them, he was reminded of his loss and his pain all over again.

"It would be my treat," Jillian said, those azure eyes luring him to forget what he'd set out to do in Houston today—and soundly winning the battle.

"Either I pay for dinner or we split it," he said. "I'm old-fashioned about things like that."

"All right. We'll split it, then." She blessed him with an appreciative smile. "I've never liked eating alone."

Riding solo—at meals or through life—had become a habit for Shane, but right now, he was looking forward to spending a little more time with Jillian, even if he knew that's as far as things would go.

"Where do you want to have dinner?" he asked.

"I have a room at a hotel down the street. Why don't we eat there?"

In her room?

Or at the hotel?

"They have a couple of nice restaurants to choose from," she added.

Okay, so she hadn't issued a dinner-with-benefits invitation.

"Eating at the hotel sounds good to me."

Besides, if the stars aligned just right, the hotel would certainly be…convenient.

And for some reason, Shane was feeling incredibly lucky tonight.

Chapter Two

Nearly four weeks later, Jillian stood in the small bathroom of her apartment and stared at the results of the home pregnancy test she'd purchased earlier that day.

Her tummy clenched as she watched a light blue plus sign grow darker and brighter, providing the news she couldn't quite grasp.

Pregnant?

How could that be? Surely there was a mistake.

She blinked twice, hoping that her vision would clear, that the blue would fade to white, that the obvious result in front of her wasn't real. But the truth was impossible to ignore. She conceived a baby the one and only time she'd slept with a stranger.

"This can't possibly be happening," she said aloud, as if she could actually argue with reality. "We used protection that night."

But her words merely bounced off the pale green bathroom walls.

Was an unexpected pregnancy fate's way of punishing her for an indiscretion she'd never have again?

If so, it didn't seem fair. After all, it wasn't as if she'd set out to find someone to help her make it through the first night of her post-divorce life. She'd been too caught up in the legal and emotional aspects of the paperwork she'd just signed, the small settlement she'd received and the pain of Thomas's betrayal to even give a new relationship a second thought.

She blew out a ragged sigh, still unable to tear her eyes away from the test results that taunted her.

The irony of it all amazed her. Thanks to Shane's quiet departure from her room that night, they'd completely avoided the typical "Now what?" questions that usually cropped up after two consenting adults had sex for the first time. But here she was, facing an ever bigger "Now what?" on her own.

Having a baby was going to change her plans to get a teaching credential and land a job right afterward. How did she expect to support herself and a child while attending school? And day care for an infant was very expensive.

"A *baby?*" she whispered. As much as she'd always wanted to be a mother, she couldn't help thinking that the timing was off—way off.

She placed the palm of her hand on her flat stomach and tried to imagine the enormous changes facing her now.

Another woman might have considered all of her options, especially adoption, but Jillian felt she would just have to figure out a way to make it all work out.

Somehow, some way, she would come to grips with her pregnancy and motherhood. She'd have to.

She moved her hand upward, from her womb to her heart, where the beat quickened as reality began to sink in.

Should she call someone? She certainly could use a confidant right now.

In the past, whenever she'd had a crisis, she'd go to her grandmother for advice. Gram had always been there for her. When Jillian had learned that Thomas had been cheating, Gram had been the one she'd turned to, the one who'd offered her full support.

"I know this hurts now," Gram had said, "but you're going to come out on top of all this. You're a survivor. You'll meet someone else someday, someone who truly deserves you."

At the time, while the idea of meeting a white knight in shining armor had put a glimmer of hope back in her heart, Jillian had feared that her marriage to Thomas might have left her skeptical of even the most loyal and honest of men.

Maybe that's why she'd invited Shane back to her hotel room that night—in the hope that her white knight wore a Stetson.

Look where *that* move had gotten her.

Jillian still couldn't seem to wrap her mind around the fact that her whole world was about to take a dramatic turn toward the complete unknown. Yet a tiny, comforting smile made its way to her lips. Finally, after years of hoping and praying that she'd conceive a child with Thomas, she was going to have a baby on her own.

Gram would be over the moon to learn that there was going to be a little one to cuddle and love, but she was also very old-fashioned. Hearing that Jillian had slept with her baby's father on their one and only date, especially when Jillian knew very little—well, practically nothing—about the man, wouldn't sit well with her. For that reason alone, Jillian didn't have the courage to call Gram and request advice on her latest "little problem."

The details of her baby's conception probably ought to bother Jillian, too, and while she felt a bit embarrassed by having a one-night stand, she wasn't going to beat herself up over what she'd done.

She'd realized at the time that she might eventually

regret her decision to invite Shane back to her hotel room. Yet even the next morning, when she'd awakened in bed and found him gone, her only regret had been that she would never experience love in his arms again.

Even now, standing in the middle of her bathroom, awed by everything that little blue plus sign represented, she couldn't help thinking back on the morning after their night together, when she should have felt regret— and hadn't.

The scant light of dawn had just begun to peek through a gap in the curtains, when she'd stretched awake in the king-size bed, the memory of an incredible night slowly unfolding.

Shane's hands sliding along her curves, hers exploring his well-defined biceps, his muscular chest…

Bodies responding, arching, reaching a breath-stealing peak…a powerful climax, the likes of which she'd never known.

A slow smile had stolen across her lips as she'd reached for the naked cowboy lying beside her…only to feel the cool sheets across an empty mattress.

For a moment, in her sleep-fogged mind, she'd wondered if the amazing sex had just been a dream. But as she'd sat up in bed and opened her eyes, the covers had slipped to her waist, and the morning air had whispered across her bare breasts.

She'd blinked several times, then scanned the bedroom of her hotel room, looking for evidence of the handsome cowboy she'd met the night before. But she'd found no sign of him—no clothes, no hat, no boots.

As she'd surveyed the king-size bed on which she sat, the comforter that had slipped to the floor during the night and the rumpled sheets, she'd realized she hadn't been dreaming. Just to be sure, she'd reached for one of the pillows on the other side of the bed, lifted it to her nose and breathed in the masculine scent he'd left behind, the proof that he'd really been with her.

Yes, she'd realized. Shane Hollister had been the real deal, and the events that had sparked it all began to unfold in her mind. The slow dance they'd shared, the sweet words he'd whispered above the music, *Your ex-husband was a fool, Jillian.*

The arousing kiss that had followed…

The haze of heat and passion…

As the memory grew stronger, she recalled threading her fingers through his hair, pulling his lips closer, his tongue deeper. And when the kiss had gotten too hot to handle, she'd taken him by the hand and led him to her room.

No, their night together had been so much more than a dream.

And now?

She glanced down at the pregnancy test that announced she was facing yet another life-altering change.

Again, she thought about calling someone, a friend maybe. But she certainly couldn't reach out to any of the women who were still part of the Wilkeses' social circle.

Katie Harris, Jillian's college roommate, came to mind. Years ago, the two of them had been exceptionally close, but they'd drifted apart after graduation.

Jillian had meant to remedy that situation as soon as she was settled in her new place, although she hadn't gotten around to it yet. She could make that call now, of course, but she didn't want their very first chat to be an embarrassing tell-all. So when she did take the time to connect with Katie, she would keep her news and her dilemma to herself, at least for a while.

What about Shane? she wondered. Telling him was probably the right thing to do. But could she even find him?

Leaving the pregnancy test on the bathroom counter, she went to her bedroom and opened the bureau drawer, where she'd put the note Shane had propped against the bathroom mirror before leaving her room that morning.

On the hotel letterhead, he'd written:

Dear Jillian,

I can't begin to thank you for a wonderful evening. I nearly woke you when I had to leave, but you looked so peaceful lying there that I didn't have the heart to disturb your sleep.

Last night was amazing. You were a gift I didn't deserve, and one I'll always cherish.

If you're ever in my neck of the woods, look me up. My friend and boss, Dan Walker, owns a spread that's located near Brighton Valley. He'll know how to contact me.

Either way, thanks for a memorable evening.

Shane

Jillian held the note for a while, studying the solid script, the bold strokes. She'd kept it as a souvenir of the magical night she'd spent with a cowboy. But now? It was all she had left of the man.

Well, that and the baby growing in her womb.

She could look him up, she supposed. And while tempted to do just that, she had to face the facts. What they'd shared had been far more therapeutic than a glass of champagne could ever be, but it was just a one-night thing. Anything else was wishful thinking on her part.

After all, she'd already given up her dreams for one man. There was no way she'd ever do that again.

Besides, what could possibly develop between her and a cowboy? Other than the physical intimacy they'd shared that night, they were pretty much strangers to each other.

Still, there was a baby to consider.

A wave of apprehension washed over her. Did she have to tell him? Would he even want to know?

She wasn't sure, but there wasn't any reason to make a game plan right this minute. Not when she was still struggling with the news herself.

A *baby*.

Once again, she placed her hand on her stomach, over the womb in which her little one grew. She had no idea what tomorrow would bring, but one thing was certain: She would raise her baby in a loving home, no matter what kind of man its daddy proved to be.

But there was something else she had to consider. Having a child together gave them far more in common than she'd even been able to imagine in the heat of the moment.

And whether she liked it or not, it was only fair to tell Shane he was going to be a father.

After a long day at the ranch and a stop at the cellular-phone store, Shane made the fifteen-minute drive home, dog-tired and muscles aching.

He'd no more than pulled his key from the front door when his new cell phone vibrated. So he pulled it out of his pocket and answered without checking the number on the display.

Out of habit, he answered, "This is Hollister."

"Shane, it's Jack."

His brother never called just to shoot the breeze. "Is something wrong?"

"I don't know. You tell *me*. We haven't heard from you in weeks. Hell, I've tried to cut you some slack after all you've been through, but things are getting worse. You've become really inconsiderate."

"Now, wait a second, little brother. I might not be living in Houston these days, playing golf with you guys and eating Sunday dinner, but I've been busy—not inconsiderate."

"Oh, no? Last month, you missed Billy's birthday party. You told us you'd stop by, but you never even showed up."

Shane turned on the lamp and shut the door, locking it for the night. "Something came up at the last minute, and I couldn't make it."

"Yeah, well you should have called to let someone know. We were worried about you."

"I *did* call, and Evan answered. I guess he didn't give you the message."

"Evan's only six years old, Shane. He can't be trusted to take messages."

"I figured that, so I asked him to put you or his mom on the line, but apparently he was too busy chasing after Emily to give the phone to someone older, so he told me to call back later." Shane took a seat on the chair nearest to the door and kicked off his dusty boots.

"Okay, so you're off the hook for the no-show at the birthday party," Jack said, "but I've tried calling you several times today, and your phone never even rang through."

"I lost my cell and wasn't able to replace it until about twenty minutes ago."

"Where'd you lose it?"

"If I knew that, then it wouldn't be lost, would it?"

Jack blew out an exasperated sigh. "All right. So that was a dumb question. But what was so important that you couldn't make it to Billy's party?"

Shane had never been one to kiss and tell. He supposed he could say that he'd met a woman and leave it at that, which would have pleased Jack and the rest of the family no end. But meeting a woman implied that he'd found her promising enough to keep seeing her, which wasn't exactly the case.

Yet Jack didn't need to know any of that. The only way to keep him in the dark was to stretch the truth, which wasn't the same as lying, but still went against Shane's grain. "Let's just say that I met an old friend, and the time just slipped away."

"A *female* friend."

Shane couldn't blame Jack for hoping that Shane had met someone special, but that hadn't happened.

"Who is she?" Jack asked, connecting the dots.

But Shane didn't want to go into it—any of it. Jillian had been more than a one-night stand. She'd been a one-night memory, and he wasn't about to share the details with anyone.

"It wasn't a woman," Shane lied. "I met up with an old friend, a guy I used to work with."

The first stretch of the truth had seemed necessary, but the actual lie gnawed at his conscience. Shane had always been straight up with his family and the people he cared about. But there really hadn't been another way around it if he wanted to maintain his privacy and keep the details from becoming Facebook fodder for the Hollisters, who were into that sort of thing.

Shane set aside his boots, then crossed the living room to the kitchen area.

"Well, you still ought to call home once in a while and let us know you're still alive and kicking. Hell, you could be laying in a morgue as a John Doe for all we know."

This was *Jack* speaking? The same brother who'd gone off to college and hadn't called home until their parents had complained to the Dean of Students?

"You're going to have to start over," Shane said. "What's the real problem here?"

"Hell, Shane. I know you're busy. But Mom's been

worried about you. She hasn't seen you in months or heard from you in weeks."

Shane, who'd just reached for a glass in the kitchen cupboard, paused for a beat—long enough to flinch from a jab of guilt. Then he released a wobbly sigh. "I didn't realize it had been so long, Jack. Tell her I'm fine and not to worry about me. Riding herd is a lot easier—and safer—than chasing the bad guys in Houston."

"Tell her yourself. She's been lighting candles and going to mass all week. Under the circumstances, what with knowing how much you liked being a cop, she's stressing about your mental health."

Shane tensed. Sylvia Dominguez, his former partner, had been a little worried about the same thing—at least for a while. And he couldn't really blame her or his family for being concerned. He'd gone a little crazy a while back, after he'd been put on suspended duty for letting his heart, his grief and his temper get away from him. But after a sobering confrontation with his dad, he realized what he was doing to himself. So he stopped closing down bars and started facing his demons instead.

Facing them?

Yeah, right. That's why his old life was in Houston and he was living in a cramped studio apartment more than two hours away. It was also why it took forever to fall asleep at night.

Of course, the insomnia might be a thing of the past now that he had thoughts of pretty Jillian to chase away the nocturnal shadows that kept the sandman at bay.

He wondered how long that was going to last.

A lot longer than their short time together, he hoped.

"Did you hear me?" Jack asked.

"Yeah." And he'd already forgotten what they'd been talking about. "I'm just a little scattered tonight. I've got a lot on my mind."

"You don't owe me an explanation, but Mom's another story."

"Tell her that my mental health is fine," Shane said. "It's amazing what a change of scenery will do."

"I'm glad to hear it. But don't be a stranger."

"I'm sorry. I'll try to check in more often."

Jack paused a beat, then added, "If you ever need anyone to talk to, you know I'm here for you."

This particular brother was a good listener, as well as a peacemaker. So in the Hollister family, that made him invaluable.

"You never should have let Cindy talk you out of the priesthood," Shane said. "You would have made a good one."

Jack laughed. "Maybe so. But give Mom a call, will you?"

Shane glanced at his wristwatch. "It's nearly nine o'clock on a Thursday night. She's probably down at the parish playing bingo."

"You don't need to call tonight. But after that mess with Internal Affairs and your leave of absence, she's been stressing something awful. You know how it is."

Yeah, he did. And he hadn't meant to cause her any more grief. He'd put the family through enough already, which had been another good reason to leave Houston.

Hoping to change the subject, he asked, "How's everyone else doing?"

"Good, for the most part. Colleen's on the dean's list at Baylor again. Stevie left for the police academy yesterday. And Mary-Lynn's expecting again."

"Is Dad doing all right?"

"Yeah, but he'd like to hear from you, too."

"I'll call home in the morning."

After disconnecting the line and putting the receiver back in the charger, Shane plunked a couple of ice cubes into his glass, filled it full of tap water and took a nice, long swig.

Any other night, he might have been tempted to fix himself a *real* drink, but memories of Jillian were still too fresh in his mind. And despite their time together being purposefully short, it was also the kind of memory that was worthy of keeping…sacred in a way. And Shane wasn't about to lessen or cheapen it.

Those magical hours spent in her bed had been a once-in-a-lifetime experience, one he'd been reluctant to end.

As dawn had threatened to break over Houston, he'd drawn her close to his chest and savored the fragrance of her shampoo, the faint floral whiff of her perfume.

She'd slept with her bottom nestled in his lap, and he'd felt himself stirring, rising to the occasion—again. But even if they hadn't gone through the only condom they'd had during the night, time hadn't been on his side.

As he'd glanced through an opening in the heavy curtains and seen the night fading into dawn, he'd carefully slid his arm from under her head, trying his best not to wake her. Because a cowboy didn't call in sick, especially if the only excuse he had was a beautiful woman in his bed. So he'd snatched his wrinkled shirt and jeans from the floor.

He'd found himself dragging his feet, not wanting to go, not ready to end what they'd shared.

Why had it felt as though they'd created some kind of invisible bond, some reason for him to linger?

Probably because their lovemaking had been so good. That had to be it.

Besides, Shane wasn't ready for a relationship. And he wasn't sure if he ever would be again.

So he'd quickly gotten dressed, wishing he could think of a better way to say goodbye. But he hadn't been able to come up with anything that wouldn't have created some kind of promise he couldn't keep. And that wouldn't have been fair to her.

Not that he didn't *want* to see her again. But they had very little in common, and their lives were headed in different directions.

His only regret had been slipping out of her bed at nearly five in the morning and leaving a note, which might have cheapened the whole thing.

Last night was amazing, he'd written. *You were a gift I didn't deserve, and one I'll always cherish.*

And while he'd struggled to choose the right words, he'd meant every one of them.

He supposed he could try to find her again. His detective skills and his connections wouldn't make it too hard. But Jillian wasn't the kind of woman who'd fit into Shane's life, whether it was in Houston or Brighton Valley.

He'd already gone through one star-crossed relationship that he shouldn't have let get off the ground, and he'd lost his son because of it.

No, he'd just have to let well enough alone. After all, if something between them was meant to be, then he'd run into her again. No need for him to chase after something that was sure to crash and burn.

But that didn't mean he wasn't sorely tempted to look her up in Houston. He'd love to spend one more night together.

They might end the evening in a blaze of glory, but what a way to go....

Chapter Three

In spite of knowing their time together had been a one-shot deal, Shane hadn't been able to get Jillian out of his mind.

Several times he'd actually thought seriously about looking her up in Houston. She hadn't given him a lot to go on, but he still had a few contacts at the police department who'd be able to help him out. Yet when push came to shove, he'd decided to let well enough alone.

That is, until he was urged to attend his niece's first communion in Houston on Sunday morning. After he'd missed Billy's birthday party a while back and created such a stir within the family, he'd decided to make a showing this time, even though he'd rather be anywhere than in a church on Sunday morning, especially if it required a confession.

It's not that he had some huge sin hanging over his head, but he wasn't ready to make things right with God when he still blamed the Big Guy Upstairs for allowing Joey to die. But he supposed he'd deal with that tomorrow morning.

Right now, he was headed to the city a day early, determined to see Jillian while he was there. Through his connections, he'd gotten her address just minutes ago: 237 Bluebonnet Court, apartment 16.

It had been exactly six weeks and a day since they'd met that magical evening in Houston, but the memory was still as strong and vivid as if it had only been yesterday.

After they'd split the bill that evening, Shane had insisted on being the one to leave a generous tip for the wait staff. Then he'd walked with her to The Rio, the hotel lounge that provided music and high-priced drinks to some of Houston's more exclusive crowd.

Shane wasn't used to hanging out at places like that, and he knew he'd been underdressed, but he'd been with Jillian, who belonged to that world.

"The music sounds good," she'd said.

At that point, being with her would make anything sound good. But she'd been right. The band was great.

As they'd made their way toward an empty table near the dance floor, Shane had placed his hand on the small of her back, claiming her in front of all the rich, fancy folks who'd gathered for an after-dinner drink.

She'd leaned against him and slid her arm around his waist in a move that seemed so natural, so right, that he wanted to hang on tight and never let go.

Then the music, something soft and slow, began to play and he hadn't been able to do anything other than to pull her into his embrace and dance cheek to cheek. As they'd swayed to a love song, as he'd inhaled her tropical scent, she'd melded into him as though they'd been made to dance with each other for the rest of their lives.

Something powerful had surged between them, something hot, soul stirring and arousing.

He'd taken her hand and brushed his lips across her wrist. As she'd looked at him, her lips parting, she'd gripped his shoulder as though her knees would have buckled if she hadn't.

And that's when he'd kissed her. Right there in the middle of that crowded dance floor.

As their lips parted, his tongue had sought hers, and they were swept away to some carnal place, where the music stopped and the room grew silent. At least, he could have sworn it had happened that way.

For a moment, he'd forgotten where they were, *who* they were. All he'd been aware of was a raging desire that promised to bring about something he'd never experienced before.

Then the music really did stop, and he'd come to his senses, albeit reluctantly. As he broke the kiss, he'd continued to hold Jillian tight, and with his lips resting near her temple, he'd confessed, "I don't normally do things like this."

"Neither do I."

As they'd slowly stepped apart, she'd closed her eyes and, after taking a deep breath, said, "I…uh…have a room upstairs."

Shane hadn't been sure he'd heard right or if he'd somehow come to the wrong conclusion, so he'd waited a beat, hoping she'd spell it out for him. Then she did just that by taking his hand and leading him out of The Rio and to the elevators.

As the memory rolled on, just as it did each time a specific clip from that night began to play in his mind, he tried his best to shake it off. But damn. What an amazing evening that had been.

If truth be told, he'd been more than a little sorry that it had ended before he'd gotten a chance to see if a long-distance relationship between two people with nothing in common but great sex could actually work.

Now, as he gripped the steering wheel of his pickup

and watched the street signs for Bluebonnet Court, the heated memory still remained front and center in his mind.

Of course, seeing her again didn't mean he was interested in starting a relationship. It was just a matter of satisfying his curiosity.

Would Jillian be glad to see him? Had she, too, found it impossible to forget all they'd shared that night?

Shane certainly hoped so. He'd just have to take things one step at a time.

As he turned and drove down the tree-lined street and approached a modest apartment complex, he wondered if the address he'd found for her was wrong. Jillian had been dressed to the nines and sporting diamonds when they'd met, and this neighborhood didn't seem like the part of town that would suit her taste or her designer pocketbook.

But there was only one way to find out.

He parked his truck in one of the spaces available for guests, then made his way to Jillian's apartment, hoping she was home.

And that she'd be glad to see him.

When the doorbell sounded, Jillian had been sitting on the sofa, reading over her college schedule. She hadn't been expecting company, and since she hadn't found time to meet any of the neighbors, she wasn't sure who it could be.

She had a feeling it might be her grandmother, though. Ever since Jillian had moved into the apartment, Gram had been stopping by with one surprise or another, such as kitchen gadgets, household necessities and decorator items.

Yesterday, she'd brought a framed watercolor print that she'd picked up at a garage sale, which was now hanging on the living room wall. That particular piece of art was a far cry from the expensive paintings and sculptures that had adorned the various homes Jillian had once shared with Thomas, but it reflected her new, simple lifestyle.

During the course of her marriage, Jillian had tried so hard to do everything Thomas and his family had expected her to do that she'd almost forgotten who she really was. So she was determined to reclaim herself and become the woman she should have been before Thomas Wilkes had come along. And creating a home for herself, decorated to her own taste and comfort, was part of the process.

Expecting to see Gram with another surprise in her arms, Jillian swung open the door with a smile. But when she spotted Shane Hollister, the smile faded and surprise took its place.

The cowboy was just as handsome as she remembered, maybe more so. And his smile, which was both boyish and shy, sent her senses reeling.

"I would have called first, but I didn't have your number." He lifted the brim of his hat with an index finger.

He hadn't had her address, either, but she was so stunned to see him again, so mesmerized by his familiar, musky scent, that she couldn't seem to find the words to respond or to question him.

But her gaze was hard at work, checking him out and soaking him in. He'd shaved, which had softened his rugged edge a bit, but he still wore a Stetson, jeans and boots—clearly a cowboy through and through.

"If this isn't a good time," he said, those luscious brown eyes glimmering as he broke the silence, "I can come back another day."

"No, it's not that." She stepped aside to let him in. "It's just that I…"

"…didn't expect to see me again?" He tossed her a crooked grin that darn near turned her inside out.

She managed a smile of her own. "How'd you find me? I didn't even have an address to give you when we met."

"It's amazing what a person can learn over the internet."

Jillian wasn't sure if she should be happy he'd found her or concerned by it. After all, she didn't know very much about him, other than the fact that he hadn't always been a cowboy, and that he was divorced.

And that he'd claimed to be a tumbleweed, while they'd had dinner that night, which was a little worrisome. If he was indeed prone to wander and not set down roots, he wouldn't be the kind of father she wanted for her baby. That alone had seemed like the perfect excuse not to contact him so far.

Not that she'd made a solid decision yet. She would need to know more about him before she could allow him to be involved in the baby's upbringing.

And as luck would have it, here was her chance. So she swept her arm toward the brown tweed sofa that had once been in Gram's den and the faux leather recliner that had belonged to her grandfather. "Have a seat."

"Thanks." He placed his hat on one side of the sofa, then sat on the middle cushion. "I hope I'm not interrupting anything."

Just her conscience and her good sense.

"No, not really." She combed her fingers through her hair, suddenly wondering what she looked like without any makeup, without having used a brush since this morning.

"I have a family function in Houston," he said, "so, while I was in the area, I thought I'd stop by and say hello. I also thought it might be nice to have dinner together."

The last time they'd shared a meal, she'd invited him to spend the night. Was he expecting the same thing to happen again?

She could certainly see where he might. When they'd danced in each other's arms at The Rio, the sexual attraction had ignited. She'd never had a one-night stand before, so she'd struggled with her conscience before inviting him up to her room. But only momentarily.

Once she'd had that sweet experience, she hadn't been sorry about it, either. Shane had been an incredible lover who'd done amazing things with his hands and his mouth, taking her places she'd never gone before. Ever.

If truth be told, she was sorely tempted to have him take her there again.

But look where sexual attraction and throwing caution to the wind had gotten her—pregnant with the cowboy's baby.

"What do you say?" he asked, clearly picking up on how torn she was between a yes or a no.

Getting involved with him again would certainly complicate her life, so she was tempted to decline and send him on his way. But what did she know about the man who'd fathered her baby? And what was she supposed to tell her child when he or she inevitably asked the daddy questions?

"We really don't have much in common," she admitted. Nothing other than a baby, of course.

"Well, we don't know that for sure. We never really had a chance to talk much that night."

He was right about that. Even though they'd known each other's bodies intimately, the rugged cowboy was pretty much a stranger to her—as she was to him.

But he'd also put her healing process on the fast track and had made her feel desirable again.

So did that make them friendly strangers?

Or strangers with benefits…?

Jillian fiddled momentarily with the silver pendant

that dangled from her necklace, then made the decision. "All right. Let me freshen up and change my clothes."

His smile nearly took her breath away, as he leaned back in his seat. "No problem. Take your time."

Thirty minutes later, she and Shane entered a little Italian restaurant he'd recommended. She'd chosen to dress casually in black jeans and a pale blue sweater.

At least on the outside, she and Shane appeared to be a better match than they had before, but for some reason she felt like a late-blooming high school senior about to enter the adult world for the first time.

"This place isn't as nice as the hotel restaurant," Shane said, "but the food is out of this world."

Jillian took a hearty whiff of tomatoes and basil, not doubting Shane about the taste. "It sure smells good."

After the hostess seated them at a quiet table for two, a busboy brought them water with lemon and a basket of freshly baked bread.

"So what do you do for a living?" Shane asked.

Jillian had planned to be the first one to start asking questions, but she supposed they both had a lot to learn about each other. "Right now, I'm planning to go back to school, but I'll be looking for part-time work soon."

"What kind of job did you have before?"

She hated to admit that she'd never worked, even though she'd kept pretty busy. But she doubted that he'd care about her philanthropic endeavors—the hospital board on which she'd served or the women's club, of which she'd been the chair. She was proud of her contributions, of course, but her heart hadn't been in the projects that had been hand chosen by Thomas—or rather, by his mother. The trouble was, until recently, her volunteerism had been her life, her work. Her only legitimate purpose in the world.

For some reason, she felt as though she ought to apologize or make excuses while explaining that she had high hopes for the future. "I didn't have a regular job, but I did volunteer work for several charitable organizations over the past few years."

He seemed to mull that over for a moment, then reached for the bread basket, pulled back the linen cloth that kept it warm and offered her the first slice, which she took.

"So you're going to take some college classes?" he asked.

"I'm getting a teaching credential."

"Oh, yeah? You must like kids."

"I do."

"But, if I remember correctly, you don't have any of your own."

It wasn't actually a question, just a conclusion he'd obviously come to after something she must have told him. She supposed there was no real reason to respond.

If truth be told, she'd always longed to have a baby— at least two or three. But she and Thomas had never been able to conceive—at least, not together.

And now here she was—unwed and pregnant.

The waiter stopped by to take their orders, which was a relief since she really didn't want to talk about babies with Shane right now. But her luck didn't hold.

Once they were alone again, he picked up right where he'd left off. "I guess teaching would be the next best thing to having kids of your own."

Not really. That thought hadn't even crossed her mind. Leaving kids out of the equation, she said, "Actually I'd like to be a high school English teacher."

Shane arched an eyebrow, his skepticism drawing another smile from her, even though she ought to be miffed that he seemed to be as cynical as Thomas had been when she'd first told him her plan to return to college and get her credential.

"Teenagers can be a real pain to deal with," he said. "Why not teach kindergarten or one of the lower grades?"

"Because I love the written word. And I'd like to make literature and grammar interesting to teenagers, especially those without college aspirations. I want to encourage them to reach their full potential." She studied his expression, hoping that he was merely questioning the age of the students she wanted to teach and not the work she wanted to do.

When he didn't seem to find her dream unusual or unfitting, she added, "And not just any kids. I want to work with bright but unmotivated teens from lower socioeconomic backgrounds who believe that college is out of their reach."

"No kidding?"

She shrugged, waiting for him to give her the same, patronizing response Thomas had when she'd shared her plans with him.

Instead, he grinned, creating a pair of sexy dimples in his cheeks. "I hated English in school, but with a teacher like you, I would have tried a lot harder."

When he looked at her like that, when he smiled, her heart soared in the same way it had the night they'd met. Just being with him again and feeling the growing buzz of sexual awareness was enough to remind her why she'd taken him back to her room, why she'd given in to sweet temptation.

It didn't take a psychic to see that she'd be tempted to take him to bed again, once he took her home.

So now what?

Why had he come looking for her? Was he interested in making love one more time?

Or was he missing her, missing *this*—their time together?

Did he want to actually date her? And if so, how did she feel about that?

Long-distance relationships didn't usually work out. Not that Jillian was ready for anything like that to develop between them. After all, she'd made one mistake by believing a man to be honorable when he wasn't. She certainly didn't want to make another one by acting too soon.

Still, spending time with Shane was making her realize that she hadn't been permanently damaged by her husband's infidelity and that the right man *would* come along someday.

Would that man be Shane Hollister?

It was impossible to know after only two evenings together. Besides, she had the baby to consider. So she might as well feel him out about that.

"How about you?" she asked. "Do you have any children?"

The spark in his eyes dimmed, and he seemed to tense. For several long, drawn-out heartbeats, he held his tongue, and she felt compelled to apologize, to sympathize—to do or say something, although she didn't have a clue what.

Finally, he answered, "No, I don't."

Something in his tone, in his demeanor, made her wonder if he liked it that way. If so, how would he react when she finally told him about the baby? Would he be happy? Uneasy? Angry?

Would he worry about being responsible—financially or otherwise—for a child he'd never intended to have?

As curious as she was, as much as his answers mattered, she didn't push for more. She wasn't ready for a full-on discussion about babies or kids right now, so she opted to change the subject.

"You mentioned that you used to work in Houston. What did you do?"

He reached for his goblet of water, then took a drink. Finally he said, "I worked for the Houston Police Department, first as a patrolman, then as a detective."

She wasn't sure what she'd expected him to say—that he'd been in sales, she supposed. Or that he'd had a dead-end job of some kind. But a police officer?

Not only did that surprise her, it made her feel a whole lot better about him and the man he was.

"Why did you quit?" she asked.

He grew quiet again, as if she'd unearthed something he didn't want to talk about. Then he shrugged. "It's complicated."

Which meant what? That she wasn't going to get any more out of him than that?

Who *was* Shane Hollister?

Before she could quiz him further, the waiter brought their food, lasagna for him and pasta primavera for her, creating a momentary lull in the conversation.

While Shane picked up his fork, Jillian asked again, this time point blank, "Why did you leave the police force?"

Shane dug into his lasagna and took a bite, hoping Jillian would get the hint that he didn't want to talk in detail about the past. There were too many mitigating factors that had caused him to leave the force, too much other stuff to reveal. And no matter how much he enjoyed her company, he wasn't ready to spill his guts yet. And he wasn't sure he'd ever be.

"Like I told you," he said, "it's complicated."

She waited a beat, yet didn't let up on him. "Okay, then tell me about yourself. Where were you born? What kind of childhood did you have?"

He supposed he couldn't blame her for being curious. He had a lot of questions for her, too.

"There's not much to tell," he said. "I was born in Houston and grew up as the youngest of three boys and two girls in a big, close-knit family."

She leaned forward, as if he'd told her something interesting. "It's nice that you have a big family."

He'd always thought so. He watched her spear a piece of broccoli with her fork. The candlelight glistened on the platinum strands of her hair, making her appear radiant and almost…angelic.

Unaware of his gaze, she looked up and smiled. "I never knew my father, so it was only my mom and me at first. After my mother died, I moved in with my grandparents. I'm afraid it's just Gram and me now."

Marcia had been an only child, too, which had made it nearly impossible for her to relate to a big, rambunctious family like the Hollisters.

Shane had a feeling Jillian would feel the same way if she ever met them. And that was just one more reason a relationship with her wouldn't work out.

But tell that to his hormones. Damn, she was a beautiful woman, even if she was mortal and prone to imperfections.

So why couldn't he spot any of them?

As she lifted her water goblet, brought it to her lips and swallowed, he followed the simple movement as it moved down her throat.

When he'd kissed her there that night, running his tongue along her neck and throat, she'd come alive in his arms.

Had the memory ingrained itself in her mind, too?

He kept reminding himself that they really weren't suited, but that didn't seem to matter right now.

"So what was it like growing up as one of five kids?"

she asked, as if she had no idea he'd been ogling her from across the table.

"It was okay, I guess." He'd idolized his older siblings until his teenage years, when he'd found them bossy and a real pain in the ass. But in retrospect, he realized they'd just been looking out for him, even if they'd sometimes overstepped their boundaries.

He'd actually thought his family had been the typical, all-American variety until he married Marcia. She'd been annoyed by them and couldn't understand the closeness they'd shared. In fact, she'd thought they were intrusive and out of line most of the time.

It had made life pretty miserable for everyone, not just her and Shane.

But it had been more than his family that had bothered her. She'd hated his job, too.

When Shane was promoted to detective, his marriage seemed to get better because he'd received a pay increase and was no longer patrolling the city streets. He'd also known better than to vent about the ugliness that he saw nearly every day. Instead, he'd stretched the truth and made his job sound safe and routine.

But Marcia hadn't bought it. When she'd accused him of cheating on her with his partner—something he *hadn't* done—he'd finally thrown in the towel.

Shane wondered what Jillian would say if she knew how many of his family members worked in one law enforcement field or another. Or if he told her that he'd wanted to be a cop ever since he could remember and that he'd once believed he'd been born to wear a badge.

Stuff like that hadn't mattered to Marcia. She'd hated everything about his line of work, which was why she'd eventually been the one to cheat, something he'd learned after the fact.

"You're not very forthcoming," Jillian said.

He hadn't meant to clam up completely. "I'm sorry. It's just that my ex-wife didn't like my family or my job. So when you start asking me about either one of them, I get a little defensive and cryptic. It's an old habit, I guess."

"I'm sorry to hear that."

To hear what? That he had old baggage and habits?

He didn't want her to think that he was still dealing with the aftereffects of his divorce. "For what it's worth, I did everything I could think of to make my marriage work. I went so far as to buy a house in a small town about an hour or so from Houston, even though that meant I'd have a big commute each day."

"It didn't help?"

"No, it was more than my family dynamics creating problems. My ex used to push me to change careers, to find a job that paid more money, a position that would allow me to spend more time at home. But that was one compromise I wasn't willing to make."

"So now you're a tumbleweed. You can come and go as you please."

"Yeah, I guess you can say that."

She grew silent, and while he was tempted to get the conversation back on track, he wasn't sure what to say that wouldn't lead him back to the things he didn't want to discuss. Like the losses he'd suffered—his wife through divorce, his son through death and his career by choice.

"I have a question I've been meaning to ask you," he said.

"What's that?" She picked up her napkin and blotted her lips.

He couldn't see any reason to tiptoe around it, so he came right out and laid it on the table. "Do you ever think about the night we met?"

Her gaze lifted from her plate, and as it locked on his,

his heartbeat rumbled in his chest. In the silence, a thousand words passed between them.

"Sometimes," she admitted.

Her expression was far more revealing, and he suspected that her musings were more in tune to his own—and that she thought about what they'd shared in Houston more than she wanted him to know.

"So what do you want to do about it?" he asked.

She paused as though giving it some real thought, then bit down on her bottom lip before saying, "I don't know, Shane."

He could have pressed her at that moment, but to be honest, he wasn't sure if it would be in his best interest if he did. After all, they had very little in common and lived nearly two hours apart.

Instead, he picked up his fork and tried to convince himself that he had an appetite for pasta, cheese and marinara sauce, when he hungered for a lot more than food.

When they finished their meal, Shane paid the bill and they walked back to his pickup, the soles of their shoes crunching along the blacktop-covered parking lot.

So now what? he wondered. Where did they go from here?

He didn't ask, though. Not when he still questioned the wisdom of getting involved in a relationship that had a snowball's chance in hell. So he decided to bide his time and see how things played out.

Ten minutes later, they were standing at her door, with a lovers' moon overhead.

"I'm sorry for prodding you earlier," she said. "I didn't mean to pry or make you relive painful memories."

"I can't blame you for being curious. You don't know me very well."

"I know you better than I did before." She smiled up

at him, revealing a shy side of herself, then reached into her purse for the keys. "I'm glad you looked me up."

Was she? Even though he hadn't been as "forthcoming" as she would have liked?

Truth was, neither of them had shared very much about themselves. Was that for the best?

Or was it an excuse to get together again?

"I'm glad I found you, too," he said.

"Thanks again for dinner."

So that was it? She was just going to let herself into the apartment and close the door?

He tried to tell himself that it was for the best, but he couldn't quite buy that with an amazing array of stars blinking overhead, with his blood pumping to beat the band, with her scent taunting him....

Unable to help himself, he skimmed his knuckles along her cheek, felt the warmth of her flush, heard the catch of her breath.

As her lips parted, his control faded into the pheromone-charged air, and he lowered his mouth to hers.

Chapter Four

Just a whiff of Shane's manly cologne, with its hint of leather and musk, stirred up an exhilarating sense of adventure. And as their lips met, Jillian's heart soared with anticipation.

She'd convinced herself to take things slow and easy until she knew him better, but at the moment, she couldn't care less about that. Not when everything they'd shared before was about to happen all over again—the passion, the heat, the pleasure.

Oh, how that man could kiss!

He slipped his arms around her, and she leaned into him as if they'd never been apart. Their bodies melded together, and the kiss deepened until desire exploded into a blast of colors, reminding her why she'd thrown caution to the wind that incredible evening in Houston.

And something told her she wasn't going to be any stronger at fighting temptation now than she'd been back then.

She'd wanted to spend more time with him so she could learn just what kind of man he really was. But at this rate, she was only going to find out what kind of lover he was. And she already knew that Shane Hollister was the best ever.

As their tongues mated, as breaths mingled and mouths grew desperate, he pulled her hips against his growing arousal, and she pressed into him as if it was the most natural thing in the world to do.

Right there, on her porch, where all her neighbors could see, she kissed him as though there would be no consequences or tomorrows.

But there would be plenty of both if she let her hormones run away with her. Making love to him this evening would only complicate things further—if that was even possible. And she couldn't afford to do that again. Not until she had a chance to actually date the man.

So she placed her hands on his chest and slowly pushed back, ending the kiss.

"You have no idea how tempted I am to ask you inside," she said, her breath a bit raspy from the arousing assault on her senses. "But I'm on the rebound, and you might be, too. So for that reason—and a few others—I think it would be best if we took things a little slower."

"Maybe," he said, although something in his eyes suggested he wasn't convinced.

Yet in spite of his apparent acceptance of her words, neither of them made a move to end their evening together.

She closed her eyes, caught up in a heady cloud of swirling pheromones, musky cologne and the vibrant and steady beat of a heart on the mend. As tempted as she was to ask him to stay the night, she had to let him go. She'd thrown caution and morals to the wind once, but she couldn't make a habit of it.

Not until she knew him better.

When she glanced up at him, he tossed her a crooked grin. Yet the hint of a shadow darkened his eyes, an emotion too fleeting for her to get a handle on.

She rested a hand on his chest, where his heart beat

strong and steady. Surely she was being too cautious. But she couldn't quite bring herself to change the stance she'd taken.

"Do you have a piece of paper and pen?" he asked.

She reached into her purse and pulled out the small notepad she carried, along with the attached ink pen.

When she handed it to him, he scratched out his phone number on the top sheet, than gave it back to her. Deciding to provide him with hers, as well, she tore out a page from the back of the booklet, jotted down her number for him.

"Well…have a good evening," she said, although she suspected that they'd both have a better one if they didn't spend it alone.

Shane brushed another kiss on her lips, this one light and fleeting. He hesitated momentarily, as if he was struggling with something. Then he kissed her a third and last time, a heart-thumping, hope-stirring kiss that would linger in her memory long after he left.

As he walked to his truck, she stood at the door and watched him go.

She ached to call him back, but if she got in too deep and too soon, she would complicate not only her life, but her baby's. And she couldn't afford to do that yet.

There was, however, one thing that she did know. Meeting Shane and experiencing the thrill of a romance had completely dulled the pain of Thomas's betrayal. And she was tempted beyond measure to hang on to what they'd found together. But she couldn't enter a full-on affair with him. At least, not at this point.

As Shane climbed into his pickup, a feeling of remorse settled over her. It took all she had not to call him back—or run after him. But it was best this way, especially since she wasn't ready to tell him about the baby.

Still, as she went into the house and locked the door behind her, she couldn't help grieving what they might have shared tonight.

Shane spent the night on his parents' sofa, thanks to all the out-of-town family members who'd converged upon the house for Becky's first communion. He'd been surrounded by his nieces and nephews, who had spread their sleeping bags all over the floor.

The kids had gotten up at the crack of dawn, so he'd merely put his pillow over his head to block out the noise and the morning light.

He had no idea what time it was now—or where they'd gone—but thankfully they were all up and at 'em.

Years ago, he'd thought that the old sofa was pretty comfortable, but he'd awakened with a crick in his neck this morning, which left him ready to snap at anyone or anything that crossed his path.

Okay, so it was more than a few aches and pains that had him out of sorts. He was flat-out disappointed that he hadn't been invited to stay with Jillian last night, although he had no one to blame but himself.

She'd struggled with the decision to send him on his way. He'd seen it in her eyes, heard it in her passion-laced voice.

If there'd ever been a couple who'd been sexually compatible, it was the two of them. So it wouldn't have taken much effort on his part to convince her to change her mind.

But the truth of the matter was that she was coming off a recent divorce, which meant that she was vulnerable—maybe even more than most women might be. She hadn't had to come out and say that, either. He'd seen that in her eyes, as well.

Only a jerk would have taken advantage of her, which was what he'd told himself last night while his conscience had warred with his libido.

"I'm on the rebound," she'd said. "And you might be, too."

That hadn't been entirely true. Shane had gotten over his divorce a long time ago.

Still, he'd been tempted to suggest that they put another temporary balm on two grieving hearts, although he'd decided against it. Why jump into anything when the future was so questionable?

Besides, if she ever came out to Brighton Valley, which was becoming home to him, she'd probably go into culture shock.

Of course, he'd been more than a little surprised to find her living in a modest apartment, instead of something ritzy. Especially since her jewelry and designer clothes suggested that she belonged in a much nicer place—and in a better part of town.

So what was with that?

He supposed it made sense that she would move closer to the university she planned to attend, but wouldn't she be happier in an upscale neighborhood?

Or had she entered El Jardin that day primed and looking for a man who had money?

Shane didn't like that particular train of thought. Had he been wrong about her?

Before he could give it any real consideration, Jack's six-year-old son ran up to him. "Hey, Uncle Shane. Can I come out to your ranch someday and ride a horse? My dad said he'd take me out there, if it's okay with you."

Shane didn't mind having Jack and his family come to Brighton Valley. It might even be fun to show them around and make a day of it. "It's not my ranch, Evan. But I can arrange a visit and a horseback ride."

"Cool! I'll tell my dad you said it was all right. Woo-hoo!"

With that, the boy dashed off, whooping it up.

Shane liked kids; he really did. But sometimes it was tough being around his nieces and nephews, especially when he couldn't help thinking that Joey would be four now and running around with them.

Using his fingers, he kneaded the stiff and sore muscles in his neck.

Once he'd attended that first communion and given his niece the charm bracelet he'd bought, he'd be history—and headed back to Brighton Valley.

In the meantime, after folding up the blanket he'd used last night, he went into the kitchen for a cup of coffee. There, he found his mom alone, standing over the stove and flipping hotcakes.

"Why are you doing all the work?" he asked as he walked up behind her and placed a kiss on her cheek.

She turned to him and smiled. "Because I enjoy having you kids home. And besides, it's Sunday morning, remember?"

"How could I forget?" His mom's special buttermilk pancakes had become a church-day tradition at the Hollister house.

"Pour yourself a cup of coffee," she said, "then get some hotcakes while they're fresh and warm."

She didn't have to ask him twice. After filling a mug and piling the pancakes on a plate, Shane took a seat at the table, where he added a slab of butter and maple syrup on top of his stack.

"Where is everyone?" he asked.

"John and Karen took Becky to the church. She's meeting up with a couple of her girlfriends there. Tom and your dad are outside, watching Trevor ride his bike. When you finish eating, you ought to join them."

Shane didn't respond either way. But for the past two-and-a-half years he'd been treading along the perimeter of most family gatherings, on the outside looking in. And truthfully it was easier that way.

He glanced at his wristwatch. Church would be starting soon, which was great. He was eager to get this day over with so he could head back to the ranch where he belonged. At least, that's how he'd been feeling lately.

It was weird, too. Back at the ranch where he worked, Dan and Eva Walker had two sets of twins. And while Shane tried to avoid his nieces and nephews, he didn't feel the same way about the Walker kids, although he wasn't sure why.

Maybe because Marcia had always blamed the Hollisters for the trouble in their marriage. And maybe in a way, he'd blamed them, too. Ever since dealing with his wife's complaints, Shane had stepped out of the family fold. And that was long before Joey had died.

Damn. Maybe Jillian was right. Maybe he *was* still dragging around some old baggage from his divorce.

He lifted the mug of coffee, savored the aroma of the fresh morning brew, then took a sip.

Making love with Jillian—and having dinner with her again last night—had been refreshing and...healing.

When he was with her, things felt different—better. And he wasn't just talking about a simple case of attraction. He'd actually been able to shed the shadows that plagued him for hours on end.

But the only way he could imagine hooking up with Jillian was if he moved back to Houston and took up his old life.

However, Jillian didn't seem to be the kind of woman who'd be interested in dating a cop—even if he wanted to go back to work for the HPD. And at this point, he really didn't.

There was something appealing about Brighton Valley and small-town life. He actually enjoyed riding fence and herding cattle.

Of course, Jillian didn't seem like the kind who'd be happy with a cowboy, either. A life in Brighton Valley would be foreign to a woman like her.

So why set himself up for failure? He'd already gone through one divorce because his wife hadn't been happy with the life he'd wanted to lead.

So why even ponder the possibility of a relationship with Jillian, either long distance or right next door?

Because, for one thing, he couldn't get her off his mind.

And because he doubted that he'd ever be more sexually compatible with another woman again.

What a shame that would be.

As he cut into his pancakes, which were growing cold, he wondered if it might be best to leave the possibility of a relationship with Jillian to fate. After all, she had his phone number, and he'd included the name of the ranch on which he worked in the note he'd left her at the hotel.

So she could find him if she really wanted to.

"I'm going to get ready for church," his mother said. "Can I get you anything else? Some OJ? More coffee?"

"No, I'm fine." Shane looked up from his plate and smiled. "Thanks, Mom."

"You're more than welcome, sweetie." She stood in the center of the room for a moment, not moving one way or the other, then added, "It's nice to have you home."

He nodded, unable to respond out loud. How could he when he was counting the minutes before he could head back to Brighton Valley and to a different way of life?

"I know that you haven't felt comfortable here for a long time," she said.

Coming from her, the truth stung. And while he

wanted to soften things, to imply that she was wrong or to blame it all on his ex-wife, he couldn't bring himself to lie. "It's complicated, Mom. But I'm working on it."

Her eyes misted, yet she managed a smile. "I can't ask for more than that."

Then she left him alone in the kitchen, wondering if he'd ever feel like a part of the Hollister clan—or even another family—ever again.

Or if he'd even want to.

Jillian hadn't seen or heard from Shane in several months—long enough for her to start college classes, visit an obstetrician and to finally share her pregnancy news with Gram.

She'd been right, of course. Gram had been thrilled to learn that Jillian was expecting, but she hadn't liked the idea of her raising a child on her own.

"What about the father?" Gram had asked. "Does he plan to be a part of the baby's life?"

"I'm not sure how he'll feel about that." Jillian had no way of knowing what Shane's reaction would be. "He doesn't know yet."

"You haven't told him that you're pregnant?" The tone of Gram's voice had indicated both surprise and disapproval.

"Not yet," Jillian had admitted.

Gram had clucked her tongue. "A man deserves to know that he's going to be a daddy, Jilly. You can't keep something like that from him. It's not fair."

"I'm going to tell him. I'm waiting for the right time."

"When is that?" Gram had asked. "On your way to the delivery room?"

Jillian wouldn't wait that long, but Gram was right. She was running out of time.

Ever since the night Shane had come by her apartment in Houston, she'd been kicking herself for letting him go without making arrangements to see him again. After all, she could have suggested that he stop by the next day on his way back to Brighton Valley...but she'd just assumed that he would.

In fact, she'd waited close to the house all day, hoping he might show up or call, but he hadn't done either.

But maybe that was her fault, not his. She hadn't meant to give him the impression that she wasn't interested in him. She'd just wanted to take things slow, to give herself some time to think.

Had he gotten the idea that she was shutting him out completely?

Or had he backed off, only to find another woman who interested him? Someone local and more his type?

That possibility sent a shiver of uneasiness through her. Had she found a knight in shining armor, only to let him slip through her fingers?

Sleeping with the handsome cowboy had just... happened. Well, that wasn't exactly true. That evening had unfolded as beautifully as a well-choreographed waltz.

She'd never been so spontaneous before, never been so bold as to suggest sex with a virtual stranger. But neither had she ever wanted to make love so badly with a man that nothing else had mattered.

If she'd actually gone to the hospital complaining of a broken heart or shattered dreams, Shane Hollister would have been just what the doctor would have ordered. He'd been sweet, sensitive, funny...and refreshing.

His kisses had been a better fix than any drug could have been; they'd made her feel whole and lovable again.

For the first time since learning of her ex-husband's infidelity, Jillian had found a way to ease the pain and to chase away the emptiness she'd lived with for months—if not for all the years she'd been married. And in the midst of it all, Shane had taken her to a place she'd never been before, a peak and a climax she'd never even imagined.

How could she not want to see him again?

More than once, she'd been tempted to call him. Yet she hadn't, which meant that Shane Hollister continued to be a mystery. Each time she'd picked up the phone, she'd chickened out.

The longer she waited, the harder it was going to be. So she would contact him today.

Didn't she owe him that much?

She reached for her purse and searched for the small notepad on which he'd written his number. It had been several months since he'd given it to her.

What if he'd gotten involved with someone else in the meantime?

Her heart cramped at the thought, creating an ache she hadn't been prepared for. After all, it's not as though she had any claim on him.

Oh, no?

She placed her hand on the swell of her belly, where their baby grew, and her thoughts drifted back to the night she'd taken him to her hotel room.

She'd never done anything so bold or brazen before and doubted that she ever would again. But *she* hadn't been sorry then, and she wasn't sorry now.

In less than five months she would be having Shane's baby. She was going to have to tell him, no matter what the consequences were. And it was only right to do that in person.

So she pulled out the notepad where he'd written his number. The page curled up on the ends, thanks to all the times she'd looked at it, tempted to place the call, then deciding not to. But this time, she grabbed the phone and dialed.

It was time to tell Shane that he was going to be a daddy.

Chapter Five

Shane stood at the mudroom sink, chugging down a large glass of water.

The hay he'd ordered last week had arrived this afternoon, so he'd spent the past couple of hours helping the driver unload a semitruck and trailer. They'd had to stack it in the barn, which meant he'd been bucking bales that weighed ninety pounds or more and stacking them more than chest high.

Needless to say, he'd not only gotten a good workout, but he'd also built up a hearty appetite in the process. So no matter what he decided to fix for dinner, he'd have to make plenty of it. Fortunately, Eva Walker kept a well-stocked pantry and freezer, so he wouldn't have any problem whipping up something good to eat.

For the past week, Shane had been holding down the fort while Dan, Eva and their four children—two sets of twins, toddlers and second-graders—were in New York, visiting a family friend.

Since Dan had asked him to look after things while he was gone, Shane had packed up his shaving gear and clothes and moved out to the ranch, where he'd spent his days working with the horses and his nights caring for the family menagerie—two dogs, a cat and a hamster.

Shane really didn't mind helping out, since Dan was not only his boss, but his friend. The two of them had met a year or so ago in town at Caroline's Diner, and Dan had offered him a job. Taking the ranch hand position had proved to be a blessing for both of them.

As Shane rinsed his face and hands in the sink, his cell phone rang. He figured it was his nephew calling to arrange the promised day of horseback riding. It had been nearly two months since Shane had agreed to let Evan come out to the ranch, but with school and T-ball schedules, they'd decided to wait until his summer vacation.

Evan was a city kid who would prefer to be a cowboy, if given the chance, and Shane couldn't help but grin at the image of the happy boy in the saddle.

Tempted to let the call roll over to voice mail until he dried his hands and poured himself a glass of iced tea, he glanced at the display, and saw an unfamiliar number. Maybe he'd better not ignore that one. "Hello."

"Shane?"

Jillian? After three months, he'd given up hope of ever hearing her voice again.

"Hey," he said, his heart thudding as though it was clamoring to escape his chest. "How's it going?"

"Good, thanks."

He'd been tempted to contact her again, either by telephone or a drive into the city, but he'd held off. If there was one thing to be said about Shane Hollister, it's that he could be pretty damn stubborn when he put his mind to it.

"How about you?" she asked.

"Not bad."

That same awkward silence filled the line again, so hoping to help things along, he said, "It's good to hear from you."

"Thanks."

Come on, honey, he wanted to say. *Just tell me why*

you're calling. Are you having a hard time forgetting that night? Or that last kiss?

He might have nearly written her off, but that didn't mean he no longer thought about her or dreamed about her. Hell, each night he slipped between the sheets of his bed, he'd never been completely alone. Her memory had followed him there.

"I'd like to talk to you," she said. "That is, if you don't mind."

"Not at all. I'm glad you called."

"Actually," she said, "I'd rather talk to you in person. Would it be okay if I drove out to Brighton Valley to see you?"

That was better yet. "Of course. I've got to work most of the day tomorrow, but I'll be finished by late afternoon or early evening." Dan and Eva were due back tomorrow around three, so Shane would take off whenever they arrived.

"Should I drive out to the ranch?"

Shane wasn't so sure that he wanted to have an audience when he and Jillian met—at least, not one that would quiz him after she returned to Houston. But he didn't think it would be a good idea to suggest that she meet him at his place, which was a small studio apartment. It might be too... Well, presumptive, he supposed.

"Why don't we meet in town," he suggested. "There's a great little honky-tonk called the Stagecoach Inn, which is right off the county highway. It shouldn't be too difficult for you to find."

"All right. Can you give me directions?"

"It's pretty easy to spot. If you drive out to Brighton Valley, it's the first thing you'll see when you hit the main drag."

"That sounds easy enough."

Shane wasn't sure why he'd suggested the Stagecoach

Inn. He supposed he also wanted to show her a good time—and in a place that was a whole lot different from her usual hangouts.

If she couldn't handle a rip-roaring cowboy bar on a Saturday night, she probably couldn't handle the small-town life in his neck of the woods. And it was best that they found that out early on.

Besides, the music at the Stagecoach Inn was enough to make most people tap their feet and whoop it up. And he hoped to see Jillian let her hair down again.

A couple of months might have passed since he'd gone to her apartment, but he still thought about her more often than not.

He wished he could say that his interest in her was strictly physical, since there'd been some real chemistry brewing between them. But as the days passed, he'd begun to realize that there was something else drawing him to Jillian's memory, something other than great sex that kept her image fresh in his mind. He actually missed hearing her voice, seeing her smile.

So even if lovemaking wasn't in the cards for them to-night, he was looking forward to whatever time they had.

"When do you want to meet?" he asked.

"I guess it depends on you, since you're the one who has to work tomorrow."

"Then why don't we say five o'clock?" That would give him time to drive home, shower and shave.

"That sounds good."

It certainly did. And since she was going to have a two-hour drive back to Houston, he wondered if she planned to spend the night.

If so, that sounded even better yet.

Jillian entered the Stagecoach Inn more than thirty minutes early—and sporting an unmistakable baby bump. Now that she'd passed her fourth month, her womb seemed to be growing more each day.

Hoping to disguise the evidence of her pregnancy until she had the chance to tell him about it, she'd found a table for two and took a seat that faced the front door. She really hadn't suffered any morning sickness, like other women, but her tummy was tossing and turning now, just at the thought of facing Shane.

She'd been dragging her feet for months, and now that she'd come to tell him, she wished she'd done so sooner. But there wasn't anything she could do about that now.

So, while waiting for him, she scanned the honky-tonk, noting the scuffed and scarred hardwood floor, the red-and-chrome jukebox, the Old-West-style bar that stretched the length of the building. If she'd ever tried to imagine what a cowboy bar would look like, this would be it.

At the table next to hers, two young women wearing tight jeans and scooped-neck T-shirts laughed about something, then clinked their longneck bottles in a toast.

Was this the place where Shane hung out in the evenings or on his days off? Is that why he'd suggested she meet him here?

"Can I get you a drink?" a blond, harried waitress asked.

"Do you have any fruit juice?"

"I'll have to check with the bartender to see what other choices you have, but I know we've got OJ for sure."

"That'll be fine. Thank you."

The bleached-blond waitress had no more than walked away from the table when Jillian's cell phone rang. She grabbed it from her purse, hoping it wasn't Shane telling her he'd been delayed, since she'd put off this conversation for too long as it was.

But when she checked the display, she spotted her grandmother's number.

"Did you get to Brighton Valley safely?" Gram asked.

Jillian pressed her cell phone against her ear, trying to block out the sounds of a Texas two-step as it blasted out of the jukebox. "Yes. It was a pretty easy drive, although it was a long one."

"Where are you?"

"At a bar called the Stagecoach Inn."

"It sounds pretty wild," Gram said. "Are you sure you're okay?"

"I'm fine."

"I don't know about that," Gram said. "I probably should have insisted upon going with you. Where will you be staying?"

"Right next door at the Night Owl Motel."

"That sounds a little…rustic. Don't they have anything nicer than that in town?"

"Not that I know of," Jillian said. "But don't worry. I'll be okay. Besides, you're the one who told me I needed to tell Shane about the baby."

"I know, but…" Gram was clearly having second thoughts.

And so was Jillian. She'd never been in a country bar before, and the Night Owl was a world away from those five-star hotels she'd been used to. But the last thing she wanted to do was to cause her grandmother any undue stress.

"The motel really isn't that bad," she said, trying to talk above a sudden hoot of laughter. "The room is clean, and the bed is soft. I'll be fine tonight. Then I'll drive back to Houston in the morning."

The waitress returned with the orange juice in a Mason jar. "Here you go. Let me know if you'd like anything else."

Jillian offered her a smile. "Thanks. This will be fine for now."

As the waitress walked away, Gram said, "I'm still uneasy about you being there all alone, Jilly."

"Don't be. Shane will be here soon."

"I'm sure he will, but you really don't know him very well."

Oh, for Pete's sake. It was Gram who'd helped her come to the conclusion that she needed to stop procrastinating and tell Shane he was going to be a father. And that wasn't the kind of news to spring on him over the telephone.

"Shane's a nice guy, Gram. You'd like him if you met him. He used to be a police officer, remember?"

"Yes, you mentioned that. But why did he decide to give that job up and go to work on a ranch?"

It probably had something to do with him getting into trouble and being suspended from duty, although Jillian couldn't be sure about that. Last night, on a whim, she'd done a Google search on Shane Hollister and uncovered an online newspaper article about him. From what she'd read, he'd gotten too rough with a man he'd arrested.

Her heart had dropped to the pit of her stomach upon that discovery, especially when she spotted a photograph that convinced her that the men were one and the same.

Just the thought that Shane Hollister, the man who'd loved her with a gentle and expert hand, might harbor a temper or a violent side, set off a wave of nausea. On several occasions, after having too much to drink, Thomas had twisted her arm or given her a shove. So Jillian had kicked herself for not conducting an internet search on Shane sooner.

She'd wanted more details, of course, but short of breaking into police headquarters and hunting for his personnel file, she didn't know how or where to look. But she certainly knew someone who did.

Katie Harris, a journalist who'd been Jillian's college roommate, now worked for a Dallas newspaper. So Jillian had called her and asked her if she could uncover any more information about the incident that had gotten Shane into trouble with the police department.

Katie had been on her way into the office and had called back within an hour. She hadn't found out too much more, other than the fact that Shane had been reinstated to his position with the HPD. But then, a few months later, he'd resigned for no apparent reason.

While tossing and turning in bed last night, Jillian had vacillated on whether to go through with the plan to meet Shane and tell him about the baby, but she'd finally decided to give him the benefit of the doubt.

Of course, she wasn't going to share any of that with her grandmother.

"Well, if you're sure you're okay..." Gram said doubtfully.

"I'll be fine."

"Okay, but call me once you're locked into the motel room for the night."

"I'll do that." Jillian glanced toward the entrance, just in time to see Shane saunter through the door, looking more handsome than a cowboy had a right to. "But I've got to go, Gram. He's here now."

And he'd just spotted her.

When Shane walked into the Stagecoach Inn, he was nearly twenty minutes early. Still, the place was already hopping, even for a Saturday night that was just getting under way. Yet he hadn't gotten two steps inside before he'd spotted Jillian seated at a table for two, looking just as attractive as ever. She was talking on the phone, but as soon as she noticed him, she hung up.

He crossed the scarred oak flooring and made his way to her table. "I see you found the place."

She smiled. "You're right. It was pretty easy, but I have to admit I've never been anywhere like this before."

He figured she meant the honky-tonk, but she could have just as easily been talking about Brighton Valley, as well. "Consider it an adventure."

"I don't know about that. I haven't felt very adventurous lately."

He wondered what she meant by that as he quietly observed her. She wore her platinum-blond hair pulled back today, and a white cotton blouse and black slacks. She'd come looking more casual, more down-to-earth.

More approachable than before, even when he'd found her at home.

As he pulled out the chair next to hers, he asked, "So what are you having? A screwdriver?"

She glanced at her glass, then back at him. "No, it's just orange juice."

The waitress, Trina Shepherd, stopped by the table to ask what he'd like to drink.

After his first visit to the Stagecoach Inn, she'd become a friend of sorts when he'd closed the place down on a slow night. But unlike most guys who'd stayed too long at the bar, he'd been drinking coffee, not throwing back shots.

As a result, Trina knew more about Shane than anyone else in Brighton Valley. But he knew more about her, too.

At one time, before heartache and a few bad choices had left her weathered and worn, she'd been pretty. If a man looked close enough, he could still see hints of it in her eyes.

"Hey," she said, brightening when she spotted Shane. "I haven't seen you in here for a while. How's it going?"

"All right." He tossed her a friendly smile. "How are the kids? Any more broken windows?"

Trina laughed. "There'd better not be. I told them I was going to quit buying groceries if they played dodgeball in the living room again."

Last week, when Shane had stopped by for some hot wings and a beer on his way home, she'd had to leave work to run one of the boys to the E.R. at the Brighton Valley Medical Center. The kid had nearly cut off his finger trying to clean broken glass off the floor.

Shane introduced the women, calling Jillian a friend of his.

"It's nice to meet you," Trina said to Jillian, before asking Shane, "What can I get you?"

"I'll have a Corona—with lime." He looked at Jillian. "Would you like something stronger than that?"

"No, thanks. I'll stick with juice."

Was she worried that alcohol might lower her inhibitions? She didn't need to be. He'd never take advantage of her, although he supposed she really had no way of knowing that. At least, not yet.

He wouldn't be opposed to taking her back to his place, though. And if she still insisted upon taking things slow, he'd let her have his bed, and he'd sleep on the sofa.

Of course, the night was still young. So who knew how things would end up?

As he cast a glance her way, he saw that she was pulling at the nail on one of her fingers. He couldn't help thinking that she was more nervous than he'd ever seen her.

Why? Was she apprehensive about seeing him again?

If so, was it the honky-tonk setting that was bothering

her? Or was it confronting the sexual attraction they'd both found so impossible to ignore?

She stopped messing with her fingernail, then leaned forward and rested her forearms on top of the table. "There's something I need to tell you."

That's what she'd said when she'd called yesterday. Yet whatever she had to say still seemed to weigh on her mind.

Wanting to make it easier on her, he tossed her a smile. "I hope it's to say that you missed me."

She returned his smile, although hers was laden with whatever had been holding her back. "It's a little more complicated than that."

Apparently so. But her nervousness set him on edge, too.

Finally, she said, "I want you to know that the night we spent in Houston was the first time I'd ever done anything like that."

He'd suspected as much, and a slow grin stretched across his face. "I'm glad to hear it."

So maybe she did have more in mind than a glass of OJ and a chat. He sure hoped so, but he was going to need a little more to go on than that.

Jillian ran her fingertip along the moisture that had gathered on the Mason jar, clearly holding back her announcement.

He couldn't help but chuckle. "Something tells me that it might be easier for you to say what you came to say if you asked Trina to put a little vodka in that glass."

"That wouldn't help." She leaned back in her chair and crossed her arms. "There's no easy way to say this, Shane. I'm pregnant."

Her statement slammed into him like barrage of bullets, making it impossible to speak, let alone react.

Was she suggesting the baby was his? Or had she met someone else in the past few months?

"I thought you should know," she added.

Why? Because the baby *was* his?

They'd used protection… Had they gotten careless that night? Was the condom outdated?

Or had she gotten pregnant by some other guy? Her ex-husband maybe?

Was that why she hadn't contacted him? Was she afraid he wouldn't like the idea of her having some other man's baby?

"How far along are you?" he asked, hoping to do the math and clarify things without asking outright if the baby was his.

"Four and a half months," she said.

That would make it about right.

He supposed there was no way around being direct. "Is it mine?"

She shot him a wounded expression. "Of course it's yours. I told you that I'd never done anything like that before."

Well, how the hell was he supposed to have known that it had to be his? She'd been married up until the time they'd met…. And maybe she'd done it a second or third time—with someone else.

"I know we used a condom," she added, "so I'm not sure how it happened, but it did."

Shane lifted his hat, raked a hand through his hair, then set the Stetson on the table. "I'm sorry, Jillian. I'm just a little…stunned. That's all."

God, he was going to be a father again…

Just the thought caused voice-stealing emotion to rise in his chest and ball up in his throat—fear and panic, pride…

"I'm not asking for anything," she said. "Like I said

before, I plan to raise the baby on my own. And other than the fact that it will probably be a little inconvenient because of school and all, I'm actually looking forward to being a mom. It's just that I thought you should know."

He would have been furious with her if he'd ever found out on his own and learned that she'd kept it from him. But right now, he didn't know quite what to say. His emotions were flying around like stray bullets at a shoot-out—each spinning toward separate targets.

For some reason, thoughts of Marcia came back to taunt him, memories of her taking their toddler and moving out of town. The reminder served to blindside him, making it even more difficult to deal with Jillian's news—and making it way more personal.

"I'm sorry," she said.

"About what?"

"I don't know. Dumping all of this on you, I guess. You must be worried about what this all means, but it doesn't have to mean anything to you. I just thought you should know." She bit down on her bottom lip, her mind undoubtedly going a mile a minute, just as his was doing.

He tried to wrap his mind around the fact that he was going to be a father again, but as he did, thoughts of Joey swept over him: the sight of the newborn coming into the world; that first flutter of a smile; the sight of the chubby baby pulling himself to a stand at the coffee table.

While he should look forward to the idea of having a second chance at fatherhood, the horrendous image of his eighteen-month-old son lying in a small, white, satin-lined casket chased away the sweet memories, and he feared what this might lead to…the anger, the pain, the grief.

After Shane and Marcia had split up, she'd moved out of state, taking Joey with her. Not only had Shane lost out on seeing his son from day to day, he'd been more than five-hundred miles away when he'd received word that he'd…lost him for good.

There was no way Shane wanted to go through that again. And while he had no idea how he would remedy that this time around, he knew he'd have to do something.

He glanced at Jillian, saw her pulling at her fingernail again—clearly worried, nervous and stressed about the situation.

It probably hadn't been easy for her to deliver the news, and he was sorry that his initial reaction had been a little harsh.

"I didn't mean to snap at you," he said, his mind still reeling.

She smiled, then glanced away. "I understand."

But she *didn't;* she *couldn't.*

He probably should tell her about Joey, about how he'd lost his son, about how he still ached with grief. But he didn't think he could open his heart like that without choking up and falling apart.

Besides, the baby news had slammed into him like a runaway train, and it was too soon for him to have a rational reaction to it.

Even if he'd been happy to learn that he was going to be a father again, he wasn't sure if he could trust her. What if Jillian took his baby away and never let him see it again?

He studied her for a moment, watched her slip her hand between the table and her belly, stroking her rounded womb as if caressing the child that grew there.

His child.

Her child.

Fear of repeating the past—the pain, the grief—threatened to suck the breath right out of him, but he couldn't let it. He had to face the truth. He was going to be a father again.

And there was no reason history had to repeat itself.

"When's the baby due?" he asked.

"December third." Her gaze wrapped around his, and she smiled, a whisper of relief chasing away all signs of her nervousness.

How had he missed seeing it before—the obvious pregnancy, the maternal glow?

Jillian might have waited too damn long to tell him about the baby, but he sensed she was happy about the situation.

"Are you planning to drive back to Houston tonight?" he asked.

She caught his gaze. "Actually, I didn't like the idea of being on the road after dark, so I got a room at the Night Owl."

"You could have stayed with me."

"I… Well, I suppose I could have, but I wasn't sure how you'd take the news. And I figured things might be a little awkward between us."

"Maybe so, but we'll need to deal with the situation anyway." And some of it was going to be tough.

Shane scanned the honky-tonk, and when he spotted Trina, he motioned for her to come to the table.

"Are you hungry?" he asked Jillian.

"A little."

When Trina reached the table, Shane said, "We'd like to place an order to go."

"All right. I'll get you a couple of menus." When she returned, she handed each of them the new, one-sided laminated sheet of cardstock that offered a few appetizers and various sandwiches. "I'll give you a chance to look this over, then I'll be back."

"Where are we going?" Jillian asked him.

"When I thought we were just tiptoeing around our attraction and a possible romance, I figured the Stagecoach

Inn would be good place to kick up our heels and forget all the reasons why a long-distance relationship wouldn't work out. But now that things have taken an unexpected turn, we need to find a quieter spot so we can talk."

Jillian didn't respond.

Moments later, Trina returned for their orders.

"I'll have the soup and salad combo," Jillian said.

Shane chose the bacon cheeseburger and fries.

"You got it." Trina scratched out their requests on her pad before taking the order to the kitchen.

While Shane and Jillian waited for their food, they made small talk about the music on the jukebox and some of the more interesting characters who had begun to fill the honky-tonk. Yet the tension stretched between them like a worn-out bungee cord ready to snap.

Before long, Trina returned with a take-home bag, as well as the bill. Shane paid the tab, leaving her a generous tip.

"Are you ready?" he asked Jillian, as he scooted back his chair and got to his feet.

Jillian stood and reached for her purse. "So where did you decide to eat?"

"You said you had a room at the Night Owl. Let's go there."

If she had any reservations about taking him back to the motel with her, she didn't say. And Shane was glad. It was important that they take some time to really get to know each other.

And the sooner they got started doing that, the better.

Chapter Six

As dusk settled over Brighton Valley, Shane and Jillian stepped out of the honky-tonk and into the parking lot, which was filling up with a variety of pickups and cars.

"Did you drive from the motel?" he asked.

"No, I walked. The doctor encouraged me to get plenty of exercise, and since I'd been in the car for the past two hours, I thought... Well, it was only a couple of blocks, and it was a good way to stretch my legs."

So she'd already seen a doctor. That was good.

"Is everything going okay?" he asked. "No problems?"

"I had a little nausea at first, but it wasn't anything to complain about."

He was glad to hear that. Marcia had been pretty sick when she'd been pregnant with Joey, although she felt a bit better by the time she was four or five months along. In fact, if he remembered correctly, Marcia had been at that stage when they'd learned that Joey was going to be a boy.

Shane assumed that, since Jillian was seeing a doctor, she was having all the appropriate tests and exams. So he asked, "Do you know whether it's going to be a girl or a boy?"

"No, I told the doctor I wanted to be surprised." She

shrugged. "At least, I'd thought so at the time of my sono-gram. But I have to admit, I'm getting more and more curious now."

As they continued walking to the street, their feet crunching along the graveled parking lot, Shane couldn't help stealing a glance at Jillian, checking out the way her belly swelled with their child.

He suspected that she was going to be one of those women who was even more beautiful when she was nine months pregnant. But he didn't want her to think his only concern was the baby, so he asked, "How's school going?"

"It took a little while to get back into the swing of taking notes and studying, but I'm doing okay now. I'm taking two summer courses, and I have finals in two weeks, but nothing too difficult."

"Then what?" he asked.

"I'll begin the student-teaching phase during the fall semester.... Well, that was my game plan before finding out about the baby. It's due right before Christmas, so I'll probably have to wait another semester."

"How are you fixed for money?" he asked.

"I'm okay." She pulled up short. "That's not why I came out here."

He stopped, too. "You need to understand something. I don't expect you to support the baby all by yourself. I'll do my part."

She bit down on her bottom lip, then her gaze lifted and locked on his. Sincerity flared in her eyes, as well as determination. "You don't have to."

Yes, he did.

Unable to help himself, he reached for her hair, touched the silky platinum-blond strands, then let them slip through his fingers. Jillian might be pregnant, and he might have been blown away by the news, but that didn't mean she wasn't a beautiful woman. Or that he'd stopped thinking about wanting to spend another night with her.

Jillian slowly turned away from him, and they continued down the street for two short blocks. Their conversation ceased, as Shane let his thoughts run away with him.

There were a lot of things to consider, a lot yet to be seen. He probably ought to ask more questions. After all, he certainly had plenty of them bouncing around in his head. But he didn't want things to get any heavier between them than they were now.

Not with a lover's moon lighting their path to the motel where she had a room.

The Night Owl, a typical small-town motor inn, sat near the highway, catering to travelers on a budget and to those just passing through. It was the only place to stay on this side of Brighton Valley.

Across town, closer to the thriving community of Wexler, builders and developers had been hard at work, creating several subdivisions along the perimeter of the lake and recreation area.

The Brighton Valley Medical Center, which served the citizens from the entire valley, was located in that part of town, too, as was a supermarket, a department store and a much nicer motel.

But since Shane hadn't wanted to give Jillian any complicated directions, he'd chosen the Stagecoach Inn because it would be easier for her to find. However, he hadn't expected her to need lodging, too. So he should have come up with something closer to Wexler.

He supposed the Night Owl wasn't so bad, even if it wouldn't provide her with the kind of accommodations she was probably used to.

As they approached the single-story building with white stucco walls and a red-tile roof, he spotted a couple of older vehicles in the parking lot, but his gaze lit upon a white, late-model Mercedes coupe in the space closet to number ten, which had to be where they were heading.

Jillian's steps slowed as she reached into her purse, then lifted an old-fashioned key instead of a more modern card and smiled. "I guess this place is in a bit of a time warp."

Her smile suggested she wasn't too bothered by the age of the motel, then she turned and led him to number ten.

Shane was reminded of the last time she'd let him into her hotel room.

As much as he'd like to wrap his arms around her again, kiss her senseless at the door, stretch out naked on the bed and make love until dawn, things were going to be different tonight.

At least, he assumed they would be.

Yet just as before, Shane held the door for Jillian, then followed her inside.

The room, which was clean but sparse, had been simply decorated with a queen-size bed and the typical, nondescript box-style furniture. Again he was reminded that she wasn't used to this kind of lodging, even if she hadn't complained.

He set their bag of food on the small Formica table in the corner, then dug inside for the takeout cartons, plastic utensils and napkins Trina had packed inside.

After setting everything out on the table, he turned to Jillian, intending to follow her lead.

She blushed, and her thick, spiky lashes swept down, then up in a hesitant way.

"What's the matter?"

"I…" She bit down on her bottom lip. "I don't know. I guess I'm just a little concerned about what the future will bring."

For a moment, he wondered if she was talking about

them having dinner together in her motel room, while a queen-size bed grew in prominence. But she probably meant the changes the baby would make in their lives, about them trying to be coparents when distance was going to be an issue.

Either way, he didn't like the idea of her being stressed—and not just because she was pregnant. So he stepped forward, cupped her cheeks with both hands and caught her eye. "If you want to know the truth, Jillian, I'm nervous about the future, too. But maybe, if we take the time to get to know each other a whole lot better, things will be easier to deal with."

Her smile, which bordered on pleasure and relief, nearly knocked him to the floor. And he found himself wanting to kiss her in the worst way—and just as he'd done before.

Who was this woman? And what was she doing to him?

Struggling to get his hormones in check, he nodded toward the food on the table. "Why don't we start by having dinner?"

"Okay." She crossed the small room in three steps, then pulled out a chair and took a seat at the table.

He followed her lead, but in spite of suggesting that they eat, he wasn't nearly as hungry as he'd once been. Not for food anyway. But making love had gotten them into this mess in the first place, and doing it again wasn't going to solve any of the problems they now faced.

Instead, it would be imperative to learn more about her.

And one thing that really had him perplexed was her financial situation, since she appeared to be ultrawealthy, yet lived in a modest apartment.

"You said that you didn't expect any financial support from me. And by the style and make of the car parked outside, as well as those diamond stud earrings you're wearing, I take it money isn't an issue for you."

She lifted the lid to her soup, then reached for a plastic spoon. "I'm afraid things aren't always what they seem. Thanks to a prenuptial agreement, the only things I got from the divorce settlement—besides my freedom—was a modest settlement, my jewelry and the Mercedes you saw out front. But I plan to trade in the car for something more economical in the next couple of weeks. And I've sold some of the jewelry already."

"Then you *do* need money."

"But I don't need *your* money," she insisted. "I didn't come here to secure child support payments. Honestly, Shane, I only came to tell you that you're going to be a father. Just so you'd know. I really wasn't trying to rope you into anything. I can make it on my own."

Shane didn't mean to doubt her. It's just that… Well, he was finding it difficult to get a firm read on her, so he asked, "Then what's the best way for me to help you? I'm afraid the ball is in your court."

Was it?

Jillian had just placed a spoonful of broth into her mouth, so she couldn't have managed a quick response if she'd wanted to, which was just as well. Her first thought was to tell him, *You can stop asking me questions and start answering a few of mine.*

After all, she'd come out to Brighton Valley to learn more about Shane, but she couldn't very well open by bringing up the incident that had caused him to get in trouble with the HPD—even if that was the main thing she both wanted and needed to know.

If she did broach a sticky subject like that right off the bat, he'd wonder how she'd found out about it. And what was she supposed to admit? That she'd not only done an internet search, which everyone did these days, but that she'd also enlisted the help of an investigative journalist?

It was too soon to do that, so she answered as honestly as she could. "I'm really not sure how you can help."

"Like I said before, I want to be involved in the baby's life."

"Well, under the circumstances, that's going to be a little tough, isn't it?"

It was the truth, although she hoped the words didn't come across as harshly as they sounded after the fact.

Shane glanced down at his uneaten burger, then met her gaze. Yet he didn't speak.

He was a handsome man and a good lover—that, she knew. But she had no idea what was under the surface—or what kind of father he'd make. And his desire to be a part of the baby's life caught her off guard, causing her maternal instincts to kick in.

"If you're thinking you'd like to share custody, that won't work. A baby needs its mother."

Shane stiffened as if she'd struck him, and she wasn't sure why. He lived two hours away. How could they possibly consider joint custody until the child was older? And even then, she wasn't willing to enter an arrangement like that until she knew him better and could determine whether he harbored either a short fuse or a violent streak.

She placed the lid back on her soup container, no longer hungry. Why had she told him she was pregnant? Okay, so it wouldn't have been right to keep it from him, but she was having serious misgivings.

Shane pushed his food aside. "Look, I didn't mean that I expected to have the baby every other weekend, it's just that... Well, I have a big family and a lot of nieces and nephews. I want them to know my son and to be able to play with him."

"Your *son?*" She smiled, assuming that he probably

thought he could relate better to a boy—playing ball, riding horses and whatever activities daddies liked to do with their children. "What if the baby is a girl?"

He paused, and that fleeting shadow darkened his eyes again, moving on as quickly as it had arisen.

"A little girl would be fine with me," he said. "I'm just trying to figure out how to make a difficult situation work out for everyone involved."

"Everyone?"

"You, me *and* the baby."

Jillian thought about that for a moment, then decided that he wasn't being completely unreasonable. "I suppose you could drive to Houston on the weekends and visit us."

Again, he stiffened, as if offended by the offer.

"I'd also be happy to invite your nieces and nephews over to spend time with their new cousin," she added.

He seemed to be mulling that over. Couldn't he see that she was willing to compromise—when possible?

She reached across the table and placed her hand on his forearm, felt the strength of well-defined muscles. "I'm sure you're a wonderful man, Shane. And that you'll make a great father. It's just that…I don't really know that yet. I don't know much about you. I'm sorry if I'm coming across as resistant or difficult. My motherly instincts must be coming into play."

At that, she could feel the tension ease in his forearm, and his expression softened.

"I already made a mistake by marrying a man I couldn't trust," she said. "So I hope you won't blame me for being gun-shy when it comes to jumping into any kind of relationship, especially when I have a baby to consider this time around."

He placed his hand on top of hers, his touch sending a whisper of heat coursing through her.

Yet it was the intensity of his gaze, the ragged sincerity in his eyes, that urged her to give him a chance—to give them *all* one.

"I can't blame you for wanting to be careful," he said. "I'm a little gun-shy, too. And since you're going to be the mother of my baby, I'd like to know with absolute certainty that you'll make a good one."

She hadn't realized that he had some of the same concerns that she had, a thought that soared crazily like a broken kite on a snapped string.

"You could be a good actress," he said, "but something tells me that you're every bit the woman I thought you were when I showed up at your house in Houston, hoping a long-distance relationship might work out between us. But back then, I figured it was worth the risk of striking out if you'd rejected the idea."

"And *now?*"

"With a baby in the balance, I think it's critical for us to know the truth about each other."

She couldn't agree more.

After a beat, she asked, "So now what? Where do we go from here?"

She expected his gaze to travel to the bed in the center of the room. After all, that's where they knew each other best. But instead, he focused on her, this time turning her heart inside out.

"You mentioned that your fall semester will be starting," he said.

"Yes, in three weeks." She'd also planned to take a class through the local YMCA on newborn and infant development in the evenings. And she hoped to start preparing a nursery.

He leaned forward, his hand still lightly pressing on hers. "Why don't you come out to Brighton Valley while you're still out of school? I'll cut back on my hours at the ranch, and we can use the time to get to know each other better."

The invitation took her aback, yet she thought long and hard over what he was proposing.

Where would she stay? Even a room at the Night Owl would get expensive after a while. She'd been trying to stretch her dollars so that her money would last until she secured a teaching position and could afford day care.

As if reading her mind, he said, "You can stay in my apartment with me. I'll sleep on the sofa—if you're worried about my motives."

She wasn't sure how she felt about any of what he was suggesting, but they did need time to get to know each other. And staying with him seemed like a logical plan, at least, financially speaking.

"All right," she said. "I'll come to Brighton Valley for a couple of weeks. And I'll stay with you."

He sat back in his seat, his eyes growing bright. "I think you've made a good decision."

She wasn't so sure about that.

Staying with him could make things a lot more complicated than they were right now.

Especially since she wasn't excited about him sleeping on the sofa when she knew how much she'd once enjoyed having him in her bed.

Two weeks later, after paying the woman who'd scrubbed his apartment from top to bottom and sending her on her way, Shane stood in the living room, surveying the results of her efforts and breathing in the scent of lemon oil and various cleaning products.

It's not as though he was a slob, but he wanted Jillian to be comfortable while she stayed with him. Of course, he had no idea how she might feel about him living in an apartment over Caroline's Diner.

When Shane had first come to Brighton Valley, he'd stopped for lunch at the small-town restaurant, where he'd had the best chicken and dumplings he'd ever eaten. His waitress had asked if he was new in town, and when he'd nodded, she'd told him about the vacancy upstairs. So after meeting Dan Walker and landing a job as a ranch hand that very same day, he'd realized that his luck had finally begun to turn.

Dan had also told him he could stay in the bunkhouse, but while Shane had appreciated the offer, he'd graciously declined. He preferred having a place of his own, where he could hang his hat and escape after a hard day's labor.

And so he'd set about making his new digs feel like home, adding a few pieces of furniture now and then, as well as a flat-screen television and a state-of-the-art sound system. He might not spend very much time at home, but when he did, he wanted a few comforts.

Hopefully, Jillian would find the apartment appealing, as well. After all, she'd be living here for the next two weeks.

Shane crossed the floor to the kitchen, where the sink, countertops and appliances all sparkled. Then he opened the fridge, which he'd stocked with food and drinks after a run to the market last night. Jillian would have plenty of stuff to choose from, including fresh fruits and vegetables.

Now all he had to do was wait for her to arrive.

After closing the refrigerator, he strode to the window and peered into the street, expecting her to arrive soon—unless she'd gotten lost along the way.

He was really looking forward to seeing her again, although he felt badly about leaving Dan Walker in a lurch for the next week. But Dan was a family man and understood the situation, once Shane had explained the surprising predicament he'd found himself in. Dan had listened, then insisted that he'd be able to handle things on his own.

Shane planned to take off only the first week of Jillian's visit. He would spend as much time with her as he could for those seven days. After that, she'd need to keep herself busy during the day. It shouldn't be too difficult. There were stores along Main, if she felt like shopping. She could even visit Darla's Salon. And there was a library in Wexler, which wasn't too far away.

He still couldn't believe that she'd gotten pregnant on their one and only night together. Yet the more he thought about it, the better he felt about it.

It didn't seem fair, though. After his divorce, he'd sworn off women who wanted different things out of life than he did. But now he'd gotten involved with another one, a woman who'd set her sights on things outside his world.

Of course, that might change with time. He had a week or two to tempt Jillian with everything a small town like Brighton Valley had to offer, although something told him it wouldn't be good enough for her.

As it neared five o'clock, the time she was due to arrive, Shane went downstairs to sit on the green wrought-iron bench in front of the diner.

He didn't have to wait long. Moments later she arrived driving a silver Honda Accord. Apparently she'd gotten rid of the Mercedes, just as she'd told him.

As she climbed out of the driver's seat, he took note of her casual clothing—jeans, a white fitted top that stretched over her baby bump and a lightweight chambray shirt.

Her hair hung to her shoulders in a loose, carefree style, reminding him of the way it had looked splayed on a pillow and the way those silky strands had felt as they'd slipped through his fingers that same night.

He was sorely tempted to greet her with a hug, but he got to his feet and shoved his hands into the front pockets of his jeans instead. No need to come on too strong, he supposed.

"Did you have any trouble finding the place?" he asked.

"No, it was pretty easy." She cast him a smile that seemed almost waifish and lost, then opened the rear passenger door for her suitcase.

"I'll get that for you," he said, stepping forward and catching an amazing whiff of her scent—something lilac, he guessed.

She thanked him, then allowed him to reach into the car. After he snatched her bag and closed the door, she hit the lock button on the key remote.

"Come on," he said, "I'll show you where I live."

He led her up the narrow stairway between the diner and the drugstore.

Once they were upstairs, he opened the door, then stepped aside and let her enter first.

As she scanned the living room, he tried to see the place from her perspective. Would she be comfortable here? Would she find it too modest, too humble?

"It's not much," he said, "but it's home."

She didn't respond, which made him wonder if she found it lacking in some way. Then she crossed the hardwood floor to the window that looked out into the street.

When she turned around, she smiled, lighting up the room in an unexpected way. "When you said you lived in an apartment, I thought it would be in a typical complex, like mine. I didn't expect something like this."

Was that good or bad?

He supposed it shouldn't matter, yet it did. "So what do you think?"

"It's got an interesting view." She walked to the sofa, which he'd purchased a couple of months ago, and placed her hand along the backrest. "I like it."

Thank goodness. It would have been tough if she were to hate the idea of being stuck here for a couple of weeks. So he returned her smile, then nodded toward the bedroom. "I'll show you where you can put your things."

"All right."

As he led her through the doorway, he said, "I made some space for you in the closet, so you can hang up some of your clothes, if you want to. And I emptied the top two drawers of the dresser. I hope that'll give you enough room."

He'd also made sure there was a brand-new tube of toothpaste for her to use, and he'd purchased two fluffy white towels, which now hung pristinely on the rack.

"I didn't expect you to go to any trouble for me," she said.

"It was no trouble." He placed her suitcase on the bed. "If you need some time to rest or settle in, I can make myself scarce. Or if you want something to eat, we can go down to the diner. I've got plenty of food in the fridge, but to tell you the truth, I eat most of my meals at Caroline's."

"It's so close. I can see where it would be easier for you."

"Yeah, but Caroline's also one heck of a cook." He chuckled. "I'd never want my mom to know this, but some of the meals at the diner are actually tastier than the ones I get when I'm back home."

Jillian smiled. "I'd like to check out Caroline's cooking and see if it holds up to my grandmother's."

Ten minutes later, after Jillian had settled in, Shane took her to the diner, where she scanned the interior, clearly taking in the white café-style curtains on the front windows, the yellow walls with a wallpaper border, as well as the wooden tables and chairs.

"It sure looks like a down-home-style restaurant," she said as she glanced at the chalkboard that advertised a full meal for seven dollars and ninety-nine cents.

In bright yellow chalk on black, someone had written, *What the Sheriff Ate,* followed by, *Meat Loaf, Green Beans w/ Almonds, Mashed Potatoes and Peach Cobbler.*

"What does that mean?" Jillian asked.

"Caroline's married to the town sheriff, so that's how she lists the daily special."

Jillian smiled. "That's really cute. And that meat loaf plate sounds good to me, especially with the peach cobbler."

"Then let's find a place to sit."

Shane and Jillian had no more taken seats at an empty table when he saw Sam Jennings enter the café. In his early sixties, with silver hair and a barrel chest, the Brighton Valley sheriff also had a belly that lapped over his belt, thanks to nearly forty years of his wife's cooking.

Sam waved at Shane, then headed for the table. The two men had become friends a while back, after a rash of robberies in town had left the sheriff perplexed. Shane had offered his help by studying the crime scene evidence, and they'd soon found the culprit, who was now behind bars.

"How's it going?" Sam asked.

"Great." Shane introduced the jovial sheriff to Jillian.

After the customary greetings, Sam stuck around and chatted for a while, mostly about the weather, the fact that the bass were really biting down at the lake and that Charlie Boswell, who'd just retired as fire chief, planned to take his wife on an Alaskan cruise.

Shane hoped Jillian didn't mind the small-town talk.

When he glanced across the table at her, she was smiling, which suggested she was okay with it all.

So far, so good, he thought.

As Sam made his way to one of the booths at the back of the diner to join another Brighton Valley old-timer, Margie, the waitress, stopped by the table with menus and two glasses of water.

"We won't need to look at these," Shane said, handing the menus back. "We'd each like the special."

Margie didn't bother taking out her notepad. "You won't be sorry. Those green beans are really fresh. So what would you like to drink?"

"I'll have seltzer," Jillian said.

Margie looked at Shane and smiled. "How about you, cowboy?"

"Iced tea."

"You got it." Margie started to walk away, then stopped. "Say, how are things going out at the ranch? I heard one of Dan and Eva's twins came down with strep throat."

"That was Kevin," Shane said. "But he's feeling a lot better now. Fortunately, he didn't share his germs with the rest of the family."

"I'm glad to hear that," Margie said before walking back to the kitchen with their orders.

"I take it she was talking about your boss and his kids," Jillian said.

"Yep. Dan and Eva have two sets of twins. I'll probably take you out to meet them while you're here."

"I'd like that."

She would? Shane took that to be another good sign that she didn't find Brighton Valley to be a hick town or a total waste of her vacation time.

"I'm wondering, though. How do your friends feel

about our living arrangement? What did you tell them about me?"

"Dan and Eva are two of the nicest people you'll meet. I told them the truth—that we met in Houston, that we conceived a child and that we need to sort through some things. They actually asked me to bring you out to the ranch."

She bit down on her bottom lip, then surveyed the diner. When her gaze returned to his, she gave a little shrug. "But what about everyone else in town? They all seem to know each other—and what's going on in their lives. What have you told them about me?"

"Just that we're friends. It's really none of their business."

As she reached for her glass and took a sip of water, he wondered if she was concerned about being fodder for gossip.

He supposed there were some people who might find her condition and her presence in town worthy of discussion, but there wasn't much he could do about it.

Opting to change the subject and to get her mind off the small-town rumor mill, he asked, "Have you ever been on a ranch before?"

"No, so it ought to be interesting. I'd also like to see where you work."

It was another way to get to know him better, he supposed. He couldn't blame her for that.

He leaned forward and placed his elbows on the table. "I've got an idea. After dinner, let's take a walk."

"All right, but where?"

"Just outside the diner. We can check out some of the shops on Main Street. I think you'd enjoy that. You might also be surprised at how much fun it is to people watch in this town."

Jillian blessed him with a pretty smile. "That sounds great."

It did? That was better news yet, especially since Shane planned to convince Jillian that Brighton Valley wasn't just a little Podunk town.

And that it would be an ideal place to raise their child.

Chapter Seven

Jillian and Shane spent the evening window shopping along the main drag of Brighton Valley. Along the way, she'd also met some of the more colorful citizens who called the small town home, like Anson Pratt, who sat outside the drugstore, whittling small wooden animals to give to the kids in the pediatric ward at Brighton Valley Medical Center.

On several occasions, her shoulder had brushed against Shane's. Each time it happened, she'd been tempted to slip her hand into his.

She'd been alone for months, determined to create a home for her baby while she chased her dream to teach. And now, as she strolled along one of Brighton Valley's quaint, tree-shaded streets, she relished Shane's musky scent and the soul-stirring sound of his soft Southern drawl.

With each step they took, the memory of their lovemaking grew stronger, triggering an almost overwhelming sense of sexual awareness and urging her to reach out to him, to take whatever he had to offer.

Instead, she continued to walk by his side, convinced that she needed to fight temptation. After all, she might want to pin her hopes on him as her lover and her baby's father, but it was way too soon for that.

What if it was all an act? What if he was only playing the part of a nice guy?

It was a risk she wasn't willing to take this early in the game.

Yet that didn't mean she wasn't enjoying their evening as they toured the shops, chatting about things as Shane gave her his tour. She'd especially found it interesting to learn that Darla Ortiz, who owned the hair salon, had been a Hollywood actress back in the day.

"Darla has a wall full of framed, black-and-white head shots of various movie stars who were popular forty and fifty years ago," Shane said, "and each one is autographed to her."

"That's so cool! I'll have to make an appointment while I'm here, just so I can see those photos."

"Do you like old movies?" he asked, as if he'd just uncovered an interesting bit of Jillian trivia.

"My grandparents raised me, remember? So I spent a lot of time watching the classics on television."

He grew pensive for a moment, then turned to her and brightened. "If you don't mind spending a quiet evening at home, I can see if there are any good movies on TV."

"Sure. That sounds good to me."

Once they were back at the apartment, Shane reached for the remote and clicked on the television. Then he surfed the channels, pausing momentarily to catch a baseball score.

"I'm not finding anything too exciting," he said, "but there's an old Cary Grant movie that will be starting in a couple of minutes. Are you up for something like that?"

"Which one is it?"

"*Father Goose,* with Leslie Caron."

"Ooh, that's a good one."

"You don't mind seeing it again?"

"Not at all."

Jillian wasn't sure how Shane actually felt about spending the evening watching classic movies, especially one he might consider a chick flick, but she'd find out soon enough.

After placing the television remote on the glass-topped coffee table, Shane went into the kitchen. A few minutes later, the microwave hummed. Before long, a popping sound let her know that he was making popcorn. She smiled at the thoughtful gesture.

"I'm going to make a root beer float," he called, as he opened the freezer door. "Would you like one, too? I can also give you plain ice cream or something else to drink."

"Are you kidding? I'd love one. I haven't had a float since my grandfather died. Do you need some help?"

"Nope. I've got it."

As the movie began, they took seats on the sofa, with the bowl of popcorn between them and root beer floats in hand, and soon fell into the story.

Shane laughed in all the appropriate spots, which Jillian took to mean that he found the old movie as entertaining as she did. But even if that wasn't the case, she had to give him credit for being a good sport.

The film was a classic romantic comedy at its best, and as Jillian reached into the popcorn bowl, her fingers brushed Shane's, sending a rush of heat up her arm.

As she glanced at him, she caught him looking at her.

For a moment, the only romance she could think about was the one brewing between her and Shane, especially since it was nearing the witching hour for lovers.

Not midnight, of course, but bedtime…

"Sorry," she said, conjuring up an unaffected smile.

"No problem."

As their gazes locked, as the sexual awareness that

buzzed between them grew almost deafening, she broke eye contact and returned her focus to the television screen. Yet even though she pretended to watch Cary and Leslie with the interest of an avid fan, it took ages to get back into the story.

When the credits began to roll on the screen, Shane got to his feet. "Are you up for another movie? Or maybe a game of cards?"

She smiled, realizing the next two weeks might prove to be more pleasant than either of them had thought.

"Actually," she admitted, "I didn't sleep very well last night, and I'm fading fast."

"All right. You take the room. I'll fix a bed on the sofa."

While she was tempted to object and tell him that she didn't mind sharing the bed with him, she wasn't sure she would be able to climb between the sheets and face the wall when he was just an arm's reach away. So she clamped her mouth shut and watched him pull a blanket and pillow out of the linen closet.

"You can have the bathroom first," he said. "I'll use it when you're finished."

"I won't be long." As she headed for the bedroom to get her makeup bag and nightgown, she realized she ought to be grateful for Shane's concessions and his obvious attempt to make her feel welcome and at home.

But for some reason, as she prepared for bed, disappointment settled over her at the thought of sleeping alone.

Jillian might have turned in early last night, but she'd lain in bed for hours, unable to sleep.

Just knowing that Shane was mere steps away had driven her crazy, and the fact that he'd been so sweet to her had only made it worse. He'd treated her with nothing but kindness and respect ever since the night they'd first met, and it was difficult to imagine him as a police officer who'd overstepped his bounds and assaulted a suspect in custody.

Of course, she didn't know that he'd done anything wrong. After all, the article she'd read said that he'd been reinstated. So that probably meant he'd been innocent of any wrongdoing.

She'd been tempted to bring it up, to ask him about it, but she'd decided to wait for her friend to report back with more details. Then she could come to her own conclusions about the man who'd shown her only kindness and understanding.

Or was she missing something?

In spite of him having a gentle side, did he resort to violence when frustrated, angry or provoked?

Thomas had on occasion, and it had been a little frightening. So even though Jillian found it hard to believe that Shane had a similar trait, the question was too important to ignore. Yet by the time she'd fallen asleep at two in the morning, she hadn't been any closer to having an answer.

And now, as she threw off the covers and rolled out of bed, she glanced at the clock on the bureau, only to realize it was after eight. So she slipped on her robe and padded into the living area.

The aroma of brewing coffee and sizzling bacon filled the air, taunting her taste buds. But that was nothing compared with the stirring ache of hunger she felt at seeing Shane move about the small kitchen, balancing his time between the skillet of breakfast meat and a mixing bowl into which he was cracking an egg.

Thomas wouldn't have been caught dead in a kitchen, let alone cooking. But then again, he'd grown up with a full household staff that had been quick to handle his every need.

Jillian placed a hand on her growing tummy and caressed the swell of her womb. If she and Shane ended up with a shared-custody arrangement, would he go to this kind of trouble for their child? She hoped so.

Before she could utter a cheerful, "Good morning," she watched him grimace and stroke the back of his neck, kneading the muscles from the top to the bottom.

"What's the matter?" she asked.

He turned, clearly not aware that she'd been watching him, then his hand lowered and a smile burst across his freshly shaven face. "Hey! Good morning."

"You were rubbing your neck. Does it hurt?"

"It's not that bad. I just slept on it wrong."

She wasn't exactly buying that, since he'd probably been cramped on the sofa and hadn't been able to stretch out all the way.

"I'm sorry," she said.

"About what?"

"Not letting you have the bed."

"Don't give it another thought. I fall asleep watching TV all the time, so when I bought that sofa, I made sure it was comfortable."

Yes, but would it have hurt to let him stretch out on the bed beside her? Sleeping together didn't mean they had to have sex.

Had to?

Yeah, right. Making love with Shane Hollister would be a privilege, not a chore.

As the sweet memories of their one night together rose to the surface, tempting her, taunting her, she tamped them down the best she could. Those were dangerous thoughts for a woman who didn't want their relationship to be complicated.

Maybe she should just wait and see what the day would bring.

"I'm making hotcakes and bacon for breakfast," Shane said, turning back to his work. "I hope that's okay. I also have cereal in the pantry and yogurt in the fridge—if you'd rather have something else."

To be honest, she would prefer to eat something lighter than pancakes, something with fewer carbs and less sugar. But how could she tell him that when he'd tried so hard to surprise her this morning?

So she said, "Hotcakes sound great. I'll have cereal and fruit tomorrow morning."

"All right." He turned the fire down on the bacon, then reached into a drawer for the egg beaters. "Would you like some coffee?"

"I've cut back on caffeine, so I'll just have a glass of orange juice, if that's okay."

"Of course. It's in the fridge."

She made her way to the kitchen area, opened the refrigerator and scanned the full shelves until she found a carton of OJ.

"You know," Shane said, while she carried the juice to the counter and reached for a glass. "I was thinking about something that might be fun to do today. How would you like to ride out to the lake? We could pack a lunch, maybe do some fishing."

"Sure." She'd had a good time when they'd strolled down Main Street last night. And being outdoors on such a lovely summer day was very appealing.

As she poured the juice, she asked, "Do I have time to shower before breakfast? I'll make it quick."

"Take your time. I can keep everything warm."

Less than an hour later, after they'd eaten breakfast and made a lunch of turkey sandwiches, grapes, chips and bottled water, they climbed into Shane's pickup and drove across town to the lake.

On the way, Shane pointed out the Brighton Valley Medical Center, as well as the new elementary school.

"The older kids have had to take the bus to Wexler for years," he said, "but that'll soon be a thing of the past. They're going to build a new high school next year."

Jillian nodded, as though he was just making casual conversation, but from the way he was singing the praises of Brighton Valley, she began to wonder if he was trying to sell her on the place.

She almost discarded the idea, then thought better of it.

Was that what he was trying to do? She had a feeling it was.

She stole a glance across the seat at the handsome cowboy's profile, which was enough to turn a woman's heart on end.

With an elbow resting on the open window, one hand on the wheel, his eyes on the road ahead and a boyish grin on his face, he didn't seem to be plotting and planning.

So she turned back to studying the passing scenery, the landscape and buildings.

Sure, the town was quaint and the people she'd met so far seemed nice. It was the kind of place she wouldn't mind visiting. But Jillian wouldn't want to move here. After all, her grandmother lived in Houston. And that's where the university was located.

It was one thing to take off a semester because she was due to have a baby, but there's no way she'd give up her plan to get a credential or her dream of teaching. Not again.

And there was no way she'd ever leave Gram all alone in the city, without any family nearby.

"Is there any chance you'd move back to Houston?" she asked.

"No, not at this point in my life."

"Why not?"

He paused for a moment, and she assumed he might be planning to sing the praises of small-town life. Instead, he said, "It's complicated."

She wondered if his move had anything to do with the reason he'd left the HPD, but his short, clipped answer was proof that he didn't want to discuss the details with her.

If that was the case, she'd let the subject drop for a while, but that didn't mean she wouldn't get the answer to her question, even if she had to draw it out of him— one word at a time.

After Shane parked in the graveled lot by the lake, he left the cooler with their lunch locked in his pickup, then took Jillian on a leisurely walk along one of the many hiking trails.

"It's really pretty out here," she said. "I'm glad you suggested we spend the day at the lake."

"I thought you'd like it." If truth be told, he hoped that she would see that Brighton Valley had a lot to offer her and the baby. Otherwise, Shane had no idea how he'd ever be able to establish a relationship with his son or daughter.

He might not have embraced the news when she'd first told him she was pregnant, and he might be afraid of what the future would bring, but if he was going to be a father, he wanted to be a part of his child's life.

When they reached the end of one trail and started toward the lakeshore, he suggested that they find a place to sit for a while. "We can watch people launch their boats and cast their lines. What do you think?"

"I'm game if you are."

They walked several yards across the lawn to a shady spot under a maple tree.

"How's this?" Shane asked. "Do you mind sitting on the grass?"

"Not at all." As she knelt down and took a seat, Shane sat beside her, tempted to stretch out instead.

"There's nothing better than a day spent fishing," he said.

Jillian smiled, her blue eyes as bright as the summer sky overhead. "My grandpa would have agreed with you. When he was alive, he loved to fish, and once in a while, he'd even take me along. But I think he actually preferred going out by himself. He used to say that it gave him time to commune with nature and to talk to God."

"I like being outdoors for the very same reason, although I haven't fished since I was in my late teens. Maybe that's why I enjoy working on the ranch. I love the fresh air, the sunshine."

"Is that why you moved from the city?"

"That's part of it." Unwilling to give her a opening to quiz him about his other reasons, he added, "This is a great place to live."

She rested her hand along the top of her pregnant belly. "Some people might argue with you there."

Was she talking about herself?

Probably.

"I guess there are those who like more glitz and glamour in their lives," he said. "More culture."

She seemed to ponder his comment a moment. "I had that kind of life once, and for the most part, it was nice while it lasted. But I gave it all up without any reservations so I wouldn't have to deal with Thomas's lies and infidelity."

Shane could understand that.

"I'm the first and only one in the Hollister family to get a divorce," he admitted, "so it wasn't easy when Marcia and I finally decided to call it quits. But sometimes two pleasant and personable people make a lousy couple."

He tossed a casual glance Jillian's way, saw her leaning back in a relaxed pose, their baby front and center.

When she caught his gaze, he said, "You know what I mean?"

She nodded.

"I was a far cry from the perfect husband," he added. "And the men in my family have always had a tendency to raise their voices when angry. But I wouldn't have cheated."

Her brow knit, as though she wasn't sure if she believed him. Or maybe she was just giving his revelation some thought. After all, he hadn't shared the details of his divorce with her before, although he was glad he finally had.

Still, he thought it was a good idea to add, "When I make a vow or give my word, it means something."

She looked out at the lake for a moment, then turned her attention back to him. "I'm glad to hear that. My mom never married my dad, but my grandparents taught me the meaning of love, commitment and family. It was a painful eye-opener to learn that not everyone is able to keep that kind of promise to a spouse."

"I guess, in a sense, we were both disillusioned by someone we considered a lifetime partner."

A pair of mallard ducks—one male, the other female— quacked as they flew overhead, then landed on the water.

"In your case," Jillian began, "who filed for divorce?"

He wasn't sure why that mattered to her. Maybe because she was trying to determine if he was a quitter.

He wasn't, although there were a few people in his family who never understood why he'd walked away from the HPD. But he'd had his reasons.

"My wife was the one who filed, although, by that time, I was ready to throw in the towel, too."

Shane studied the ducks, wondering if the feathered mates had as much trouble getting along and sticking together as some humans did.

"Did your ex-wife ever remarry?"

"Yes, she did. And I think she's better off now. She found someone who was more her style. He also has a nine-to-five job that's safe."

"I can see where she'd worry about you while you were out on patrol."

Shane tensed for a moment, remembering the unfounded accusations Marcia had often thrown at him, then chuffed. "I think her biggest fear was that I was away from home so much, that I would screw around on her."

"And you honestly didn't cheat?"

He'd already told her that he hadn't, but since her faith in the male species had been seriously undermined, thanks to the jerk she'd married, Shane didn't take offense when she challenged his honesty.

"No," he said, "I didn't cheat."

Okay, so his tone had betrayed him. He *had* been a little offended, after all.

"I'm sorry," she said. "I didn't mean to imply you weren't telling me the truth."

"I guess that's the result of having a spouse lie and cheat." He removed his Stetson and placed it on the grass beside him. "For what it's worth, I don't plan to make any of the same mistakes again, either. If I ever remarry, it'll be to a woman who's happy with my line of work, whatever that is."

"Does that mean you don't plan to be a cowboy the rest of your life?"

"I'm not sure. But that's not the point. I think couples need to be a team."

"I agree."

They continued to sit there, locked in silence. Then she turned again. This time her knee brushed his—taunting him with her touch, with her nearness.

"Do you think you'll *ever* move back to Houston?" she asked.

"Only for visits. Sometimes I miss my job. I was very good at what I did. But I'm happy with my life here. Things are more laid-back, more real."

As the silence stretched between them again, Shane glanced at his watch and noted the time.

"Are you ready for lunch?" he asked.

"Actually, I *am* getting a little hungry."

"Then let's go." He grabbed his hat, got to his feet, then reached out to help her up.

The feel of her hand in his was enough to make him rethink his stance about living in Brighton Valley permanently—if it meant a relationship was completely out of the question. There was something about Jillian that made him wonder if things could be different, that made him *want* them to be.

As they headed back to the parking lot to get the cooler, they approached the playground, where several local families had gathered to spend a few hours with their kids.

They'd yet to pass by it when Jillian reached for Shane's arm and pulled him to a stop. Her fingers gripped his flesh—not hard—but with enough emotion to cause his blood to warm and his heart to race.

When he turned toward her, their gazes locked.

"Let's watch the kids play for a while," she said. "Do you mind?"

Yeah, he minded. The last time he'd been with Joey, he'd driven to Marcia's house and got to spend the afternoon with him. They'd gone to get lunch at McDonald's, then to the park.

But if spending time by the playground convinced Jillian that she'd like to bring their baby here to play in the sand or on the swing set, then he'd agree.

He nodded toward an empty bench. "There's a place to sit over there."

After they'd settled into their seats, Jillian pointed to a mommy showing her preschool-age girl how to blow dandelion seeds in the air. "Isn't that sweet?"

But Shane's gaze went beyond the woman and child to the daddy helping his chubby-legged toddler climb the slide, taking care to follow the boy up each step.

He turned his face away, looking for a bird, a tree, a rock—anything that he could focus on so she wouldn't see the crushing grief in his eyes.

"Is something wrong?" she asked.

Would Jillian understand if he told her about Joey, about how he'd died? How Shane had blamed himself somehow, even though he hadn't been in the car that day, hadn't been the one behind the wheel?

She reached out and touched his hand, sending a warm, healing balm to his bones.

"I…uh…" He cleared his throat, yet his voice retained a husky tone. "My wife and I had a son. A baby boy."

Her fingers probed deeper on his hand, gentle but firm. "What happened?"

"He…was killed in a car accident." Shane cleared his throat again, yet he couldn't seem to shake the rusty, cracked sound in his voice. "My, uh…his mother was driving, and Joey was in the car seat in back when she hit a patch of ice and fishtailed into the path of a semitruck."

"I'm so sorry, Shane," Jillian said softly. "I don't know what to say."

"I…" He cleared his throat for a third time. "I took it pretty hard."

"I can't even imagine what you've been through."

"Yeah. It was tough." He blew out a tattered sigh. "And I wish that I would have handled it differently."

She brushed her thumb across the top of his hand, grazing the skin near his wrist as if trying to offer what little comfort she could.

"I'd expected the overwhelming pain and sadness," he said, "but I hadn't been prepared for the anger."

"I think that's only natural. And part of the grieving process."

He shrugged. "I was upset with my ex-wife and said some things I shouldn't have. She was devastated by Joey's death, too, and didn't need me to lash out at her like I did."

"People say things when they're hurting that they don't always mean."

"That's the problem. I meant them. And I still do. I just wish I hadn't said anything out loud."

"What did you say?"

"I resented her for moving out, for not trying to make the marriage work for Joey's sake. And when he died, I blamed her, saying it was all her fault. And not just because she'd been driving the car, but because she'd taken him away from me, and I'd missed out on the last three months of his life."

He turned his hand to the side, taking hers with it and clutching her in a warm, desperate grip. "I'm sorry for rambling."

Her words came out in a soft whisper. "You didn't ramble."

"Yeah, well, I don't usually talk about it."

"Maybe you should."

"You might be right."

Yet even though he'd finally said it, Jillian didn't leave it alone. "How long has it been?"

"About a year ago. It's still hard."

"How long have you and his mother been divorced?"

"It's been final for about five months. Joey's death sort of slowed the legal process. Neither one of us was really able to deal with anything for a while."

Jillian didn't say a word. Instead, she continued to hold his hand, to offer comfort. And for a moment, he accepted it.

She might sympathize with him, but she'd never understand what he'd dealt with, thanks to Marcia's refusal to compromise.

Did she realize that now, after spilling his guts, that he feared grieving for two children—a son he'd lost through death and a baby he'd yet to meet?

What if Jillian refused to let him be a part of their son or daughter's life? What if she, like Marcia, hooked up with someone else and moved away?

As unsettling as that thought was, he couldn't help but think that Jillian would probably be better off with a guy who could provide all the nicer things in life—a guy who wasn't a cowboy *or* a cop. And that fact didn't sit any better.

After all, Jillian had said the same thing Marcia had once told him. *Babies belong with their mothers.*

All right. Maybe they did. That's the reason he'd stood by and watched Marcia take Joey from him in the first place.

What would stop Jillian from doing the same thing?

Was it any wonder he was torn between insisting that Jillian let him be a part of the new baby's life and letting go before his heart had the chance to break all over again?

Chapter Eight

As Jillian listened to Shane's heartfelt disclosure and gazed into his watery eyes, something frail and broken peered out at her, clenching her heart.

A wave of sympathy surged from her womb to her throat, making it difficult to breathe, let alone respond. So she took his hand, trying to connect with him on some level, trying to ease his pain.

He wrapped his fingers around hers, clutching her in a warm, desperate grip. At the intimacy they'd broached, at the strength of their bond, her pulse raced and her emotions soared in a hundred different directions.

There was nothing she could say to ease the pain he'd suffered. And now that it lay before them, there was no way to roll back time, to go back to the carefree day they'd been having—the warmth of the sunshine, the birds chirping overhead, the children laughing...

Jillian hadn't meant to stir up his sorrow when she'd asked about his son, and as a result, she felt somehow to blame for his sadness, for the tears he struggled to hold back. The only thing she could think to do was to thread her fingers through his, tightening their connection.

Clearly, sitting by the playground, watching the happy

children and families at play, was just making things worse.

"Come on," she said as she stood and drew him to his feet. "Let's go back to the truck and get the cooler."

They returned to the picnic area in silence, joined together by more than their clasped hands.

She kept the conversation light while they ate lunch, something she continued to do on the drive back to his apartment. Yet even though they'd managed to maintain upbeat subjects, her thoughts were lugged down by the heart-wrenching disclosure.

Shane had said he hadn't taken his son's death very well. Had he fallen apart? Found it difficult to put one foot in front of the other and make it through the day?

That's the way Jillian had felt, after she'd first learned of Thomas's affairs. But there was no comparison. Losing a baby would have been unspeakably worse.

Once they were back at his place, Jillian went through the motions of making dinner. Then they'd topped off the tasty meal—baked chicken, rice pilaf and broccoli—with ice cream sundaes.

On the outside, they'd both forgotten about Joey, about the grief and sadness. But she suspected it was something that would always be buried in Shane's heart, ready to erupt at any time.

After they washed the dishes, he asked, "How about a movie?"

"Good idea."

Twenty minutes later, Jillian and Shane sat on the sofa, watching an action-adventure flick. Jillian had forgotten the name of it, since she didn't normally like much violence. But this one wasn't too bad.

He'd asked her to choose the movie they were going to watch, and she felt that it was only fair to opt for something he might like—something that would get his mind off kids and families.

For a moment, she'd wondered if Shane's move from Houston to Brighton Valley had been some kind of escape for him, too.

Maybe. But it didn't explain him assaulting a suspect in his custody. Though, to be honest, she had yet to see any sign of temper or mean streak in him. Ever since she'd met him, he'd been nothing but sweet and thoughtful.

She tried to focus on the television screen, where bullets continued to fly and ricochet off brick walls, where the good guy was surrounded by the bad guys. When she glanced at Shane, she saw that he had leaned forward, caught up in the tension created by a Hollywood gunfight. But Jillian just couldn't lose herself in the story or the action.

Finally, when things were headed for a showdown of one kind or another, she stood. "I'm going to take a shower, if you don't mind."

"Now?" he asked. "You'll miss the ending."

She smiled, not at all concerned about that. "I have a feeling it's going to all work out just fine."

And, if luck was in their favor, real life would offer them that same guarantee.

Thirty minutes later, Jillian returned to the living room, wearing a pale blue robe over a white cotton gown. Her hair was wrapped in a towel turban, and her feet were bare.

Shane had been watching a baseball game on ESPN, but he reached for the remote, more interested in the beautiful woman standing before him, the woman who threatened to turn his life inside out. So he lowered the volume and gave her his full attention.

"Are you going to bed now?" he asked.

"I think so." She bit down on her lip, lifted her hand and fingered the lapel of her robe, clearly nervous.

Was she holding something back? Or trying to build up the courage to spit it out?

Instead of pressing her by asking what was on her mind, he waited until she found the words.

"I'm not sure when you plan to turn in tonight," she finally said, "but you don't need to sleep on the couch again. There's plenty of room for you in the bed."

Shane again reached for the remote, this time shutting off the television completely. "Are you sure about that?"

Her cheeks flushed, and a shy smile crept across her face. "I wasn't talking about sex, but it certainly won't hurt for us to sleep in the same bed."

Shane wouldn't argue with her there, and while he'd be more than willing—in fact, more than eager—to have sex, he counted her concession as progress just the same.

The way he saw it, sleeping together—even if there wasn't any sex involved—meant they might be getting closer to working things out between them.

Was she willing to consider having a relationship with him, after all? One that went beyond coparenting?

"I realize that I was the one who wanted to take things slow and to get to know each other better before we consider dating." She gave a little shrug. "But we took a big step toward intimacy and friendship today, so it seems silly to have you sleep on the couch, all cramped up."

By intimacy, was she talking about him spilling his guts at the park, getting all teary-eyed and laying open his broken heart for her to see?

In the long run, revealing the details of Joey's death had probably been cathartic for him, but it also had shown Jillian a weak and vulnerable side of him that he wasn't proud of having. And one that might have scared off another woman.

Still, he figured they were taking another step in the right direction.

"You don't have to come to bed now," she said. "Your side will be waiting for you whenever you're ready."

He'd rather hear that *she'd* be waiting for him, but there was no need to press for more at this point. They had twelve more nights together, which meant that there was still plenty of time for a sexual relationship to bloom.

Their lovemaking had been too good for it not to.

"I'm ready to turn in, too," he said. "But I'm going to shower first."

Ten minutes later, Shane entered the bedroom wearing a pair of boxer shorts, even though he usually slept in the raw.

Jillian, who smelled of shampoo, lotion and lilacs, was lying on her side, facing the wall.

Was she asleep? Or only pretending to be?

It was hard to know for sure, but either way, she was tempting as hell. Still, he'd always been able to hold firm when he wanted to, so he climbed into bed, careful not to bounce or jiggle the mattress.

He lay still beside her for the longest time, tempted to reach out to her—with his words or his arms—and deciding not to do either.

But, interestingly enough, when dawn broke over downtown Brighton Valley, bringing a faint light to the bedroom, Shane woke to find himself cuddling Jillian as if their bodies had minds of their own.

They lay spooned together, her back pressing against his chest. One of his arms was under her head, the other lay over her waist.

He'd awakened like this before—in her suite at the hotel. On that morning in early March, he'd slipped out of bed quietly. So now, given a second chance to sleep with her, he had an almost overwhelming urge to wake her with a kiss and a gentle yet eager caress.

Just the thought of drawing her closer to him, pressing his growing erection against her bottom, brought a smile to his face.

As he continued to hold her, relishing her lilac scent, she stretched in his arms, like a waking cat that had been snoozing in the sun. Then she rolled over, facing him. As her eyes opened, as she woke to the reality of where she was and who she was with, her lips parted.

Shane smiled, but he didn't move either his arms or his hands. "How'd you sleep?"

She blinked, and surprise swept across her face, yet she didn't pull away. "I slept okay. How about you?"

He'd certainly woken up a lot better than he'd slept, but he wasn't about to reveal that.

"Much better than the night before last," he said.

She slowly pulled away, as if reluctant to leave his arms.

He wasn't ready to let her go, either, and once again, he fought the urge to give her a blood-stirring, heart pounding kiss.

But he didn't want to push her. Waking up in a lover's embrace would have to be good enough for now.

As the sun stretched high in the East Texas sky, Shane and Jillian drove nearly ten miles outside downtown Brighton Valley to the Walkers' ranch. He was looking forward to showing her the place where he worked, but he also wanted her to meet the couple who had become his close friends.

While traveling along the county road, they passed the Sam Houston Elementary School, Roy's Feed and

Grain, and the Flying K Auto Parts Store before reaching open land again.

"How much farther is it?" Jillian asked.

"Just another couple of minutes."

She nodded, then glanced out the passenger window at the passing scenery.

"Like I told you before," Shane said, "Dan and Eva are great people. You'll really like them. Of course, Eva might ask about our plans for the future, but if she does, she'll do it gracefully." He chuckled. "In fact, she'll be so nice about it that you might not even know that you're being quizzed."

Jillian placed a hand on her distended womb and turned to him, her brow furrowed. "It's hard enough talking about the future with *you*. I'm not sure I want to discuss it with anyone else at this point."

"I can understand that. But keep in mind that if Eva asks, it's only because she wants everyone to be as happy as she and Dan are."

Of course, Shane had reason to be skeptical of the whole white-picket-fence dream and to be leery about making the same mistakes all over again. And Jillian certainly did, too.

"Are you sure they're going to be okay with…*things?*" she asked.

"You mean about us staying together in a one-bedroom apartment? Or about you expecting my baby when we're not married?"

She nodded. "And maybe for us having a one-night stand."

"First of all, that night in Houston was incredible. And it fulfilled a need in both of us that went beyond sex. So it wasn't a one-night stand, especially with a baby on the way. And even if it was, it's no one's business but our own." He stole a glance across the seat, saw her nod in agreement. Yet her expression remained pensive.

For a woman who'd once hobnobbed with Houston's high society, she appeared to be more self-conscious than Shane had expected her to be. But then again, maybe it was her experience with that particular social circle that had her so apprehensive now.

"What did those people do to you?" he asked.

Her eyes widened in surprise. "What people?"

"Your ex-husband, his family and friends."

"What makes you think they did something?"

"Because I don't see you as normally self-conscious, but I figure your self-esteem probably took a hard blow when that jerk cheated on you."

She arched a brow. "What makes you think that?"

"I have good instincts when it comes to reading people."

He reached across the seat, took her hand in his, then gave it a gentle squeeze. "Don't worry about what other people think. You're ten times the person most of them are."

"Maybe you're right." Jillian shrugged. "But I'm more to blame than anyone. I got caught up in a fairy tale. And while my life might have appeared to be picture-book-perfect on the outside, it was actually sad and lonely most of the time."

"Do you want to talk about it?" he asked, thinking that he'd actually felt a little better after telling her about Joey.

She seemed to ponder his question for a moment, then eased back into her seat. "Our wedding was really over-the-top—almost fit for royalty. We took a three-week honeymoon in Europe, and Thomas and I moved into a spacious family-owned estate in Houston. I was given carte blanche to decorate the house any way I wanted to, but after that was done, I had very little to do, other than getting dressed up and going to various charity events."

"Were your in-laws good to you?"

"Outwardly, yes. They were very generous. But they were also very controlling and pushy. They interfered more times than not."

Marcia had said the same thing about Shane's family, and for a moment, he wondered how Jillian would feel about the outspoken Hollisters, but he didn't dwell on it.

"So your in-laws created problems in your marriage?"

"I guess you could say that—although indirectly."

"What do you mean?"

"I wanted more out of life than attending social functions, and Thomas couldn't understand that. Instead, he insisted I get involved with his mother's philanthropic projects. And he implied that we'd both be miserable if I didn't yield to her wishes."

"So you gave up your dream for his world."

"More or less." Jillian was quiet for a moment. "I'd always been a good girl who'd never given my grandparents a bit of trouble, so rebellion never came easy for me. And as a wife, I fell into the role Thomas—and his mother— expected of me. And it was a lonely, unfulfilling life. I'd hoped having a baby would be the answer, but after a couple of years trying, I wasn't able to get pregnant."

Shane glanced at her swollen belly, then smiled. "I guess it's safe to say you weren't the one with the fertility problem."

"Apparently not. I'd begged Thomas to go with me to a specialist for testing, but he refused."

"Didn't he want kids?"

"He said he did. But maybe he was afraid to find out that he was infertile. I don't know. Either way, things were always tense when he was around. And when he began to travel on business, I was actually relieved to have him gone."

"Is that when he started messing around?"

"I think so. He was gone more often than not. And then one of his girlfriends called him at home, instead of the office. And...well, his secret was out."

"He was a fool," Shane said.

"Thanks." As she glanced out at the passing scenery, a smile chased away her pensive expression.

"What's so funny?" he asked.

"When I confronted him, I was so angry that I did something completely out of character for me." Her eyes glimmered, and a pair of the cutest dimples formed on her cheeks. "I called him everything but his given name, then threw an expensive vase against the wall, shattering it into a zillion pieces."

"I can't blame you for that." Shane chuckled. "It seems to me that he had that and a whole lot more coming."

Shane understood only too well how emotion could come into play and make someone want to break something—or hit someone. And he wasn't just talking about all of the domestic violence calls he'd gone on, when a cop never knew what to expect.

Shane had lost it once, too. But he wasn't going to tell Jillian that he'd been enraged to the point of striking a perp several times.

Instead, he reached out and took her hand. "You won't meet nicer or more down-to-earth people than the Walkers. So don't worry about impressing them. They're going to like you and accept you—just the way you are."

She gave his hand a squeeze, letting him know she trusted him and making him feel almost heroic. But unwilling to let it go completely to his head, he focused on the road.

As they neared the entrance to the ranch, he pointed

to the right and then to the left. "See those cattle grazing in the pastures along both sides of the road?"

"Yes."

"They're part of Dan's spread."

Moments later, they reached the entrance to the ranch, which was marked by a big green mailbox—a plastic replica of a John Deere tractor.

Shane turned in, drove through the open gate and followed the tree-lined driveway until he reached the house and the outbuildings. Then he parked by the barn, next to Dan's white flatbed truck.

He shut off the ignition and turned to Jillian with a smile. "This is it. What do you think so far?"

"It's nice." Jillian scanned the yard, turning to the yellow clapboard house with white trim, where Dan's uncle, the man who'd raised him, sat on the porch in a rocker.

"Who's that?" she asked.

"That's Hank Walker. He can be a little cantankerous at times, but don't let his gruff exterior scare you. He's actually as gentle as a spring lamb."

Before they could open the pickup doors, Jack and Jill, the cattle dogs, ran out of the barn, barking to announce the arrival of guests.

As Shane and Jillian climbed out of the truck, Kaylee and Kevin came out of the barn, following the dogs.

Shane introduced the twins to Jillian, then while she greeted the kids, he gave the dogs each a rub behind the ears.

It had taken him a while to warm up to the Walker twins, but not nearly as long as he'd thought it would. He wasn't sure why that was, but he'd been giving it some thought lately and had come up with an interesting possibility.

Marcia had never met the Walkers, and she'd never blamed them for her unhappiness.

"I've never visited a ranch before," Jillian told Kevin, "so this is a real treat for me. Thanks for letting me come see it."

"No problem," Kevin said. "We like having company and showing them around. Do you want to ride one of the horses? I can saddle it for you."

Shane stroked the back of the eight-year-old cowboy's head. "Kevin is a good hand with the horses. And he's learning how to rope and cut cattle, too."

"That's really impressive." Jillian rested her hand on top of her pregnant tummy. "And thanks for the offer, but I don't want to ride today. Maybe you can take me out the next time I come to the ranch."

When the front door swung open, two-year-old Sofia stepped out on the porch, followed by her brother Steven. Together they ran toward Shane.

About that time, Hank got to his feet and grabbed his cane. Then he shuffled across the porch, his gait a bit unsteady. As he approached, he reached out an arthritic hand to Jillian. "Shane told us you'd be coming. When's the baby due?"

Jillian blessed the old man with a smile. "December third."

Hank whistled. "Before you know it, this place is going to be bursting at the seams with little ones."

Apparently, he was assuming that Jillian would be a permanent fixture on the ranch, although the jury was still out on that. Either way, Shane didn't correct him.

Hank gave Shane a nudge with his arm. "Did you know Eva's expecting again, too?"

"No, I didn't."

Hank chuckled. "I'm not sure how they're going to handle another little rug rat around here. The baby will make five. 'Course, they got me to help 'em."

About that time, Dan and Eva Walker came out of the

house, crossed the porch, walked down the steps and approached Shane and Jillian with welcoming smiles. Shane introduced them as his friends, rather than his employers, since they'd become like family to him in the past six months.

"And this is Jillian Wilkes," Shane said, turning to the woman who was pregnant with his child.

Jillian didn't usually like to be the focus of so much attention, but when Dan reached out, she took his hand and gave it a warm shake. He was a ruggedly handsome man with light brown hair and blue eyes. Yet there was a gentleness about him.

"It's nice to meet you," Jillian said, before turning to his wife.

Eva Walker, whose olive complexion and long dark hair suggested she might be Latina, was a beautiful woman, in spite of a rather ugly burn scar that ran from the underside of her chin down to her throat. Yet it was the sincerity in her warm brown eyes that drew Jillian's attention and set her mind at ease.

"We're glad you came," Eva said.

"If you don't mind," Shane told Dan, "I'd like to show Jillian around the ranch."

"Not at all." The rancher slipped his arm around his wife's waist and drew her to his side.

"We'll have lunch when you get back," Eva said.

With that, Shane took Jillian by the hand, and they were off.

After checking out the stalls, the horses and the office, they walked along the outside corral that fenced a couple of mares. Shane explained that they were working horses—trained to cut cattle out of the herd.

Next they continued on to the pasture, following a path that led to the creek.

The sun was especially bright, the temperature warm,

the breeze light. And after a tour that took more than an hour, Shane brought Jillian back to the house and into the kitchen, where Eva was making lunch.

She had bread spread upon the countertops, as well as apple slices and oatmeal cookies. And when she spotted Jillian and Shane, she brightened and gave them her full attention—at least until the kids came running.

"Kaylee, will you and Kevin take the little ones into the bathroom and wash up? I'll have your lunch ready in a few minutes."

The older girl nodded, then helped her brother herd the younger twins out of the room.

About that time, Dan opened the back door and entered the mudroom. "Shane, I've got something I'd like you to see. Do you mind coming out to the barn?"

"Sure." Shane turned to Jillian. "I'll be right back."

"Take your time. I'll help make lunch."

Moments later, Eva opened up the fridge and pulled out lunch meat, cheese, mayonnaise, mustard, lettuce and tomatoes. Then she placed them on the countertop.

"You have beautiful children," Jillian said.

"Thanks. Things can get awfully hectic around here, and they can be a lot of work, but I can't imagine my life without them. I'm sure you'll find that to be the case, too." She glanced at Jillian's baby bump, then smiled. "Do you know if you're going to have a girl or a boy?"

"I'd told the doctor I wanted to be surprised when I had my last sonogram, but that's no longer true. I'm really curious now. And since I'd like to set up a nursery, it would be nice to know whether I should focus on trucks and cars or butterflies and kittens."

Before Eva could comment, Kevin dashed into the kitchen. "Mom, can we watch that new SpongeBob movie until lunch is ready?"

"Why don't you watch that Mickey Mouse DVD until

I put Sofia and Steven down for a nap. Then you and Kaylee will be able to watch TV without them bothering you."

He seemed to think about her suggestion, then said, "Okay" and dashed out of the room.

Eva reached for the peanut butter and jelly. "I'd better get the little ones fed first."

"I see that there's a lot of careful orchestrating that goes on around here."

Eva grinned. "That's for sure. Dan and I try to stay a step ahead of them whenever we can, but every once in a while, something unexpected happens to really throw us off stride."

"Like what?" Jillian asked.

"Well, a couple of months ago, Kaylee came home from school sick with the intestinal flu." Eva blew out a sigh. "It wasn't more than an hour later when Kevin's stomach began to bother him, too. And by morning, both Sofia and Steven had it."

"That must have been awful. Passing germs around has got to be the downside of having a big family."

Eva chuckled. "You can't believe what that day was like. Dan and I were moving from one sick kid to the next. And when Shane stopped by the house to check on us, he felt so sorry for us that he spent the morning helping us clean up after the kids and doing tons of laundry. He was amazing. And a real blessing."

"I can see how having a second pair of hands would be helpful in a family with two sets of twins."

It was also nice to know Shane had gone above and beyond. And that he hadn't been scared off by sick kids. That had to be a plus, didn't it?

"What can I do to help?" Jillian asked.

"You can peel and slice the apples, if you'd like."

Jillian reached for a knife from the wooden butcher block on the counter, then carried the fruit to the sink. Before turning on the water, she said, "Hank mentioned that you and Dan are expecting again."

Eva smiled, and her eyes brightened. "We haven't made an official announcement yet, but it's true. We hadn't planned on having another child, but I guess God had other ideas."

"You seem happy, though."

"Oh, I am. Babies are a gift, especially the unexpected ones."

Jillian placed a hand on her tummy. Her baby hadn't been planned, either, but she considered her pregnancy a blessing.

Before long, Eva brought the children into the kitchen for lunch. After wiping sticky fingers, she took the little ones off to bed for a nap.

Kevin and Kaylee went into the living room to watch the DVD they'd been waiting to see, just as the men returned from the barn.

Lunch was pleasant, and so was the conversation. Jillian was glad that she'd met the Walkers. Shane had been right about them. They were nice people, a loving couple and a wonderful family.

As Shane drove her back to Brighton Valley, she reflected upon her time at the ranch. "Thanks for bringing me today. I had a really good time."

"I thought you would."

More than that, Jillian realized that she now had a woman to talk to about pregnancy and babies. Her friend Katie, as sweet as she was, had never been married. So it was nice knowing that she had Eva.

"The Walkers are sure going to have their hands full when the new baby comes," Jillian said. "I can't even imagine what it would be like to have five kids. Wow."

When they arrived back at the apartment, Shane parked in back of the diner. Then they headed for the stairway that led to the rear entrance.

As Jillian made her way up the steps, something pulled low in her belly. Something sharp and painful. She stopped abruptly, gasped and put her hand on her stomach.

"What's the matter?" Shane asked.

"Something hurts."

"What?"

"I don't know." She stood there a moment, stroking low on her belly.

Deciding to continue on, she took two more steps before it happened again. "Whoa."

"Was it a cramp?" he asked. "Or maybe a contraction?"

"I don't know. I've never had a baby before."

They stood in the stairway, not moving up or down.

After a beat—and another painful twinge—Shane clicked his tongue. "That's it. You need to see a doctor."

"But he's in Houston."

"We're not making a two-hour drive for medical advice. I'm taking you to the E.R. at the Brighton Valley Medical Center."

She wanted to argue, to downplay the pain, but the whole baby experience was new to her, and she had to admit she was a little worried herself.

But was this something that required a visit to the emergency room?

"We could go upstairs and wait to see if it goes away," she said.

Shane reached for her waist. "Don't take another step, Jillian. I'm going to carry you down the stairs and put you in the truck."

She wanted to object, to say that she could walk, but

as Shane scooped her into his arms, as she caught a whiff of his musky scent, she let down her defenses for the first time since the night they'd met and let the cowboy have his way.

Chapter Nine

Shane drove Jillian straight to the Brighton Valley Medical Center and followed the sign to the emergency room.

"How are you feeling now?" he asked, as he pulled into a parking space.

"I'm okay." She glanced out the window at the white stucco building, then rubbed her belly. "It's feeling a little better now. It's probably nothing."

"Maybe, but it won't hurt to have you checked out by a doctor."

After Shane parked, he slid out from behind the wheel, circled the pickup and opened Jillian's door. Then he took her hand and held it until they entered the E.R. and Jillian was directed to a triage area, where a nurse determined which patients needed to be seen first.

While Jillian explained her pain and the details of her pregnancy, Shane scanned the waiting room, which didn't appear to be especially busy today, thank goodness.

He couldn't count the number of times he'd experienced busy E.R.'s in Houston, when he'd brought a perp or a victim in for treatment. And he knew that some patients waited for hours to be seen.

Shane figured it wouldn't hurt to remind the nurse what was at stake, what could go wrong. "Under the circumstances, since she's pregnant and might be in premature labor, she'll see a doctor right away, won't she?"

"No," the triage nurse said. "We'll be sending her up to the obstetrical floor. They're better equipped to examine and treat her up there. Just give me a minute or two, and we'll have an orderly take her upstairs in a wheelchair."

Shane gave Jillian's hand a gentle squeeze, hoping she felt as relieved as he did at the news.

"In fact," the nurse added, "why don't you take a seat in the waiting room for a few minutes? It won't be long."

After a clerk from the reception desk took Jillian's insurance information, they released her to find a chair with the others who waited with hacking coughs, stomachaches and visible wounds.

It seemed like ages, but was probably only a matter of minutes, before a tall, slender nurse with black spiky hair called Jillian's name. Five minutes later, after an elevator ride and a trip down several corridors, they arrived in the obstetrical unit, where Jillian was assigned to an exam room. After her vitals were taken, she was given a gown and told to undress.

Thinking she would probably want some privacy, Shane said, "I'll wait outside."

He'd hoped she might stop him, which would mean that their friendship—or whatever their relationship was—had made a turn of some kind, growing stronger and more intimate than before. Yet she let him leave.

The nurse followed him out, but they didn't have to wait long. Once Jillian had changed out of her street clothes, he and the nurse returned to the room.

When the two of them were left alone, he asked, "So how are you feeling now?"

"Better. In fact, I'm afraid I might have made a bigger deal out of those pains than I should have."

"Don't worry about that. This is just a precaution."

Moments later, they were introduced to Dr. Selena Ramirez, the resident obstetrician, an attractive woman of average height. She was young—probably only in her late twenties or early thirties, with expressive green eyes and a reassuring smile.

After asking Jillian about the pain she'd had, the doctor had her lie back on the table while she pressed on her stomach to feel the size of her uterus. Then she reached for a pair of gloves, explaining that she would need to give her an internal exam.

"I'll be right outside," Shane said, as he stepped into the hall again, leaned against the wall and waited next to the door.

Being on an obstetrical floor—the smell, the sound of a newborn's cry, the happy smiles of pregnant women or new mothers walking the halls—caused memories of Marcia's pregnancy to surface.

Shane had been thrilled to learn he was going to be a father. He'd always adored his many nieces and nephews, and had been glad to know that his child would soon be a part of the happy-go-lucky Hollister brood.

He'd also hoped and prayed that having a baby would make his wife happy and more content to stay married. But by the time Joey had taken his first steps, Marcia again asked for a divorce. At that point, Shane had finally been ready to throw in the marital towel, too. The only thing that had torn him up was the fact he wouldn't see his son on a daily basis.

To make matters worse, Marcia met another man and moved to Arizona with him, taking their son with her.

Of course, Shane had objected, but she'd argued that a baby needed its mother, and that he had no right to stop her from being happy. So he'd reluctantly let her go and poured himself into his work, seeing Joey as often as he could.

"Code Blue—Neonatal Nursery."

The overhead announcement of an emergency affecting one of the newborns sent a chill through Shane, along with an unexpected wave of fresh grief.

After Joey's death, as one day stretched into the next, the only thing that had kept him going had been his family and his job. Then, one day, his temper and his grief had gotten the best of him.

He and Sylvia Dominguez, his partner, had been hunting day and night for Lyle Bailey, a suspected child kidnapper who'd killed his latest victim. Knowing the details of the crime had served to make Shane focus on nothing else but prohibiting the perp from hurting another child, destroying another family.

Following a lead, he and his partner had found him holed up in a woodshed behind a house, and when Lyle had tried to run, Shane had tackled him to the ground. He could have held him there, locking on a pair of handcuffs, but for some reason, Shane had snapped and hit the guy a couple of times, something he'd never done before.

It had been the first—and only—time he'd ever felt so out of control.

Bailey's attorney had filed police brutality charges against the department, and Shane was suspended from duty with pay. Internal Affairs finally let him off with a warning. But after that incident, his job no longer helped to keep his mind off his troubles and his grief.

So he'd taken a leave of absence, left town and eventually ended up in Brighton Valley, where he found work on Dan Walker's ranch.

"Code Blue—canceled."

Thank God. He hated to think of any parents having to go through what he'd gone through.

Now here he was, expecting another child and no closer to having the happy family he'd always wanted.

"You can come back now," the nurse said to him from behind the slightly opened door.

When Shane entered the exam room, Dr. Ramirez explained that there was no sign of labor.

"Sometimes, one of the ligaments that holds the uterus in place is pulled. So that's probably what happened today." She turned to Jillian, who was sitting up on the exam table. "Why don't you go home and take it easy tonight. But give me a call if that pain comes back."

Jillian seemed to be okay with both the diagnosis and the instructions, so Shane was, too.

Not that he wasn't still worried about her and the baby.

"There's just one more thing I'd like to do," Dr. Ramirez said. "If you'll lie back on the table, we'll give you a sonogram and double-check to make sure everything is okay on the inside."

Shane was about to excuse himself and leave the room, just as he'd done before, but he wanted to see the baby—*his* baby.

If Jillian had any objections to him staying in the room, she didn't say anything. Instead, she lay down on the exam table.

As the nurse wheeled in a machine, Dr. Ramirez lifted Jillian's gown, then squeezed out a dab of gel and smeared it on her rounded belly.

As the sonogram began, the doctor studied the screen. And so did Shane. Just like the time Marcia had the very same test run, he was intrigued by the image of the growing child in the mother's womb.

"The baby looks good," Dr. Ramirez said. "Strong heartbeat, healthy umbilical cord."

"Can you tell if it's a boy or girl?" Jillian asked.

"It's…" the doctor said, as she zeroed in on the screen, "…a girl."

A *girl*.

As much as Shane had missed Joey, as often as he'd imagined himself coaching a Little League team or taking his son fishing at the lake, the thought of a girl nearly took the breath out of him.

He hadn't wanted to replace Joey. He'd just hoped to recover those paternal feelings, like pride and love. And with the doctor's announcement that it appeared as though his daughter was healthy, all those hopes and dreams came rushing back to him.

Without giving it a thought, he bent down, placed his lips near Jillian's ear and whispered, "Are you okay with us having a girl?"

Jillian looked up at him and smiled. As their gazes met and locked, happy tears overflowed and streamed down her face, convincing him that she wasn't just cool with it, she was over the moon.

"What about you?" she asked. "Are you up to being the daddy of a little girl?"

He smiled, then brushed a kiss on her brow. "Absolutely. As long as she's as pretty as you."

For a moment, everything seemed perfect, and Shane couldn't help thinking that life would be beautiful this time around.

How could it not be?

At least, as long as Jillian agreed to let Shane be involved in his daughter's life.

Once Shane had gotten Jillian home and comfortable, he went downstairs to Caroline's Diner and ordered dinner to go—the pot roast and apple pie that the sign claimed the sheriff had eaten.

Shane had plenty of stuff in the pantry, as well as the refrigerator, to cook for dinner. But he didn't want Jillian to even think about getting up or helping out. She was reclining on the sofa, with her feet up on a stack of pillows, the television remote in her hands.

Now, as he took a seat at an empty table near the front of the diner, he waited for Margie to bring out his order.

He'd been more than relieved to know that Jillian's pain hadn't been an indication of preterm labor and that the baby—a girl, imagine that—appeared to be healthy.

Jillian had mentioned on the way home that she'd really liked Dr. Ramirez. In fact, she thought the Brighton Valley obstetrician had spent more time with her than the doctor she had back in Houston.

Shane wondered if there was any chance she might want to switch obstetricians and stay in town until she delivered. He sure hoped so.

When the front door of the diner opened, he looked up to see Sheriff Jennings enter. He lit up when he spotted Shane, moseyed up to him and reached out his right arm in greeting.

"How's it going?" Shane asked, as the two men shook hands.

"Not bad." Sam folded his arms around his ample belly and grinned. "You're just the guy I wanted to see."

"Oh, yeah? What's up?"

"I told you about my buddy Charlie Boswell, the fire chief who just retired."

"Yes, you mentioned that he was taking his wife on a cruise of some kind."

"He's also been getting in a lot of fishing lately, something I haven't had time to do since last August."

"Sounds like the life to me," Shane said.

"Me, too. In fact, Caroline and I were talking last night, and she asked how I felt about retiring. I'd never expected to turn in my badge, thinking they'd have to pry it from my hands. But I thought about it all night long, and when morning came around, I started to make a list of all the things I'd do if I had a little time off."

"So why'd you want to talk to me?"

"Well, now I'm not saying that I've made up my mind. But if I did decide to give up my position here in town, how would you feel about taking my place—even if it was just in the interim?"

"Until a permanent sheriff could be found?"

Sam nodded. "I'd have to talk to the county commission, but they were impressed with the help you gave me on that burglary case. I'm sure they'd appoint you in a heartbeat."

"I honestly don't know," Shane said. Thing was, if he agreed, even for a while, he'd be leaving Dan in the lurch. And that didn't sit well with him. Besides, he really liked working on the ranch. But there was a part of him that missed police work, and he didn't want to be too quick to decline the offer. "I'd have to think about it, I guess."

"You do that," Sam said, before waving at some people in the rear of the restaurant and heading over to join them, leaving Shane to his thoughts.

If he had reason to believe that Jillian would consider settling in the valley, if there was any future for them together, he'd need to find some kind of job that provided health benefits.

Of course, if she insisted upon living in Houston, he was going to be in a real quandary. Because with each passing day he spent in a small town, he became more and more convinced that he'd never want to return to life in the big city.

But what if Jillian decided Brighton Valley would never be her cup of tea? Where would that leave them?

Right back in the same place he and Marcia had once been. And Shane couldn't figure out what he'd do this time around.

* * *

As Jillian climbed from the shower and dried off with one of Shane's white, fluffy towels, she glanced at her image in the mirror. Her tummy seemed to be growing bigger every day, but the baby wasn't anywhere near ready to be born. She was so glad when Dr. Ramirez told her that everything was going well, that the baby wasn't going to come early and that…

I'm going to have a little girl.

Her heart had filled to the brim with love for the child she'd yet to meet, and Shane seemed to be pleased at the news, as well. In fact, he'd been so supportive during yesterday's health scare that it was difficult not to believe that he truly cared about her and the baby.

But was he insisting upon being a part of the baby's life because he hoped their baby would replace the little boy he lost?

She certainly hoped that wasn't the case.

There were other things to consider when it came to contemplating any kind of life together—love for one thing, and loyalty for another.

Sure, a healthy sexual relationship was important—and it wouldn't be a problem for them. But there was more to life than sex.

After slipping on her cotton gown, she went into the living area of Shane's small apartment and waited for him to bring dinner upstairs. While she had the chance, she picked up her cell phone and dialed her grandmother's number.

"Hi, Gram. I just called to say hello."

"I'm so glad you did."

"Are you feeling okay?" Jillian asked, concerned at the hoarse sound of Gram's familiar voice. "It sounds as though you might be coming down with a cold."

"I have a scratchy throat and a bit of a cough, but it's

nothing I can't deal with. How are things going? Are you okay? You really don't know that man very well."

"He's a nice guy, Gram. You have nothing to worry about."

There was no need to tell her about the visit to the E.R. today, especially since it had proved to be no big deal.

"Is he treating you well?"

"Shane's been a perfect gentleman." In fact, he'd been…wonderful.

"He hasn't tried to take advantage of you, has he?"

On the contrary. "He's been very sweet and respect-ful." In fact, he'd been everything Jillian could have hoped for.

"I'm glad to hear that," Gram said. "Since the two of you will be having a child together, it's important that you be friends."

That was true. And little did Gram know, Jillian would be sleeping with that "friend" in an hour or so.

Of course, the doctor had said to take it easy, so there was no chance that they'd end up having sex tonight. But would they eventually become lovers again while she was staying with him?

Just the thought sent a delicious shiver that pooled low and warm in the depths of her.

It was still too soon to tell if they would pick up where they'd left off, she supposed—even though it would be incredibly easy to succumb to temptation.

Maybe she should make an extra effort to stay strong. Their relationship as friends and coparents was going to be difficult enough, especially with them living two hours away from each other. Trying to be sometimes lovers, too…?

That might be too much to handle.

Would Shane consider moving back to Houston? If so, could something permanent work out between them?

"When will you be coming home?" Gram asked, her graveled voice reminding Jillian that she might be sicker than she'd let on.

"I'd planned to stay two weeks, which is right before my next appointment with Dr. Allan." Jillian had been looking forward to that appointment, since she wanted to make sure the baby was healthy, that her pregnancy was going well. But she'd just had confirmation from Dr. Ramirez that the baby—her *daughter*—was growing as expected, that all seemed to be fine.

For a moment, she wanted to share the news with Gram. But that would mean she'd have to admit to having that pain earlier today, and Jillian didn't want to worry her any more than necessary.

"I assume you asked Dr. Allan for permission to travel," Gram said.

"Yes, he was fine with it."

Dr. Allan was one of many doctors in a large and prestigious obstetrical group in Houston, although Jillian sometimes got the feeling that his practice was too big, that he was too busy and rushed her appointments.

Dr. Ramirez, on the other hand, had been both thorough and reassuring. Maybe it was because she was a woman herself and was more nurturing by nature. It was hard to say.

Gram coughed into the phone, then apologized.

"I don't like the sound of that cough," Jillian said. "Have you called the doctor?"

"Not yet."

As heavy, booted footsteps thumped on the stairway outside, Jillian realized Shane had returned with dinner.

"Listen, Gram. I have to go. But promise me you'll see the doctor if you're not feeling better in the morning. And that you'll call me, either way."

"I will, honey. Don't worry about me."

It was hard not to. Gram had not only raised Jillian, but she was the only family she had left.

After the line disconnected, she set her cell phone on the lamp table, then met Shane at the door. As he scanned the length of her, his gaze zeroed in on her breasts.

Oops. The thin cotton fabric of her white cotton gown was probably a little more see-through than she'd realized.

As his gaze lifted and met hers, a shot of awareness rushed through her. For a moment, she was tempted to let her hormones take the lead, but it was the maternal hormones that kicked into play and insisted she heed them.

What if having sex caused that pain to return? What if Dr. Ramirez was wrong about it being something minor?

So in spite of wishing things were different, she tried to put a platonic spin on things.

"So what did the sheriff eat tonight?" she asked.

"Pot roast with all the fixings and apple pie."

As Shane set out the food on the table, he asked, "How do you feel about going for a little drive tomorrow?"

"Where?"

"I thought I'd take you to Wexler. There's a store that sells baby stuff. And since we know the baby's going to be a girl, I thought it might be fun to check things out."

Jillian hadn't planned to purchase anything until she got back to Houston, since it wouldn't do her any good to buy things in Brighton Valley and haul them home—or have them shipped. But it might be nice to see what was available and to get some decorating ideas.

"Sure, that sounds like fun." As she started for the table, where he'd set out their meal, he looked up, his gaze again sketching over her.

With the light behind her, she suspected that he was taking in every curve of her body, from her breasts, to her hips, to her belly. And while she really ought to be a little concerned by the raw hunger in his eyes, she felt a sense of feminine power, too.

Of course, as heady as that was and as tempted as she was to make love to him again and experience all the passion she'd felt in his arms, that wasn't going to do her any good this evening, when she was determined to follow the doctor's orders about taking it easy.

Of course, Dr. Ramirez hadn't said anything about being careful tomorrow morning.

And by the way her body seemed to gravitate toward his while they slept, she had a feeling that it was only a matter of time when they'd wake to find temptation too strong to ignore.

Chapter Ten

Although Shane's bed was plenty big enough for two, Jillian woke up the next morning on his side of the king-size mattress, her left arm draped over his shoulder, her leg entwined with his.

Yesterday, when they'd shut off the TV and turned in for the night, she'd purposely faced the wall. But for some reason, by the time morning rolled around, their bodies had seemed to find each other.

At least, her body had sought out his.

She probably ought to move before he opened his eyes and realized that she'd somehow crept from her side to his, but it felt so natural to lie with him, so good to snuggle up against him.

It seemed as though they hadn't slept together in ages, even though it had only been the night before. And she tried to figure out why it felt as though such a long time had passed.

The connection they seemed to share? The healing she'd found in his embrace?

Meeting Shane last March had been the first step in getting over the effects of her divorce and restoring her confidence as a woman, something Thomas's infidelity had sent reeling. And now that she and Shane had come together again, now that they were developing a...

What? A friendship?

As she lay stretched along the length of him, her body pressed against his and taking comfort in his warmth, his strength, his presence, it seemed as though there was more than friendship going on here, although she was reluctant to admit just what it was.

The scare she'd had yesterday, even though it had proved to be unfounded, and the trip to the E.R. had bonded them in an unexpected way. And the sonogram that had revealed their baby growing in the womb, their *daughter,* had locked them into their roles as parents.

Was there even more going on than that?

As Shane began to stir, Jillian wanted nothing more than to caress his cheek, to trail her fingers along the morning stubble on his jaw that gave him a roughened edge. To watch his eyes open and know that his very first vision upon waking would be her. But that was a little too risky at this point, a little too...*married.*

Still, whatever it was that she was feeling for him, including the physical attraction that she'd never been able to shake, was too tender and new to analyze. But one thing was clear. She didn't want to risk falling heart over head for him yet, even though she had to admit that the possibility of that happening was growing by leaps and bounds.

It was too soon for her to forget that he'd assaulted a suspect he'd taken into custody.

Of course, he'd been nothing but sweet and kind and gentle to her since she'd arrived in Brighton Valley. But that didn't mean he didn't have a temper, that it wasn't lurking somewhere, under the surface and ready to snap.

His breathing changed, and he moved, reaching for her

hand. Then he brought it to his lips and pressed a kiss into her palm, sending a tremor of heat to her feminine core.

Had a move so simple, so sweet, been such a turn-on before?

"Good morning," he said, his voice still laden with sleep. "How are you feeling?"

Hot. Aroused. And maybe even willing to see where this morning takes us.

Before she could deal with the temptation, the urge to throw caution to the wind and come up with a response, he asked, "No more of those pains?"

Now she could answer in all honesty. "None whatsoever."

"That's good to hear." He turned slightly, so that his back was on the mattress, and he turned his head to allow his eyes to meet hers.

She appreciated his concern for her, for the baby. Bracing herself up on an elbow, she rose up and offered him a good-morning smile. "How'd you sleep?"

"Great." When he lobbed her a crooked grin, she no longer seemed to care whether he had a temper or a short fuse.

Instead, she was tempted to skim her fingers along his chest. To brush her thumbs across his nipples, knowing—*remembering*—how he reacted to that particular stimulation. But before she could lift her hand and place it on his chest, he rolled to the side and climbed out of bed, leaving her in a pool of disappointment.

"Do you want to use the bathroom first?" he asked.

No, she wanted to stay in bed, to experiment with the thoughts and feelings that had been playing on her mind since waking this morning. And while she'd assumed he'd sense where her thoughts were heading, it was clear that he wasn't a mind reader.

For that, she supposed she should be grateful, since her head was urging one thing and her body another.

"No," she told him, "I can wait. Go ahead."

Maybe he planned to come back to bed as soon as he was done, and when he did—that is, *if* he did—she'd...

Well, she wasn't exactly sure what she'd do. But she doubted that he'd put up an argument over anything she might suggest.

He yawned and stretched, flexing muscles in his chest and forearms she'd discovered in Houston and had nearly forgotten about.

"What time do you want to go into Wexler?" he asked.

Seriously? He was ready to start the day and wasn't planning to return to bed?

Again, she tried to tell herself that she should be grateful, that it was too soon for the ideas she'd been having. Yet the strangest sense of disappointment settled over her.

"I don't care," she said. "It's up to you."

"Then let's shower, have a quick breakfast and get out of here. I'm actually looking forward to seeing the kind of stuff they have at that store for baby girls."

To be honest, so was Jillian. But she couldn't help thinking that he seemed to be more excited about the baby than he was in having Jillian in his bed.

And for a moment, she felt both abandoned and rejected.

As Shane headed for the bathroom, leaving her to deal with the confusing emotions, she tried to shake them off, telling herself that she should be happy that he was looking forward to their child's birth. That her pregnancy hadn't made him uneasy about what the future might bring.

But now Jillian had something else to worry about, something about Shane's past that gave her pause.

If he saw the baby as some kind of replacement for the one he'd lost, then maybe Jillian was merely a means to the end for him....

As Shane drove Jillian into Wexler to check out The Baby Corral, a store that sold furniture, clothing and other items new parents might need, he couldn't help noting how quiet she'd been this morning—unusually so.

It might have been only his imagination, he supposed. But something seemed to have her in deep thought, and not knowing what was bothering her left him a little unbalanced, since there was so much riding on her plans for the future.

As his marriage to Marcia had begun to unravel, the two of them had grown more and more introspective, so to see Jillian doing the same thing was a little disconcerting.

Earlier, when he'd woken up wrapped in her arms, he'd been tempted to kiss her, to run his hands along her hips, to venture into a little morning foreplay. And while he'd noted a spark of passion in her eyes, in her smile, he'd decided only an insensitive jerk would suggest a romp in bed when the doctor had told her to take it easy the day before.

So he'd headed for the shower before she could see how primed and ready he was for sex.

When he went to the kitchen to put on a pot of coffee and whip up some scrambled eggs, she'd gone into the bathroom. It seemed as though she'd stayed in there for hours, and when she came out, as pretty as any woman he'd ever seen, her makeup just right and every hair in place, he'd tried to coax a smile out of her.

But all she'd been able to muster was a makeshift grin, which hadn't been what he'd expected, what he'd wanted. And that's when he'd realized something was off.

So even now, as they entered Wexler city limits and he turned down the main drag, she still hadn't opened up.

"Are you sure you're feeling okay?" he asked, hoping that a shopping trip wasn't going to be too taxing and wishing he hadn't suggested it.

"I'm fine." She'd offered him another smile which didn't quite reach her eyes.

Shane couldn't see pursuing it any further, so he focused on the road until they reached the store.

After he parked in front, they headed to the door. Once inside the trendy baby shop, she seemed to brighten at the variety offered.

"Let's check out the cribs and dressers," he said, as he led her to the back of the store.

"All right."

They took time to check out the various furniture styles, as well as the colorful comforters and matching mobiles that would entertain the baby while she was small. Jillian seemed to favor one with teddy bears, each one sporting a different-colored bow tie.

"Do you see anything you like?" he asked, thinking he'd buy it for her—although maybe not today.

"This one is nice." She touched one of the spindles of a light oak crib.

As they continued through the store and they passed a display of bottles and nipples, he asked, "Do you plan to nurse?"

"Yes, I'd like to." She turned to him and offered a shy smile, which made him decide the quiet spell might be over. "I know that December seems like a long time off, but it's getting closer every day, especially after seeing the baby on that sonogram screen yesterday."

"I know what you mean." The baby had sure become real to him over the past twenty-four hours. And her due date would be here before they knew it. In fact, for the first time since Joey died, he found himself looking forward to Christmas and all that it brought…stockings on the mantel, presents under the tree. A new baby…

As they continued down one aisle and up another, he decided to throw out an idea he'd been tossing around, just to see what she would say.

"Would you consider sticking around in Brighton Valley a little longer? After all, you mentioned that you might postpone your student teaching until next term. And you said that you liked Dr. Ramirez. If there was a problem, you'd be in good hands."

As she turned to him, a swath of confusion crossed her face. "You want me to extend my visit?"

"Why not?" He certainly found the idea appealing. "I've been thinking about getting a bigger place anyway, so if the quarters are too tight for you, that won't be an issue for long."

"I…" She tilted her head slightly, as though the movement might help her wrap her mind around his suggestion. "But my doctor is in Houston."

"You said you weren't all that impressed with him."

"Actually, Dr. Allan has a great reputation and a degree from one of the top medical schools in the country. It's just that he's so busy, I sometimes feel as though my appointments are cut short." She continued down the aisle, just as pensive as ever, then she stopped and faced him. "I really like Dr. Ramirez and wouldn't mind having her deliver the baby. But it's really not feasible for me to stay in Brighton Valley."

"Why not?"

"Because my life is in Houston, Shane."

He'd figured as much, and even though he'd expected that to be her answer, it still left an ache in his chest, a twist in his gut.

As they reached a display of rocking chairs, she

stopped by one in particular and took a seat. Then, as she set the chair in motion, she looked up at him and smiled—one that lit her eyes this time. "I really like this one."

"Good. Let's get it."

"Today?"

"Sure, why not?"

"Because I've been trying to conserve my money. And while I plan to buy some things new, I figured I could pick up some furniture, like a rocker, at a consignment store in Houston."

"I was offering to buy *that* rocker—as a gift."

"You don't need to do that."

"I want to."

She didn't object any more, yet she continued to sit, to sway back and forth. Then she caught his gaze again. "Can I ask you a question?"

"Sure."

"Do you miss working as a cop? Do you think you'll ever go back?"

"I miss parts of it," he admitted. "I was good at what I did. But in the last year or so, I've found small-town life to be a lot more appealing than living in the city."

"You don't miss the excitement?"

"Sure, sometimes." There was an adrenaline rush that came with pursuing and arresting a suspect, of knowing that he'd gotten a dangerous perp off the streets. But Shane wasn't sure if Jillian would understand the complexities of his job, of missing it, yet not wanting to go back.

Marcia certainly wouldn't have.

"I was ready for a change in my life," he said. "And working on Dan's ranch and living in Brighton Valley suits me right now."

He couldn't really explain why that was the case when

a part of him did miss the excitement, the thrill and the knowledge that he'd made the streets a little safer. But here in Brighton Valley, he seemed to have shaken the bad memories, the reminders of why his marriage had fallen apart and how he'd come to lose Joey.

Out here, where the Texas sky seemed bluer, the air cleaner, the sun brighter and warmer, he'd found a sense of peace that he doubted he'd ever be able to find in the city. So going back to Houston wasn't in his immediate plans—if ever.

He'd hoped that Jillian would find something comforting about small-town life, too. But that didn't appear to be happening. And if it didn't, it was going to make it a real challenge—if not completely impossible—to work out a way to coparent and share custody of their daughter.

He supposed he'd have to at least consider moving back to Houston, but that meant he'd be forced to make a life choice that didn't appeal to him, all because a woman he cared about wasn't willing to find a compromise they could both deal with—like splitting the distance and making a commute work.

Yet even if he gave up his happiness for hers, there was still no guarantee that things would turn out the way he wanted them to.

But how did he want it to turn out?

He wanted to be a part of his child's life. That was for sure. But what about Jillian?

His feelings for her went beyond the fact that they'd conceived a child together and that they would be involved with each other one way or another for the next eighteen years or longer. He still wasn't sure just how far those feelings went, but he'd go so far as to say that he'd like for them to be lovers again.

"Uh-oh." Jillian's rocker came to a halt.

Damn. Had her pain come back? Had Dr. Ramirez

been wrong when she'd said there probably wasn't anything to worry about?

"What's the matter?" Shane asked.

Jillian hadn't meant to gasp—or to forget that she hadn't talked to Gram yet today. So she said, "I'm sorry. My grandmother wasn't feeling well last night, and she promised to call me this morning and let me know how she was doing, but she hasn't."

She glanced at her wristwatch, noting that it was nearly noon, so she reached into her purse and pulled out her cell. Then she dialed her grandmother's number.

As she waited for Gram to answer, Shane took a seat in the rocker next to hers.

Again, Jillian couldn't help thinking about how supportive he'd been, how understanding. Yet was his kindness a result of his concern for her—or for the baby?

About the time Jillian was ready to hang up and call one of the elderly woman's neighbors, Gram answered, her voice almost a bark.

"You forgot to call me. How are you feeling?"

"I'm not feeling any better. And my cough might be worse. I have a call in to the doctor, and I'm waiting to hear from him."

"How's your throat? It sounds as though it still hurts."

"It does, but don't worry about me. I'm sure it's just a cold."

How could Jillian not worry? Gram was a widow in her mid-seventies, and she didn't need any more health issues than the ones she already had: diabetes, high blood pressure and high cholesterol.

"I was hoping the doctor would phone in a prescription to the pharmacy," Gram said. "I really don't want to drive to his office. I don't have much energy."

What about driving to the pharmacy?

Jillian clucked her tongue. She couldn't help thinking that she ought to head back to Houston and make sure Gram got to her doctor's office, as well as to the pharmacy, to pick up any prescriptions she might need.

"I'm going to come home. I can be there by two o'clock or a little after, so when the doctor does call, try to set up an appointment in the late afternoon."

"You don't need to cut your visit short. I can call Margie, my neighbor, if I need a ride. Or I can drive myself. I really don't want to be a bother to anyone."

"You're not a bother," Jillian said. "And this isn't up for negotiation. I'm coming home."

After ending the call, Jillian looked at Shane, saw him watching her intently.

"What's the matter?" he asked.

"I need to take my grandmother to see the doctor. She's getting older, and I'm all she has."

"I understand. Why don't I drive you?"

As tempting as his offer was, as much as she'd like for him to meet the woman who'd raised her—and maybe get a second opinion about his character—she slowly shook her head. After all, she'd nearly jumped his bones this morning, and he hadn't seemed the least bit interested.

He might have made it clear that he wanted to be a part of his child's life, but he hadn't said anything about the importance of being a part of hers.

Besides, he didn't want to live in Houston, and because of Gram, that's where Jillian needed to be. She couldn't very well jump in the car and make a two-hour drive every time her grandmother needed something.

As if that wasn't reason enough, the university was located there. And Jillian was more apt to find a good job or a teaching position in the city.

She'd already given up her dreams, as well as her independence, for a man once. There was no way she'd do that again.

No, she had to remain in Houston. And the sooner Shane realized that, the better.

"Thanks for the offer," she told him, "but I'd rather take my own car and drive myself."

His eyes narrowed a bit, as if he wasn't at all pleased by her decision. Or was he finally revealing a bit of the darkness or anger that might lie under his surface, ready to break free?

Shane shifted his weight, glanced down at his feet, then back to her, shuttering any shadow she might have detected just seconds ago.

"Okay," he said, "then let's go. I'll take you to the apartment to get your things and your car."

"Thanks, I appreciate that."

But he didn't comment further. Instead, he led her out of the store, leaving the rocker and anything else he'd planned to purchase for the baby behind.

The ride back to Shane's apartment was a quiet one. But what was there to say?

Jillian was leaving and unlikely to return. He'd hoped that she would have enjoyed staying with him, that she would have liked small-town life, that she might eventually consider moving in with him over the fall and becoming a family.

But apparently, that wasn't going to happen.

While Shane wanted to stop her from packing her things and leaving permanently, to insist she give him a shot to prove he could be a good father, he clamped his mouth shut.

He wasn't about to be put into the same no-win position that he'd been in with Marcia. And he even went so far as to wonder if walking away now might be easier to distance himself—before he had a chance to bond with the baby, before he had a chance to see more than a grainy, black-and-white image of his little girl. Maybe then it wouldn't hurt as badly as it had when Marcia had taken Joey away.

He'd been backed into corners before, when he'd been faced with two choices—one was bad, the other was worse. And this was clearly one of them.

After parking the truck behind Caroline's Diner, Shane walked behind Jillian as she climbed the stairs and entered the small apartment that had once seemed like home.

He waited while she packed her bags, then carried them out to her car for her.

"Thanks so much for having me," she said.

"No problem. I'm glad you had a chance to see Brighton Valley and to get to know me a little better."

She went up on tiptoe, placed her hand on his cheek, then planted a sweet, it-was-nice-while-it-lasted kiss on his lips.

It took all he had not to wrap his arms around her and pull her close, kissing her senseless in one last attempt to keep her here—or to encourage her to return.

But the memories of the past—of the fights he'd had with Marcia over his family interference, his job and Joey—everything that was important to him—came pummeling down on him, and he took a step back, letting her go.

Jillian had never met his family, but he remembered the conversation they'd had on the way home from the ranch, when they'd talked about the Walkers expecting a new baby.

Eva's going to have her hands full, Jillian had said. *I can't even imagine what it would be like to have five kids. Wow.*

If she couldn't imagine herself having a big family, how could she ever accept the boisterous Hollister clan?

Marcia certainly hadn't dealt very well with all of Shane's siblings, their spouses and the twelve-at-last-count nieces and nephews. Hell, even Shane had distanced himself from them—although he wasn't sure why.

Because Marcia had accused them of being outspoken and intrusive, he supposed, and to avoid trouble at home, he'd tried to cut the cord. But even that hadn't worked.

So why did he avoid being around them now?

He wasn't sure. Guilt maybe—for staying away so long.

What had they ever done to hurt him—at least, intentionally?

He wondered if she'd feel any differently about them than Marcia had—and hoped she would.

"Did your ex come from a big family?" he asked.

She shook her head. "And thank goodness for that. Dealing with his mother was tough enough as it was."

He remembered her saying the woman was controlling. Interfering.

"Well, I'd better go," Jillian said. "Thanks again."

"Keep in touch."

"I will." Then she climbed into her car.

As much as Shane might have hoped that Jillian would be open to meeting his family, he was beginning to realize that he'd only be opening a can of worms to introduce them. And as he watched her drive away, he came to the sad conclusion that he'd probably been right all along.

Their relationship had been doomed from day one.

Chapter Eleven

Although Jillian had been gone only a few days, Shane missed her more than he'd ever thought possible. But he'd be damned if he would chase after her like a love-sick puppy.

He'd called her a couple of hours after she'd left, just to make sure that she'd gotten home safely, then again later that evening, to ask about her grandmother's condition.

"She has pneumonia and is in the hospital," Jillian had told him, "but the doctor assured us that she was only being admitted as a precaution. He expects her to respond to antibiotics, and as soon as she does, she'll be discharged."

"Then it was good that you went home," he said, in spite of his disappointment that she'd ended her visit early and his belief that she probably wouldn't come back— even if she could.

"You're right. I really had no choice. My grandmother had hoped to get by with only a prescription and no office visit, so I'm glad I insisted upon taking her in."

At that point, Shane could have asked Jillian to come back to Brighton Valley after her grandmother was feeling better, but why bother? She'd clammed up that morning, before she'd even made the call to the older woman, so something else had been bothering her. Something she hadn't wanted to share with him.

Shane had chased after a woman before, and it hadn't done him a bit of good. So he wasn't about to do it again.

When they'd said their goodbyes and ended the phone call, he'd turned on the TV, hoping to shut Jillian out of his mind. But it hadn't done the trick. When he'd finally turned in for the night and slipped between the sheets, her lilac scent teased him, until his bed had never felt so empty. Not even after Marcia had left him, which had come as a bit of a surprise.

The next day, he'd gone back to the ranch, hoping that some hard work would help him get his life back on track.

Dan had asked why he'd come back before the week was up, but all Shane had said was that there'd been a family emergency, and Jillian had to return home.

Now it was the weekend—Sunday morning to be precise. And without having any physical labor to ease his mind, he'd decided to drive into Houston to see his parents, who typically barbecued on weekend afternoons for anyone who cared to show up.

They'd be surprised to see him, since he lived so far away and had used the distance as an excuse more often than not. But it was finally time for him to stop avoiding the family get-togethers and join the Hollister fold once again.

He hadn't planned to drop in on Jillian, even though he'd been tempted to give her a call every five minutes on his two-hour drive to the city. So much for keeping her out of his mind. Who was he fooling?

Now look at him. In spite of his best efforts to leave well enough alone, he found himself heading for her apartment rather than to his parents' house.

After parking in one of the visitor spaces, he made his way to her front door and rang the bell. When she answered and spotted him on the porch, her bluebonnet eyes widened and her lips parted.

He'd been envisioning her for days on end, remembering her lilac scent and her pretty smile, yet he hadn't realized the actual sight of her would steal the breath right out of him.

"What a surprise," she said.

He grinned. "I was in the area and thought I'd stop by."

She stepped aside to let him into the small living room.

"How's your grandmother doing?" he asked.

"Much better. She only stayed in the hospital overnight, then I brought her here to stay with me for a couple of days. I took her home this morning. She wanted to water her plants and check on things."

"I'm glad she's feeling better."

"Me, too."

He waited an awkward beat, then said, "I hope you don't mind me stopping by."

"No, not at all. Why don't you have a seat?"

He scanned the room, deciding upon the sofa. "Thanks."

"Why did you have to come to Houston?" she asked, as she sat, too, and rested one hand in her lap, the other on her pregnant tummy.

"My folks live in the Woodlands," he explained, "just off Arbolitos Drive. And since they've been complaining that they don't see me often enough, I decided it was time to pay them a visit."

"That's nice."

Nice? That's it? As much as Shane had wanted to see her, to hear her voice, he'd hoped to get more than that out of her. But as the initial awkwardness stretched between them, he wasn't sure what to say, what to do.

He probably ought to make an excuse and leave, but decided to give it one more shot. And since he was going to lay his heart on the line once—and *only* once—he decided to level with her about his feelings and ask what she wanted from him.

"You know that I plan to be a part of the baby's life, which means I'll be a part of yours, too."

"I know." She offered him a smile. "You can't very well be one or the other, can you?"

Yeah, he supposed that was true.

"I want you to know that I wouldn't be opposed to getting married."

Her smile faded, although he couldn't blame her for being a little surprised by a semiproposal like that. So he added, "Not right away, of course. We'd have to work through things, but I see a future for us as a couple."

She crossed her arms, as though bracing herself. Or distancing herself. Hell if he knew.

Should he have mentioned anything about love?

Women were funny about things like that. But how could he profess to loving her when he wasn't all that sure about the depth of his feelings himself? And even if he was, he wasn't sure he could admit to something like that without hearing it come from her first. Throwing those three little words out there would really put him behind the emotional eight ball.

So why wasn't she saying anything?

Damn, he was botching this all up. He'd never been comfortable talking about feelings, not to his family or to Marcia, when the two of them had been married. So what made him think he'd learned to open up about that stuff now, when there was so much riding upon him and Jillian working out some kind of relationship?

"I really care about you, Shane. And I think you'll make a good father. So I'm okay with you being a part of the baby's life, but marriage is…well, it's a big step. I just got divorced. I'm not ready for that kind of commitment, not yet." She tucked a strand of hair behind her ear.

Shane wanted to object, although he wasn't sure why. Jillian clearly wasn't interested in marriage or a future together. And, apparently, being his lover again was out, too. Otherwise, she wouldn't have put him off each time they'd taken a step in that direction.

But there was one thing he would take a stand on, without giving a damn whether he was compromising himself or not. And that was being a father to their baby.

"For what it's worth," Jillian said, "I'm still trying to prove to myself that I don't need a man to rescue me, even if that means going without and struggling financially. It's important for me to know that I can support myself and my daughter."

"She's my daughter, too."

"I realize that."

Did she really? Then why did she think she had to call all the shots?

The past, it seemed, was repeating itself. And Shane wasn't about to go through that frustration all over again. So he glanced at his wristwatch, then got to his feet. There wasn't any reason for him to stay. He'd offered marriage—well, at least he'd brought it up as a possibility—and Jillian had pretty much thrown it right back in his face.

He wasn't going to beat a dead horse, at least when it came to Jillian. On the other hand, he wouldn't give up his child without a fight.

"Are you leaving?" she asked.

"Yeah, I need to go." But not because anyone at his parents' house was expecting him. Right now, his heart was knotting up inside because of all he stood to lose—and he wasn't just talking about his daughter.

He'd fallen for Jillian. As much as he'd like to dispute the possibility, he couldn't. Not here. Not now.

As he walked to the door, she followed him. But he let himself out.

Then he headed for his pickup without looking back.

As Jillian watched Shane climb into his truck, she wanted to call him back, to tell him that they had more to talk about. But fear caused her tongue to freeze and her feet to root to the floor.

After she and Thomas had split, she'd been determined to protect herself from getting involved in another bad relationship—and the pain and disappointment that went with it. So she'd resisted Shane and her growing attraction to him.

So how's that working for you? a small voice asked.

To be honest? Not so well. Her heart ached at the thought of losing him for good, and she wasn't sure how to make things right. Was it too late to even try?

She had to admit that she'd handled things badly when he'd stopped by, but his surprise visit had thrown her off balance, and so had his mention of marriage.

Yet somewhere, deep in her heart, she'd hoped that they could have become a couple someday—and a family. But Shane hadn't said anything about love, and there was no way Jillian would ever consider making a lifetime commitment without that one critical ingredient.

So she closed the front door, locking herself into her apartment.

Yet instead of gaining the sense of security she'd been expecting, a cold, lonely chill settled within her, leaving her feeling lost and more alone than ever before.

For nearly twenty minutes, she continued to struggle

with her emotions, as well as her plans for the future, but she was still no closer to a resolution.

Jillian could certainly use a friend right now, but Katie, her old college roommate, wasn't going to fit the bill this time. She didn't just want to chat and vent; she needed some guidance from someone who loved her unconditionally.

So she picked up the telephone and called the one person in the world she could always depend upon for level-headed advice.

When Gram answered, Jillian gripped the receiver as though she could reinforce their connection, strengthening it.

"I've got a problem," she told the older woman.

"What's the matter?"

In the past, while talking to Gram about the night she'd met Shane and invited him back to her room, Jillian had held back a lot of details, but she wouldn't do that now. If she wanted her grandmother's advice, she would have to lay it all on the table, letting the older woman know just what the problem was—and how it was tearing her apart.

So Jillian told her grandmother everything—about the romantic dinner they'd had, the arousing kiss they'd shared on the dance floor and the fact that Shane had turned her broken heart on end, jump-starting the healing process and making her feel like a desirable woman again.

She didn't go into the specifics of their lovemaking, of course, but she did admit that they'd been sexually compatible.

Compatible? that small voice asked. How about downright *combustible?*

There was no disputing that, but she did her best to shake off the heated memories. Then she mentioned that Shane's young son had died. She also shared what she'd read about his assault of the suspect who'd been in his custody, the resulting suspension from the force and, of course, his reinstatement after a thorough investigation. She ended by telling Gram that he'd ultimately left the HPD altogether.

Jillian even went so far as to admit that Thomas had been abusive at times, although he'd never gone so far as to strike her. And her concern that Shane might have a short fuse or a violent streak, too.

"Has he given you any reason to believe that about him?" Gram asked.

"Honestly? None at all."

Gram seemed to ponder that response for a moment, then asked, "When did he lose his child? Was it before or after the incident with that suspect?"

"His son died first, I think. Why?"

"Because that time in his life must have been filled with grief."

"I'm sure it was."

"When he snapped with that suspect, he might have been in a bad place emotionally. And if that's the case, then maybe you should cut him a little slack, honey."

Jillian hadn't thought about that, even after that day at the park when he'd told her about Joey's death. For some reason, she hadn't put the two incidences together, and she probably should have.

Either way, how could she make an assumption about Shane's character without even asking him what had happened that day? Or to consider the reasons that may have led up to it?

"Thanks for talking to me, Gram. You've given me a lot to think about."

"I haven't met that young man, Jilly, but I trust your judgment. And it's time that you started to trust yourself again, too."

After saying goodbye and ending the call, Jillian sat back on the sofa.

Gram had been widowed after losing the love of her life, so it wasn't any wonder that she had a romantic streak, that she believed marriages and relationships could go the distance, even though Jillian's personal experience suggested otherwise.

As hope began to rear its head, Jillian couldn't help thinking—and *believing*—that the older woman might be right.

Had she made a big mistake by letting Shane leave before telling him how she felt—even if she wasn't entirely sure?

She could have told him how much she'd appreciated all the little things he'd done to make her visit in Brighton Valley special—and enjoyable. Having him with her in the E.R. that day had been comforting, too.

As she thought about the sonogram, about her and Shane watching their baby move within the womb, she remembered his excitement, his support.

And in spite of her fear that he considered their baby a replacement for the son he'd lost, she realized that he'd seemed pleased to learn that their child was a girl.

He'd even been willing to get a bigger place to live and to purchase a brand-new rocking chair for her to put in the nursery she planned to create.

As Jillian took it all in, she blew out a sigh. Why hadn't she realized that there was far more to Shane Hollister than met the eye, although what met the eye was enough to set her heart soaring and her hormones pumping?

In fact, even though she'd been dragging her feet about getting physically involved with him, she liked sleeping with him and waking in his arms. She even wanted to make love to him again.

And again.

Did all of that mean that she could fall in love with him?

Or maybe she already had.

So now what? she wondered.

The urge to talk to him grew until she had no choice but to act upon it.

He was probably already at his parents' house by now, with his family. Maybe she should call him, discuss her thoughts and feelings over the phone. But a face-to-face conversation would be best.

My folks live in the Woodlands...just off Arbolitos Drive.

Jillian didn't know exactly which house belonged to Mr. and Mrs. Hollister, but she could certainly find the street. And then she could drive up one side and down the other until she spotted Shane's pickup.

There would probably be a party in progress, but she wasn't going to let that stop her. She was going to walk right up to the front door—baby bump and all. Then she would ring the bell and ask to speak to Shane.

He hadn't said much about his family, and she wasn't sure why he hadn't. So she wasn't sure what his family would think of her showing up unannounced, unwed and pregnant. But she didn't care. She needed to talk to Shane and make things right.

She just hoped it wasn't too late.

After climbing into his pickup and leaving Jillian's house, Shane had sworn under his breath, ashamed of himself for practically groveling.

Right then and there, he'd been tempted to head back to Brighton Valley, with its clear blue skies and wide-open spaces, where he'd created a new life for himself.

Instead, he drove across town to the Woodlands,

turned onto Arbolitos Drive and proceeded until he arrived at his folks' house.

There were a couple of cars parked in front already, as well as two of his nephews playing catch on the lawn. He sat in his truck for a moment or two, watching his brother John's sons.

The boys were getting bigger, Shane noted. It was nice to see the oldest coaching the youngest. John must be really proud of them.

Deciding he'd sat in the truck long enough, he climbed out of the driver's seat and headed for the house. As he made his way up the sidewalk, he stopped long enough to say hello to the boys and to add, "Good arm, Trevor."

"Thanks, Uncle Shane. You want to play with us?"

"Maybe later. I have to check in with your grandma first, or I'll be in big trouble." Then he made his way to the front door and let himself in.

He'd barely entered the living room when his sister Mary-Lynn spotted him.

"Hey, Mom," she called. "Come quick. Look what the cat drug in." Then she wrapped Shane in a hug, which he held on to for a beat or two longer than necessary.

For some reason, it felt especially good to have a physical connection with another human being, especially since Jillian had sent him on his way earlier. Not that she'd asked him to leave, but she hadn't done anything to convince him to stay.

"You're certainly a sight for sore eyes," Mary-Lynn told him, as they stepped apart. "You really should come around more often. We miss you."

"I missed you, too." And at that very moment, as the words rolled off his tongue without any conscious thought, he realized they were true.

"So what's new around here?" Shane asked his sister,

knowing that she was the go-to girl when it came to learning the scoop about the comings and goings in the family.

"Well, let's see… Colleen's setting a wedding date—November tenth. And Andy will be heading for Camp Pendleton soon, although I'm not sure when."

Before Shane could question whether their baby sister was old enough and wise enough to tie the knot, or whether Andy should have considered another branch of the military, his mother entered the room and clapped her hands.

"Shane! I've been hoping and praying that you'd surprise us one Sunday and come home." Then she wrapped her arms around him in a mama-bear hug, letting him know just how glad she was to see him.

After the welcome-back embrace ended, his mom and his sister headed back to the kitchen, just as Jack, his oldest brother, came into the house from the backyard.

"It's good to see you, little brother."

"Same here."

"So what's new?" Jack asked.

Nothing Shane was ready to talk about yet. So he said, "Not much."

"Are you dating anyone special yet?"

"Nope. I'm too busy riding fence and mucking stalls for that."

"Sounds like a crappy job, if you ask me. If I were you, I'd much rather be chasing after the bad guys—and dating the ladies." Jack, who loved his work with the police department, nodded toward the sliding door that led out to the patio. "Come on outside. I'll buy you a beer and let you know what's been going on at the HPD."

As Shane followed his brother out to the yard, he thought about the dating question and his lack of honesty.

Of course, he and Jillian weren't what you'd call an

item. In fact, after today, they weren't really anything—other than coparents, he supposed.

He'd been a fool to stop by her place earlier, and he'd been an even bigger fool to mention marriage or to hint at them having a life together.

From day one, he'd known that a permanent relationship with Jillian wasn't in the cards—even if he'd wished otherwise.

Jack handed Shane a can of beer, and they made small talk for a while. A few minutes later, their father, who'd been napping, joined them outside. They greeted each other, then talked about the scuttlebutt down at the precinct.

As Shane scanned the yard, watching the kids play tag and the adults crack jokes, listening to the bursts of laughter and the escalating voices, he realized that it would take a special woman to appreciate a Hollister get-together.

Marcia certainly hadn't been able to. And Jillian, who was an only child, too, didn't seem able to handle it, either.

Besides that, Jillian had also experienced the best that life could offer when she'd been married, so how could she ever live happily in a blue-collar world?

She'd be miserable. And Shane would find himself back in that same marital turmoil he'd been in before.

No way would he ever want to live like that again.

"You ready for another beer?" Jack asked, as he dipped his hand into the ice chest.

"No, I'm good for now." Shane turned back to the game of tag that his nieces were playing on the grass.

"Shane?" his mom called out.

"Yeah?" He turned to face the sliding door, where his mother stood.

He assumed that she wanted him to do her a favor, like

carry something heavy outside or reach a bowl in the top shelf of the cupboard.

Instead, she said, "You have company."

"Me?" He wondered who knew that he'd be here today, since he hadn't told anyone in the family that he was going to show up.

"Yes, *you,*" she said.

"Who is it?" he asked.

"That's what *I'd* like to know." His mother crossed her arms and raised her brow. "She's a beautiful blonde who's obviously pregnant. And she's asking for you."

"Uh-oh," Jack said. "Sounds like you might have been doing a little more than riding fence and mucking stalls while you were in Brighton Valley."

Shane might have had some kind of snappy retort if he hadn't been floored by the news that Jillian was here. And it had to be her. Who else did he know who was blond, beautiful and pregnant?

Trouble was, when he went inside the house and headed for the front door, everyone else seemed to follow him like a string of ducklings.

Chapter Twelve

Jillian stood on the Hollisters' front porch, waiting for Shane's mother to call him to the door.

She'd been invited inside, but until she had a chance to talk to him and he issued the invitation himself, she thought it would be best if she waited here.

But when footsteps sounded—a lot of them—she glanced past the entryway and into the living room, where Shane strode toward her, several of his family members following behind.

Certainly she wouldn't have to tell him what she'd come to say in front of an audience, would she?

He wore a slightly bewildered expression, although she had no idea what her own looked like—uneasy? Embarrassed? Contrite? Maybe a little bit of each?

Still, as he approached, she managed a smile. "I… uh…need to talk to you." She glanced beyond him—at Mrs. Hollister, as well as a man who could be his brother, and several children.

Shane peeked over his shoulder, at the curious on-lookers, then back to her. "Do you want to take a walk around the block?"

"Sure."

"It might be the only chance we have at some privacy."

Then he turned to his mother and said, "Don't wait for me to get back. Go ahead and eat whenever those steaks are done."

Then he stepped onto the porch and closed the door behind him, shutting out the audience.

They started down the sidewalk to the curb, then proceeded down the shady, tree-lined street.

"How'd you know where my parents live?" he asked.

"You told me the neighborhood, as well as the street. I took a drive, then looked for your truck. Actually, I knocked at one of the neighbor's houses by mistake, and a lady told me to go next door."

The sun had risen high overhead, and a breeze ruffled the leaves in the trees, as they continued a casual walk.

"I hope you don't mind that I came by," she said.

"No, that's fine."

"It's just that I wanted to apologize to you—in person."

He pondered her comment for a half beat. "About what?"

"For not being completely open with you about the way I feel. For holding back and for not trusting you."

His steps slowed, and hers did, too. As he turned to face her, as their gazes met and locked, she braced herself for what she'd driven across town to say.

"I think you'll make a wonderful father for our baby. And I'll be happy to share custody with you. But I plan to nurse her, and so… Well, you can understand why I wouldn't want you to take her away from me or keep her overnight."

"I never planned to do that. At least, not when she's little. That's one reason why I…" He glanced down at his boots, shifted his weight, then looked back up again. "I guess that's why I suggested that we work something out, where we could… Well, eventually where we could raise her together."

"You mean move into the same house?" she asked. He'd mentioned marriage, so that's what he must have been thinking.

"I'm willing. But if you're not ready or even interested, I understand."

"It's not that." She cleared her throat, hoping to cut through the complicated feelings she was struggling with, then pressed on with the honesty he deserved. "I enjoyed my time at your place in Brighton Valley. You were a perfect gentleman and… Well, you seem to be too good to be true, and that scares me."

"Why?"

"Because I'm afraid of getting hurt again."

"I can understand that."

"Can you? Because I can't. And it doesn't seem fair to you. I mean, my ex-husband was a lying jerk. And I've been holding you at bay because I'm afraid that you might not be the man I want you to be."

Shane reached out, caught a strand of her hair, letting it slip through his fingers as though it were spun gold. "You scare me, too. I had a lousy marriage, and my wife never could appreciate my family or my job. Hell, most of the time, she didn't even appreciate *me*. So now I find myself involved with a woman who lives in a world two hours from mine, and she's having our baby."

"So how can we work this out?" she asked.

"Are you willing to compromise?"

"That's what I came here to tell you. I should have said something earlier, but my fears got in the way, even though you've given me nothing to be afraid of."

"Are you saying you'd consider marrying me?" Shane asked. "Maybe someday?"

"That's the problem." She bit her lip, then sought his

gaze, his understanding. "Marriage is hard enough when people love each other."

"And you don't think you could ever love me?"

She tilted her head slightly. "I *do* love you, Shane. I'm not sure when it happened—maybe that night at the hotel. All I know is that my feelings for you continue to grow, and I don't know what to do, other than face them head on."

She *loved* him? Shane couldn't believe his ears. He wasn't the only one wrestling with those feelings, with that mind-spinning attraction.

He reached out and cupped her beautiful face, skimming his thumbs across her cheeks, breathing in her lilac scent, basking in her presence. "You have no idea how happy I am to hear that, Jillian, because I love you, too."

"You do?"

He nodded. "I was afraid you wouldn't be able to accept me and the lifestyle I wanted to provide for you. But if we love each other, maybe we can come up with a compromise that will work out without either of us having to give up our dreams."

"I'd like that. And while I wasn't sure how this conversation was going to turn out, I did some thinking about possible solutions on my drive across town."

"So what'd you come up with?"

"Since school is out, and the baby is due in December, there's no reason for me to be in Houston, other than my grandmother. And maybe, if I tell her I'm moving to Brighton Valley and taking the baby with me, she'll consider relocating."

"No kidding?" Shane had hoped she'd feel that way, yet it had all seemed too much of a stretch.

"I'd have to make some phone calls, but I might be

able to do my student teaching at the new high school in Brighton Valley—or even the old one in Wexler."

If she was willing to compromise, to go to that extreme for them to be together, then he'd do the same for her. "If it doesn't pan out, if you can't get the position, then I'll do whatever I have to do—even if it means moving back to Houston or taking a desk job. I want us all to be together—as a family."

"It just might work out," she said. "I'd have some meetings and classes I'd have to attend at the university sometimes, but not every day. So I can probably commute."

"I know it'll work out," he said. "One way or another. We'll find a way."

Then he lowered his mouth to hers, sealing the commitment they intended to make with a kiss that began sweet and precious, then deepened into something soul stirring and filled with promise.

When they came up for air, he drew her tight, amazed at his good fortune.

"I don't know when I've ever been so happy," he said.

"Neither do I."

"I don't know about you," he said, "but Christmas came early this year."

"Speaking of Christmas…" She broke into a radiant smile. "There's going to be three of us by then. Can you believe it? We'll be writing letters for Santa and leaving cookies under the tree before you know it."

Shane thought of Joey, of the first Christmas after his birth. And while the memory was bittersweet, it wasn't nearly as painful as it might have been—before he'd met Jillian and had realized that time really did heal, that life went on.

"I can't wait," he said. "Come on, let's go back to the

house and tell my family. We won't have to stay long, but I'd like them to know. I think it'll make them happy."

"All right."

He reached for her hand, then she gave it a tug. "Wait a minute. I have something I want to confess."

"What's that?"

"After I found out I was pregnant, I looked you up on the internet. I was curious and wanted to know more about you."

"I can understand that. I actually did some checking of my own." He gave her hand a gentle squeeze, knowing what she'd probably learned and ready to deal with it now. After all, with her in his corner, he could handle anything. "So what did you find out?"

"An online newspaper account reported the trouble you had with the police department. At the time I read the article, I wondered if you had a violent side. But the more I got to know you, the more I realized you weren't the kind to snap like that. Not unless provoked."

He couldn't blame her for being concerned. And he was glad that she'd come to the conclusion that she and the baby would always be safe with him.

"You don't have to tell me what happened that day if you don't want to. It doesn't matter to me anymore. But I want it to be out in the open, since I want us to always have an open relationship."

He remained silent for a while, rewinding that scene and watching it all over again as it played out in his mind. Then he let it go, wanting the honesty, too.

"His name was Lyle Bailey. And he brutally murdered a little boy. My partner and I had been looking for him, and when we found him, he ran. I took chase, knowing that there'd be no way in hell I'd let him get away. No way I'd let him hurt another child again, ruin another family. And when I caught him… Well, I snapped. All I could see were two little boys in small caskets, the boy he'd murdered and Joey."

Jillian reached up and cupped his cheek, then she drew his lips to hers, kissing him softly, sharing his grief. "I understand."

"I don't have a temper," he explained. "Although I've got to admit that I'm not sure what I would have done to that guy if my partner hadn't stopped me."

It seemed like a dark and horrible thing to share, yet because of the intimacy and honesty that stretched between them, it was the perfect time to set it out there.

"I was suspended, with pay," he added. "You probably read that, too."

"Yes, and I also know that they reinstated you."

His lips pressed together, and he nodded. "But after that, after I assaulted Bailey, I thought it would be a good idea to take a leave of absence to wait until Joey's death wasn't so fresh on my mind."

"Do you ever want to go back to work as a cop?"

"Would it bother you if I did?"

"No, I'm going to support you in whatever you want to do."

Shane couldn't believe his good fortune. How lucky he'd been when he'd spotted Jillian in that bar, when he'd gone back to her hotel room. And he couldn't wait to start their life together, to get ready for their Christmas baby.

"Come on," he said, taking her by the hand. "I need to introduce you to my family before they come looking for us. They might get a little loud and boisterous. And they'll be full of questions. But if you can handle it for a little while I'll follow you back to your place, where we can be alone."

And where they could seal their love with more than a kiss.

"I hope they like me," she said.

Shane reached for her hand, giving it a gentle squeeze as they headed back to his parents' house. "Don't worry about that. They're going to love you. I'm more concerned about you liking them."

"Why? What's wrong with them?"

"They can be a little quirky at times. And intrusive. And generous and loving, too. You know what I mean?"

"I think so."

As they reached the house, he spotted movement near the shutters, realizing that someone had been peering into the street.

So as he opened the door for Jillian he said, "Okay, you guys. The gig's up. No need to be snoopy, we have an announcement to make."

His mother swept into the room as though she'd just now become aware of their return, although Shane had a feeling she'd been the one doing the peeking out the window.

"This lovely woman is Jillian Wilkes," he said, "and she's expecting my baby—a little girl. We're going to get married, although we haven't decided when."

As the family closed in on them, their smiles revealing their happiness and their willingness to welcome Jillian into the Hollister fold, Shane's heart filled with love—for her, for their child and for the family that only wanted him to be happy.

Jillian opened the door to her small apartment and let Shane inside. She wasn't sure why he'd felt so uneasy about her meeting his family. Sure, they were a little loud and outspoken, but their love for each other was apparent and seemed to spill over into everything they did or said.

They'd ended up staying nearly an hour, since Jillian had felt so welcome and had wanted to join them for dinner.

Now they were back at her apartment, where she scanned the small living area, realizing that this place was only a temporary abode. She had no idea where she and Shane would end up living, but she knew that as long as they were together, anywhere would feel like home.

"Did you get enough to eat?" he asked.

She laughed. "More than enough. Your mom and sisters kept offering me seconds."

Shane slipped behind her and wrapped his arms around her waist. "They mean well."

"I know they do." Jillian turned to face him and stepped into his warm embrace. "But there's something you need to keep in mind."

"What's that?"

"I'm not anything like Marcia. And while I've never had brothers or sisters of my own, I'm actually looking forward to being a part of the Hollister clan—even if they're a little quirky or become intrusive at times."

Shane kissed her, and as her lips parted, as their tongues began to mate, she drew him close, relishing all she'd found in his arms, in his heart.

Somehow, some way, this was all going to work out beautifully.

As she threaded her fingers in his hair, she leaned into him, relishing the feel of his mouth on hers, wanting more. Needing more.

Would she ever get enough of *him*—the man she loved? The man who offered her everything she'd always wanted in life—a family, a home?

As the kiss intensified, as the physical hunger that always simmered between them kicked into high gear, she reached for his belt buckle, letting him know she was ready for more than just a kiss, that she wanted a replay of the first night they'd met.

He followed her lead, undoing his jeans and tugging at his shirttails.

This was what they'd been waiting for since that night in March, when two lonely people met and set about to heal each other.

She reached for his hand and led him to the bedroom, where she began to undress, removing her light jacket and letting it flutter to the ground, unzipping her slacks, pushing the fabric over her hips.

As Jillian shimmied out of her pants, Shane stood transfixed, caught up in an arousal of epic proportions and mesmerized by the provocative way she removed her clothes.

When she stood before him in a pair of lacy white panties and a matching bra, the swell of her pregnancy added a sweet innocence he hadn't quiet expected. He swallowed hard as the woman he loved bared herself to him, offering herself as a gift he would cherish the rest of his life.

With his heart pounding in both love and need, he eased before her, slowly. Reverently. "You're beautiful."

"So are you." She unbuttoned his shirt, sliding the fabric off his shoulders. Then she skimmed her fingers across his chest, sending a shiver through his nerve endings and a shimmy of heat through his blood.

As he removed his shirt completely, he watched as she reached behind her back and unhooked her bra, releasing her breasts. He bent and took a nipple in his mouth, tasting, suckling, taunting until she gasped in pleasure.

Then he scooped her into his arms and laid her on top of the white goose down comforter, where they began to work the magic that had been sparking between them ever since the first time they'd spotted each other at El Jardin, the upscale bar in Houston.

Then, after removing the rest of his clothes, Shane climbed beside her on the bed, never missing a beat, as they picked up right where they'd left off.

When their breathing grew ragged, when they were unable to wait any longer, he entered her, giving her everything he had, loving her fully—with his body, heart and soul.

As they reached an incredible peak, as she gripped his shoulders and cried out with her release, he let go, too, riding the waves of an amazing climax.

When it was over, they continued to hold each other, basking in their love and in the amazing chemistry they shared. Finally, Shane rolled to the side, taking Jillian with him. As they faced each other, drawing sated smiles, she placed her hand on his chest, over his heart.

"I can hardly believe this," she said, "but making love with you was even more amazing than I remembered."

"I was just thinking the same thing." As he ran his hand along the slope of her hip, a slow smile stretched across his face. "And the best part about it is the fact that it's only going to get better."

She knew he was right, although it was hard to imagine how they could improve perfection. She brushed a hank of hair from his forehead, amazed at the depth of her love for him.

Somehow, it seemed as though they'd always been meant for each other.

"It's too bad we didn't meet each other before we fell into bad first marriages," he said.

"I'm not so sure about that. Maybe all those struggles we dealt with before made us into the people we are today, people who can fully appreciate and love each other."

"Maybe so, honey. But I promise you this. I'm in this for the duration."

"So am I."

With that, he kissed her one more time, with everything he had, everything he was, everything he ever hoped to be.

Epilogue

Three weeks after Jillian and Shane brought Mary Rose Hollister home to their four-bedroom tract house in Brighton Valley, they hosted the family Christmas party as a way to welcome their new daughter into the Hollister fold and to show off their new digs.

Outside, while storm clouds gathered overhead, a December breeze stirred the dried leaves still on the trees. Yet inside, the flames of a small fire in the hearth cast its warmth throughout the living room.

A Christmas tree with blinking white lights and colorful ornaments stood near the bay window that looked out into the street, while the faint scent of pine mingled with the aroma of a turkey baking in the oven.

Along the mantel, adorned with small boughs of pine and a nativity scene, hung three handmade stockings, each filled with goodies that Santa had brought the night before.

Jillian's grandmother, who'd decided to move into the apartment over Carolyn's Diner after Shane and Jillian had found a larger place, was seated on the new rocking chair near the fireplace. As Gram held the eight-pound baby girl, who'd been dressed in a red-and-white sleeper, she marveled over the tufts of dark hair and blue eyes.

"I swear to goodness," Gram said, "Mary Rose is the most beautiful baby I've ever seen."

Jillian thought her daughter was adorable, too, although she and Gram were probably just a wee bit biased.

"Honey?" Shane called, as he came in from the backyard. "Did Jack get here yet? He called a while back, and I gave him directions."

"Not yet," she said. "Do you think he's lost?"

"Maybe not. But he should have gotten here by now."

Dan and Eva Walker had been the first to arrive, along with both sets of twins and Catherine Loza, a friend of theirs who'd been living in Manhattan.

According to what Eva had told Jillian earlier, Catherine had gone through a recent breakup and had wanted to get away. Jillian didn't know the details—and she wouldn't ask—but she couldn't imagine a better place than Brighton Valley to heal a broken heart and to get one's life back on track.

She'd come to love this town and looked forward to starting her student-teaching at Washington High School in Wexler when the winter semester began in mid-January.

Shane, who'd been appointed sheriff when Sam Jennings retired, was happy with the position, saying that it allowed him the best of both worlds.

When the doorbell chimed, Shane announced, "I'll get it. That's got to be Jack."

All of the Hollisters would be arriving within the next twenty minutes or so, but Jack had started out sooner than the others. And Jillian couldn't wait to see them. Shane's family had been wonderfully supportive, accepting her as a new daughter-in-law and going so far as to include Gram in all of their family gatherings.

Jillian wasn't sure who was happier to hold the family

Christmas dinner—her or Shane. They'd been decorating and planning the meal since Thanksgiving.

"Come in," Shane told his brother, who entered along with his wife and two sons.

"Trevor," Shane said to the oldest boy, "why don't you take Evan out to the backyard? The Walkers are back there, checking out the swing set that came with the house."

As the Hollister boys dashed outside, Jillian met Shane at the door to welcome her brother-in-law and his wife. "Thanks for agreeing to have Christmas in Brighton Valley this year. I know it's a long drive for you."

"We wouldn't have missed it," Cindy Hollister said. "Now, where's the baby? I can't wait to hold her. They grow up so fast."

As Jillian pointed to Gram, Jack scanned the living room and said, "Nice house."

"Thanks." Shane slipped his arm around Jillian and pulled her close. "We like it."

And they truly did. Their new home might be miniscule in comparison to the estate in which Jillian had once lived with Thomas, but it resonated with the love and laughter she'd been longing for during those sad, lonely years.

As Jack and his wife followed the kids out to the backyard, Shane drew Jillian into a warm embrace. "Thank you for making this Christmas my best ever."

"I'm the one who should be thanking you."

Then she kissed her husband with all the love in her heart.

* * * * *

A Baby For Christmas

JOANNA SIMS

Joanna Sims lives in Florida with her husband and their three fabulous felines. Joanna works as a therapist for the public school system during the day, but spends her evenings and weekends fulfilling her lifelong dream of writing compelling, modern romances for Mills & Boon. When it's time to take a break from writing, Joanna enjoys going for long walks with her husband and curling up on the couch to watch movies (romantic comedies preferably). She loves to answer any questions or provide additional information for her readers. You can contact her at Joannasims2@live.com.

Chapter One

Captain Luke Brand was home for the holidays. Against his will. As far as he was concerned, First Recon was still in Afghanistan, so *he* should still be in Afghanistan. Bottom line. And it didn't matter that an insurgent had blown a bullet clean through his left leg. It didn't matter to him that he had almost lost the leg. *Almost* didn't count. His leg was still attached; he should return to active duty. But the Marines sure as hell didn't see it that way. They denied his request, patched him up and shipped his butt back to the States for medical leave. Like it or not, he was on his way home.

And he didn't like it. Not by a long shot.

The military had gotten him as far as Helena; now Billy Whiteside, an old high school buddy, was taking him the rest of the way to his family's Montana ranch. Bent Tree was less than an hour away. Luke wished it were two hours. Three would be even better. He wasn't in a hurry to tangle with his sister-in-law, Sophia; from his point of view, fighting the Taliban for control of Afghan towns seemed like a much easier task.

"He's found a good spot to hang out." Billy glanced over at the black kitten perched on Luke's left leg. Luke looked down at the scrawny kitten and grunted in response. The kitten had started the trip in a box situated between Billy and Luke. Once the kitten caught Luke's eye, he made a determined escape from the box, and a beeline for Luke's leg. Luke had always liked an underdog, and this kitten certainly qualified; found in a ball of toilet paper in a truck stop restroom, half starved, half frozen. He was lucky to be alive. He was a survivor. Luke liked that about him. So, when the kitten had gingerly sat down on the exact spot where his leg was wounded, Luke didn't have the heart to make him move. In fact, the warmth of the kitten's body and the vibrations of his purr seemed to ease the pain a bit.

"He's lucky he didn't end up in the Dumpster...." Billy's naturally round face had gotten even rounder with weight and age; he still easily wore a giant grin that split his face. Billy reached over and banged on the dashboard of his Chevy to get the heater kicked on again. "Cindy swept him right up into the dustpan. Can you believe *that?* 'Course, she didn't know what was in that mess'a paper. How could she know, ya know? 'Course, Cindy can't keep him. What with four kids, two dogs, a couple of cats and that pig her youngest is raisin'! And, I don't know, man... I think my ol' lady will put me out in the barn if I bring anything else home. But what else could I do? I couldn't just leave him there..." Billy banged on the dash again. "And, it looks like he picked you... Cats pick their owners, you know. Didn't you tell me that? No! It was your mom who told me that! Your mom told me that...."

Luke didn't bother to reply. He knew what Billy was getting at. He was trying to pawn this scruffy orphan off on him. Not a chance! The little fur ball would just have to go back into the box when the ride was over. As for Billy, his old friend wouldn't expect him to say much, about the kitten or otherwise. That's why he'd hit

Billy up for a ride in the first place. He was in no mood for small talk. And Billy would understand that without being told. All Luke wanted to do was to be quiet and think about Sophia. All he wanted to do was figure out what he was going to *say* to Sophia. So, while Billy kept up both sides of the conversation, Luke stared morosely at each passing mile marker and thought about what he was going to say to his brother's widow.

What in the hell am I going to say to you, Sophia? What the hell *could* he say?

By the time Luke caught a glimpse of Bent Tree over the horizon, he still hadn't thought up a good answer to that question. Maybe there wasn't one.

"This's good." Luke gestured for Billy to pull over at Bent Tree's entrance.

"Are you sure, man? I can take you all the way in." Billy had the good sense not to mention Luke's leg or the cane he had to use to get around.

"This is good." Luke repeated. The slow walk up the long drive would push back his arrival time. Anything to stall the inevitable was okay with him. He had no idea how Sophia was going to react to him. Was she going to hug him or hit him? It was a hard one to gauge. Luke gently picked up the kitten and put him back in the box. The kitten immediately started to cry, but Luke refused to look at him again. He grabbed his cane and pushed the door open. Once his feet were on the ground, he paused for a minute, balanced, and then pulled his sea bag out of the bed of the truck and hoisted it onto his shoulder.

"Thanks, brother. 'ppreciate it." Luke reached across the seat, over the crying kitten, and shook Billy's hand.

"No problem, man. Anything I can do to help," Billy said, and Luke knew he meant it. "And don't be a stranger while you're here. Drop by. Meet the wife and kids."

Luke leaned on his cane for support. "I'll see what I

can do. Things are…" His voice trailed off for a moment as he searched for the right word. "Complicated."

For the first time, Billy's grin faded. He looked down at the steering wheel. "You know, we were all real sorry to hear about Danny. I mean… We all knew it could happen. Lots of folks are headin' over to Iraq and not comin' back. But you never expect it to happen to someone you know…." Billy shook his head slowly. "I just didn't expect it to happen to Danny."

"I know. Me, neither." He had seen a lot of death in the past six years, but to lose his brother, his *twin,* was… unbearable. If he was back in action, he could bury the pain and forget it for a while. But here? In Montana, with his grieving family and Daniel's grieving widow? The pain was going to be front and center, in his face, all the time. With a definitive nod, Luke ended the conversation. "Give my best to your family."

"Will do, Luke. Will do. To yours, too." Billy shifted into gear. "And if I don't see you, Merry Christmas, man."

"Merry Christmas." The kitten wouldn't stop crying. Luke shut the door.

Billy saluted and started to pull away. Without thinking about it, and without knowing why he did it, Luke reached out and banged the side of the truck with his cane.

Billy's brakes squeaked; the truck stopped. Luke yanked open the door.

"Dammit, Billy. Give me the damn kitten!"

Sophia Lee Brand was beginning to think that she had made a *huge* mistake. At first she had thought it was a great idea to stay behind while her in-laws went elsewhere for Thanksgiving. She had thought, *foolishly,* that the peace and quiet would do her a world of good. Not to mention that a three-hour car ride while she was eight months pregnant seemed like a slow form of torture. She had to pee *all the time*. So, she had stayed behind. Insisted upon it, in fact. And now she was bored senseless! One week of solitude was more than enough for a Boston girl stuck in the west, thank you kindly. Week two was going to be excruciating! Thank God for her to-do lists!

Sophia leaned over the kitchen counter and perused her latest list. It wasn't even close to supper time and she had already checked off most of the items.

"I really need a longer list!" She stood upright, stretched backward a bit to ease the pressure from the small of her back. She rubbed her hands over her rounded stomach in a circular motion, looked down at her growing abdomen and laughed. "I'm one big belly."

"All right, Danny boy," she said to the baby nestled in her stomach. "There's no time like the present." She moved over to the fridge and started the next project on her list: make a giant salad. She dragged every raw vegetable out of the fridge that she could find, rummaged through drawers and moved bottles and jars out of the way. Once she had located every last veggie, she carefully and methodically sharpened a knife. She took her time. It was only a little after 3:00 p.m. and she had absolutely no idea what she would do with herself until bedtime.

"Let's have a little 'get in the mood' music, shall we?" Sophia read the titles on the CDs stacked at the end of the long counter. "No. No. Really, no. Seriously, no! And… ah…yes. Mr. Van Morrison." She slid the CD into the player and turned up the volume.

She waited for the first notes to play before she turned up the volume even louder. "I can play it as loud as I *want* to. Who's gonna complain way out here in the boonies?" She patted her stomach. "Are you going to complain, my baby? No, you're not, because you're gonna *love* Mr. Morrison just like your daddy did."

On the way back to the veggies, she grabbed a large salad bowl and then got busy chopping and dicing. The music helped get a rhythm going, and before she knew it she was moving on to the pile of carrots. While she worked, she thought of Daniel.

She paused her chopping for a minute, closed her eyes and conjured his face. In her mind's eye, she could easily see his strong, squared jaw, the bright, sky-blue eyes and his trademark smile.

"Hmm. So handsome." This was said with a sigh as she continued with her chopping.

Sophia had a theory, and it had actually helped her cope. She figured that if she thought about Daniel all of the time, she would burn into her brain the little details that made him so incredibly special. She never wanted to run out of things to tell her son about his father. And, of course, she never wanted to forget the little details of Daniel that had always been just for her, like the natural sweet almond of his skin and the sensation of his fingers on her neck as he brushed her hair over her shoulder. And his voice. The sound of Daniel's voice always sent a shiver up her spine. Especially the husky way he would say her name when he reached for her in the morning....

"Hello, Sophia."

Sophia was in midchop of a very hardheaded carrot when the sound of her name startled her. She simultaneously spun her head around and pressed the knife down hard. The knife missed the carrot and cut the tip of her finger.

"Ow! Shoot!" Sophia jerked her hand away from the cutting board, but otherwise ignored the wounded finger. Instead, she stared at Luke. He was standing in the kitchen doorway wearing his dress blues and a long gray overcoat; feet planted apart, shoulders squared, sky-blue eyes slightly narrowed. He stood before her proudly in his uniform. Strong. Unyielding. Totally masculine. He looked so much like Daniel that her heart started to thud in her chest, the muscles in her legs gave way, and she had to force herself not to cross the room, throw herself into his arms and squeeze the breath right out of him.

That's not Daniel! That's Luke. Stay put! You and Luke don't hug.

"You're bleeding," Luke said.

"What?"

"Your finger." Luke didn't move from his spot. "It's bleeding."

Sophia looked at her finger. Luke was right. It was indeed bleeding. Quite a bit, actually. The blood had trickled down the length of her pointer finger and was pooling into the palm of her hand; some had gotten smeared on her mother-in-law's counter. Under normal circumstances, she would have quickly fixed the finger, cleaned the counter and gotten back to work. But these weren't normal circumstances, and it appeared that she had temporarily lost control over her body. She couldn't seem to move.

But Luke could. In two long strides he was by her side. She saw him wince whenever he put pressure on his left leg. It was strange to see Luke hurt. He had always seemed so invincible to her. Luke flipped on the cold water and guided her finger beneath the stream. She was still pondering on the warm brand his fingers had left on her skin while he moved down the counter to search a nearby drawer.

"Right corner cabinet, top shelf, all the way in the back." Sophia pointed with her good pointer finger.

"Band-aids?" Luke gave her a quizzical look.

"Your mother's been rearranging since the day we got the news about your leg."

Once Sophia said that, it made perfect sense. Barbara Brand didn't cry when she was upset. She rearranged stuff. Luke located a step stool. "Okay, where are they again?"

"All the way to the right." Sophia waved her hand for him to move farther down. "Top shelf. Behind the olives."

Luke stabbed the off button on the CD player before he forced himself up the steps. He ignored the pain in his leg and concentrated on working his way through the maze his mother had set up between himself and the Band-aids. Luke grabbed the box, threw them onto the counter and got down off the step stool.

Luke put the box of Band-aids on the counter next to Sophia. "Not exactly the most convenient place to put *first aid* stuff."

That made Sophia laugh. "No. It's not. But none of us were about to argue with your mom. Not your dad, not me. Certainly not Tyler, he's so easygoing."

One side of Luke's upper lip curled into something that vaguely resembled a smile. "I don't blame you." He knew better than to argue with his mother, too. Most people did. He unwrapped a Band-aid. "Here. Give me your finger."

Something clicked on in her brain and she went from foggy to full throttle. She didn't want him to touch her again. The heat from his body, the smell of his skin, made her feel light-headed. He was too much like Daniel. She didn't know how to react to him, and that ticked her off!

She held her finger away from him. "I can do it myself."

Luke gave her a look that she was certain was meant to intimidate her into cooperating. "Sophia. Don't be a pain."

She narrowed her eyes. "I'm not being a pain."

"That would be a first," Luke said under his breath. Then, more loudly, "Just give me your finger."

"Just give me the stupid Band-aid." She held out her hand. His voice, so much like *Daniel's* voice, sent a shiver right up her spine.

Luke grabbed her arm firmly, held her hand in place and put the Band-aid on her finger. "Now, was that so difficult?"

God, Luke irritated her! He always had. He was so *bossy.* Domineering. Why had she thought, for *one minute,* that things would be different between them now? She grabbed a rag off the kitchen faucet and wiped up the blood from the counter. "Thanks," she said sullenly.

"You're welcome," he replied, with a hint of sarcasm. He wasn't about to climb up on the step stool again. Instead, he tossed the box of Band-aids down the length of the counter.

Silently, she rinsed the rag and wrung it out before she turned back to him. "What are you doing here, anyway? Your parents said you wouldn't be here for another week."

He almost told her the truth, that he had come home early to see her. That he knew his family was away and she was alone. But he didn't. Instead, he said plainly, "Change of plans."

A flash of anger flushed Sophia's cheeks. "Well, I wish you *hadn't* changed your plans. Not if all you intend to do is fight with me the entire time you're here. If you hadn't noticed—" she pulled her sweater tightly over her belly and splayed both hands over her stomach "—I'm a little bit busy here with your nephew, and the last thing I need is to have you hanging around, bullying me."

When she stopped talking, the anger ebbed as quickly as it had risen. The last bit of her energy slipped away with the anger. Suddenly, she felt exhausted. She always felt exhausted now because of the baby, but she did her best to fight it all day long until the fatigue finally won out. Sophia moved over to the table and sat down heavily.

Sophia's words struck him as if she had slapped him in the face. The last thing he *ever* expected Sophia to call him was a bully. He raised an eyebrow at her. "Bullying you?"

He would have joined her at the table, but his leg was killing him. Instead, he leaned back on the counter and crossed his arms over his chest.

Sophia waved her hand before she rested her chin on it. "All right. Perhaps *bullying* is the wrong word. But you know what I mean. You've always looked for a reason to pick a fight with me. Always. And to tell you the truth, now that Daniel's gone, I thought things might be different. I thought you might actually make an effort to be nice to me. Stop giving me such a hard time all the time."

Next to his mother, Sophia was the only person who could easily cut through his B.S. and make him feel like crap. They were the only two women whose opinion actually mattered to him. And she was right. He was doing exactly what he had promised himself he wouldn't do with her. He had promised himself that he wouldn't fall into the same old pattern with her. He'd stop looking for reasons to fight with her and handle her gently. Things would be different. He would change his ways and get along with Sophia. That's what Daniel would have wanted. That's what he needed to do, for everyone's sake, including his own.

"Okay." Luke's tone was steady and quiet. "We've obviously gotten off on the wrong foot here."

Sophia drew her eyebrows together. "We?"

Luke eyed her, blew out his breath and then started over. "Okay...*I* got off on the wrong foot here. Let me go upstairs, take a shower. We'll try it again later."

Sophia nodded. Seemed like a good idea. The two of them were going to be under the same roof for the next month or so. They were going to have to learn how to get along. She was willing, if he was willing. "I'm in Daniel's room. Your mom fixed up your room for you, of course. We're sharing the bathroom. That a problem for you?"

"No." He took a step forward, but stopped abruptly. A sharp pain ripped through his left thigh.

Sophia saw Luke's tanned face pale as he bent over to put his hand on his leg. She forced herself to stand up. "Should you be walking around so much? Why don't you have a cane?"

Luke straightened upright and took in a deep breath through his nose. He *should* be using his cane, but he had some stupid notion that he didn't want Sophia to see him with it. He hadn't wanted her to think he was weak. Screw it! She was going to see him use it eventually anyway. It might as well be now. It had to be now. "It's in the hall. With my bag."

Sophia went into the hall, grabbed the cane and brought it to Luke. "A whole heck of a lot of good it was doing you over there."

Luke leaned on the cane. He suddenly looked beat. "I don't like the damn thing."

Sophia didn't like Luke's pallor, or the beads of sweat that had popped out along his forehead. Luke had always been so combative with her, but she still cared about him.

"Do you need help?" she asked.

Luke had to stop himself from snapping at her. He measured his words, regulated his tone. "No. I've got it." Offhandedly, he added, "Thanks."

Luke slowly made his way to the hallway. He looked between the narrow stairs and his duffel bag at the entrance. He considered leaving the bag behind. His leg was throbbing. He just wanted to get to his room and get off his feet.

"Luke?" Sophia's voice made him stop.

"Yes?"

"Is your coat meowing?"

Chapter Two

For a moment, Luke stared at Sophia and tried to make sense of her words. Then it hit him. The kitten! "Shit! I mean, shoot!" He was going to have to start watching his mouth in his mother's house. And in front of Sophia. One raised eyebrow in his direction made Luke acutely aware of Sophia's displeasure with his use of profanity in her presence. Luke looked down into his gaping pocket at the sleepy-eyed kitten. "Sorry, little guy. You were so frickin' quiet I forgot all about you."

"What do you have?" Sophia peeked into his pocket. "A kitten? You have a *kitten?* Where'd you get him? Or her?"

Luke leaned his cane against the wall and used both hands to scoop the kitten out of his pocket. "It's a 'he.' Billy suckered me into taking him. That ride from the airport wasn't free."

"Ah, yes. I've heard about Billy and his strays." Sophia moved closer, her face delighted. She loved kittens. So had Daniel. "Hi," she said to the kitten. Then, to Luke, "What's his name?"

Luke examined the kitten, took in his coal-black fur and his giant golden eyes. Black and gold were Ranger colors. "Ranger." The name popped out of his mouth, and it seemed to fit.

"Ranger," Sophia repeated. Daniel had been a ranger in the army. Briefly. "I like it. Daniel would have liked it, too. He loved cats."

Luke put the kitten on his shoulder. "Yes, he did." He supposed that was the real reason he had decided to keep the little guy. It's what Dan would have done.

Luke reached for his cane, accidentally pushed it, and the stupid thing slid down the wall and landed on the ground. Sophia and Luke both eyeballed it. With her hands on her hips, Sophia finally said, "I can get myself down there, but I'm gonna need help getting back up." She patted her bulging belly with a self-effacing smile. "I'm a little top-heavy nowadays."

Luke used one hand to hold the kitten on his chest. "I'll get you back up."

Sophia tilted her head. "Teamwork, then." She carefully lowered herself down onto her haunches and picked up the cane. With her other hand she reached out and clasped Luke's outstretched fingers. Luke braced himself and used the strength of his biceps to bring her up steady and smooth. As he pulled her up, while her eyes were averted, Luke took the opportunity to admire the angles of her beautiful face. How many times had her image kept him company while he was away? He knew her face well. He had memorized every landmark years ago. The slightly upturned tip of her nose, the smattering of freckles across the bridge. The honey tone of her skin that perfectly matched the honey highlights in her long, straight hair. Her full mouth. She had married his brother, but he had seen her first. Fell in love with her on the spot. Had loved her ever since; secretly and from a distance. Always from a distance.

"Here ya go." Sophia handed the cane over and then

scratched the back of Ranger's neck. "Why don't you leave him with me while you take a shower? I could use the company."

Luke had been wondering how the heck he was going to get himself, his bag, and now the kitten all upstairs. Her suggestion sounded like a good one. "What about the whole pregnancy-and-cat thing..."

Sophia waved it off. "Oh, please. We'll just trim his nails so he won't accidentally scratch me and you'll handle all the kitty-box duties. My mom had cats when she was pregnant with me, and I turned out fine. Not to worry..."

"All right." Luke tried to pull Ranger from his shoulder, but the kitten was determined to stay put. Ranger used his claws to cling to Luke's overcoat as if it was Velcro.

"Here, let me help you." Sophia carefully extracted Ranger from Luke's coat. She held him in the crook of her arm and gave Luke the once-over. She moved her finger up and down. "Why do you still have your coat on, anyway? Here, take it off and I'll hang it up. No sense in you taking it upstairs."

Luke shrugged out of the overcoat, glad to have it off, and handed it to Sophia. She nodded her approval and hung it up on the coat rack by the door.

"One more thing," Luke said with a gruff tone. He checked himself and adjusted his tone. "If you don't mind."

"Hmm?"

"Drag my bag over here for me, will ya? I'll get it on my shoulder from here. I don't want you lifting it. It's too heavy."

"No prob." Sophia dragged the bag over to Luke. She smiled up at him. "Teamwork!" That smile of hers was rarely aimed his way. It caught him off guard, made his stomach clench in response. Without a word, he bent over at the waist and lifted the bag up with a grunt. Once he hooked it onto his shoulder, he headed up the stairs.

"Take your time," Sophia called after him. "I'll just close the door to the kitchen so he has to stay in there with me. We'll see you when you come down."

Luke awakened from his nap, groggy and disoriented. At first he didn't know exactly where he was; it took him a minute to figure it out. He had no idea how long he had slept. All he knew is that it had been light outside when his head hit the pillow and now it was dark. He reached over and fumbled for the lamp on the bedside table. Then he squinted at his watch. It was still on Afghan time. His fuzzy brain calculated the time difference and figured it was closing in on 9:00 p.m.

He couldn't believe he had slept so long. Nearly six hours. He had popped a couple of pain pills before he crashed on the bed. Those pills must have done the trick; he usually could sleep for only an hour or two at a time.

Luke hung his legs off the side of the bed for a moment before he slid off the mattress. He stripped off the rest of his clothes, undressed his wound and headed for the shower. He examined the antique claw-foot tub, with unreasonably high sides, and worked out the most practical way to get himself in it. Once in the shower, he pressed his hands against the back of the wall and let the steaming water run down his back. The water stung as it hit the wound, but it was a good pain.

As the water pummeled his skin, Luke's mind drifted, as it often did, to Sophia. She had surprised him. Honestly, he had expected to find a sniffling, hormonal, wretched woman who spent her waking moments blaming him for Dan's death. He blamed himself, after all, so why shouldn't she? If he hadn't chosen a military life, perhaps Dan wouldn't have joined the army out of the blue. And if he hadn't joined, he'd still be alive today.

He'd thought for sure that Sophia would blame him. He had counted on it. Planned for it. But she didn't seem to. And she certainly wasn't wallowing and weeping. That was a major relief. There were a lot of things that Luke knew how to do. If he had to jump out of a plane to get the job done, he could do it. If something needed to be blown up, not a problem. But comfort a hysterical female? Not his area of expertise.

Luckily for him, Sophia had her act together. He should have known she would. He had no idea what possessed him to doubt her in the first place. Sophia had always been headstrong, determined and upbeat. In the ten years he had known her, he'd never once seen her let life get her down. It was one of the things he had always loved about her. So had Dan, for that matter. Dan and he had disagreed since they were kids, about everything, all of the time. But they had always agreed about the merits of Sophia.

Out of the shower now, Luke dressed the wound, pulled on jeans and a white undershirt. He was starved. He headed downstairs to raid the fridge and see how Sophia and Ranger were getting on.

Sophia was sitting at the table, writing. Ranger was sitting on the table next to her pad of paper, legs tucked up beneath him, eyes closed. He opened his eyes when he heard the kitchen door open, stood up, stretched into a back arch and then sat down on his haunches.

"Mom would have a fit about that," Luke said. Sophia knew he meant Ranger sitting on the table.

Sophia wrinkled up her nose. "I know." She sighed, heavily. "I know. But to tell you the truth, I was so impressed with his determination to get up here, I didn't have the heart to tell him no."

Luke remembered Ranger's valiant escape from the box. He had felt the same way. "He has that effect." Luke moved to the table and reached out to stroke Ranger's fur. The minute he touched the little guy, he started to purr.

"How's your finger?"

Sophia held up her bandaged finger. "Still attached. How's your leg?"

Luke shot her a wry expression. "Still attached."

Sophia smiled at him, which made the dimple on her left cheek appear.

"What are you doing?" Luke asked. He picked Ranger up and held him next to his heart.

"Making a list of things to do tomorrow. I swear, these lists are the only thing that's kept me sane while your family is at your uncle's for Thanksgiving. He's in pretty bad shape after that surgery he just had. Did you know about that?"

Luke took a seat at the table. He nodded yes.

Sophia clicked the pen so the tip came in and out. "You know, you should really call your folks and let them know you're here."

"I'll let it be a surprise."

"Okay," Sophia replied, skeptically. "If you say so. But you know how your mom is…."

"She'll be fine."

Sophia made a noise and went back to her list. After a minute, she slapped the pen down on the paper. "Wow. My brain is really fried. You haven't eaten." She pushed herself up. "You've gotta be famished."

"I am."

Sophia opened the refrigerator. She twisted to the side and looked at him. "Chicken and stuffing okay? I made myself a little impromptu Thanksgiving dinner yesterday. Happy belated Thanksgiving, by the way. It's a bummer you had to spend your holiday traveling." She paused to take a breath and then continued. "So? Chicken and stuffing okay?"

"That's fine," Luke said. You always had to wait for Sophia to come up for air before you spoke. "I can fend for myself, you know. I don't want you overdoing it on my account. You're...you know."

She pulled out some Tupperware. "Pregnant? I know. Kind of obvious. But it's not like I'm disabled or an invalid."

Luke's shoulders stiffened. "Neither am I."

Ah yes. The infamous Brand family pride. She knew it well. She found it as equally annoying in Luke as she had in Daniel. "You'd think you wouldn't be so cranky after such a long nap." Of course, the Brand men were well-known for being impossible to get along with if they were hungry. Sophia stopped what she was doing and leaned back on the counter. "I wasn't calling you an invalid, but the truth is the truth. Your leg is screwed up. Mine isn't. So, do you want me to help you out or not?"

The expression on Luke's face undoubtedly sent his military underlings running for cover. She knew him well enough not to be impressed. "Yes? No? What shall it be, Captain?"

"Do you always have to be so dramatic over every little thing?" Luke answered a question with a question; another Brand family trait.

"I'll take that as a yes." She popped the lids off the containers and piled food high on a plate.

While Sophia prepared his meal, Luke couldn't take his eyes off her. Thoughts of her had been his constant companion, but this was the first time he'd ever been alone with her. This was the first time he'd ever had her all to himself. The circumstances weren't ideal, but having Sophia with him now felt as if the planets had aligned for him. And he was enjoying just sitting back and watching her.

"How are you feeling?" he asked her.

Sophia's ponytail swung to the side as she spun her head around to look at him over her shoulder. "Honestly, I've had a great pregnancy…all things considered. I've been exercising, of course, staying active. I have a friend who's a personal trainer and she helps me choose the right foods, pick safe exercises. I haven't even been all that tired, until recently." She shrugged one shoulder. "The worst of it is missing Daniel, wanting him to be here with me. He always used to say that he couldn't wait to see me pregnant." Sophia paused for a minute to compose herself. At times, the emotions would well up without warning and she would have to push back the tears. "I suppose we shouldn't have waited so long to have a family. We were waiting until he finished school and my practice was more stable." Lower, almost under her breath, she added, "Stupid."

"You couldn't have seen this coming, Soph. None of us plan for this sort of thing. No one would get out of bed, if we did," Luke said in a low, even tone. "But you're right about one thing, though. He always wanted to see you pregnant. He always thought you'd make a great-looking pregnant woman." His eyes swept her body unbeknownst to her. "He was right."

"Thanks," Sophia said with a small smile. The timer dinged and Sophia pulled the plate out of the microwave. "Of course, my face is puffy, my ankles are swollen and I have to urinate *constantly*." She put the plate down in front of him and smiled. "TMI, right?"

Luke shook his head; as she set the plate down, he noticed the simple gold wedding band that still encircled her left ring finger. He wasn't surprised that she still wore her wedding band; she had always been loyal to Dan. In life, and now in death.

The minute she moved her hand away, he hunched over his plate and started to dig in.

"Something to drink?"

Luke chewed fast, and then swallowed hard before he spoke. "Water's good."

She brought a glass of water back to the table with her and then sat down beside him. Ranger had found his way back to the food Sophia had scrounged up for him. The Brand family had taken in so many strays over the years that it was standard operating procedure to have emergency pet supplies on hand.

"The moral of this story is, I feel pretty good and I have to stay active in order to maintain a modicum of sanity out here in the boonies. So, I don't mind helping you out while you rest your leg a bit…if you can put your male pride aside for a second or two."

Luke wasn't really paying attention to what she was saying; he was shoveling in his food as if he hadn't eaten for days. He ate like a man who was used to being surrounded by other men vying for the same food. He protected his food with one arm, leaned forward and got the food to his mouth as quickly as possible.

"Luke," she asked with surprise, "what happened to your table manners?"

Luke paused from his shoveling for a second, sat up and moved his arms off the table. He glanced up at her. "Better?"

"Much." She shook her head at him. "I take it you like the food? Or, were you just that hungry?"

Luke gulped the water down before he said, "It was pretty damn good."

Sophia picked up the plate and rinsed it in the sink.

"Glad you liked it." When she returned to her spot at the table, Luke had Ranger in his lap.

"Find any clippers when you found the cat food?" Luke was examining the kitten's claws.

"Yes. Finally. I wish your mom would find a different outlet when she's upset. None of us can ever find anything when she's done." Sophia chuckled and shook her head. "I put them over there on the counter." She made to get up again. Luke's warm hand on her arm stopped her.

"You sit. I'll get them."

She decided to let him win this one and didn't protest. He returned with the clippers and the kitten. Once seated, he flipped Ranger over on his back and put him down gently on his lap.

"You've done this before."

"Yes, I have," Luke replied. His mom's soft spot for animals was well-known in the community; everyone knew where to drop off the strays.

Ranger was crying and squirming on Luke's lap. "If you steady his hind legs, we'll get this done quickly."

She scooted her chair closer and reached out to stop Ranger from kicking his legs, while Luke started to trim his front claws. She was so close to him that the fresh scent of his skin invaded her senses. He smelled just like Daniel when he was straight out of the shower: almonds mixed with the scent of soap. She couldn't stop herself from taking his scent deeply into her lungs. Her long intake of breath caught Luke's attention. He looked up from his task, caught her eye and said, "Teamwork."

Nothing in his face read humor, but she saw a glint of mirth that lurked behind the intense depth of his light blue eyes. She leaned back a bit and resisted the urge to bury her nose in his neck. That's what she used to do with Daniel. It used to be one of her favorite things to do.

"There you go, little man. All done." Luke easily turned

the kitten upright and let him down on the ground. Ranger hopped forward a couple of steps before he stopped and licked his shoulder to release some of his irritation.

Sophia watched Ranger, glad for the distraction that pulled attention away from the way Luke's nearness made her heart race. "I was actually starting to think that you were going to sleep through the night."

"I'm surprised I got any shut-eye at all, to tell you the truth." Luke leaned back in the chair and stretched out his left leg. He rubbed his hands across his cropped hair. Daniel had always worn his light brown hair shaggy and long. Sophia couldn't remember the last time she had seen Luke without what she termed "Marine hair." Looking at him now, she was reminded of the first time she had seen Daniel after he had enlisted in the army; he had looked just like Luke in that moment. When they had made love, conceived the child she was carrying, for a split second, she had thought of Luke.

"What?" Luke asked her, an eyebrow raised in question. She must have been giving him an odd look.

"Just thinking."

"Anything interesting?"

"No."

Just remembering that I had thought of you when Daniel and I conceived this child…

Luke was growing a goatee; there was a faint outline of stubble that encircled his mouth. Her fingers had the strangest urge to reach out and follow the goatee trail around his lips, of all the stupid things!

"I think we should put Ranger in the hall bathroom upstairs. What do you think?"

"What?" She hadn't been paying attention to the conversation; she had been distracted by his lips.

"The hall bathroom. Ranger. The kitty box. What do you think?"

"Oh. Yeah. Makes sense." Those words were followed by a wide yawn. "I think it's time for me to start thinking about bed. It's been a long day."

It took several slow trips, but between the two of them, they managed to get Ranger, his food and the kitty box upstairs into the hall bathroom. Sophia molded a bed out of towels and turned on a low nightlight before she shut the door. Ranger was hooked up.

Luke and Sophia faced each other outside of their respective bedroom doors. There was an awkward moment of silence before they both finally said good-night. Once inside their rooms, they ran back into each other on their sides of the adjoining bathroom.

Luke held on to his door. "Ladies first."

Sophia agreed. She stepped into the bathroom. She added, "Make sure you knock, mister. Let's not have any unfortunate moments."

He knew what she was getting at. She didn't want him to accidentally walk in on her while she was naked in the head.

"Understood," he said before he closed the door firmly shut. He heard the lock click, and that made him smile a bit.

Fifteen minutes later, she knocked on his door. "Okay. Your turn."

He got himself in and out of the bathroom as fast as possible. He popped a couple of painkillers into his mouth and then waited impatiently for them to knock him out. He tossed and turned; he tried to find a comfortable way to position his leg, but he never found it. Instead, he lay on his back with his hands folded behind his head, and imagined Sophia in her bed. It took all of his willpower not to cross to her room and pull her into his arms.

God, he loved her.

God, he wanted her.

But she loved Dan. In her eyes, he would always be second best to his twin. He knew that. Had always known it. Now, he would just have to continue to live with it.

Sophia wasn't having any better luck sleeping than Luke. It was almost impossible to find a comfortable position to sleep at this stage of the pregnancy game. She had three pillows jammed along her back for support, and one pillow jammed between her legs to keep her knees from digging into each other. Little Danny had decided, for some unknown reason, to change his position the minute she lay down to go to sleep. He had seemed perfectly content in his original position the entire night, but once she closed her eyes, he stuffed his feet up under her rib cage and started to spin around. It felt as if he was trying to make a break for it!

So, when Ranger started crying at the top of his lungs, she was awake to hear it. She sighed heavily and rolled herself out of bed. The wood floor was cold on her bare feet as she quietly made her way to the door. She opened the door, stepped outside of her room and bumped right into a nearly naked Luke. The only thing the man had on was tight white boxer briefs. She hoped that her expression didn't change as her eyes flitted up and down the length of him.

The frame was the same as Daniel's, yes. But this build was all Luke. His body was lean and muscular from years of fighting and surviving. Her eyes settled on the bandage that encircled Luke's sculpted thigh before she swung them back up to Luke's face. At that moment, she was genuinely grateful for the dim light in the hall. She had no doubt that her face was stained bright red with a blush.

"I'll get him," Luke said. "You go back to bed."

"Are you sure?"

"Yeah. I got it."

Sophia removed herself quickly back to her room. The

racing of her heart, she suspected, had absolutely nothing to do with her husband and everything to do with Luke. And she hated it. What kind of woman would bury her husband, carry his child and then respond physically to another man?

"A seriously disturbed one," Sophia scolded herself as she pounded the pillows behind her, squeezed her eyes shut and willed herself to fall asleep.

Luke was having his own issues. Ranger was curled up in a ball next to his ear on the pillow, happily purring his fool head off. Luke, on the other hand, was wide awake and fully aroused. Seeing Sophia in her nightgown, her long silky hair spilling over her shoulders and onto her breasts, made blood flow rapidly into parts of his body that had no business waking up. But she had just looked so damned sexy in her modest cotton nightgown with the light from the stairs revealing the outline of her shapely legs. Even the bulge of her pregnant belly was a turn-on.

"God... You're sick, man," Luke said to himself. He balled his hands into a fist and waited for the arousal to ebb. He had no business horn-dogging after Sophia. No business at all! Luke felt like hitting something, so he pounded the mattress with his fists. Why hadn't the pills kicked in? Only sleep would annihilate the vulnerable, sensual image of Sophia fresh out of bed that was now scorched into his brain. Sleep couldn't get here soon enough. Not by a long shot.

Chapter Three

Luke woke up the next morning feeling hungover from the meds. He had managed to sleep off and on, but for the most part, he had tossed and turned all night. He couldn't get his leg comfortable and he couldn't get Sophia out of his mind. Being so close to her, without Dan as a buffer, was not something he had been prepared to handle. She made him feel *out of control*. He didn't like it.

"Square yourself away, marine. Real quick," Luke said to his reflection before he flipped open the hinged bathroom mirror and looked for a razor in the medicine cabinet. He knew he'd find one; his mom was always prepared. What he wasn't expecting to find was a neatly organized row of Sophia's favorite fragrances.

The first time he had ever laid eyes on Sophia, she was working behind a fragrance counter in a local department store. She had been talking with a customer, a perfume bottle loosely held in her hand. Her hair was swept up into a haphazard twist and her lovely face was completely devoid of makeup. The sight of her throwing her head back as she laughed stopped him in his tracks. She laughed without reservation; her positive energy sucked him in. He couldn't seem to take his eyes off her. In an instant, he was crazy, head over heels for her, and he had been ever since.

Luke glanced over at the adjoining bathroom door that led to Sophia's bedroom. He had heard her moving around a couple of hours ago, so he knew she was already downstairs. He reached over and checked to make sure the door was locked before he pulled the first fragrance bottle down.

"Stalker," Luke said quietly to himself with a self-effacing half smile. He popped the top off the first bottle and brought it up to his nose. The minute the perfume reached his senses, he thought "Sophia." To Luke, Sophia always smelled like something he wanted to eat. She never wore the same fragrance two days in a row, but she did have a lineup of favorites, and Luke recognized them all.

One by one, Luke spent a moment with each of Sophia's fragrances. Each one conjured up a memory of Sophia. From Luke's vantage point, Dan had won the ultimate prize the day he married her. Luke snapped the top onto the last bottle and got back to the business of shaving the stubble off his face. He moved his head side to side and checked out the goatee that was taking shape. A couple of days more and it might actually look like something. He wondered if Sophia would like him with it. The minute that thought crossed his mind, he gripped each side of the sink, dropped his head and shook it.

Unacceptable, Brand!

The sooner he got back to his life in the corps, the better off he'd be. He didn't make sense in civilian clothes. He sure as hell didn't make sense when he was around Sophia; he needed to figure out a way to shove his feelings back into place. He had been doing it for years; it should be second nature. But it wasn't. Keeping his heart closed to Sophia was like trying to stop his lungs from wanting to take in air. Whenever she was near him, he had an overwhelming urge to hold her face in his hands, look into those sweet hazel-green eyes and tell her that he loved her. That he had always loved her. Which would, of course, be the worst mistake of his life. His confession would freak Sophia out, and any plans he had to play a big role in his nephew's life would get eighty-sixed. He couldn't risk that happening. He just couldn't risk it.

Luke stared down his own image in the mirror. "Maintain your military bearing, marine. That's all you have to do. Maintain your military bearing."

Luke pushed himself away from the sink and headed downstairs. Sophia smiled at him in greeting. She was on the phone; she mouthed the name "Tyler" and raised her eyebrows at him. He shook his head. There were five kids in the Brand clan, including him. Tyler was the middle child; he was sandwiched between two sets of twins; Dan and Luke were the oldest, and Jordan and Josephine were the youngest. Out of the three boys and two girls, Tyler had turned out to be the only true rancher in the bunch. He took after their dad, from his tall, lanky build to his love for the land. Luke was proud of him, looked forward to seeing him, but he wasn't ready for a reunion just yet. His entire focus was on Sophia. The rest of the family had to take a backseat.

"Okay." Sophia said into the phone after a pause. "Thanks for checking up on me. Tell your mom and dad that I'm fine. Danny and I are doing just fine." She rested her hand on her stomach as she spoke those words. "Okay. I'm glad your uncle's feeling better. And listen, have some fun while you're there. Stop worrying about me. I'll see you when you guys get back. All right. Bye, Tyler."

Sophia hung up the phone. "You could have at least told *Tyler* you're here. He's as tight-lipped as you are."

"And ruin the surprise?"

Luke said this with a deadpan expression. She could rarely read him, and this time was no different, but something in her gut told her that Luke's early arrival didn't have much to do with surprising his family. She just couldn't figure out what else it could be.

She put the kettle on for tea. "I already got the third degree from my parents this morning…again. They want me to have this baby in Boston. I can't really blame them, this is their first grandchild. But this is your parents' first grandchild, too. And I don't know…I think it's more important for your parents because this is Daniel's son."

"No matter what you do, someone's always gonna be ticked off." Luke shrugged. "Do what's best for you, make yourself happy; everyone else will fall in formation. Or not."

Sophia smiled faintly. "You're right. Not always easy to do, though. For me, anyway. Coffee?"

Luke nodded. She brought him a cup of black coffee. He was surprised she remembered that he didn't take cream and sugar.

"Eggs okay?"

"I wish you'd stop waiting on me."

"I wish you'd stop giving me a hard time about something I want to do. You're actually doing me a favor. My days are packed in Boston with clients and meetings, friends, shopping. I'm used to being on my BlackBerry all of the time at home. I swear I'm having serious withdrawal because the reception is so bad here. I actually have to stand up on the window seat in my room and smash myself up against the wall in order to get just one lousy bar! I *have* to find stuff to do here, or I swear to you I'll go stark raving mad." She pulled eggs out of the fridge and located a pan. "I mean, your family's great. Your mom, your dad, Tyler…all of them. They've been wonderful to me. But I'm a city girl. I'm used to keeping up the pace all day long. Coming and going as I please. Out here, I feel like I'm stuck in slow motion." She paused from her task for a minute so she could punctuate her words with her hands. "Quite frankly, it's driving me nuts. There are only so many sunsets I can admire, so much foliage I can appreciate. I never thought I'd hear myself say this, but bring on the traffic and the noise." She dug in the cabinet for a bag of decaffeinated green tea. "And I can only hope that your parents aren't going to want me to make this a permanent situation once Danny is born."

Luke nodded. His mom just might try to convince Sophia to stay. His mom was all about family, and she would want to see Dan's son grow. "It's gotta be tough to be away from your business. Who's taking care of your clients while you're away?" Luke asked, before he took a sip of coffee.

Sophia started to scramble the eggs, just how he liked them. Another thing she had remembered about him. Dan only ate his fried.

"It's the hardest thing I've ever done, leaving the business. I've had horrible abandonment issues. What kind of therapist abandons her patients? Luckily I have a great group of therapists in our office who were willing to take on my patients. I still feel bad, though. Like I'm letting them down. Especially during the holidays. I'm booked between Thanksgiving and New Year's. A lot of depression." Sophia took the kettle off the stove and poured the piping-hot water over the tea bag.

"Dealing with your family can do that to a person." Luke nodded.

"The holidays are a tough time. People get depressed if they have to spend time with family, and then other people get depressed if they don't *have* family to make them miserable during the holidays. Either way, the holidays are a therapist's busy season. Kind of like tax season for CPAs." Sophia put the finished eggs on a plate and brought them to Luke. "Here ya go."

"Tax time's probably busy for you, too."

That made Sophia smile. Lately, Luke had been having that effect on her. She liked it. "Come to think of it, I do get a boost during April."

When Sophia leaned over to set the plate on the table, her arm brushed against Luke's. The sensation of his skin against hers set off an instantaneous chain reaction; the fine hairs on her arm stood straight up on end, and wherever his skin had touched hers a trail of goose bumps popped up. Horrified, she immediately started to rub her arm to smooth the goose bumps away.

Luke admired the food on his plate. "This looks really good. Thanks."

"My pleasure." She turned away from him. "Hey... Where's Ranger?"

"I put him in the bathroom. He needs to use the head," he said, then corrected himself. "I mean the *facilities*."

"Gotcha." Sophia smiled; she continued to rub her arm.

Luke noticed the rubbing, of course. Had to comment, *of course*. "You cold? I'll get a fire started if you want."

Sophia looked down at her arm. She wasn't cold, but what was she going to say, "The feel of your skin on mine gave me goose bumps, Luke"? Not likely! Instead she said, "I'd like that. Tyler or your dad would always build me a fire. I've missed them. Do you need anything else? Toast? Orange juice?"

"I'm good. Thanks."

"Then I'm gonna check on Ranger. Maybe he'll be brave enough to explore downstairs today." That little kitten had been a great distraction. She needed a reason to get away from Luke and the bizarre, completely unacceptable feelings he kicked up inside of her; Ranger was a perfect excuse. This reaction she was having to Luke was starting to get really old. She was obviously having some sort of emotional transference brought on by the fact that Luke looked exactly, for the most part, like Daniel. And it was obvious that she missed Daniel and was transferring some of her unrequited desire on to his twin! It had to be that. She didn't want Luke.

"No. Of course you don't," she said under her breath as she climbed the stairs.

Luke had always been a pain. He had always given her a hard time. He was *nothing* like Daniel, except for the outside package. And even that wasn't exactly the same. Case in point: a nearly naked Luke had looked quite a bit different than a nearly naked Daniel. Okay, perhaps that wasn't the best example she could have thought of. But still!

Sophia reached the top of the stairs and put her hands on her hips as if she were scolding a small child. "You want him to *be* Daniel. But he's not Daniel. He never will be Daniel, so you really need to get a grip, Sophia!" Her psychology degrees were starting to come in handy; she could psychoanalyze herself.

Sophia opened the bathroom door, and Ranger was more than ready to be let out. He dashed out with a trill, wound his way around her ankles and rubbed his head against her leg.

"Hi, buddy." Before Sophia could reach down over her belly to pet him, Ranger voiced another excited trill, stuck his tail straight up in the air and zoomed down the stairs without a moment of hesitation.

She stared after him for a moment, bemused. "He's going to be an absolute terror."

He'd probably do the family a lot of good during the holidays. This would be the first Christmas without

Daniel. Perhaps having a crazy kitten in the mix would distract them all.

Before she went back downstairs, Sophia stopped off at the medicine cabinet to pick out the day's fragrance. Unfortunately, none of the self-talk up the stairs stopped her from wondering which fragrance Luke would like.

Irritated, she reached for Daniel's favorite, sprayed it on and went downstairs with a renewed determination not to have any bizarre reactions to Luke.

She found Luke standing in front of the giant bay window that overlooked the ranch. He was staring out at the horizon and seemed to be lost in thought.

"Mission accomplished with the kitty box. Did he come through here?"

"Yeah." One side of his mouth lifted. Sophia could tell by that one small gesture that the kitten cracked Luke up. "He went tearing through here, ran headfirst into the cabinets, shook it off like nothing happened, jumped up a foot in the air, spun around and went flying back toward the library."

"That kitten is a menace. Your dad is going to hit the roof when he sees him." Sophia laughed. She picked up her tea and walked over to stand next to Luke. Perhaps she stood closer to him than she should have, but once she was there, she didn't have any desire to be anywhere else.

"At first. But he's always the one who gets attached the quickest," Luke said as he continued to stare at the horizon.

"It must feel good to be home, especially with all of this," she said of the snowcapped mountains in the distance. "It's getting a bit old for me, but this is your home."

Again, Luke was quiet, as he often was. He stood stock-still, but Sophia could feel his body become tense beside her. She almost moved away, worried she was invading his space, but something made her stay put.

All Luke could do was keep his eyes trained forward. He wanted nothing more than to drape his arm around Sophia's shoulders and pull her close until her body was molded into his. She was wearing his favorite fragrance. She smelled like citrus and freshly cut grass, and he wanted to bury his face in her neck and breathe her in.

And then she would slap me.

Luke shook his head at himself before he drained his cup.

"What?" Sophia noticed him shaking his head.

"Nothing. I think it's time for a fire."

There was something raw in his voice that quickened her pulse. She nodded her head and put some distance between herself and Luke. "I'm going to check my email real quick and then I'll be back down."

They both went their separate ways, headed in two completely different directions. No matter how hard Sophia tried, she couldn't stop her body from reacting to Luke. And it seemed that little Danny was having his own reaction to his uncle's voice. Was it her imagination, or did her baby seem to get more active whenever Luke was around?

Being around Luke was tying her up in knots on the inside. She felt like an absolute lunatic. She was hormonal and grieving, away from her friends and family, and now she was faced with her husband's twin. No wonder she was confused. But she had to make sense of it all and do it quickly. After all, Luke had never liked her, not from the very first day that Daniel had introduced them to each other. If he had even a remote clue what was in her head, he'd dislike her even more. This tentative truce he had forged with her for Daniel's sake would be ruined.

She smoothed her hand over her stomach. "We're not going to let that happen, are we, Danny boy? No. We're not."

More than anything, she wanted Luke to be a big part

of her son's life. She couldn't screw it up. She wouldn't *let* herself screw it up. Instead of booting up her laptop, Sophia did something she rarely allowed herself to do; she curled up on the bed, buried her face into a pillow and cried.

After she cried, she slept. And both activities seemed to do her a world of good. When she awakened an hour later she felt a million times better, and she went downstairs with a renewed sense of purpose. It wasn't like her to let things eat at her. She liked to bring things out in the open; clear the air. That was just the way she was; that was the therapist in her. And, even though Luke wasn't exactly the most approachable guy in the world, she wanted to believe that his bark was really much more serious than his bite. She was just going to have to tell him how she was feeling, and he was just going to have to listen. Like it or not.

Sophia found Luke in the library. The fire had died down and the library felt to her as if she was slipping into a warm bath. It was the perfect temperature. Luke was sitting on one end of an overstuffed couch, head back, eyes shut. Ranger was perched on the armrest beside him. When Ranger saw her, he trilled but didn't move.

"Nice fire," she said.

"Hmm." That was the extent of Luke's reply.

Sophia sat down at the other end of the couch. She sank deep into the cushions and realized that she wasn't getting back up unless Luke agreed to pull her out. Sophia slid her butt forward and leaned back. She rested her hands on her belly.

"My friends tell me it's perfectly normal to get tired of being pregnant." She sighed. "I look like I swallowed a basketball, but at least I have a comfortable place to rest my hands." She smiled at herself after she said that.

"Hmm."

"Are you even listening to me?"

Luke cracked an eye open. "No."

Sophia grabbed a pillow and smacked him in the head with it. "Thanks a lot, Luke. That's really sensitive!"

She saw his chest moving; saw the corner of his upper lip lift. The man was actually chuckling. Amazing. Rare. She hit him again.

Luke glanced over at her. "When has anyone ever accused me of being sensitive?"

Sophia raised an eyebrow at him. "Good point."

After a minute, exasperated, she said. "Luke! Aren't you going to say 'you don't look like you swallowed a basketball'?"

Luke pushed himself up so suddenly that it caught her off guard. He leaned forward and turned his head toward her. He had a hard, exasperated look on his face. "You don't look like you swallowed a basketball, Sophia," Luke said in a clipped manner; his hand sliced the air as he spoke. "And, honestly, I don't like to hear you say sh... stuff like that about yourself. You're a beautiful woman who looks better eight months pregnant than most women I know who *aren't* pregnant. If you need to put yourself down, don't do it around me anymore."

Sophia was taken aback by Luke's words. Shocked, actually. Just when she thought he was a total jerk, Luke would throw her a curve ball and prove her wrong.

She saluted him. "Aye, aye, el Capitan."

Luke shook his head slightly at her sarcasm before he leaned back into the couch once again. "Can we enjoy the fire now?"

Sophia didn't agree because she had an agenda, but Luke didn't seem to require her consent. He closed his eyes and sighed deeply.

She wasn't completely heartless; she would give him a few moments of quiet before she approached him about the main issue on her mind. He seemed to be in a pretty good mood; no time like the present was a personal motto.

After a couple minutes, Sophia pushed herself up into a more upright position and turned her body so she could look at Luke's profile.

"Luke?"

"Hmm."

"There's something I want to talk to you about."

It took several long seconds for Luke to respond. No doubt he didn't like the phrase, "I have something to talk to you about."

"This isn't what I meant by 'enjoying the fire.'"

"It's important to me." She tapped her finger to her chest, not deterred by the abrasive tone of his voice.

With a sigh, Luke rubbed his hands over his face several times. "What's on your mind?"

Sophia had been mulling over in her mind how she should bring up the subject. There didn't really seem to be any diplomatic way to broach it. Honestly, the direct approach seemed to be her only real option. Besides, Luke was a more "in your face" kind of guy. He was a marine. He'd probably appreciate her not beating around the bush.

"Well, it's like this." She held out her hand. "And I really hope you don't take offense, Luke, because I'm not trying to hurt your feelings…"

"Before I'm ninety, Soph."

"Quit rushing me!" she replied, "I want to make sure that when I've said what I have to say that you're not going to feel bad…."

"Sophia…"

"*Fine*. Here goes." Sophia paused, took in a deep breath, then let the deep breath out, before she said, "Luke… I don't want you to take this the wrong way, but your face really bothers me."

Chapter Four

After the words popped out of her mouth, Sophia felt immediately relieved. Unloaded. It felt really good to get that off her chest.

There, she thought proudly. *It's good for relationship growth to get things out in the open.*

She had absolutely no doubt that this would be good for both of them. They would have an open and honest dialogue about their feelings; about Daniel. About being together without him. Of course, she had never had a serious discussion with Luke before, but after all, Luke and Daniel were twins, right? There had to be *some* similarities in the way they resolved problems.

Daniel was great when it came to hashing things out. And he always had something relevant to say that let her know that he'd really listened to her and that he'd thought about his answer. He never dismissed her. It was one of the many things that she had truly admired about her husband.

Just like Daniel, Luke was taking his time before he responded. He hadn't moved; his eyes were still closed, his head was still resting on the cushion. No doubt he was trying to think of the perfect thing to say....

Sophia sank back into the couch, rested her head in

her hand and, for the first time she could remember, she really *looked* at Luke. Her eyes roamed his profile and naturally took an inventory of all of the little Daniel details she loved.

Those were Daniel's ears. One of her favorites spots to nibble on when they made love. So sensitive. It made her wonder, irrationally, if Luke's ears were sensitive, too.

Silly thought.

Of course, the dent in the middle of Luke's nose, which made him look like a prizefighter, didn't mirror Daniel's nose. Daniel's nose had been unaltered from the original design.

By the time her eyes landed on the faint, long scar that ran the length of Luke's jawline, it hit her that Luke was taking an excessive amount of time to respond to her statement.

Sophia opened her mouth to say his name, but clamped it back shut when she heard Luke take in a deep breath through his nose that sounded suspiciously like a snore.

Sophia reached over and poked him in the arm with her finger. "Luke!"

"Hmm?"

"Did you just fall asleep?"

After a long pause. "No."

"Yes, you did!"

"Are you sure?"

"Yes!" she snapped. Typical Luke behavior! Once again, she had given him more credit than he deserved. She had opened her heart, revealed something very personal to her, and he was *snoring!*

She would have thought at this point the man would have the decency to open his eyes. He didn't. Luke didn't move, but Ranger did. The kitten used his back leg to scratch an itch underneath his chin before he moved over to sit on Luke's chest. Ranger plopped down and curled up into a tight ball. Luke didn't bother to move.

"Luke!" she said forcefully.

"What?" Now *he* sounded irritated.

"You fell asleep!"

After a few ticks of the grandfather clock and a few loud Ranger purrs, Luke cracked an eye open and looked at her. "Then, why'd you wake me up?"

Her mouth dropped open. "Are you *serious?*"

"You bet."

He used that abrasive tone that always rubbed her the wrong way, and she felt her blood pressure soar. She wasn't here to play naughty "recruit" to his bad boy "drill sergeant"! She felt like punching him and she wished, at the moment, that she had a violent streak.

Was this some sort of bizarre pregnancy rage, or was Luke just that infuriating to her?

"Luke." Her tone was snappy and she didn't try to curb it. "We were in the middle of a conversation."

Luke stretched, yawned and then stretched again. Finally, his eyes were open. He turned his full attention to Sophia, examined her through heavy-lidded eyes.

"We were?"

Sophia lifted up both her hands and splayed out her fingers. "Yes! We were! I said that your face bothered me." When she repeated the phrase out loud, it sounded comical to her own ears, but she didn't laugh as she continued. "Didn't you hear me?"

"I heard you." He had the audacity to sound irritated with her. She wasn't the one who had fallen asleep in the middle of an important conversation.

She found herself glaring at him. "And?"

"And *what?*"

"And... What do you have to say about it?"

Luke rubbed his hands over his face, sighed heavily

and finally turned his intense gaze back to her. "What do you want me to say? Oh, wait… How 'bout this. You're the therapist. Why don't you tell me what I should have said, since you obviously have my response all planned out for me."

"No." Her words were clipped and articulated with precision. "I didn't have your response planned out for you, thank you kindly. I was waiting for you to add something constructive to the conversation. A temporary lapse of reason, quite obviously!"

"That was a conversation?"

"Luke! Now you're just being thickheaded! Do you have anything to say or not?"

"No."

"Nothing at all?" Her tone was incredulous; her eyebrows were lifted in disbelief. She told the man that his face bothered her and he had nothing to say?

"What's your problem?" she demanded.

Finally, Luke was paying full attention to her. He held on to Ranger as he sat upright. The features of his handsome face hardened; his lips were downturned into a frown. His eyes were dark and unreadable.

"I'm not the one with the problem." His tone was sharp, controlled. Slightly mocking. "Your face doesn't bother me all that much."

Sophia was silent; her mind raced to craft the perfect sarcastic retort. She stared at him; he stared back at her. Finally, she let out an exasperated noise and tried to push herself into a standing position. She wanted to stomp out of the room in a flurry of righteous indignation, but her belly was in the way, so it just wasn't happening for her. Instead, she held out her hand with an irritated sigh.

"For crying out loud, Luke!" She waved her hand at him. "Help me up!"

Luke stood, clasped her hand in his and pulled her out of the overstuffed couch.

They were standing close together, too close. She could smell that intoxicating almond scent on his skin. It made her heart race even faster, and she couldn't understand why he wasn't budging. She pushed on his chest.

"Move it, Luke!"

She needed to find something to do, anything, to take her mind off Daniel's arrogant, sarcastic, pain-in-the-ass brother. The farther away from Luke she could get, the better off she'd be.

Luke didn't budge.

"Move!" She reached out and pushed him again. She was being rude and she didn't care. For some reason, no matter what, Luke always brought out the worst in her. Just when she would start to think they had found some common ground, he went and screwed it all up.

This time, Luke turned to the side and let her by. She sent him a slit-eyed look before she lifted up her chin and breezed by him.

Luke watched as Sophia disappeared in the direction of the kitchen. He stood in the same spot for several seconds and felt as if he'd just been mugged. One minute he was enjoying the fire with Sophia, and the next thing he knew she was picking a fight with him. Why did that woman always have to make everything so damned complicated?

Luke looked at Ranger sitting on the edge of the couch cushion. "What the hell just happened here? Can you tell me that?"

Luke sat back down on the couch to contemplate his next move. One option was to not move at all. Normally, with any woman in his life, that's the only option that would have been on the table. He would have stayed put and let them come back to him. They always did come back.

But there wasn't anything *normal* about his situation, and he wasn't dealing with just any woman. He was dealing with Sophia, and she definitely had to be handled with care.

What would Dan do in this situation?

He'd follow after her and eat crow! That's what he'd do. Dan knew how to keep Sophia happy. And now, that was his new mission. Keep Sophia happy.

Luke dropped his head into his hands; that woman was giving him a massive headache. "So, go eat crow, marine."

He dropped Ranger off in the bathroom and popped a pain pill into his mouth before he went to find Sophia in the kitchen. She was sitting at the table, writing in a determined fashion. She didn't bother to acknowledge his presence.

She obviously still wanted to wring his neck.

He tried to break the ice by stating the obvious. He felt like an idiot trying to cajole a woman; it was out of character. "Working on your list?"

Sophia glanced up and narrowed her eyes at him. He had just been trying to lighten the mood, but Sophia looked as if she might want to do him bodily harm.

So much for breaking the ice.

Luke sat down at the table across from her.

"What's on that list of yours, anyway?" Persistence was going to be a key element in this situation. He'd seen Sophia hold a grudge.

Sophia stopped writing and tapped her pen on the table. "Is there something you want?"

Luke rubbed his hands over the top of his shaved head. "God, Sophia, gimme a break, will ya? How was I supposed to know you wanted me to say something?"

She made a face. "Please."

Luke let his arms drop onto the table with a thud. "Okay. How 'bout this? Why don't you tell me what I should have said, because I sure as hell don't know! Tell me what I should say when someone tells me that my face bothers them."

It didn't seem possible, but her eyes narrowed even more. She dropped her head and went back to her list. "Just forget it."

"No. I'm not going to forget it." God, she was a royal pain in the ass! "You wanted to talk about this. Let's talk. I'm telling you flat-out—I didn't know your statement required an answer. You don't want to believe me, that's your problem. But that's the truth. Bottom line."

Sophia chewed on his words for a bit. She glanced up. "You really didn't think you should add something? Really?"

"That's the honest truth. What do you think, that I sit around the campfire with my men singing Kumbaya and talking about our feelings? Come on...I just came out of a war zone, Sophia. You're the shrink. Shouldn't you be able to figure out that there may be an adjustment period for me?"

"You act as if you aren't civilized anymore," she said sullenly. The man did have a good point; there was no denying it.

"Maybe I'm not," Luke said harshly without hesitation. "Because I sure as hell don't know what I should have said to you back there."

Sophia waved the pen in the air. "You could have said something like, 'Gee, Sophia, I didn't know that. I'm sorry that me looking like Daniel is making you feel confused and upset. Thanks for the info. Thanks for sharing.' Something like that. Anything would have been better than *snoring!*"

When the woman had a point, she had a point.

Luke rubbed his hands over his face before he dropped them onto the table in surrender. Emotional conversations had never been his strength; that was a fact. He could have done better with Sophia. He *needed* to do better with Sophia. She deserved it.

"You're right. I could have done a little bit better."

Sophia snorted. "*A lot* better."

"All right. A lot better."

"Substantially better," Sophia added.

Luke got up and pulled a glass out of the cabinet. He filled it up with tap water and chugged it. He turned his back to the counter and crossed his arms over his chest. Sophia was back to her list, and back to ignoring him. It was strange. He hadn't really gotten a good look at her after she came down from her nap. He could see now, in the light of the kitchen, that her eyes were puffy. Sophia had been crying.

He felt like an even bigger jerk, if that was possible. He supposed it *was* possible, because he *did*.

Sophia always seemed so tough. In control. In charge. But right now she appeared vulnerable. He didn't know quite how to deal with this version of the woman he loved. He'd never encountered it before.

"Sophia." He said her name softly.

She ignored him.

Stubborn woman.

"Sophia." He said her name as he always wanted to, like a caress. This grabbed her attention. It got her to look up.

"What?" Still a bite in her tone.

"I'm sorry."

"For what? You don't even know what you did wrong."

"Dammit, Sophia… Can you let a guy apologize without crucifying him?"

Sophia put her pen down. Luke took this as a good sign. "First of all, an apology is useless if you don't know what you're apologizing for. Second of all, watch your mouth."

"First of all, it's not easy switching from marine life to civilian life. I'm sorry about the profanity; all I can say is that I'm working on it." Luke jammed his hands into his front pockets. He lowered his tone back to an acceptable level. "Second of all, I know what I'm apologizing for."

Sophia raised an eyebrow. "Really?"

"Yes."

"What for?"

"For being an insensitive jerk."

Sophia cocked her head and eyed him contemplatively. "For one thing."

That's the Sophia he knew. The woman didn't give an inch. Then again, neither did he. This time, he raised his eyebrow at her. "Are you going to let me finish?"

Sophia waved her hand. "By all means. Please do."

Her defenses were still up. Luke could see it plain as day. He had been working to get her defenses down since the moment he had walked through the door, had even managed to make a bit of progress with her, and then in two seconds he was right back to square one. Less than square one!

Nice going, Brand.

Luke knew what he had to do. There wasn't a choice. If he wanted to see that guarded look leave Sophia's eyes, he was going to have to open up to her.

"You know, sensitivity isn't exactly a quality the Marines look for in a man," Luke began.

In spite of herself, Sophia felt like smiling at that comment. She didn't actually do it, but she felt like it.

Luke continued. "So, talking about feelings and sh…

stuff like that isn't my area of expertise. Never was, really. Dan was the talker. You know that."

Sophia nodded in agreement.

"I never knew what the heck to say to anyone about anything. Dan always knew. That's why he did most of the talking for the both of us when were kids. Unless the talking that needed to be done had to be done with a fist..." Luke cracked a smile when he said that. "Then, it was my turn to talk for the two of us," he continued. "I guess what I'm trying to say is that I didn't know *what* to say to you, Sophia, so I didn't say anything. From my experience, sometimes it's best just to keep your mouth shut."

Sophia raised her eyebrows again.

"It didn't apply to this particular situation, I admit. Normally, it works out just fine for me. But just because I didn't know what to say to you doesn't mean I didn't hear what you said, and it doesn't mean that I didn't understand why you said it."

That was the statement that grabbed her total attention. He saw the look in her eyes change. She was listening to every word now.

"I came home early for you, Sophia."

Sophia was rendered speechless for a moment, which was unusual. Even more unusual was a string of more than two sentences coming out of Luke's mouth. And even more unusual than that, was Luke saying that he had come home early for her.

"What do you mean you came home early for me?"

"Do you really think I didn't know you were going to have a hard time being around me? Come on, Sophia... I'm not that much of a jerk. You know that. Or, maybe you don't, which is my fault, no doubt. You're pregnant, you've just lost your husband, and now here comes his twin? That would screw with anyone's head."

Sophia saw something she had never seen in Luke's eyes before. Or, maybe she had never bothered to notice. Compassion. For her.

"So, I came home early, so we could get this——" he moved his hands between them "——this weirdness between us out of the way without an audience."

Sophia rubbed her hands over her belly in a circular motion. It took her a minute to respond. Now it was her turn to not know exactly what to say.

Luke watched her closely. He wanted the trusting look she had given him just this morning to return to her sweet, hazel-green eyes.

"I don't know what to say," she finally admitted.

Luke chuckled. "You might not believe this, but that's happened to me before. Just recently."

He finally got a smile out of Sophia. "Is that so?"

"Yes," he said, relieved to see the stiff set of her jaw soften.

She twisted her wedding ring and studied Luke. "I suppose it never occurred to me that you ever gave me that much thought. You never seemed to like me all that much. I didn't think you'd care one way or the other how I felt about anything, much less something like this. Thank you."

"You're welcome. Am I forgiven now?"

"Of course. What else can I do after all of that?" She waved her hand. "You haven't left me much choice, now have you?"

He winked at her. "That was the plan."

"Well, it worked." For several minutes neither one of them had anything to say. Then Sophia said, "It's really strange being here without him, don't you think?"

Luke nodded. He crossed his arms over his chest and examined the tip of his boot.

Sophia went on. "Everywhere I go in this house,

there's a memory of Daniel attached. Weird things bother me, too, things that you wouldn't think would hit you... Like a coffee mug that he used to like to drink out of, or a book in the library he liked to read. And the pictures everywhere, of course." She continued to twist her ring. "The truth is, I don't like being here without him."

In that moment, it hit Sophia that maybe all of this was even harder on Luke than it was on her. She had memories of Daniel in this house only as an adult. Daniel and Luke were born under this roof. Almost all of Luke's memories of this house were intertwined with his brother. Why hadn't she thought of that before? Was she really that insensitive when it came to Luke? Did she think he was a man without feelings?

"I'm sure you feel the same way," she added.

Luke continued to examine his boot. "I expect him to come walking through that door. And when he doesn't..."

"It makes you feel a little crazy inside."

Luke locked eyes with her. "That's right."

"Me, too," Sophia admitted. "Some days it's all I can do to get myself out of bed I feel so lonely for him. But it's not good for the baby. Taking care of our son has actually given me something to fight for. It's given me a purpose other than just myself. Just going to work. This is the biggest job I've ever had to do, and I fully intend to do it right. That's why I refuse to let myself get depressed. Of course, I cry. But I won't let myself wallow. Daniel wouldn't want me to, anyway."

"You're going to be a great mom."

"I hope so," Sophia said. "None of this has been easy. And, honestly, having you here has made it really hard on me. And I know it's not your fault, and I don't expect you to fix it, but whenever I see you, Luke..." She stopped.

"What?" He didn't want her to stop.

"Whenever I see you." Her voice was trembling again.

"You look so much like Daniel…I want to hug you. I want to kiss you. I want you to take me in your arms and tell me that you're okay. And I know that sounds nuts, but that's how I feel. I know you're not Daniel, but sometimes…" She stopped again and pressed the heels of her hands into her eyes to stop the tears. She regrouped and started again. "Sometimes, my heart forgets you aren't him, and it's hard not to reach out and touch you. Or, to want you to touch me, for that matter. Does that make any sense to you at all?"

It took all of Luke's willpower not to grab her and crush her in his arms. That's what she needed from him. That's what he wanted to give her. But she would have to come to him. He couldn't risk blowing the truce by overstepping some invisible line. And, if he was honest, he didn't want to know what it could feel like to have Sophia push him away.

"I'm not Daniel," he finally said quietly.

"I know you're not…" she interjected.

He continued on. "And I can't ever be him for you. Even if I could, I wouldn't."

"I know that, Luke," Sophia said, her brow furrowed. "Don't you think I know that?"

"Yes. I do." Luke took his hand out of his pocket and put it on his chest. "But do you know that *I'm* here, Sophia? Do you? I'm right here. Right *here*. My heart's still beating." He emphasized his words by hitting the part of his chest that housed his heart. "I'm still alive and I'm still here. So, if you need someone to hug, Sophia, hug me. You can hug *me*."

Chapter Five

For a split second, Sophia stopped breathing. She didn't move. She didn't blink her eyes. She encouraged her foggy brain to make some sense of the scene unfolding before her. Luke was opening up his heart to her. He was allowing himself to be vulnerable in her presence, and it was something she never expected to happen. He was offering to comfort her, yes. But she knew that he was asking for comfort in return.

Luke needed her. Luke needed comfort from her. Every cell in her body responded to his request. She couldn't have turned him down if she wanted to. And she didn't.

Supporting her belly with one hand, Sophia stood up. Luke had crossed his arms back over his chest, and he was staring at her with a look that Sophia could describe only as suspicious. Why he would be suspicious of her didn't seem to matter. Their eyes were locked as Sophia moved slowly toward him.

She couldn't look away.

She didn't want to look away.

And, for some inexplicable reason, being caught up in Luke's eyes didn't make her uncomfortable. Quite the opposite. It made her feel connected to him in a way she had never known possible. And without thought, without reason, she liked it.

Sophia reached out and tugged on Luke's crossed arms. After a moment of resistance, Luke's arms fell down to his sides. Their eyes were still locked; they were so close that she could see his pupils dilate as she reached out and wrapped her fingers around his wrists. As her fingers made contact with his skin, Sophia watched as his nostrils flared. Her brain registered that he had taken a sharp breath in the moment she touched him. His strange reaction to her touch didn't deter her; her only focus was to hold Luke in her arms. They shared a common sadness. They shared a common loss. It made perfect sense that they should find solace with each other.

Sophia guided Luke away from the counter and stepped into his arms. She wrapped her arms around his waist, pressed her swollen belly against his washboard abdomen and rested her cheek over Luke's rapidly beating heart. His heart was beating so strongly that she could feel the sensation of it against her cheek. She closed her eyes and sighed. His natural scent was so much like Daniel's. It made her feel safe. It made her feel secure. She couldn't figure out where Daniel ended and Luke began, and she didn't care. She just didn't care.

At first, Luke stood stock-still. Every muscle in his body tensed as Sophia melted against him. He had fantasized about having Sophia in his arms since the first moment he saw her. And now, here she was. He could feel her warmth through the cotton of his shirt. He could smell the sweet lilac scent of her hair. She was so close, he would only have to tilt up her head and he could easily press his lips against her full, soft mouth.

"Hug me back," Sophia said softly.

He felt her words vibrating through the wall of his chest as much as he heard them. Her wish was his command. He wrapped his arms around her shoulders and pulled her tightly into his body. He closed his eyes; his body came alive everywhere Sophia's body touched his. It was intoxicating; Sophia was melting in his arms. The feel of her swollen belly pressed against his body only made the experience more intense, made his desire for her ignite.

He could force himself not to kiss her, but he couldn't stop his body from reacting to hers. Luke tightened his arms around her and buried his face in her hair. One hand moved up to cradle the back of her head, the other moved down to the small of her back. The distance her belly put between their hips saved him; Sophia couldn't feel how his body was reacting to her. His body craved a release that only Sophia could provide. His body wanted something that just wasn't possible.

Luke fought to refocus. He willed his body to cooperate; he shifted his concentration from his frustration to the fluttering feel of Sophia's heart beating against his body. Luke rested his chin on Sophia's head; heard her sigh and relax into his arms even more.

He wanted to push Sophia away; he wanted to pull her closer. He felt as if he had lost his mind in Sophia's arms. Perhaps he had…

"What was that?" Luke untangled himself from Sophia's arms and held her away from him. He looked down at her stomach.

Sophia looked up at him and smiled. "That was Danny." The surprised look on Luke's face made her laugh. "He kicked. You must have felt it because we were close."

"Is that normal?"

The moment was broken; she stepped away from him. "Perfectly normal."

"So, he's okay?" Luke asked.

It was the first time he'd shown real concern for the baby, and it made Sophia soften toward Luke in a way that she hadn't known was possible.

"Sure. He kicks me all the time. And often when I don't *want* him to." She continued to smile up at him. Then, she added with a laugh, "It seems whenever I'm ready to rest, that's when he decides it's time to do somersaults."

Luke's expression changed from concerned to neutral. With a definitive nod, he turned away from Sophia. "I'm going to check on Ranger."

"Okay." She tried very hard to stop her disappointment from reflecting in her tone. For whatever reason, Sophia didn't want this moment with Luke to end.

"I'll be back," Luke threw over his shoulder as he disappeared into the hall.

For a moment, Sophia didn't move. She had just shared an extremely intimate hug with Luke, and the experience had left her feeling odd. Luke hadn't even hugged her at the wedding. He had shaken her hand, for crying out loud. And now this? It was a shock to the system.

The truth was undeniable: she had loved every minute she had been in Luke's arms. He was strong and warm and hugged her back as if he meant it. For a split second, she had imagined she was with Daniel, but surprisingly, that moment was fleeting. There was no denying Luke. He was a force to be reckoned with.

Danny kicked her again and it drew her attention back to her baby. She rubbed her hands over her belly and smiled down at her rambunctious son. "Like father like son, eh, Danny boy? You just can't stand it if you aren't the center of attention."

Luke let Ranger out of the bathroom, then went to his room and closed the door firmly behind him. He locked the door and rested his forehead against it. He had to get out of the kitchen fast. His body refused to stop thinking about making love to Sophia, and the last thing he needed was for Sophia to notice the obvious bulge in his pants.

There wouldn't be any way to explain that one away.

Luke shut the blinds, shut the adjoining bathroom door and spread out on the bed. The kitten curled up in a ball on the pillow, while Luke let out a frustrated growl. His body wasn't giving up. He was still aroused, and it was starting to hurt.

A cold shower was the only plausible solution.

Luke stripped off his clothes and let the frigid water pelt his skin. Luke looked down at his body in disbelief. His problem refused to go away. What had Sophia done to him?

"Come on!" he said through gritted teeth. He closed his eyes and leaned back so the water could pound him on the chest.

If this didn't work, he was going to have to get rid of it the old-fashioned way. He had been without a woman for too long; he wanted Sophia too much. Under the circumstances, it was a horrible combination.

It took longer than he would have liked, but the freezing water did the trick. Luke stepped out of the shower, dried off, yanked on some boxer-briefs and flopped back onto the bed. He didn't bother to finish dressing or bandaging his wound. He just wanted a minute to get his head straight. Being around Sophia was driving him nuts. More times than he'd like to admit, he had thought about walking away from her. Anything would be easier than this. He'd rather be dropped into a hot zone from a perfectly good plane one hundred times a day than spend the next week sorting things out with Sophia. It was just too damn hard not to let her see how he felt about her. It was a minute-by-minute struggle not to just get it out in the open and let the chips fall where they may.

But he knew he couldn't do that. He had to keep himself under control no matter what. His feelings couldn't matter. He had his whole family to consider.

He had Dan's son to consider.

Luke rubbed his hands over his face. That kick was the first time it had truly sunk in that Sophia was carrying a real person inside her. Of course, he could see that she was pregnant; he could see the fullness of her breasts, the roundness of her belly. Her face was fuller, yet still incredibly beautiful. He could easily see the changes, but for some reason, it took *feeling* it, feeling the baby move, for the whole thing to become real.

That kick came at the right time. It helped him get his head clear, helped him get his brain back on track and back into reality.

As Luke was lulled to sleep by the rhythmic sound of Ranger purring in his ear, he felt more determined than ever not to screw things up with Sophia. More than ever, Luke wanted to get to know that little boy who had just given him a swift kick in the gut. That kick had done more than just wake Luke up; that kick had made him fall in love for the second time in his life. Luke was head over heels crazy about little Danny. Bottom line.

Sophia checked her cell phone. One missed call. It must have gone straight to voice mail; it hadn't bothered to ring. "Stupid reception," she said bitterly as she punched the buttons and pulled up her missed calls list.

"Allie." Sophia read the name out loud. Allie was her best friend and one of her most valuable "baby" assets. Allie had three children of her own and had an extremely busy career as a speech-language pathologist. She was

Sophia's inspiration to find a balance between motherhood and work in her own life.

Sophia dialed Allie's number on the landline and waited while it rang.

Allie picked up the phone on the third ring. "Where have you been? Why didn't you answer your phone? You're supposed to have it with you at *all times!* All times!" That was just like Allie; forceful, to the point. "I've been worried sick, thank you very much. You could've been carried away by thieves, carved up and left on the side of the road, for all I knew!"

"Thanks for the graphic image, Al." Sophia leaned against the counter. "The reception is a nightmare here. This is the home phone number. Use that if you need to get ahold of me."

Allie retorted, "Thanks for making me panic, lady! I was just about to make a call."

Sophia smiled. "Who were you going to call?"

"I don't know," Allie snapped, but Sophia knew her well enough to know she was starting to soften. "There has to be someone you can call out there in the middle of absolutely nowhere." According to Allie, if there wasn't an outlet mall within a ten-mile radius, the place wasn't civilized. "Could the National Guard reach you out there?"

Sophia laughed. Allie always made her laugh. "I'm in Montana, Al...not the jungle. Half of Hollywood lives out here."

"What's that supposed to mean? Does that make it safe? Is L.A. safe? I don't think so. But you've gotten me way off the point. You're out there, in the middle of nowhere, pregnant, *alone*..."

Sophia interjected. "Not alone."

There was a pause on the other end of the line. "Is the family back early?"

"No," Sophia said, dragging out the word for a while.

"Who's there?" Allie asked suspiciously. "You haven't picked up a hitchhiker or are feeding some homeless guy, are you?"

"Okay… That's something *you* would totally do…"

Allie chuckled. "That's true. I would. But I'm not eight months pregnant and stranded in the middle of nowhere." Every time Allie said the phrase "in the middle of nowhere," she had to really emphasize it. "Who's out there with you?"

"Luke's here."

Another pause. "Luke? As in Daniel's brother, Luke?"

"Yes."

"You're kidding."

"No. He showed up the day after Thanksgiving."

She didn't have to see Allie to know that her eyebrows were raised at the juicy news. "Wow. So how's that going? If I remember correctly, the two of you are like oil and water."

Sophia smiled. She supposed her rocky relationship with Luke wasn't exactly a well-kept secret. "We still are…sort of. He's making an effort to get along with me…"

"Are you making an effort to get along with him?" Allie interjected.

"Yes. Of course. For my son's sake, if for nothing else."

"You know what…?"

"What?"

"I'm really glad to hear it. Luke could be incredibly important in your son's life. Your son has an advantage that most children who lose a father don't have. His uncle is a twin. Danny can actually see what his father looks like, what he sounds like, and I have no doubt that Luke is full of stories about Daniel."

"You're right. I think Luke feels the same way. And, I have to tell you, there's a lot about Luke I never knew...."

"Like...?"

"Like he isn't as much of a...jerk...as I once thought. He's actually quite..." Sophia paused to think of the right word to fill in the blank. "Nice."

"I never thought he was a jerk, anyway. He was always very polite to me. And I loved to see him in his uniform. Handsome. If I hadn't been married at the time, I would have insisted that man show me a good time...."

"Allie!" Sophia said, caught off guard. "Really?"

"Oh, please...like you haven't noticed how handsome Luke is? You married his twin."

"Yeah, but I never really thought of Luke in that way. Daniel was the handsome one, at least to me he was. Besides, Luke was always a pain in my neck...."

"Like the little boy who pulls on the girls' pigtails in school..."

"What's that supposed to mean?"

"You know... When we were little, boys were always mean to the girls they liked. It's the same with Luke. I always thought he had a thing for you."

Sophia's stomach twisted into a knot. "That's crazy. Luke doesn't have a thing for me. Trust me! I would know."

"No, you wouldn't. You're blind as a bat when it comes to stuff like that. You have absolutely no radar for that sort of thing whatsoever. I, on the other hand, do. And, I tell you, Luke has always had a thing for you. I saw him giving you 'the look' a couple of times."

"What 'look'?"

"*The* look. Like he's trying to imagine what you look like naked kind of look!"

That made Sophia laugh out loud. "Now I know you're delusional. Have you been getting enough rest? Are you sleep deprived? Taking any new medications I should be aware of?"

"You can laugh all you want, Soph. But I'm serious. Luke has feelings for you."

Sophia shrugged off Allie's words. Usually her friend did have an uncanny ability to spot stuff like that, but this time she had to be way off base. Luke didn't have a thing for her. No way.

Allie spent the next half hour giving Sophia Boston highlights, which only made Sophia more homesick for her life back home. She couldn't wait to get back to her city and make a new life with her son.

"Tell Luke 'hi' for me. Oh, and tell him the next time he's in town to bring his uniform and I'll let him take me out on a date," Allie said with a laugh. "You have to love a man in uniform. And I've always had a soft spot for marines. Especially sexy marines like Luke."

For some inexplicable reason, Sophia's gut clenched at the thought of Luke and Allie dating. Allie was just joking around, but she didn't like the idea one bit. She'd never cared one iota before; she sure as heck shouldn't care now! And yet…she did.

To Allie she said, "I'll tell him."

To herself, she said, *get a grip, Sophia!*

After she hung up, Sophia went into the library and sat down in her favorite double chair. She pulled a blanket over her legs and stared into the fireplace. It was chilly in the room, and she found herself wishing Luke would reappear and build a fire for the both of them. She wanted the warmth of a fire and Luke's company. A couple of times she thought about getting up and building the fire herself, but she didn't want to take the job away from Luke. He seemed to like filling that role, and she enjoyed watching him.

As she waited for Luke, her mind drifted to the conversation she had earlier with Allie. She still couldn't understand where the jealousy had come from, but it was undeniable. And for some inexplicable reason she hadn't told Allie about the hug she had shared with Luke. That wasn't like her at all; normally she confided stuff like that to her best friend. This time, she hadn't. She had wanted to keep the moment she had shared with Luke and her *reaction* to the moment to herself.

"You look like you could use a fire." Luke walked into the room followed by Ranger.

Sophia leaned her head back against the chair. "I was hoping you'd come down soon."

"Why didn't you come get me?"

"I didn't want to disturb you. Figured you were resting." She shrugged one shoulder. "And I was being incredibly lazy. I could have easily done it myself…."

Luke leaned his cane against the couch before he threw a couple of logs into the fireplace. He interrupted her. "You shouldn't have to do stuff like that while I'm here. That's my job. If you need something, don't hesitate to ask. Are we clear?"

"Okay," she agreed with a faint smile. His bossy tone, which normally set her teeth on edge, didn't seem to bother her this time. It felt good to have Luke looking after her. She twisted her wedding ring as she watched Luke build the fire.

After the fire was lit, Luke sat down on the couch. "Listen, I hope I didn't overstep some invisible line earlier. I'm trying to stay on your good side."

"You didn't. Trust me. If I knew you were hug-friendly, I might have attacked you the first day you arrived!"

That got a half smile and a chuckle out of Luke. He winked at her, and something about that wink made her heart skip a beat. "Consider me officially open for business."

Chapter Six

Sophia couldn't seem to get enough of Luke's company. After they enjoyed the fire they went for a walk, which was absolute heaven for her. She loved the outdoors, and with Luke's arm to hold on to she had navigated the icy porch stairs, and the icy patches on the ground, without a second thought. She hadn't felt that invigorated in a week, and by the time they had returned to the house she had a renewed sense of purpose. The walls didn't seem to be closing in on her any longer.

Now that it was just the two of them it was easy to see how compatible they were together. And they seemed to gravitate toward the same part of the house: they both loved to sit in the library in front of the fire. So, after dinner, Luke headed toward the library to throw some more logs on the fire, and she found herself hurrying her movements to get back to Luke more quickly.

She could imagine Daniel looking down on her and smiling right now. He would have a hard time believing his eyes, but he would have been thrilled. Next to her, Luke had been Daniel's best friend, and it always hurt him that the two of them didn't get along.

"It took this to bring us together, my love," Sophia

said softly as she pulled the mugs out of the cabinet. "I wish you were here to see it."

But, the truth was, if Daniel had been here, she and Luke would still be keeping their distance from each other. It had taken a tragedy; it had taken them losing the most important person in both of their lives for them to put aside their petty differences.

Better late than never, she supposed.

"Here ya go." Sophia walked into the library; she carried a full cup in each hand. Ranger jumped out from the side of the couch and batted at her feet with his little paws. She stopped, surprised, and the liquid in the cups sloshed.

"Here, I got it...." Luke reached out for his cup.

Sophia shook her head and smiled at the kitten. "What are you doing, stinker?"

Luke sank down into his spot on the couch and took a sip of his black coffee. As usual, Sophia had it right. The fact that she remembered his likes and dislikes didn't surprise him anymore; it just made him feel good. It let him know, for the first time, that he was a part of Sophia's life. He mattered, and had always mattered enough for her to take notice of, and remember, small details about him.

Sophia sank down into her favorite chair across from the couch and put up her feet. The fire was just starting to crackle and she could feel the warmth of the blaze on her face as it took the chill off the room. "Ah. This is perfect. Thank you." She took a sip of her tea before she added, "This is becoming a regular thing for us, isn't it?"

"Seems that way." Luke's eyes were on her in the dimly lit room. "Thanks for the coffee."

"You're welcome." She heard the sincerity in her own voice. She had actually started to enjoy bringing small pleasures into Luke's life. At first it was just to stave off boredom, but it had quickly become something she enjoyed doing. That made her smile.

Luke noticed the small smile and asked, "What?"

Sophia shook her head softy. "I was just thinking about how civil we are with each other now. We've been like oil and water for years, and now…"

"Not so much," Luke filled in.

"Yes. Not so much," Sophia said before she brought her cup up to her lips and blew on the hot liquid. "Daniel would be proud of us, don't you think?"

"Dan would be proud," Luke agreed. "Speechless actually, which would've been a switch."

"True." Sophia laughed.

As Sophia slowly sipped on her tea and focused her eyes on the fire, Luke focused his eyes on her. His eyes traveled over every feature of her face; he loved the way the firelight cast a golden hue across her honey skin. She was the most beautiful woman he had ever seen. He loved every angle of her face, every laugh line around her eyes; the quickness of her smile. As far as he was concerned, Sophia had always looked like an angel. And he adored her.

The harsh truth was that he had imagined himself in this very situation with Sophia many times over the past ten years. Of course, in his fantasies, she was never across the room from him; she'd be right next to him, where he could keep his hands on her at all times.

This fantasy come to life was more bitter than sweet, because his brother was gone. But nothing would change the fact that he loved being with Sophia. And, for him, being with her now put a much-needed salve on the wound that Dan's death had carved into his heart. Now that baby boy Sophia was carrying was another much-needed salve. He already loved the boy as his own.

"What are you thinking about?" Sophia had turned her face toward him, and now their eyes were locked.

"Dan."

A small smile lifted her bow-shaped lips. "Me, too. What were you thinking?"

"I was wondering if he knew he was going to be a father."

Sophia took a deep breath in and felt her gut clench. It took her a minute to compose herself before she gave a small shake of her head. "He didn't. It's strange how life works out, isn't it? We hadn't planned on having a family until he was finished with his Ph.D. We had everything planned out, you know? Everything. Then, the next thing I know, Daniel comes home and says he's joined the army. Just like that." She snapped her fingers. "I was *literally* blown away. And furious, to tell you the truth." She glanced away from the fire to Luke for a split second. "I've never been that angry in my life! And, believe me, I let him know about it every chance I got. I wish I hadn't now."

"You can't blame yourself for that, Soph. If I had been within arm's length of him, I would have personally strangled him myself! I don't know what the *hell* he was thinking."

"I know you're right, but I can't seem to forgive myself for that fight. I play it over and over in my head, and sometimes I can't sleep. I know I shouldn't drive myself nuts like that, but my brain just won't give it a rest. I said some pretty horrible things to him that night. Things that I should never have said…"

She paused her story for a minute while she pressed her fingers to the corner of her eyes. After a minute she shook her head and continued. "He'd never even mentioned joining the army, Luke. Not *once,* in all the years we had been together. It was like boom, boom, boom."

Sophia hit the arm of the chair with her hand. "One minute he had joined, and the next minute he was gone to officer training. Then, the next thing I know, he's saying he's going to Iraq. It was like being on a rollercoaster ride against my will and I couldn't get off!" She looked at Luke with a slightly accusatory set to her mouth. "He never told you why he joined?"

"No," Luke said flatly, but she heard anger creep into his voice. "I was hoping you had an answer to that question."

She crossed her arms over her chest and stared sullenly into the fire. "Well, I don't." She could hear that same old bitterness in her tone, never far from the surface. "I thought if he had told anyone why he did something that *crazy,* something that totally out of character, it would've been you. If it hadn't been me, at least he could have told you." She forced the bitterness that had bubbled up back down. It was pointless to be bitter, so she squashed it. Temporarily if not permanently. "I asked him, of course. I was like a bloody broken record...."

Luke made a noise in the back of his throat. "I bet you were...."

"But time and time again he wouldn't give a straight answer. He kept on saying that he thought it was his duty as an American, which is exactly the kind of crap I used to hear you say about being a marine." She held up her hand to him. "No offense."

"None taken."

"I even blamed you, but he denied you had anything to do with it...."

"He didn't tell me until after he'd already done it. I've never been that damned angry in my life...."

"I knew in my heart that you hadn't talked him into it, you know." She shrugged one shoulder. "I just wanted someone to blame. For a while that someone was you. Sorry."

"No apology needed. I blamed myself. Why shouldn't you?" Luke asked angrily.

"It wasn't your fault." Her reply was quick and firm. "Daniel had a mind of his own. Why he did it, none of us will ever know. But, in the end, it was his choice, his price to pay. Anyway, we didn't have many pleasant conversations right up to the time he left. I couldn't accept what he had done, and I picked fights with him every chance I got."

"You were scared."

"I was. But I still feel guilty about it. We fought at the end more than not. But he blindsided me, and that wasn't fair either. We discussed everything, *everything,* in our marriage, or at least I thought we did. And here I was so smug about my marriage whenever my friends would complain about their relationships. I never had anything bad to say about Daniel." She smiled. "Other than the fact that he snored and hogged the bed."

She rested her head in her hand and took a minute to imagine Daniel in their bed: naked, lean, totally sexy. Luke watched the expression on her face change from sweet to almost sensual. The lids of her eyes dropped, her full lips parted, and he could see that her breathing had deepened almost imperceptibly. But he noticed. He noticed everything about her.

"But you still never got it out of him," he said to jump-start the conversation again.

Sophia slid her eyes toward him. "Hmm? Oh, no. I never did. The only decision he ever made without me, and it turned out to be the most important decision of our lives." Her hand moved over her stomach. "All of our lives."

"And the baby?" Luke prodded.

Sophia's hand stilled and rested on her stomach. "Daniel surprised me with a visit right before he shipped out. I hadn't been expecting him, we were out of condoms, and one thing led to another…."

"You're kidding…"

The look on Luke's face was comical in its surprise and she couldn't help but laugh at the situation. "My husband had just shipped out. Why would I restock the condoms?"

Luke leaned back and propped his hands on the top of his head. He nodded toward her stomach. "It's a good thing you didn't. Now we have a piece of Daniel."

Every time Luke said something positive about her son, it made her soften toward him. She couldn't help herself. "Just think, if he hadn't come home for a visit, I wouldn't be having his son right now."

"Or, if he had stopped off for condoms."

"Touché. But I think I'll keep that little fact from Danny… Why give him a complex, right?"

"Good call."

"You know, I have no idea why I told you that…I haven't told anyone that story, not even my best friend!"

"Your secret is safe with me."

She narrowed her eyes playfully at him. "Do you swear?"

Luke reached down and made an X over his heart. "Cross my heart. Dan Junior won't hear it from me."

"I'd appreciate it," Sophia bantered back. She was beginning to understand Luke's sense of humor. It was irreverent and it made her laugh. It felt good to laugh, and with Luke, she had been laughing wholeheartedly for the first time since Daniel's death.

After a moment, when they both stopped laughing, Luke prompted her to continue. "So, he didn't know you were pregnant?"

"No. I didn't know myself until I was two months along. By then…"

"He was gone," Luke filled in for her as her words trailed off. Dan wasn't made for combat. He had been the sensible one of the two of them. He had been the brains; Luke was the brawn. He had been killed in an explosion soon after he had arrived in Iraq.

"Yes," Sophia said softly. "By then he was gone." Sophia paused and then glanced over at Luke. "Don't worry, Captain, I'm not going to start crying."

"If you won't, maybe I will," Luke said dryly.

Instead, it was Ranger who cried at Luke from beside the couch; Luke scooped him up and the kitten happily curled up on Luke's chest, closed his eyes and promptly fell asleep.

Sophia pulled the blanket tight under her chin and curled up in the chair. Once again, little Danny insisted on jamming his feet underneath her ribs; it felt as if he were using her ribs as a springboard in order to do a full somersault.

"Hey," she said as she poked the baby in her belly with her fingers. "Why do you have to be so rough in there?"

"Like father, like son," Luke murmured, his eyes closed.

"Exactly," Sophia said. Then added, "Like uncle, like nephew, too, I think."

Luke said proudly, "Brand boys." He moved his head sideways and looked at her.

"You know," Sophia continued, "one of the strangest things about this whole pregnancy thing is that the minute I stop moving, that's when he decides he wants to have a little party in there. It'd be nice if we could both be still at the same time!"

"That'd be too easy," Luke said, and then, after a brief

pause, "could I feel him moving? You know, like I did before?"

Sophia shrugged. "It could happen, I'm sure, but another strange thing about it is that for some reason, when someone touches my stomach, he stops moving. Thank God for the internet so I know all of this stuff and don't freak out when it happens."

"I'd like to feel him moving around again."

"You sound like you love him."

"I do," Luke said easily and without hesitation. "Dan's son is my son, too."

If she hadn't sworn off hormonal crying, this would have been a perfect time to indulge. Luke's words made her feel more secure than she had felt in a long time. For some reason, at that moment, it seemed to her that she wasn't going to have to raise little Daniel without a strong male influence.

"I'm glad," Sophia finally said once she felt safe to talk without crying. "I'm really glad to hear that."

"I know you can't trust it yet, Sophia, but I'm here for you. That's a fact."

They spent the rest of the evening in comfortable companionship. She asked Luke to tell her Daniel stories, and after a good dose of strong coffee, Luke told one story after another until the caffeine started to wear off. Sophia had closed her eyes while Luke talked, and occasionally allowed herself to drift into a place where she could imagine that Daniel was in the room talking to her. Luke's voice was so similar to Daniel's that it wasn't hard to do; in that moment, she had Daniel back with her, and it was priceless.

She didn't know when she fell asleep, but the next thing she knew, Luke was gently shaking her leg to wake her up. She slowly opened her eyes and blinked at him.

"Did I fall asleep?"

"Yes," Luke said wryly. "So much for my riveting storytelling."

Sophia glanced over at the fire. It had died down and Luke had the grate back in place. "Sorry."

He offered his hand. "You ready for bed?"

"You're not mad, are you?" She held out her hand.

"Please," he said as he engulfed her hand with his strong, warm fingers. He pulled her up. "I'm used to women falling asleep on me."

She wrinkled her forehead at him and said groggily, "Now I'm gonna say, 'Please…give me a break, Captain Brand.' You had women crawling all over you in college. I'm sure it's not any different now."

Just not the one I wanted to crawl all over me.

He offered her his arm and out loud, he said, "There were a lot of women with very bad taste at that school."

She took his arm and frowned at him playfully. "That's a *horrible* thing to say. I thought most of your girlfriends were really pretty and nice. Except for that cheerleader you dated, remember her? She was a real tramp."

He looked down at her. "Why don't you tell me how you really feel about her?"

She frowned. "Well, she was. But, other than her, I thought you had really good taste. Honestly, I never understood why you didn't settle down with one of them eventually."

Because none of them were you.

"I wanted to save them the trouble of divorcing me," Luke said dryly as he looked over his shoulder and whistled for Ranger. "Come on, little man."

The kitten trilled, stuck his tail straight up in the air and raced to catch up with them.

Sophia liked the feeling of having her hand on his forearm. She liked the feeling of walking beside him. And it wasn't just because he reminded her of Daniel.

This time, this particular evening, she discovered that she was enjoying walking next to Luke; standing this close to Luke, just for Luke.

She was just too tired to try to analyze it. It just *was*.

A question was formulating in her fuzzy head, and the curious side of her brain was fighting with the cautious side. Finally, the curious side won out and she tried to sound nonchalant when she asked the question. "Are you seeing anyone now?"

She didn't sound half as casual as she would have liked. And, for some reason, her heart was beginning to thump in the most annoying way as she anticipated his answer.

Luke cocked an eyebrow at her as he helped her up the stairs. "Why do you ask?"

Sophia shrugged as if she couldn't care less. "No reason, really. Other than the fact that my friend Allie...remember her?" Luke nodded. "Well, I told her you were here and she said that she thought you were handsome...."

"Ah...I see. You're trying to fix me up..." There was a bite in his tone that made her glance at his strong, handsome profile.

"Well..." Sophia said slowly, "if you aren't with anyone...and she's single..."

"Allie is a beautiful woman," Luke said easily.

Sophia's eyes quickly found his face again. There was something in his tone she didn't like. He sounded interested, and the compliment made her feel a pang of jealousy.

"Yes, she is," she agreed quickly, and meant it.

"And a great mom," he added.

Another pang. "The best. You should give her a call sometime. She's single now and..."

He cut her off. "I'm not in the market for a woman like Allie."

Relief flooded her body. "Why not?"

"Allie's the type of woman you settle down with."

"And you aren't ready to settle down?"

"No," he said decisively. "I'm not."

She just couldn't give up the conversation, even when she knew she should leave it well enough alone. "But you do date...?"

"What's with all of the questions about my love life?" Luke evaded the question.

"What's with the secrecy?" she countered, and wondered if her cheeks were starting to redden with embarrassment.

"No secrecy. I have several women who I...keep company with."

She knew exactly what "keeping company" meant. And why not? Luke was an unmarried, red-blooded, American male. Why shouldn't he be involved sexually with women? And yet, she didn't like the idea at all.

At the top of the stairs, Sophia's brain was whirling with possible images of the women in Luke's life. Who were these women? How many were there? How often did he see them?

She shouldn't care one bit if he was seeing ten thousand women! She had zero reason to be jealous. No right. None whatsoever.

But she was so filled up with it at the moment that she was surprised her eyes hadn't turned a bright shade of green.

She should keep her mouth shut, and yet she couldn't seem to do just that. Nor could she keep the disapproving tone out of her voice when she asked, "So, what is it...a 'woman in every port' kind of thing?"

Luke was examining her with a curious, slightly amused expression on his handsome face. "Something like that," he said easily. Too easily for her taste.

Sophia tried to stop herself from frowning and failed. Then she managed to muster a tired smile. "Good night, Luke."

He had the distinct feeling that he had hurt her in some way, but he would be damned if he knew what it was. He didn't want her to leave on a bad note, not after such a great day together. "You don't approve?"

She paused in her doorway. "It's your life, Luke. Who am I to judge?"

"Your opinion matters."

"It shouldn't," she said wearily as she started to shut her door.

"I feel like I've done something to upset you, but for the life of me, I can't figure out what it is...."

Sophia mustered a weak smile; she was acting like a lunatic. "You haven't done anything, Luke. Your personal life is really none of my business. I was just passing along the message from Allie."

"So, you aren't mad?" Luke asked.

"No. I'm not mad at you, Luke. I'm exhausted, pregnant and just a little bit nuts. I'll feel better after I get some sleep. Good night."

"Good night." Luke watched as Sophia disappeared into her room before he went into his. By the time he made it into his room, Sophia had already closed the adjoining bathroom door and was preparing for bed. He sat on the edge of the bed and listened to her go through her nightly routine. He liked being this close to her, and something as simple as listening to her prepare for bed gave him a sense of intimacy with the woman he loved. There had been a lot of women in his life; he loved women and they seemed to gravitate toward him. But he'd never found another woman who could replace Sophia in his heart. He had tried. Many times. He had always failed.

Sophia crawled into bed feeling exhausted and confused. Luke kept on tying her into knots in one way or another. She was hoping in time things would make sense, because right now they didn't. She listened as Luke prepared for bed and wondered about the women in his life.

She didn't have any doubt that they were all gorgeous creatures. Most likely, they were exotic women who had great bodies and lots of brains. Luke always wanted the entire package and he was a man who always got what he wanted. The image of a willowy brunette with pouty lips, blue eyes and a Ph.D. was the last unfortunate image she had in her head before she drifted off to sleep.

The sound of a man's voice jarred her awake.

Sophia jerked her head off the pillow and stared confused into the darkened room. The digital clock on the nightstand read 2:15 a.m. She had been asleep for several hours.

Had she dreamt the male voice?

She was just about to think that the voice *had* been a part of a dream when she heard it again.

It was Luke's voice. The words were unintelligible, but the tone was unmistakable. He was yelling and his voice was commanding, urgent.

She pushed herself out of bed as quickly as she could and crossed to his room through the bathroom. She flipped on the bathroom light and tapped on the door lightly.

"Luke?"

He didn't answer, but she heard him mumble something she couldn't understand.

"Luke?" She tapped louder this time. No answer.

Impatient, she opened the door and peaked inside the room. Luke was sprawled out on the bed in his underwear. One arm was flung over his forehead and the other dangled off the side of the bed.

"Luke?" She said his name again, and walked quietly over to the bed. As she got closer, she could see that his body was covered with a thin sheen of sweat; his face was flushed.

Concerned, she stopped at the edge of the bed. He was still mumbling; she strained to make out the words.

"Luke," she said more forcefully as she reached out her hand to touch his arm.

In an instant, Luke's eyes popped open and his fingers closed over her wrist. She could see by the confused look in his eyes that he didn't recognize her. His fingers were like a steel band around her wrist; it didn't hurt, but she couldn't move away either. She was trapped, and if this hadn't been Luke holding her wrist so firmly, she would have been afraid. But this was Luke, so she had nothing to fear.

Chapter Seven

Luke was looking at her so strangely; she'd never seen this look in his eyes before. It was unnerving. He still held her wrist in his hand. The pressure didn't hurt, but she had the distinct sensation that it wouldn't take much for Luke to change that situation.

"It's Sophia, Luke," she said quietly; she kept her tone even and calm.

The look in his eyes shifted; he recognized her. "What are you doing in here?"

"You were having a…" She paused to find the right word. "A nightmare, I think."

Luke's eyes moved to his hand on her wrist. He released her as if he had been burned.

Instead of taking a step back, she leaned forward and touched his forehead. His body was tense, the muscles coiled as if he was about to spring into action. He could have avoided her hand, but he didn't.

"My God, Luke, you're burning up. Do you feel sick? Is it your leg?"

Her cool hand felt so good on his forehead, it took a minute for him to remember himself. He could distinctly see the outline of her full breasts barely concealed behind the thin material of her nightgown. Her hair, long and loose, drifted over one shoulder. She smelled so good; so fresh and clean. He wanted to reach up and bury his hand in her hair, bring her face close to his, breathe her in.

Luke pushed himself up and swung his legs over the side. Sophia stepped sideways and let him by as he stood up. He marched over to the bathroom, with a slight limp, and ignored the cane. He jerked on the faucet, bent over the sink and splashed the frigid water on his face and over his head, which washed away the sweat from his brow and neck.

Sophia watched him from the doorway. After a minute, she reached over and pulled a hand towel from the cupboard and handed it to him.

"Here." She shook the towel.

"Thanks." This was said gruffly as he wiped the towel over his head, his neck and his chest. Sophia didn't avert her eyes as he dried himself off. It didn't take much for the psychologist in her to figure out what she had just witnessed. In fact, before she had left Boston for Montana, she had counseled several veterans; she was acutely aware of how active combat could impact a person's psyche. She wondered if Luke was aware of post-traumatic stress, or if he had chosen to ignore any negatives that came along with his blind dedication to the Marines.

Luke caught her eye; he rubbed the towel over his chest one last time before he threw it over the tub. They stood face-to-face, neither one of them spoke, neither one of them moved. There was something raw and intense in the way he examined her. She could feel the heat of his body radiating onto her skin.

"Did I hurt you?" he demanded, finally. His tone was commanding, but she detected the underlying concern in the question.

"No," she said quickly. "Don't be ridiculous. You would never hurt me."

Luke's face hardened; his jaw clenched. "You have no idea what I'm capable of."

She could tell that he was done with the conversation, but Sophia didn't budge. She scoffed. "Yes, I do. You would never hurt me. Not ever."

He took in a long, deep breath through his nose while he examined her through narrowed, contemplative eyes. In the light, his eyes had turned a dark, sapphire blue, and she found it impossible to look away. Whenever he caught her up in his gaze, she became mesmerized by the power, confidence and control that lurked behind his shocking blue eyes.

"Finally," he said. "You'd be wise not to sneak up on me again."

Her hands went immediately to her hips. Defensively, she retorted, "I didn't sneak up on you, Brand. I came to check up on you. There's a huge difference."

"Either way." Luke stepped toward his bedroom, but she still didn't feel inclined to move.

"Don't you think we should talk about what happened here? There is obviously something wrong that needs to be addressed...."

"Christ, woman!" Luke snapped. "Why can't you ever just give it a rest? Why can't you ever just let something go? I'm not one of your patients. Don't psychoanalyze me to death!"

"I'm not *psychoanalyzing you to death*. I'm trying to help. Perhaps you need to acknowledge the fact that being a marine can have some negative consequences." As the words came out of her mouth, she could see the muscles tighten in his chest and neck. The man was truly unreasonable when it came to his career.

"My life is on the line every day... Death is a pretty serious negative consequence, don't you think?"

"Yes, I do, and I..."

Luke's face had become a granite mask again, but there was fire in his eyes. "So, what the hell is it that you don't think I know about the negatives of being a marine?"

"First of all, don't interrupt me. Second of all, don't curse at me. And third of all, some of my patients believe it would be easier to die in combat than to live with the memories for the rest of their lives!" Now her voice was raised, and she felt her heart as it pumped harder in her chest.

"You just like pushing my buttons, don't you? Is that it? You just can't stand it if we're getting along, can you? Perhaps you're the one with the problem here. Did you ever think of that? Why don't *you* stand here and get some self-reflection time while I get back to bed?"

"I'm not pushing anything...." Sophia felt her own jaw set.

"Good. Then, if you don't mind stepping aside—" Luke stepped toward his bedroom again "—I'd like to get some more shut-eye."

Sophia crossed her arms over her chest, but she moved out of his way.

"You should go back to bed, too," he said in that commanding tone that she had always hated. What in the world had *ever* given Luke the impression he could boss her around? He gave her a cursory once-over with his eyes that made her thumping heart skip a beat, partly from irritation, partly from some other emotion she'd rather not admit to. "You need your rest."

"I *was* in bed. I would still be in bed, *asleep,* if you hadn't awakened me!" she snapped. The man had the audacity to tell her to self-reflect when it was *his* nightmare that had jarred her out of her own sleep. The man was *infuriating!*

Luke sat on the edge of his bed and grunted his displeasure. He looked as if he were sculpted out of marble; every muscle was hard, defined, and rippled with his slightest move. There wasn't an ounce of fat on his body; the man was built to fight, there was no doubt about it.

"Go back to bed, Sophia." He gave a shake of his head and said quietly, "You're concerned; I get it. But I've got it handled. You don't need to worry."

"I don't need to worry?" She repeated it as if she hadn't quite heard him correctly. "You wake me up out of a sound sleep…you're shouting, you're burning up…"

Luke interrupted her with a low growl in the back of his throat. She clamped her mouth shut and watched him through narrowed, irritated eyes. She wasn't going to get anywhere with Luke tonight. It was time to quit. But she sure as hell wasn't about to let it drop for good. Luke should at least know her better than to expect that.

"Fine." This was said in a disgruntled tone. "I'm going back to bed."

"Sleep well." Now that he had his way, he was being polite.

"Bug off, Brand," she snapped as she shut the door behind her.

Sophia woke up feeling lousy. Of course, being a typical female, she had been awake for the majority of the night stewing over what had happened with Luke. She had changed positions, meditated and even tried to count sheep; nothing had worked. The more she tried to sleep and failed, the more irritated she felt toward Luke. Her irritation only increased when she heard him snoring from the other room. He had awakened her from a sound sleep, yet he fell back asleep with no problem, while she spent the rest of the night tossing and turning. Typical man!

Sophia shuffled into the bathroom and looked at her reflection. Her eyes were baggy and her face looked

puffy. She leaned forward for a closer look, frowned at
her reflection as she pulled down the skin on her cheeks,
and made a displeased noise.

She broke from her usual routine of a morning yoga
stretch, brushed her teeth, threw on a comfortable sweat
suit and yanked her hair into a haphazard ponytail. She
had been up all night thinking about Luke and she was
determined to talk to him about what happened.

Whether he liked it or not.

Sophia opened the door to her room, noted that Ranger
was already on the loose and the door to Luke's room
was ajar. She knew he was an early riser, but since he had
been home, she had beaten him downstairs every day.
She found him in the family room; the cane was propped
against the wall and Luke was bending over one of the
boxes filled with his mother's Christmas decorations.

"You're up early," she said from the doorway.

He looked annoyingly well rested.

"You're up late," he retorted easily; if she hadn't seen
the slight upturn of his lip that signaled he was kidding,
she would have thought that he was trying to pick a fight.

"I wonder why," she countered. She seriously missed
caffeine at this particular moment. She rubbed her back
and winced a bit. She hadn't had backaches until recently.
But as her belly grew, so did the back pains. "Did you
already have breakfast?"

"I grabbed something."

"I'm going to grab something, too, and then I'll be
back to help you. I was thinking about tackling this today.
You must've read my mind."

"Close. I read your list...."

It hit her like a flash: this was Luke's way of apologizing for what had happened between them the night
before. He knew how she felt about her to-do list, and he
was pitching in as an apology.

It was a nice gesture, and it certainly soothed her ruffled feathers, but it didn't change the fact that she was going to talk to Luke about what had happened. He wasn't getting off the hook that easily.

She wolfed down a piece of toast, a hardboiled egg and a glass of orange juice before she headed back to the family room. Luke had opened all of the boxes, and Ranger was pouncing on a piece of tissue paper that had fallen out of one of them.

"We can't have tinsel this year." Sophia surveyed the open boxes.

"Why not?"

She nodded her head toward Ranger, who had just discovered that his tail was following him.

Understanding lit Luke's face. "Good point. No tinsel." He waved his hand over the boxes. "I can't believe the stuff my mom has held on to. Look at this."

Sophia came over and took an ornament from Luke's hand. It was a gingerbread man made out of dough and painted haphazardly with food dye. One of his legs was broken off.

"That is an official Dan creation," Luke said.

Sophia studied the ornament with a faint smile on her face. "He wasn't really an artist, was he?"

Luke actually cracked a smile on that one. It was the first time he had smiled with his teeth showing since returning from Afghanistan. The military had changed him. He had always been more serious than Daniel, but he used to smile more readily when she first met him in college.

"No. Art wasn't either one of our strongpoints."

She pointed to the missing foot. "Is this your handiwork?"

Luke looked up from unpacking the other ornaments. "That's Jordan's handiwork, not mine."

"It blows me away every time I think about your mom and dad raising five kids. Five! And two sets of twins, no less. Did your mom tell you that Jordan and Josephine are coming for Christmas? They're flying in the week before. How long has it been since you've seen your baby sisters?"

Luke thought for a minute. "It's been a while." It seemed like a lifetime ago since he had seen his twin sisters. They were the youngest of the five and sometimes they seemed like complete strangers. He loved them, of course, but most of the time he didn't get them at all.

They unpacked all of the boxes and put out a few items that were a family holiday standard: the giant Frosty the Snowman candle was positioned on the fireplace mantel, a sprig of mistletoe was hung at the threshold of the family room, and an ornately dressed Santa Claus was placed in his usual spot on the coffee table. The rest of the items were placed neatly on one side of the room. Once Luke's younger twin sisters arrived from college, they would bring in a live tree to decorate.

Sophia gave the room a final visual inspection. She wasn't surprised anymore that the two of them made a good team; she was just grateful. But because they were getting along so well, she found it hard to rock the boat and bring up what had happened the night before. She wasn't going to forget about it, but it seemed like a good idea to postpone the talk.

"Do you think your mom would let me have this?" She held up the footless gingerbread man ornament.

Luke straightened upright and squinted his eyes a bit to examine the ornament. "I don't see why not."

Sophia nodded and held the ornament in her hand; she rubbed her finger over the rough surface. She could imagine a young Daniel painting the ornament, and it made her think about her own son. One day, Danny would make a homemade ornament for her. She brought the old ornament up to her nose and breathed in.

She let her mind take a trip down melancholy lane, which was a mistake. The minute she started to think about all of the Christmases her son would have without his father, her emotions took over, and the tears started to well up in her eyes.

"What are you doing?" Luke was looking at her with a horrified expression.

Embarrassed, she swiped at the tears, which fell unchecked onto her cheeks.

"Are you crying?" Luke asked. His tone now matched the horrified expression.

"No." That was a ridiculous thing for her to say.

"Yes, you are." He took a step closer. "You're crying. Why are you crying?"

The absolute horror in his voice bordered on panic, which actually made her laugh. If she had been bleeding from her eyes, Luke could handle that without any problem. But tears? The man was like a deer caught in headlights. Now she was laughing and crying at the same time, which was a very odd thing to experience.

She laughed for a minute and then started to cry harder.

"Christ, Sophia! Stop that!" Luke reached over and grabbed something from the top of the Christmas pile and was at her side. He sat down on the couch beside her and began to roughly rub the tears from her face. He swiped the cloth over her entire face, smashed her nose down, and covered her mouth in the process. A piece of lint broke loose and was sucked into her windpipe. Caught off guard, she started to cough; she reached up and stopped Luke. She pulled the item from her face.

"Hey, hey, hey…a little rough, Captain Brand!" She glared at him accusingly before she looked down at his makeshift tissue. "What is this? What are you wiping my face with?"

"I don't know."

Sophia turned it over in her hand and saw the word *Barbara* embroidered on it. "It's your mom's Christmas stocking from when she was a kid! Your grandmother made this, Luke! It's a family heirloom! How could you use it to wipe my face!? And none too gently I might add…."

"How did I know what it was? It was available. I grabbed it."

"There's a lot of stuff available all over the place! That doesn't mean that you wipe a person's face with any of it! Especially not the stocking your grandmother *hand-stitched* for your mother! Geez!"

"The situation called for action." This was said with total seriousness.

Sophia took the tail of her shirt and dabbed it over the stocking to blot the tear-stained material. "And the stocking got in the way, is that it? A casualty of war?"

For a minute, the two of them sat on the couch together and looked from the stocking to each other. They both started to smile. "Well," she said, "that's one way to get me to stop crying. Thank God you didn't tell me to blow!"

Luke cracked a smile. "That was next."

Sophia held out the stocking in front of her. "Can you tell that I cried all over it?"

"It's fine."

"You didn't even look."

"What do you want me to look at?"

"I want you to look at the stocking. What's the matter with you? Could you focus for *one* second? Why are you being so difficult? Just look at the stupid stocking, already."

Luke looked at the stocking.

"Well?" she prompted.

"It's fine."

She sighed in exasperation and waved it at him. "Just put it back where you found it, will you? I just pray that your mother doesn't notice, but we both know that Barbara Brand notices absolutely everything! And if she does I will throw you right under the bus without any hesitation or guilt!"

Luke dropped the stocking on top of the pile. "You'd do that, wouldn't you?"

"Yes, I would."

"I always knew you had a mean streak, Soph. I always knew."

Luke sat down beside her and the mood in the room lost the humorous edge. Luke's eyes swept her face, his sharp, blue eyes concerned.

"What was that crying stuff all about, anyway?"

She let out a long breath. "Self-pity. Plain and simple. I started to think about my son and all of the Christmases we were going to have without Daniel..." She shrugged and sniffed loudly. "There are a lot of mental roads I know better than to let myself travel down, because in the end, feeling sorry for myself doesn't change anything, you know? But knowing better and actually not doing something are two entirely different things."

Luke slid his arm around her shoulder, gripped her shoulder tightly and pulled her into his body. "I'm proud of you."

Sophia found herself sinking into his hard, warm body without a second thought. She tipped her head back. "You're...proud of...me?"

"You bet."

"Why?"

"You're a tough woman and you're handling this situation like a marine...."

"Well, thank you, Captain." This was a compliment of epic proportions coming from Luke.

"Except when you're leaking all over the couch," Luke added as he gave her arm a squeeze. "Then, you're just another weepy dame."

She pulled back and punched him on the arm. "Thanks a lot, Brand. You know, you aren't exactly good at the 'providing comfort' thing. You almost rubbed my nose right off my face with that stocking!"

"In my own defense, I don't have a lot of practice. My men don't typically cry. But, if one of them did, I sure as hell wouldn't gently wipe away his tears."

"Hey…*gentle* is a matter of opinion."

"You're just a chick. What do you know?"

"I know if someone is trying to rub my nose right off my face, I can tell you that!"

Luke glanced over at her. "You're never going to let me live that one down, are you?"

"I doubt it," she said easily. "Hey! Perhaps you should pack some Christmas stockings in with your gear just in case one of your men has a moment."

"I'll put it in the suggestion box."

"See that you do," Sophia bantered. "Do you think I could become an honorary marine for submitting a winning suggestion like that? I could *literally* change the face of the military."

"Sergeant Sophia Brand," Luke played along.

"Ooh-rah," she said with a smile.

He tugged on her ponytail. "Ooh-rah."

They smiled at each other for a moment and then Sophia's stomach growled loudly. They both looked down at her belly.

"Lunch?" she asked.

"That works."

Sophia accepted his offered hand. "You know…I was

about to go stark raving mad just before you arrived. At that point, I was glad to see any sign of human life..." She paused.

Luke filled in the rest for her. "Even me."

Sophia glanced up at him to gauge his mood and then she laughed. He was teasing the both of them. "Yes. Even you. And I wouldn't have thought it could be possible, Luke, given our rather rocky past... But I'm having a great time with you, and I'm glad that you came home early to see me." She stopped at the threshold of the room to look up at him. "I really am."

Luke met her gaze. He knew that he had to stop closing his heart to her, so he said, "I'm glad to be here with you too, Sophia. There's no place on earth I'd rather be than right here with you now."

She planted her hands on her hips. "Not even back with your men?"

"Not even back with my men."

Sophia was once again caught off guard by Luke's words. She had been teasing him, but his response had been serious.

"You keep me on my toes, Brand, that's for sure. Just when I think I have you figured out, you say something that surprises me." She smiled up at him, before she began to walk toward the kitchen.

Luke reached out and grabbed her wrist. He tugged it gently to get her to stop. She looked over her shoulder questioningly. He had a mischievous twinkle in his striking blue eyes as he glanced upward. She followed his eyes up to the sprig of mistletoe.

She felt a blush race up her neck to her cheeks. Her heart started to beat in the most ridiculous way. Did he mean to kiss her? Did she mean to let him?

She tried to make light of the situation. "What would

your girlfriends, *plural,* think?" She tried to keep her tone casual, but she heard an annoying waver in her voice.

Luke quirked up his lip and his eyes radiated a heat that she had never experienced before from him. No wonder the women threw themselves at Luke. When he turned that gaze on her, she started to forget herself and felt inclined to melt into his arms.

"I'm not going to make love to you, Sophia." When he said "make love," a shiver raced right up her spine. "It's just a kiss."

"Between friends," she said on a rush of air; she wished that her heartbeat would slow down. Something odd flickered in his eyes, but it came and went before she could pin down the emotion.

"Something like that," Luke murmured as he brought her hand up to his lips. Sophia watched him press his mouth to the back of her hand.

The moment came and went quickly, and when he released her hand, she felt like a real lunatic. She couldn't believe that she actually thought Luke was going to kiss her on the mouth. Of course, he wasn't going to do that! And she was glad that he hadn't. Sort of...

That simple kiss had made her feel sensations in places throughout her body that hadn't been revved up since Daniel last touched her. It was unnerving and exciting all at the same time. She had the distinct feeling that Luke knew how to love a woman's body like nobody's business. Allie was right: Luke was a seriously sensual, sexy, handsome man.

How could she have missed that?

Why was she noticing *now?*

Chapter Eight

Several days had passed since Luke had kissed her beneath the mistletoe, and Sophia couldn't seem to stop thinking about the sensation of his lips pressed against her skin. It had been an innocent gesture that had left an indelible mark on her brain.

Of course, Luke hadn't meant anything by it. And yet... Her pulse would quicken whenever her mind replayed the moment over again. And she hated to admit it, but the moment was never far from her mind. Her brain had conjured a slow-motion image of his piercing blue eyes as he bent his head down to press his lips to her hand.

His eyes had locked on hers, drew her in and held her motionless with their intensity.

Once Luke locked his eyes on you, he had you. It was the first time she had felt the power of his gaze; it was magnetic. Animalistic. That one look had made her heart race in a way it hadn't raced in a very long time. Perhaps not ever. She felt a tingle in her stomach whenever she remembered the feel of his warm breath as it brushed across the back of her hand just before his lips made contact with her skin. The minute his lips had touched her, goose bumps had cropped up on both of her arms and she had involuntarily sucked in her breath. Even now, if she closed her eyes, she could still imagine the soft tickling sensation the stiff hair of his goatee created as it brushed past her knuckles.

And she closed her eyes often.

Reliving that innocent kiss had become somewhat of a favorite pastime. Had she conjured up all of this romantic euphoria out of boredom or grief? She couldn't be certain. All she knew was that for the past couple of days, Luke had made all of her bells and whistles go off, and she flat-out enjoyed it. Enjoyment laced with a heavy dose of guilt.

"You okay?"

Sophia opened her eyes; Luke was staring at her over his paper. They had fallen into a comfortable routine; Luke with his coffee, she with her tea. He would read the paper while she wrote out endless items on her to-do list. Luke had blended in with her daily routine seamlessly.

He seemed to fit her in a way she hadn't imagined possible. He wasn't Daniel, and yet he fit her just as well, in his own unique way.

"I'm fine," she replied quickly, irritated with herself that Luke had caught her daydreaming about that stupid kiss. And, to make matters worse, she hadn't been able to get Allie's words out of her mind. She couldn't stop herself from trying to catch Luke giving her "the look." She had caught Luke looking at her many times, but never with "the look." Most of the time the "look" he was giving her was one of curiosity, because he was probably wondering why every time he looked up, *she* was staring at *him*.

Damn Allie for sticking that ridiculous idea in her brain!

She looked back at her list and tried to shove the kiss back into the recesses of her mind. She wrote another item on the list and then stared at the words she had written.

Take Luke to Daniel's grave.

She stared at Luke and tapped her pencil on the paper while she thought. Finally, she made a decisive circle around the latest item and drew an arrow to point to the top of the list.

Luke had been home for nearly a week and he had yet to make any mention of visiting Daniel's grave. His family was due home in a day. And just as Luke thought it best that their reunion be a private event, she *knew* that it should be just the two of them present the first time Luke visited his brother's grave.

It needed to be done.

"What now?" Luke asked in an exasperated tone. He had bent the corner of the paper down and was examining her through slightly narrowed eyes.

"What do you mean?"

"I know that look; I know that tapping. Whatever's on that psychologist's mind of yours, just spit it out so I can deal with it."

He was blunt, so she was blunt.

"We need to go visit Daniel's grave."

Everything in Luke's body tensed. Sophia was watching him closely; she saw his jaw clench and the pallor of his face whiten. The long scar that ran along the edge of his jaw became more prominent. He studied her for a moment before he snapped the paper back into place and returned to his article.

She wasn't about to be deterred by him. She knew that Luke was good at intimidating people; he was a soldier first and a man second. But he didn't intimidate her. And he was going to visit Daniel's grave if she had to drag him there herself!

She had always believed in divine intervention, and

she realized now that Luke was here to help her cope with Daniel's death, and in return, she was here to help him. And she intended to do just that.

"It needs to be done," she said, before she drained the rest of the tea from her cup.

He ignored her and she didn't care. She had put off her discussion with him about the nightmare he had experienced several nights before, but she couldn't put this off. It was just too important.

She stood up, rinsed out her cup at the sink before she returned to the table. She scooped up Ranger, who had been upside down on the table between them, gave him a scratch on his chops and then put him down on the ground.

"No time like the present." She stood next to Luke. He didn't bother to look at her.

Silly man! He actually was under the mistaken impression that she was going to give up!

She poked his shoulder with her finger, which got a snarl out of him but no verbal response.

She poked him again. This time he sighed heavily, dropped the paper and glared at her.

"Are you trying to pick a fight with me?" he asked, disgruntled.

Sophia crossed her arms over her chest. "Do you want a fight?" She threw the question back at him. Her tone was razor sharp.

He leaned back a bit, his eyes still narrowed. "Maybe."

She didn't back off. "Fight all you want, Lucas. You're going to go see your brother. It needs to be done, and it's going to be done today!"

Luke picked up her list, glanced at it and then tossed it back onto the table. "Why? Because you have it written down on your damned list?"

Sophia had zero intention of budging. Luke needed to

see Daniel. It needed to be real for him. And it needed to be done without a crowd.

Sophia set her jaw. "You're going, Luke. Your father gassed the truck up for me before they left, and you only need your right leg to drive. There isn't one good reason why we shouldn't go."

Luke pushed back from the table abruptly and stood up. She saw him wince slightly when he put full weight down on his left leg. "I can think of plenty," he said in a low, controlled voice.

She cocked her head to the side. His eyes were narrowed, and so were hers. "Name one."

He clamped his mouth shut and said nothing. She knew she was pushing him, that he was uncomfortable. But his discomfort would grow a thousandfold if he saw Daniel's grave for the first time with his entire family as witnesses. He needed to go now, and she wasn't going to stop until he agreed.

He'd thank her later. Most likely.

After a minute of Luke staring her down, he said in measured words, "Why do you always have to do this, Sophia? Why can't you leave well enough alone? Were we getting along too well, is that it? Too calm for you? You had to get in there and stir up the pot?"

"Don't try to put the blame on me so you can avoid this," she retorted. "I'm not doing this to pick a fight with you because I'm bored." She waved her hands when she talked. "I'm doing this to *help* you, for all the thanks I'm getting!"

He grabbed for his cane and moved away from the table. "Thanks," he said with a large dose of sarcasm.

"You're welcome," she snapped back as she followed behind him. "Let's get ready to go."

Luke stopped abruptly, spun around, and she nearly

bumped into him. They were face-to-face. She had her hands on her hips; he wore a scowl.

She nodded her head toward the cane. "You know, it doesn't do a whole heck of a lot of good being held in your hand like that. It actually has to touch the ground for it to be effective."

He ignored her comment and said through gritted teeth, "I'm not going."

"Yeah," she said easily, "you are."

Luke gave her a look that she supposed was meant to stop her in her tracks. He turned back to the stairs with a frustrated growl.

At the bottom of the stairs she said, "You have to do this, Luke."

Luke paused on the third step and she waited. Finally, he turned back around. His handsome face was hard and tense. "Why are you pushing this?"

"You need to see Daniel's grave," she said simply, quietly.

"Why?

"It won't be real until you do."

Luke ran his hand over his head in a frustrated gesture. He pinned her with his bright blue eyes. "Did it ever occur to you that I don't *want* it to be real?"

"Yes."

"It occurred to you?"

"Yes! It's what I do for a living, for crying out loud."

He moved down one step. "If it occurred to you, then why are you pushing me so damn hard?"

"I'm doing this for you."

"You're doing this for me?" His eyes were blazing. "This kind of favor I can do without!"

"No, you can't!" Sophia raised her voice and waved her arm toward the door. "Do you think that I wanted to watch them bury my husband? No! I didn't! But it needed to be done. I needed to see it, Luke, so I didn't spend the rest of my days waiting for him to come walking back through that door! You have to stop pretending that he's just away, on a trip. He's not away on a trip! He's gone!"

"I know that."

"Do you?"

"Yes," he said in an oddly quiet voice.

"Do you?" she repeated more forcefully.

"Yes!"

"Have you even cried for him, Luke?"

He looked at her as if she was crazy. "I'm a marine."

"He was your twin!" she snapped back. "Marine or not, you need to say goodbye to him. You need to cry for him. Of all the stupid things we teach our boys in this country, that men don't cry is about the most idiotic!"

"What in the hell do you think it will prove? You think that if I *cry* for Dan I won't feel like someone has yanked out half my guts? It doesn't work that way, sweetheart!"

"Don't you patronize me, Lucas Brand! I'm not your 'sweetheart,' I'm your friend, and I deserve a little respect from you."

When the word *friend* came out of her mouth, Luke felt his stomach clench into a tight knot. No matter how many times he told himself to think of her that way, he couldn't. Even now, when she was ticking him off beyond belief, he wanted her. His body ached for her. Especially now, when she was riled up and her lovely face was flushed pink with emotion, and her hazel eyes had turned a dark shade of forest green.

She was everything he wanted in a woman: strong, independent, incredibly smart, and sexier now than she had ever been. She wasn't intimidated by him. She wasn't afraid to stand up to him, or call him on his crap. It was a turn-on. His hands wanted to strip her down and stroke every silken inch of her curvaceous body. That was his idea of heaven on Earth.

It took every last ounce of his willpower not to close the distance between them, mold her body into his and taste those full, tempting lips of hers. He wanted to kiss the breath right out of her. Kiss her until the word *friend* was permanently eradicated from her brain. But whenever he came close to crossing that line, Luke would look down at her belly, and that would stop him cold.

His nephew was the only thing that sobered him up and helped him keep his hands, and lips, to himself.

Sophia watched the expression in Luke's eyes as they roamed her face. She had to admit that the look he was giving her was more sensual than "friendly." He was looking at her with the same hungry expression he had given the apple pie she had baked the day before.

She shifted uncomfortably under his scrutiny. He wasn't saying a word; he just stood there and stared at her with an undeniably provocative look in his eyes. She opened her mouth to break the silence, but Luke broke the silence for her.

"You really know how to piss me off."

That shattered the tension, and she laughed out loud. Her hands went to her hips again and she smiled up at him.

"You really tick me off too, Luke."

He took another step down. "No one speaks to me the way you do."

"I know," she agreed easily.

"Then why do I let you?" he asked, his eyes never leaving hers.

She shrugged. "I'm your friend." For some reason, she felt that she needed to establish that boundary between them.

Luke's eyes took in the features of her face until they

finally stopped at her mouth and lingered. She involuntarily licked her lips. His eyes traveled slowly back up to her eyes, and there was a satisfied glint in his.

"I don't have any female friends." There was a husky quality in his voice that sent a shiver right up her spine. Her heart started to thud and she felt weak in the knees.

She touched her hair nervously and wondered how he had turned the tables on her so quickly. "There's a first time for everything."

"Perhaps…" Luke said softly; she had the distinct feeling that he was saying that just to shut her up. Either way, Sophia was thrown off by the predatory look in Luke's eyes. She had never seen it before, but every nerve in her body was responding to it.

For a split second she wondered if this was "the look" Allie had mentioned, but her brain immediately rejected it.

The lengths this man would go to get out of something! It had to be that. He wasn't so hard up that he would desire a woman as pregnant as she was. She was nearly bursting at the seams and getting bigger by the minute!

She took a step back; she wanted to put a bit of space between Luke and herself. Her body was betraying her, but her mind was on task.

"Are we going, then?"

His expression shifted from predatory to amused. "You're relentless."

"Yes. I am."

He leaned back against the railing. "Why is this so important to you?"

"Why was it so important for you to come here a week early so we could work things out between us without an audience?"

"I knew it was best for you. For us."

"Exactly." She finally had him right where she wanted

him. Luke never argued with logic. "I know this is best for you. For us. You need to say goodbye to Daniel without an audience. Once your family gets here, you know how your mom will react. It's not like you will be able to avoid the cemetery forever. Let's do it now."

"All right."

He conceded so easily that Sophia had to confirm it. "All right?"

"Is there an echo in here?" Luke started up the stairs. Sophia followed. So did Ranger.

"Oh, be quiet!" Sophia said playfully. "If you weren't such a stubborn pain in the rear end, we would already be halfway there!"

They parted at their doors. He saluted her. "Touché."

They threw on their winter clothes and loaded into his father's dark blue Ford truck. Sophia wrapped her arms tightly around her body and watched her breath materialize as a curl of steam in front of her face. She pulled her scarf up over her mouth and nose.

The tires crunched on the packed snow as Luke slowly drove the truck up the driveway to the main road. "It's a snow sky," he said.

Sophia nodded but didn't uncover her face. Luke glanced over at her with an amused look. He didn't seem the least bit bothered by the frigid air in the truck.

She pulled down her scarf. "I thought it was hot in Afghanistan."

"It is. But it's freezing in the mountains. This is nothing."

She pulled the scarf back over her face and waited for the heater to start working. They were halfway to the family's church before Sophia felt the heat blast into her eyes. It was right about the time her stomach started to churn with nerves. She had been so determined to get Luke to the gravesite that she hadn't considered her own feelings about seeing Daniel's grave again. His mother went to the site every week, no matter what the weather. Hank and Tyler hadn't been back since the funeral. She had made the trip a few times, but she always felt like crying when she did, so she had stopped. Until now. Until Luke. This was something that she simply had to do, tears or no tears.

Her hands started to sweat inside her gloves and she felt nauseous as they pulled into the abandoned church-yard. Most of the headstones in the small graveyard to the left of the church were covered with snow and ice. Some had been cleared by relatives.

Luke shifted the truck into Park and he leaned forward to rest his weight on the steering wheel. He looked at the headstones, his expression unreadable.

But Sophia could imagine what he was thinking. It never occurred to either one of them that Daniel would leave them so soon. Luke had tempted death for a decade, and yet his brother was the one to lose his life to war.

No doubt Luke couldn't make sense of that contra-diction.

None of them could.

"No time like the present," Luke finally said and switched off the engine. He met her at her side of the truck and helped her out. "Lead the way," he said, and she complied.

They walked together slowly, arm in arm. She held on tightly to Luke's arm so she wouldn't slip. The baby, who had started to kick her furiously during the ride to the church, had suddenly quieted.

She pointed ahead. "He's down this row. At the very end. Under that tree."

The short walk seemed to take forever, until they fi-nally reached Daniel's resting place. Luke's face was de-void of expression as he stared down at the snow-covered headstone that marked his twin's grave. He stood perfectly still, at attention; both of his hands gripped the handle of his cane as he stared at the grave.

Sophia unhooked her hand from his arm and bent down to brush the snow from the headstone.

"Careful," Luke ordered, softly.

Sophia nodded and continued with her task. She wanted Luke to see Daniel's name. She lowered herself down, used the headstone for support, before she brushed the snow from the name.

When Daniel's name was exposed, Sophia shook her head slightly. "Hello, my dear husband…my dear friend." She pressed her fingertips to her lips and then pressed her fingers to the headstone.

She looked over her shoulder. Luke hadn't moved. She reached her hand out to him and he helped her to her feet. They stood side by side; neither of them said a word. Luke's arm came around her shoulders and he squeezed her. She leaned into him, glad for his offer of comfort and warmth.

Words didn't help. Words didn't change anything. They both knew that. But being there with Luke did make her feel better, and she could only hope that he was feeling the same way about her presence.

Finally, silently, Luke walked over to the headstone and touched it with his gloved hand. He said something under his breath that she couldn't make out before he turned back to her and nodded his head.

She knew he'd seen enough. So had she.

It was a quiet ride back to the ranch. It was a quiet walk back into the house. After they dropped their coats and boots at the front door, Luke went to the stairs while Sophia paused at the kitchen doorway.

"I'm going to take a shower," Luke said. "Are you okay?"

Sophia nodded. This was the caring side of Luke she was starting to get to know. That she was starting to love. "I'm okay."

"I'll get a fire going when I'm done."

"Sounds good," she said. "Luke?"

"Hmm?" When he turned toward her, she could suddenly see how weary he was. How his leg and Daniel's death had worn on him. She could see it because he wasn't bothering to hide it from her.

"It really is a stupid thing our society tells boys about crying. Men should cry if they lose someone they love. I'm not going to fill little Danny's head with that nonsense. If men weren't supposed to cry, why would God give them tear ducts?"

Luke gave her a halfhearted smile. "I'll get that fire going soon."

"Okay." She had said her piece; time to let Luke work things out for himself.

In the shower, Luke pressed his hands against the wall and let the hot water run down his face. It burned and the burn felt good. What was Sophia doing to him? What was that woman doing?

She seemed to be able to see right through him. No one had ever been able to read him this well, other than Dan. Dan knew him inside and out. Now it seemed that Sophia knew him, too. The woman had pushed him right up to the edge, and then, when they had gotten home, she had booted him right over it.

He bent his head down and closed his eyes. Tears squeezed out of his eyes and blended with the steaming water from the showerhead. It felt right to cry for his brother.

It was the release he needed. And the fact that Sophia had given him permission had somehow made it possible.

That woman already had his heart; now she had wormed her way right into his brain.

He loved her more now than he ever had before. Perhaps he was truly loving her for the first time; perhaps before, he had loved the woman he had thought she was, and now he was loving the woman he knew her to be.

Either way, that woman had him, heart, mind, body and soul. He was hers. She might not want him. But she had him.

Chapter Nine

She found him later in the library building the fire he had promised her. He greeted her with his version of a smile, and she could see that he was clean-shaven and refreshed. She curled up in her favorite chair and pulled the comforter over her legs. Ranger, who had been keeping her company in the kitchen, dragged himself up onto the ottoman and shared a corner of the comforter with her.

"How's it going?" she asked him as she watched him build the fire. His back was wide and the muscles rippled beneath the cotton of his T-shirt as he loaded wood into the fireplace. The man was covered in hard, thick muscle, where Daniel had been a lean runner. Both were very appealing physiques in their own way. With his back turned, her eyes roamed over his body without censure. There was something she particularly enjoyed about how the muscles bulged in his arms whenever he tensed them in the slightest way.

She also enjoyed the feel of his strong, thick arms beneath her fingers whenever she had to hold on to him for balance. In the beginning, she had spent all of her time with Luke picking out all of the details that reminded her of Daniel. Now she found that she spent most of her time noticing the little details that made Luke distinctly Luke.

Luke held on to his cane and levered himself up. He watched the fire for a moment, made certain that the flame caught, before he set himself down on the couch. Then, he answered her question.

"I've recovered from our little field trip, if that's what you're getting at."

"That's what I was getting at." There was a smile in her voice. She snuggled farther down into the chair, pulled the comforter up to her chest and sighed happily.

"I'm so glad that you showed up, Luke. These fires are the best part of my day."

He didn't respond with words, but he did give her a slight nod. That was another thing she had to become accustomed to with Luke; he was a man of few words. His actions were his words, and it had always been the exact opposite with Daniel. Daniel would talk your ear off without thinking twice. It was hard to pry a full sentence out of Luke most of the time, but she was learning to enjoy the silences between them. She was also learning to pay close attention to what Luke *did* say, because each word counted for something, and he never said anything he didn't mean. She loved that about him. As it turned out, there were many things that she loved about Luke. She loved his strength, she loved his honesty and she loved the fact that he thought of her baby as his own.

Perhaps she had always loved him, in her own way; she just hadn't realized it until Luke had come home early for her sake. That one act opened her eyes. And her heart.

"Can I ask you a question?" she broke the silence.

"Shoot."

"Have you ever thought about getting out?"

"Out of what?"

"You know…the military?"

Luke glanced over at her. He had rested his chin in

the palm of his hand; his legs were stretched out in front of him. "No."

"Not once?"

"Not once," Luke said without hesitation.

She paused for a minute before she continued. "Not even after your leg?"

"No."

For some ridiculous, unknown reason, her heart sank. What did she think? That one week with her would make him quit his military career? One week with her, and he would be willing to stop putting his life in danger, come to Boston and get to know his nephew in a way that his brother would never be able to do?

Unfortunately, there was a part of her that didn't think this sounded all that unreasonable.

"Not even after Daniel?" Yes, she went there. She didn't know why she went there, but she did.

"No," Luke replied smoothly. "Not even then."

"Why not?" Her voice sounded shrill.

"The military is my life. It's the only life I know. I wouldn't know who I was without it."

"So, you're going to retire a marine?"

"That's the plan. God willing."

"Or die a marine." There was a bite in her tone.

That got his attention. His eyes were focused directly on her. "Either way, I'm going to die a marine."

"And what happened the other night doesn't bother you?"

"Nothing happened." Luke's granite expression was back in place.

"Something happened."

Luke leaned forward and rubbed the palms of his hands together. "You need to learn when to leave well enough alone with me, Soph. I'm not Dan."

"I never said you were," she said in a low, calm tone.

"All I'm doing is having a conversation with a friend. Perhaps you should ask yourself why you're getting so defensive."

Luke sliced the air with his hand. "I'm not going to ask myself a damn thing when it comes to the other night."

"That's where you and Daniel are one and the same... You're both so pigheaded. There's no reasoning with either one of you! Stubborn jackasses right to the core!"

Luke sat back and crossed his arms over his chest. "Is that your professional opinion?"

Sophia felt her blood pressure skyrocket. "You might not want to hear it, but I work with men and women coming back from combat, and all of them have some sort of post-traumatic stress. I've seen it time and time again. You're tough, but you aren't immune. And being a soldier isn't everything you crack it up to be. Most of the time, the military just chews you up and spits you out when they're done. A lot of the veterans I see don't ever get the help they truly need."

Luke didn't respond for a minute, let the silence drag on. Then he said stiffly, "Are you done?"

"Yes."

"Are you sure?"

"I said yes, you royal pain in the butt!"

Sophia stopped talking and started watching the fire. She hadn't liked any of his answers, but she hadn't been a bit surprised. Any thoughts she had conjured up recently of Luke leaving the military in order to get to know her son was all a bunch of fantasizing. She had only herself to blame for the disappointment she felt. She wasn't being reasonable.

He was still staring at her, probably sizing her up, trying to figure out her angle. Finally, he restarted the conversation.

"What would you have me do? Give up my life? To do what, exactly? I'm no rancher."

She shrugged beneath the comforter. "I wasn't thinking of anything specific. I was just wondering if you thought you should give your family a break. Your mom shouldn't have to worry about losing another son."

"And what about you?" There was a gravelly quality to his voice that made her move her eyes from the fire to his face.

"What about me?"

"I thought maybe you didn't want to lose another Brand man."

Another bull's-eye. Did the man know absolutely everything that was in her head? It was unnerving!

Sophia pushed herself up a bit and met his gaze head-on. "I suppose I was talking about myself, too. More about my son, actually. You are the closest thing to Daniel he's ever going to have. It'd be nice if you didn't go off and get yourself blown up, as well."

What she had said sounded harsher in words than it had in her head, but it was the truth, and she couldn't make herself regret saying it.

To her surprise, Luke said, "I've thought about that."

"You have?"

"Quite a bit. That boy you're carrying is the closest link I have to my brother. He's my top priority, and whether you believe it or not, that's a strange concept for me. Nothing has ever taken priority over my career, and I sure as hell didn't expect it to happen now." He pinned her with his sky-blue eyes. "But it has happened, and I want little Danny to know me. I want to know him. Without my damned consent, you and your boy have changed everything!"

Quietly, she said, "I didn't know you'd given it that much thought."

"How could you unless I spelled it out? We've never been great at getting to the heart of things with each other...."

"Past tense," she added.

"I hope that's the case." Luke rubbed his hands together. "I'm trying here, Soph. I don't always do the right thing, and I sure as hell don't always say the right thing. But I *am* trying."

"I know you are, Luke. And I'm trying, too. You don't know how good it is to hear you say you want to be a big part of Danny's life. It means more to me than anything. It's a blessing."

"He's the blessing," Luke said without hesitation. "That boy—" he nodded toward her belly "—is the blessing. To me."

"It makes me feel good to hear you say that, too. Honestly, because of our past, I didn't really know how you'd feel about this baby. And, no matter what I tell other people, or what kind of brave front I put on, I'd be lying if I said that I'm not scared that I won't be able to raise Danny on my own without..."

"You're not on your own," Luke broke in. "You have me. The two of you have me. I'll help take care of Danny any way I can." He rubbed his hands together and dropped his head. "And, if you let me, I'll come to Boston and visit the two of your whenever I can."

Her words caught a bit in her throat as they came out. "I'd like that. You're welcome anytime."

Luke sat back and gave a nod. Business was conducted, and concluded, satisfactorily. "Good. I'm glad we worked that out."

She could still feel his eyes on her, and then he said, "You aren't going to start crying again, are you?"

"You're not going to let me live that down, are you? I'm pregnant, you know. I do have hormone issues!"

Luke held up his hand in quick defeat. "Hey, I was just going to offer you a box of tissues or something."

"Or a Christmas stocking, Captain?" she threw back quickly.

He winked at her. "Whatever works."

The next morning, Luke was the one to answer the phone when his family made their daily "checkup" call to Sophia. It was time to give them fair warning that he was at the ranch, and from the anxious sound in his mother's voice, he had no doubt that they would be moving up their arrival time. His family couldn't wait to welcome him home, and he was grateful. But there was a very real part of him that didn't want to deal with anyone other than Sophia. Selfishly, as much as he loved his parents and his siblings, this time alone with the woman he loved had been a dream coming true. He hated for it to end.

Once his family arrived, the dynamic between them would change. It was inevitable. The minute you threw other people into the mix, that was the result. And Luke didn't want things to change between Sophia and him. He liked things just as they were. Other than the fact that he wasn't at liberty to hug her, caress her and kiss her anytime he pleased, which would be his ultimate and impossible scenario, things couldn't be better.

But, on the flip side, having his family as a buffer might just be the very thing he needed. His desire for Sophia was escalating every day. He went to bed wanting her and he awakened wanting her. And the more receptive she was to him, the more she began to warm to him, the harder it was for him not to act on the impulse radiating from the lower half of his body.

Making love to Sophia was never far from his mind. No matter what time of the day. No matter what they were doing. He wanted to make love to her. He wanted to show her, with his body, how much he loved her.

In fact, day by day, it was becoming less of a want and more of a need. It was starting to become a worst-case scenario. Time to adapt. Time to change up the environment.

His family might just be the dose of reality he needed to get his libido under control. He was certain that having his mother fussing over him as if he was a child would kill his lust quicker than just about anything else could.

"Whatcha reading?" Sophia breezed into the kitchen looking well rested and perky. Her ponytail swung behind her as she walked and her cheeks were flushed, which gave him the impression she had already gotten in her daily yoga stretch.

He held up the baby book he had found in the library.

She gave him a bemused smile. "A little light reading, Captain?"

He didn't seem the least bit embarrassed for having been caught with the book. Instead, he pointed to something he had just read. "Says here that the baby can hear and recognize voices in the womb." He pointed at the page with his finger and looked at her. "So, Danny there will be able to recognize me once he makes an entrance."

She pulled some fruit out of the fridge. As usual, she had misjudged Luke. She would never have expected him to pick up one of her baby books. And yet, not only had he picked up, he was actually *reading* it!

"Feel free to talk to him whenever you want." She dumped some fruit into a bowl and brought it over to the table.

Before she could sit down, Luke gestured for her to walk over to where he was sitting. "Bring him over here, then." This was said gruffly, before he added, more softly, "Please."

She laughed at him and he liked the sound. "Okay."

Sophia stood directly in front of Luke and he looked up at her. "Do you mind if I put my hands on your stomach?"

She shook her head at him. "Be my guest." This was the strangest conversation she had ever had with Luke.

"I wouldn't expect this from you, Captain Brand," she said as he positioned his large, warm hands on both sides of her stomach.

"What?"

"What do you mean 'what'?" she asked incredulously. "This! You and me! You talking to my stomach." She laughed out loud again. "You have to admit that this is a bizarre scene, considering our history."

Luke held up his finger to his lips. "Shh. I'm trying to have a conversation with my nephew."

"Well, excuse me," she said with playful sarcasm. "Far be it from me to interrupt a personal conversation you're having with *my* stomach!"

Luke cleared his throat and acted as if he were about to give an important speech.

"You aren't handing down orders, you know. Just speak normally," she said as she watched him with curiosity. The marine in him was always near the surface; everything had to be planned and executed with precision.

He glanced up at her. "Are you being quiet?"

"Are you hurrying up? I'm hungry, and if you don't mind, I'd like to take my belly over to that chair and eat." She pointed at her bowl of fruit awaiting her arrival.

He drew his brows together and gave her a slightly disgruntled look, but he complied. After he had a brief conversation with his nephew, he sat back in his chair and seemed satisfied. Sophia didn't move away immediately. Instead, she reached out and put her fingers on each side of Luke's lips and lifted up the corners into a makeshift smile.

"How come you don't smile anymore? You used to smile. Remember? You used to have a nice smile before you became a marine and lost the ability to do it. Do the Marines discourage smiling, too?"

Luke gave her that "you are slightly off your rocker" look that made her smile at him broadly. She pushed up his lips up a little bit higher and said. "There. See? Doesn't that feel better?"

When she dropped her fingers, Luke's lips dropped back into their normal, unsmiling position. Sophia sat down and began to wolf down her breakfast.

He hadn't responded, so she prodded him again. "I'm serious. Your face doesn't move most of the time; it's strange. You used to smile all of the time. Now you don't. Is it against Marines protocol? Do they *frown* upon it... no pun intended."

True, she was teasing him, but she was genuinely curious about the fact that Luke had forgotten how to smile.

Luke took a sip of his coffee. "If the Marines wanted us to smile, they would have issued us one."

"Ah. I see," Sophia said before she savored her last bite of fruit. "More Marines logic. I still think you could smile once in a while when you're *not* in a combat zone. I like it when you smile. You're handsome when you smile."

Without hesitation, he said, "Then I'll smile more when I'm around you."

"Good. Start now." He was trying to please her and she was going to let him. Why shouldn't she?

"How's this?" Luke lifted up the corners of his mouth.

"Oh, my God!" Sophia shook her head. "Really bad. *Really* bad! You have to show your teeth. Okay, try again."

Luke wiped his hand over his goatee, smoothed it

down, as if that would help him smile more success-fully. He pulled his lips tightly over his teeth and bared them quickly.

"How was that?"

Sophia sighed dramatically and dropped her hand to the table. "You looked like you were in pain. Or crazy. Or both."

"It couldn't have been that bad." Luke crossed his arms over his chest.

Sophia nodded her head several times. "Oh. Yes, it was. Worse. I've never seen such a pathetic excuse for a smile. What have they done to you? You can't even smile properly anymore!"

Luke drained his cup and then winked at her play-fully. "But I can jump out of planes and blow stuff up."

She rolled her eyes. "Fine. Good. Wonderful. You still need to remind your face muscles that they have the abil-ity to move."

"I'll get right on it, ma'am," he said with another wink and his trademark half smile.

After breakfast they spent the rest of the morning pre-paring for the family to arrive the next day. Sophia was a good housekeeper who bordered on compulsive now that she was pregnant. On the other hand, Luke's mom was an *impeccable* housekeeper who knew where everything in her house belonged, right down to the last matchbook.

When the last pillow was plumped and put back into place, Sophia looked around the room with a satisfied nod. "Your mom should approve, don't you think?"

Luke leaned against the doorway to the sitting room and watched her. He had helped her right up to the last room, but now she could tell by his body language that he was done cleaning for the day. No doubt he was in the mood for an afternoon fire and a nap with Ranger.

"Mom will always find something out of place. It's just her nature."

"That's true. But I'd rather give her less to spot than more." She looked around again. "And we have the Christmas stuff unpacked. That was a big chore."

"Relax, Soph. Mom wouldn't want you wearing yourself down on her account."

She couldn't disagree with him, and yet there was something in her that didn't want to disappoint Barbara. Barbara had always embraced her as her own from the very beginning, which only made her want to please her more. But Luke was right. She had done enough. Her back was starting to ache and she felt weary.

With one last look, Sophia gave in and walked over to where Luke was standing. She faced him and rubbed her back with a sigh.

"It's going to be strange having everyone here with us. I'm used to it just being the two of us."

"Me, too."

Her eyes snapped open wide. His bluntness surprised her. "You, too?"

"I'm not big on crowds. Not even if the crowd consists of my own family."

"Hmm."

"Your back hurting?"

She gave a self-effacing laugh. "You know what…it is. I shouldn't have been so cocky about the fact that it hasn't for most of my pregnancy."

"Perhaps you're doing too much. Maybe you need to take it easy." He was concerned about her. She heard it in his voice. She could see it in his eyes. "Come here and I'll rub it for you."

Sophia hesitated. The thought of Luke putting his hands on her again made her feel nervous; she had such a strange reaction to his touch. But the lure of a back rub won out; she moved closer to him and turned around so he could reach her back. She closed her eyes as his large hands touched her lower back; she could feel the warmth of his hands through the material of her shirt. She pressed back into his hands as his fingers found the spot that bothered her the most. She heard herself spontaneously moan with pleasure.

"I suppose I don't have to ask how that feels."

"Uh-uh." That was all she could say. She didn't want to talk; she wanted to enjoy.

Luke didn't tire quickly, and finally, she was the one to end the massage. She stepped away from him, broke the contact between them. Beneath the material of her shirt, her skin felt hot where his hands had touched her.

She turned around to face him. "Thank you. You have no idea how good that felt."

"My pleasure," he said in a soft, low tone. "Any time."

Her laugh sounded a bit nervous even to her own ears. "I may take you up on that."

After a minute she changed the subject. "You know, all of my friends worked *and* went to school when they were pregnant. All I'm doing is hanging out here at the ranch. I feel like a real wimp when my body wants to rest."

"You're too hard on yourself, Sophia. Why don't you give yourself a break? You're a good woman. I don't know too many women who would put their lives on hold in another state so their in-laws can be a part of their grandson's beginning. Maybe I don't know *any* who would do that, who would be that selfless. You're helping ease my parents' pain over losing Dan by being here, and I'm telling you, I have a lot of respect for what you're doing."

"Thank you. It just felt like the right thing to do."

"Like I said. You're a good woman. The best."

Sophia cocked her head to the side and looked up at

him. "Thank you, Luke. Really. It means a lot to hear you say that. I never thought you liked me much, and I suppose I didn't think much of you in return; I'm glad those days are behind us. I owe you an apology, I think."

"You don't owe me anything."

"Yes, I do." She shifted her weight and continued to look up at him. "I misjudged you and I was wrong. You are a good man, Lucas Brand. A truly good and decent man. And for the first time I know why Daniel loved you so much, because, to be perfectly honest, I never got it. But this Luke—" she pointed at him "—is the Luke he knew. Now I know him, too."

After she finished, they both fell silent. She waited for him to reply, and she supposed he was waiting for her to continue. After a minute, she saw an amused glint enter his eyes.

"What?" she asked in response.

"Sometimes you look at me like you're looking at something under a microscope," he said, and she felt a blush of embarrassment creep up her neck. "Makes me wonder if you're trying to figure out where Dan ends and I begin."

Now he was looking at her as if *she* was something under a microscope.

She knew she was turning bright red in the cheeks, and the turn of the conversation was starting to make her feel flushed all over. There was something in Luke's eyes that made her feel like a desirable woman instead of a woman about to give birth. He was looking at her as if she was a woman worth wanting, and she just couldn't deny it anymore. Luke found her attractive. And, whether she thought it was appropriate or not, her body was responding to him. All he had to do was sweep her up in that predatory gaze of his and she would start to tingle all over.

Sophia licked her lips and thought about taking a step back from him, but her feet refused to move. Finally, she said, "You're right. I can't deny it. In the beginning, I did try to figure out where Daniel ended and you began. I think it was only natural for me to do that. But now... there isn't anything to figure out. When I look at you, Luke, I don't see Daniel anymore...I only see you."

Something primitive flashed in his eyes; something primitive in her nervous system exploded. She should have moved away, but she didn't. Instead, Luke pushed away from the wall to close the distance between them.

"I'm glad to hear it," he said in that low, gravelly voice of his that sent her pulse racing.

His hands moved to her face; his fingers pushed the tendrils that had escaped from her ponytail away from her forehead. The minute he touched her, the blood started rushing through her veins, and her breathing suddenly felt shallow; she took a sudden deep breath in through her nose. Every fiber in her body wanted to have Luke continue. Every thought in her head was screaming for him to stop.

"What are you doing, Luke?" she heard herself ask in a husky voice that didn't seem to belong to her.

"You're standing under the mistletoe."

She let out a nervous laugh. Truth be told, he was making her feel a bit giddy. "Do you want to kiss my hand again? Is that it?" It was a feeble attempt to put a humorous spin on the uncomfortable situation she found herself in.

"No," Luke said as he gently titled her chin up so he could look directly into her eyes. "I don't."

"What are you doing, Luke?" she asked again, this time more urgently. One of them had to stop, and for some reason that person wasn't her.

"I'm going to kiss you, Sophia." Her name rolled off his tongue like a caress.

Her heart skipped a beat and she felt herself lean toward him against her brain's explicit instructions. "Do you think that's a good idea?"

His lips hovered just above hers. "No," he said huskily, "I don't."

She was about to continue the conversation when she heard the slam of a car door. It gave her the out she needed, and she took it. "Did you hear that?"

"Yes." He didn't budge.

She made an irritated sound and pushed on his chest before she stepped around him. She walked over to the window and looked outside.

"Your mom said that they'd be back tomorrow, right?"

Luke had returned to his spot in the doorway. He seemed irritatingly relaxed as he leaned against the doorjamb, while she felt like a scrambled egg.

"That was the plan." Luke didn't seem the least bit distracted by the interruption. He was watching her in an observatory fashion, as if she were some fascinating animal at the zoo. His nonchalance really ticked her off.

Her voice became shrill as she threw her hands up into the air. "Then *why* are they in the driveway right now?"

Chapter Ten

Sophia glared at Luke in accusation. "Did you know about this?"

Luke shook his head. "Apparently Mom couldn't wait to welcome me home."

Sophia peered out the window one more time before she threw up her hands. "Well, a *little* warning would have been nice."

It was out of character for her to be flustered. She didn't like the feeling. And the fact that Luke seemed completely undisturbed by this sudden change in plans served only to irritate her more.

"Look at me!" Sophia waved her hands in front of herself. "I'm a mess!"

"You look fine," he said in a slightly dismissive tone that sparked off her temper.

She snapped at him. "What do you know?"

"I think I can tell if you look okay or not. I have eyeballs in my head," Luke replied. "Why are you getting hysterical?"

Hands on her hips, Sophia stopped in front of him. "I am *not* getting hysterical!"

Luke raised one eyebrow. "You're a little hysterical."

"Oh, zip it, Brand!" Sophia snapped. She struck the

palm of her left hand with her right hand in a slicing motion to emphasize her words. "I like order. I like a plan. Your family was supposed to be here tomorrow! And now that they're here early..."

"You're hysterical," Luke broke in.

"I am *not!* And even if I am *a little*...you're one to talk, Mister Marine, who has to have everything in perfect order and perfectly planned!"

"I was trained to adapt to any situation," he said seriously. "This one included."

At this moment, she really did wish that looks could kill. Luke was having an awfully good time at her expense, and if he hadn't tried to kiss her just a minute before, she wouldn't be feeling so wigged out.

"If you so much as say one more pro-Marine thing, I'm going to personally wring your neck!"

Her threat had the exact opposite effect on Luke that she wanted. His mouth curled up into his half smile and he had the audacity to wink at her. "Ooh-rah."

Sophia balled up her fists and let out a frustrated noise.

"That's it! We're not speaking!" Luke was incorrigible, and there was absolutely nothing she could do about it. When she realized that she wasn't going to convince Luke to join her emotional unraveling, *and* that her emotional unraveling was giving him a platform to irritate her more, she quit the conversation.

Unfortunately, she was never successful at the silent treatment. So, it lasted for about thirty seconds.

"It's your fault I'm freaking out, anyway!" Sophia stomped over to a mirror in the hallway.

"I thought you weren't speaking to me...."

Sophia leaned into the mirror and examined her face. There were smudges of dirt on her forehead and on her cheek. Perfect!

"God, you are *annoying!* You just couldn't leave well enough alone, could you?"

"Hey, I'm just standing here minding my own business." He had the gall to sound genuinely innocent of any wrongdoing.

Sophia took one look at her haphazard ponytail and threw up her hands again. There was no covering up the fact that it needed to be washed. She looked a mess. And she looked guilty! That was the real problem.

"Do you call trying to kiss me minding your own business?" she hissed at him under her breath; she didn't want anyone to hear her from the other side of the door. "Why would you *do* that? What were you thinking?"

Luke actually smiled with his teeth. "I was thinking that I wanted to kiss you." He was really enjoying this. His enjoyment served only to send her frustration shooting through the roof.

With one last disgruntled look at her own reflection, Sophia spun away from the mirror and returned to her spot in front of him. "Well, you shouldn't have!"

"Probably not," he agreed easily. Too damned easily! "Is that why you're coming unhinged? It wasn't a big deal. You gotta calm down. You look like you're breaking out in hives." He gestured to her neck.

"Not a big deal?" she asked, incredulously. "*Not* a big deal!"

"Nothing happened."

"Thanks to me!" she pointed out as she narrowed her eyes at him. "You know, it's really helpful that you've picked *this moment* to say more than two sentences in a row to me after a decade of one-liners!"

"Glad to be of assistance."

"I was being sarcastic!" She heard how shrill her own voice sounded to her ears; she immediately closed her eyes and took in a sharp, soothing, calming breath.

In her mind she repeated the phrase "I am calm, I am at peace."

"What are you doing?" Luke's annoying voice punctured her mental mantra and rendered the phrase useless.

Through gritted teeth, she said, "I'm calming myself by using a meditative phrase."

A few seconds later, Luke replied, "You might want to try something else. The blotches are still there."

Sophia opened her eyes and swiveled her head toward the object of her irritation. "Blotches? I should have a big red A stamped on my belly, thanks to you! How's that for a blotch!"

With one last hateful look at Luke and his stupid, smug, handsome face, Sophia plastered a welcoming smile onto her own face, walked over to the door and pulled it open.

She was greeted at the door by a cold blast of air and the family's German shepherd, Elsa. The minute Elsa spotted Luke, she raced into the entryway.

"Hey, girl!" Luke patted his chest for Elsa to put her paws on his shoulders. When she complied, Luke roughed up the fur on her neck and back.

At the moment, Sophia wanted to strangle Luke, but when she watched him with Elsa, it reminded her that he wasn't *completely* rotten to the core.

"Sophia, my dear! Hello!" Barbara Brand breezed into the foyer with her husband, Hank, following closely behind.

"Could you grab this, dear?" Barbara said to her tall, lean, silver-haired husband. She slipped out of her full-length faux-fur coat and handed it to Hank. As soon as Barbara was free of her winter trappings, she wrapped Sophia into her arms. "I've been so worried about you, my darling. How is my grandson?"

"We're both doing well. I'm glad to see you."

For a moment Barbara admired her with Luke's same clear, bright blue eyes. No matter what the weather, Barbara always looked as if she had stepped out of a fashion magazine; her blond hair was smoothed back into a flawless chignon and her ears were adorned with her signature pearl drop earrings. She had followed her husband to Montana, but she never let go of her Chicago roots.

Barbara pressed a kiss to Sophia's cheek before she turned her attention to her son. She moved quickly to Luke's side. She reached up and put her hands on both sides of his face. "Lucas. Lucas. You're finally home." Then, she wrapped her arms around her son and hugged him tightly.

Sophia watched as Luke engulfed his mother in a bear hug. "Hi, Mom."

When Barbara pulled back slightly to get a better look at her boy, she said, "You're so thin, Lucas. My goodness! Why are you so thin?" Then Barb reached up and touched Luke's goatee. "And this isn't my favorite!"

"He looks good, Barb! Leave the boy be." Hank slapped Luke on the back and clasped his hand with his.

"Good to see you, Dad."

"How's the leg, son?" Hank asked in his gruff, bass voice.

"Yes. How is your leg?" Barbara stepped back a bit and looked down.

"It's getting better. Don't worry."

Barbara gave him a stern look. "I'll be the judge of whether or not I should worry." She looked at her husband. "Imagine your son telling me what to do in my own house!"

For the first time in a long time, Sophia saw Luke look sheepish. His mom could put him in his place quicker than anyone she had ever seen. Luke went from surly soldier to compliant son when Barbara was around.

Barbara didn't make a move to let Luke go. She looked over at Sophia. "He hasn't been giving you too hard of a time, has he?"

Sophia and Luke locked eyes for a brief second. She shook her head. "No. He's been on his best behavior."

Until just before you arrived.

"Shame on you for not telling me you were coming home early!" Barbara said to her son.

"I wanted to surprise you," Luke said easily.

Before she could retort, Tyler, six foot four like his father and heartthrob handsome, walked through the door with the bags. "Hey! There he is!" he said as he dropped the bags on the floor and shut the door with his foot. He walked through to the entryway and engulfed both his mother and brother in a giant bear hug.

"Good to see you, man!" Luke looked genuinely happy to see his younger brother.

Tyler slapped his brother on the back several times before he swept Sophia up into a bone-crushing hug. "Hey, sis! Miss me?"

"You have no idea." Sophia laughed. Tyler was so handsome, with an easygoing cowboy charm, that it was hard for anyone to dislike him.

"Hank, what is she *doing* in there? Do you hear hissing…?" Barbara asked in an irritated tone. Elsa was whining excitedly in the kitchen.

Sophia and Luke looked at each other, and knew exactly what was occurring in the kitchen. Elsa had found Ranger, and Ranger had decided he did not *like* being found by the German shepherd.

Barbara stopped talking and walked decisively over to the kitchen doorway. She looked in for a moment, analyzed the situation and then turned her gaze to Luke.

"Lucas, darling?"

"Yes, Mother?"

"Why is there a kitten in the kitchen?"

Hank walked over to stand next to his wife. He seemed perplexed. "There's a kitten in the kitchen, Barb."

"I see that," she replied to her husband, and then she readdressed Luke. "There's a kitten in the kitchen, Lucas. Why is there a kitten in the kitchen, Lucas?"

"That's Ranger," Luke said nonchalantly; he winked at his brother.

"Why is *Ranger* on my kitchen table?" Barbara asked in a steady, precise voice.

Hank was shaking his head. "Why is there a kitten in the house? That's what I'd like to know. There wasn't a kitten here when I left two weeks ago, and there shouldn't be one here now!"

Sophia chimed in. "It's my fault he's on the table, Barb. I'll get him off."

Sophia moved toward the kitchen, but Tyler had already threaded his way past his mom and dad to scoop Ranger up; he held him in the air to get a good look at him. "Hey, Ranger! You're a funny-looking little cat, aren't you?" He held Ranger to his chest. "Who does he belong to?"

"Us," Luke said simply.

"He's going to grow into those ears." Sophia defended Ranger.

"Of course he will," Tyler agreed easily.

"Well." Hank said, "he's going to have to grow into them somewhere else."

That sparked off a loud, boisterous debate amongst the family. Barbara and Hank lead the charge for Ranger to find a new home, and Sophia, Tyler and Luke defended the gangly kitten's right to stay at Bent Tree.

"There isn't another place. This is it," Luke reasserted. He wasn't backing down. He was determined that Ranger was going to make his home at the ranch.

"Oh, for heaven's sake, Lucas! You know that we have so many other responsibilities to attend to. What possessed you to do such a thing?" Barbara asked, but her eyes softened when she looked at Ranger tucked into the crook of Tyler's arm.

"He's just one kitten, Mom," Luke said.

Hank shrugged out of his coat and pointed his finger at his son. "That kitten needs to find another place to call his own, Luke. You tell Bill to come back over and get him. Now, that's all there is to it."

Hank gave his wife one last look before he disappeared into the sanctuary of his study.

"Are you really going to throw an orphaned kitten out into the snow at Christmas, Ma? Is that the spirit of the season?" Tyler asked before he winked at Sophia.

All of them knew that Ranger was staying. Even Hank knew it. The Brand family had never turned their backs on a stray, and they weren't about to start with Ranger.

Barbara shook her head with a heavy sigh. It was a sound that signaled to Sophia that her mother-in-law had given in without much of a fight. Barbara walked over to Tyler, took the kitten into her hands and looked into his eyes. "And where did Billy happen to find you?"

"Truck stop bathroom," Luke filled in.

Barbara made a displeased noise. "Who would do such a thing? He's just a baby."

"He's a baby who needs a home," Luke added.

Barbara eyed her son over Ranger's head for a moment. "The battle is already won, Lucas. Anything at this point would simply be a waste of artillery. Haven't those Marines taught you anything?" Barbara ended her sentence with a raised eyebrow at Luke before she turned her attention back to the kitten that had melted in her hands. "Oh, for heaven's sake…" she said again, with another shake of the head. "I suppose Ranger will do."

Luke gave Sophia a satisfied look. Barbara was hooked and Ranger had a home. It was as simple as that.

The family had gathered for a celebratory dinner in Luke's honor. Barbara planned the menu and Sophia was happy to pitch in. She was grateful for the company and the distraction. She still couldn't believe what had just happened to her. She couldn't believe that Luke had tried to kiss her; and more important, she couldn't believe that she had actually considered *letting* him kiss her!

This *must* be a rebound reaction. It had to be! There was simply no other explanation for her behavior. Yes, she had discovered a very lovable, nurturing side of Luke she hadn't even seen before. And yes, she was enjoying his company. And yes, her body was responding to him in ways that could not be considered platonic. But, and this was a very big but, that didn't mean that she wanted anything more than friendship with Luke. And certainly, he didn't want anything more from her! The man had spent the better part of a decade giving her a stony expression and a hard time. And that was when he wasn't outright avoiding her!

Obviously the two of them were turning toward each other for comfort because they had both lost Daniel. It made sense. And it had to stop.

That's why, after she had gotten over her obsessive-compulsive meltdown, she was very glad that Luke's family had arrived when they did. Just in the nick of time!

After the dinner mess had been cleaned away, the family dispersed. Sophia, who hadn't been able to keep from seeking Luke out with her eyes all night, had been internally champing at the bit until the evening had ended and she could have a minute alone with him to set things straight. She was determined to find out what had happened between them, and to make certain that it never happened again.

Of course, whenever she had sneaked a glance at him, he wasn't looking back at her. In fact, he seemed completely relaxed and unaffected by their brief encounter. No doubt it had been meaningless to him, with his "woman in every port" attitude. No doubt he was just missing out on some random female companionship after a tour of duty, and she just happened to be convenient.

Whatever the reason, whatever the motivation, she was going to make certain it didn't happen again.

Sophia made it back to her room before Luke and claimed the bathroom first. She scrubbed the day's dirt off her body and face. Then she twisted her long wet hair up into a towel before she slathered moisturizing cream on her face.

For a minute she looked down at her belly. She was getting more pregnant by the day. She had a checkup this coming week, and she was starting to feel very impatient to have the pregnancy over so she could start getting to know her son. She also wanted to get back to her life in Boston. Whenever she emailed or spoke with her friends on the phone, she felt horribly homesick. She wanted to go home.

After she had finished her nightly routine, Sophia sat in a rocking chair next to the crib and scrolled through her emails. She was just wrapping up her responses when she heard Luke enter his room next door. She clicked on the send button, logged off and closed the laptop, then stood and pulled the towel off her head. On her way to Luke's room she dropped the towel over the tub, then ran a comb through her wet hair. Finally, with one last look in the mirror, she took a deep breath and tapped lightly on the door.

"Yeah?" Luke responded to the knock.

"You decent?" Sophia asked through the door in a hushed voice. Now that the rest of the family was milling around in the old farmhouse, she was going to have to watch the volume of her voice.

"Not likely," Sophia heard him say as he pulled the door open. His eyes gave her a clinical once-over that set her teeth on edge, before he turned back to hanging up his shirt.

She took one step inside the room and leaned her back against the wall. She watched him while he finished his chore. He was stripped bare to the waist and the top button of his jeans was undone. In spite of herself, she just couldn't stop admiring the way Luke's muscles rippled as he hung up his shirt.

Luke shut the closet door. "What's up?"

His face looked different. It took her a minute to figure out why. "You shaved your goatee."

Luke propped himself against the end of the bed. He reached up and rubbed his hand over his freshly shaven face. "No sense lighting Mom's fuse over nothing."

Sophia nodded. After a moment of uncomfortable silence, she found another way to avoid getting to the point.

"You aren't using your cane as much as you should," she replied, suddenly hesitant to start the discussion she knew they needed to have.

"Is that what you came in here to say?" he asked her. He was looking at her in a very odd way. He looked relaxed enough, but something in her gut told her that Luke was wound up tight as a drum beneath his nonchalant exterior. It was if he was waiting for something unpleasant to happen.

"No." Sophia didn't like the pouty quality to her voice, so she cleared her throat and started again. "No. It's not. But you should be using it anyway."

Luke crossed his arms over his chest and didn't bother to button his jeans. "I'll keep it in mind. Anything else?"

She didn't like his dismissive tone. "Yes, as a matter of fact, there is."

Instead of answering her verbally, he waved his fingers at her, as if to say, "Bring it on."

He was being rude, dismissive. She didn't like it. Sophia pushed away from the wall and closed the door to the bathroom behind her. She stepped closer to him and said in a low, demanding tone, "I think I deserve an explanation."

"For what?"

Now they were face-to-face. His arms were crossed over his chest; her hands were on her hips. "Are you serious?"

"You bet." He didn't bother to keep his voice down.

She waved her hand. "Shhhh."

"No one can hear us."

"You don't know that!"

Luke pulled the conversation back on track. "What's up, Sophia? What's on your mind?"

"The kiss," Sophia said bluntly.

Luke's eyes narrowed and he moved away from her. He put some distance between them before he turned back to her. "Jesus, Sophia. You're relentless. Once again you just can't leave well enough alone. Why do you have to go over and over the same issue again and again? We've already discussed this. It's over. Let it go."

"Don't put this off on me, Lucas. You tried to *kiss* me and you expect me to just forget about it?"

"Yeah. I do. Nothing happened." Luke jammed his hands into his pockets. "And my name is Luke. Not Lucas."

"I want to know why you tried to kiss me, *Lucas*. And don't try to put this off on me, implying that I'm a crazy pregnant woman! You owe me an explanation. After a decade of barely tolerating me, ignoring me and avoiding me, you try to *kiss* me? And if you don't want me to give you the third degree about something, then don't do it in the first place! I'm not one of your bimbos you can use up and toss aside like garbage. Now, explain it to me as if I'm stupid, because I really don't get it. What in the *hell* were you thinking?"

Chapter Eleven

Without a word, Luke stepped around her and jerked open the door to the bathroom. The look he gave let her know, in no uncertain terms, that he was finished with the conversation.

But she certainly wasn't. She turned slowly to face him and didn't move from her spot.

She shook her head. "Nice try. But I'm not leaving."

Luke shrugged nonchalantly and walked over to the bed with only a slight limp. His leg was noticeably stronger.

"Suit yourself," he said smoothly.

"What do you think you're doing?" Sophia asked as she watched him reach for the zipper of his worn jeans.

He pinned her with his ice-blue eyes, and she could have sworn that she detected a taunting glint in them.

"What does it look like I'm doing?" His tone was unmistakably suggestive. As those words came out of his mouth, he unzipped his pants in one quick, fluid motion.

"It looks like you're taking off your pants," she responded robotically. She knew she should admit defeat and return to her room, but she couldn't seem to move her feet.

"Your powers of observation are impressive." He said this while his pants were dropping to the ground. Luke stepped out of his pants and stood before her without any sign of modesty. He was trying to get her to leave by embarrassing her, but it wasn't going to work.

"I want an answer, Luke. Are you going to give me one?" She tried. She really did. But she couldn't take her eyes off him. She was a woman, and he was a man to be admired; she was tempted to run her hands over his skin, just to feel the strong muscles underneath. He was rock-solid and incredibly appealing.

She forced herself to jerk her eyes away from his taut abs just as he jerked the blanket back and climbed into his bed. He stopped briefly and stared her down; unsmiling, silent, he slipped onto his back. He sighed deeply as his head sank into the pillow. She watched as he pulled the blanket up to his waist and closed his eyes. She was actually glad for his closed eyes; her face felt as if it were burning up from embarrassment and...

Desire. There was no mistaking it. Her body was tingling all over; her heart was beating hard in her chest. There went those bells and whistles again, ringing loud and clear!

The room was silent for several moments while she pulled herself together. Sophia stared at Luke sprawled out in his bed and felt completely frustrated and inept to deal with him. Daniel and Luke were nothing alike when it came to stuff like this. Daniel would never do this sort of thing, and she had to admit that when it came to handling Luke, she was failing miserably.

"Oh, my *God,*" Sophia finally blurted out as she moved from her spot to stand next to the bed. She could tell by his deeper breathing that he was about to fall asleep with her standing in the middle of his room! "You are unbelievable! Truly unbelievable. Why do I even bother trying to talk to you about anything?"

Luke didn't bother to open his eyes. "If you stay in my room much longer, Sophia, I might just start to think you want me to pick up where I left off under the mistletoe...."

It took a minute for his words to sink in, but when they did, Sophia was overrun with guilt and embarrassment. The words hit too close to home. She opened her mouth and then shut it. She opened it again and then shut it again. She couldn't think of the perfect retort fast enough, and it was really ticking her off that she was standing in the middle of Luke's room acting like a beached guppy.

Finally she said through gritted teeth, "Go to hell, Luke."

She turned, walked into the bathroom and firmly shut the door behind her.

It was easy to avoid Luke for the next couple of days, and Sophia was glad, for the most part, that they could take a break from each other. There was so much to do in preparation for the holidays, and most of it required her to fill her time helping Barbara. Luke spent most of his time in the barn with his brother and father, which made keeping him at a distance an easy thing to do. There seemed to be a silent agreement of avoidance between them at this point, and even though she had zero desire to speak to him after his rude behavior, it irked her no end that Luke had decided to avoid her, as well.

And, truth be told, she missed his insufferable company. She actually felt a sense of loss without him near. She didn't understand how she could have allowed herself to get attached to him so quickly. But it made her believe that this sudden break was a good idea. After all, he was going back to active duty as soon as he was healed. He was a military man and nothing was going to change that fact. Certainly not her and her baby, no matter how much he cared for her son. Luke was Luke, and the Marines always came first.

But she couldn't stop herself from missing the jerk no matter how hard she tried, and it was that feeling of missing him that drove her to cross the threshold into his bedroom on the third morning of their unspoken pact to give each other space. He was long gone; she had heard him leave near the crack of dawn to go into town with his brother to pick up Jordan and Josephine. She walked over to the bed, picked up his pillow, and brought it up to her nose. She breathed in deeply. It smelled like Luke. She couldn't remember why his scent had ever reminded her of Daniel. He had his own very distinctive scent that seemed to drive her senses crazy.

Sophia hugged the pillow to her chest and walked over to the uniform hung on the outside of the closet. She ran her hand over the stripes on the sleeves and the rows of medals pinned to the breast. As her fingers touched each individual medal, a very disturbing thought passed through her mind: *Am I falling for Luke?*

"Am I?" Sophia asked softly, out loud. She hugged the pillow tighter to her chest for a minute, stared at the uniform for several seconds, before she threw the pillow back onto the bed.

"I could be falling for Luke," she said to herself as she returned to her room. When you stand in a man's room smelling his pillow and touching his clothing, you're either falling in love or you are a stalker.

How in the world could this have happened? Was she that weak? That hard up? That susceptible? The last thing she should be doing is developing feelings for Luke.

"Pathetic," Sophia said to herself as she slumped into her rocking chair. It took a full hour, but Sophia tired of her own self-pity and headed downstairs. Barb was busy in the kitchen preparing for her daughters' arrival home, and Hank was in his study with Ranger, his new faithful companion.

"I was wondering when you were going to show up," Barb greeted her. "Here, have some juice."

Sophia sat down at the table and gratefully accepted a tall glass of orange juice. "What time do you expect them back?"

Barb popped some bread into the toaster. "Two more hours. It's going to seem like twenty." Barb smiled at Sophia as she opened the fridge. "What kind of jam? Grape, strawberry…?"

"Do we have raspberry in there? I can't remember."

Barb pulled out a jar. "Raspberry it is."

Sophia slowly ate the toast and polished off her juice while Barb peeled a bowl of potatoes. "Can I help you with something?"

"I can always use an extra set of hands," Barb said with a smile. She put down her peeler and wiped off her hands with a dish towel. "But first, I found something you may be interested in."

"What's that?"

"Follow me and I'll show you."

They moved into the family room and Barb pointed to a book box on the coffee table. "I found this last night in the attic. I couldn't believe I had overlooked it."

"What is it?"

"Some things Daniel saved from college."

Sophia's eyes widened. "You're kidding?"

Sophia sat down and pulled the box toward her.

"I'll give you some time to go through it."

"Thanks," Sophia said off-handedly as Barb disappeared. Her focus was completely on the box. It was like finding a hidden treasure.

Sophia slowly opened each flap of the box, pushed them down and ran her hand over the rough cardboard. She had no idea what was in the box, or how it would make her feel to explore the objects treasured enough by her husband to save them.

Carefully, and with reverence, Sophia pulled the items out of the box. Most of the items were standard and expected: his trophy from his favorite swim meet, an A paper from a political science class, an unframed picture of the two of them at their first college dance, and plastic gold beads from their trip to New Orleans Mardi Gras. He also had items in the box that didn't make any sense at all. There was a large gold paper clip, a broken fountain pen and a black marble.

Sophia spread the items out on the table and looked them over. It was strange to see her husband's college years reduced to a few random items. She would give anything to ask him what in the world possessed him to save a paper clip and a black marble. After a while, Sophia pulled the box toward her and tipped it on its side so she could load the items back into the box. At the very bottom of the box, Sophia noticed a weathered white envelope. She reached in and grabbed it. She pushed the box back to the middle of the table as she looked at the return address on the envelope.

"Second Lieutenant Lucas Brand," Sophia read aloud. The postmark was dated the year of her engagement to Daniel.

Why would Daniel hold on to this letter for so long?

Sophia peeked inside the envelope and eyed the single handwritten note. She carefully pulled the letter from the envelope and unfolded it slowly. After she read the first couple of words, her heart began to thud harder in her chest, and she felt chilled all over her body.

Dan,
Mom tells me you're engaged. Congratulations. I wish you had told me yourself, but I guess you were

waiting for the right time. I want you to know that
I'm really happy for you. You know me well enough
to know that if I say it, I mean it. The last thing I
want is for this to come between us. Nothing has
ever come between us; I'm not going to let anything
start now. You're my twin brother and that comes
first with me. The fact that I'm in love with Sophia
doesn't change the fact that I want my brother to
be happy. She makes you happy, and I'm happy
for you. I can't help how I feel about her any more
than you can. It is what it is. I love her, but if I can't
have her, then I'm at least glad that she's with a
man who will take good care of her. You want me
at the wedding as your best man, and I'll be there
if I can get leave. I'd do anything for you, brother...
even marry you off to the woman I'm in love with.
I have one stipulation as your best man: never tell
Sophia how I feel about her. Take it to your grave.
I'll have your word on this. I love you and I'll see
you soon if I can....

The letter continued, but Sophia stopped reading. She
sat in stunned silence and tried to make sense of what she
had just read. In his own handwriting, in his own words,
Luke had written that he was in love with her. Suddenly
everything she had been feeling from him over the past
couple of weeks became crystal clear: the attempted kiss,
the smoldering look in his eyes when he looked at her
and the very fact that he came home early out of concern for her. As it turned out, Allie and her instincts had
been dead-on accurate. Luke loved her. For all of these
years, since they were in college, he had loved her. And
Daniel had kept his secret. How could he have kept that
from her for their entire marriage? Twin or not, he wasn't

supposed to keep secrets like that from her! What else didn't she know?

With the letter in hand, Sophia went to the kitchen.

"Anything interesting in that box?" Barb asked over her shoulder. "My boy was such a pack rat. No telling what junk he thought was essential to save."

Sophia held up the letter. "I found this."

"What is it, darling?"

"A letter that Luke wrote to Daniel."

"Really? Anything sordid I should know about?" Barb joked, but when she turned her attention from the stove to Sophia, her expression changed from humor to concern. "What's wrong, honey? You look pale. Here, sit down."

"I don't want to sit down, Barb. I want you to read this."

Barb took the letter with a furrowed brow. Barb quickly scanned the letter, but her face lacked the surprise that Sophia expected.

Without a word Barb refolded the letter, put it back in the envelope and handed it to Sophia.

"Well?" Sophia prompted.

"Come here, darling. Let's sit down. There's no sense in you getting yourself all upset. It's not healthy for the baby."

Sophia's mouth dropped open. "Don't get upset? Are you kidding? You did *read* it, didn't you?"

"Yes." Barb slid a chair back and patted it. "Here, honey. Sit down and we'll sort this out."

Reluctantly Sophia sat down at the table. Once Barb was seated, Sophia said, "Why do I get the feeling that you aren't surprised by what's in that letter?"

"Here, have a cookie. It will make you feel better." Barb offered her a plate of chocolate chip cookies that had just come out of the oven.

"No. Thank you." Sophia couldn't imagine ever feeling hungry again. Her stomach was tied up tightly into knots. A cookie certainly wasn't going to make anything better.

"To answer your question, no, I'm not surprised by the content of that letter."

"You're not?"

"No."

Sophia took a minute to digest the response. Then she asked, "So you're telling me that you knew that Luke is in love with me? Or, at least he *was* in love with me back in college?"

"Yes." This simple response sliced through Sophia's chest.

"How do you know?"

"Luke told me," Barb said simply, as if she were reading off a recipe.

"Luke told you," Sophia repeated dumbly. After a second anger bubbled up inside her and was reflected in her voice. "Who else in the family knows about this?"

"There just isn't any need to get so upset...."

"Barb, I don't want to be rude to you, but please don't tell me how to feel right now. I already had my fair share of emotional minutiae to work through when Daniel was killed and I found out I was pregnant. I honestly don't need this on top of everything else. Could you please just tell me, who else knows about Luke being in love with me when we were in college?"

"I don't believe that the past tense is appropriate. I believe that he is still very much in love with you."

Sophia could feel her skin flush bright red on her cheeks. She ignored Barb's last comment and stuck to the original question. "Who else knows?"

"Directly?"

"Directly, indirectly, through osmosis..."

"Hank knows, of course.

"Because you told him…"

"Because I told him."

"Who else?" Sophia demanded. Her stomach started to ache.

After a few long seconds, Barb said, "I suppose everyone knows in their own way. We're a tight-knit family." This was said with pride. "Secrets have a way of working their way out into the open. But none of the siblings have been told directly, to answer your question." She paused for a second before she added, "Not that anyone would need to be told. When Luke looks at you, it's there in his eyes for anyone to see."

"So what you're telling me is that I'm the *only one* in the entire family who *didn't know* that Luke was in love with me?" Sophia quieted her voice and shook her head. "How is that possible?"

"You didn't know because you didn't *want* to know, dear, which is perfectly understandable. You were in love with Daniel…."

"Still am," Sophia broke in.

Barb gave a quick nod as she continued. "But in your heart, if you look back, you've always known on some level. You're a smart cookie." She reached out and gave Sophia's arm a pat. "I'm going to make some tea."

"I don't want any."

"Of course you do." Barb stood in front of her cabinets. "Now, where did I move the tea bags?"

"Second cabinet on the left. Behind the spices." Even to Sophia's own ears, her voice sounded robotic. She felt numb all over, as if her limbs had turned to lead. In one moment her reality had been altered; the sky was green, the grass was blue.

Sophia watched as Barb put on the kettle. She sat perfectly still, but her mind was racing. Her previous encounters with Luke were rolling through her mind like a motion picture. She tried to remember every look, everything he had ever said to her. As hard as she tried to conjure up a memory that would have given her some inkling that Luke was in love with her, all she could remember was his surly attitude, and his constant disapproval of her.

Barb placed a steaming cup of tea in front of her. "Lemon?"

Sophia shook her head.

"Honey?" Barb asked.

Another quick shake of her head. "No. Thank you."

Barb rejoined her at the table with her own cup of tea.

"I can't seem to make any sense of this, Barb." Sophia ignored the tea. "Luke has always disliked me. *Always.*"

"No. He has never disliked you. He could never dislike you. He's pushed you away. For a good reason. For his own sanity. For his relationship with his brother. What better reason is there? Can you think of one?"

"Are you saying that Luke has been giving me a hard time for a decade because he's in love with me?"

"Yes," Barb said simply. "That's exactly what I'm saying."

Sophia and Barb stared at each other and for several moments neither said a word. In that brief moment of silence Sophia was able to read the sincerity in Barb's eyes. This wasn't a joke. Barb had just confirmed the content of the letter.

Sophia shrugged her shoulders with a sense of helplessness. Her entire insides were shaking, her armpits were sweating and she felt as if she wanted to scream, but instead she asked, "What am I supposed to do with all of this?"

"That depends."

"On what?"

Barb pinned her with those bright blue eyes of hers. "On how you feel about Luke."

How did she feel about Luke? At this point, she had absolutely no idea!

"I'm in love with Daniel, Barb. That hasn't changed." This was a dodge and she didn't care.

"I have a theory about being in love," Barb said after she took a small sip of tea. "Being in love is a dynamic experience. One that requires interaction between people. A living thing, if you will. I know how much you love Daniel. I know how much you will always love Daniel. But my dear boy is gone, God rest his soul. And you—" Barb looked at her with steady, wise eyes "—are here. Among the living. You have a heart. You have needs. And there's absolutely nothing wrong with that! It takes two people to be in love. You love Daniel, yes. But you are 'in love' with Luke."

"I'm not *in love* with Luke," Sophia denied quickly.

"Oh, my dear. I beg to differ. I've been watching the two of you ever since I returned home. I believe that you return Luke's feelings. Perhaps you don't want to. Perhaps you think it's inappropriate…."

"To say the least!"

"But you love him nonetheless."

Instead of denying it again, Sophia took a different approach. "And you approve? Is that what you're saying? I'm pregnant with Daniel's baby and you are giving me the green light to date your other son? Don't you think that's a little…"

"Modern?" Barb asked with a mischievous smile.

"*Bizarre* is more the word I was searching for."

Barb's demeanor took on a more serious affect. "I don't think it's bizarre at all. If you ask me, it's the best thing that could happen to my family. Yes, I've lost one of my boys, and I will miss him for the rest of my life, but Luke is still here. He's alive. And he deserves to find happiness with the woman he has always loved." Barb's hand was on her arm again. "Daniel would approve. Daniel would want Luke to raise his son. How could that be wrong, or *bizarre,* as you put it? How could it be anything but wonderful, if God wills it?"

"And you don't think the rest of the family would object? Hank? He wouldn't object?" Sophia asked, and then added quickly, "Not that I'm saying anything is going to happen between Luke and me…I'm just curious."

"Everyone loves you. Everyone loves Luke. It's a match the entire family would get behind."

It took several minutes for Barb's words to sink in, but when they did, Sophia felt more confused than ever. She rubbed her temples with her fingertips. "My head aches."

Barb reached out. "Here. Let me have your hand."

Sophia stopped rubbing her head and extended her hand to her mother-in-law. Barb gave her fingers a reassuring squeeze. "Dear Sophia. I have loved you since the day Daniel first brought you home. You know that, don't you?"

Sophia nodded.

"You trust me not to lead you astray, don't you?"

Again Sophia nodded.

"Good! Then listen to me now. You're so young! You have so much living to do. Don't throw away happiness with both hands just because you think the timing is wrong. Life isn't like that. You have to go for it when you can! Grab the brass ring and don't let go. Luke loves you. He's a one-woman man, and you are *that* woman. You have always been that woman. And whether you believe it or not, Luke is the romantic one out of my twin boys. Not Daniel. Once he gives his heart away, there's no turning back. Why do you think he's been single all of these years?" Barb gave her fingers another squeeze. "His heart belongs to you, Sophia. And if I'm correct and you have given your heart to him, the only advice I can give you is go for it. Go for it, Sophia, and never look back!"

Chapter Twelve

The conversation with Barb had sent Sophia reeling. She retreated back to her bedroom to get her head screwed on straight. She tried everything to calm herself down, to make sense of what had just happened to her. Nothing worked. She paced, she tried to meditate and she took a hot bath. None of it helped; she felt as if a sinkhole had just opened and swallowed up her life. She couldn't seem to wrap her head around what had just happened to her.

Luke *loved* her.

"And Daniel knew."

All she could do was sit in the window seat, stare out at the driveway, and wait for Luke to return home from the airport. The minute he got home, they were going to have it out. Her shock had long since turned to anger.

How could she have been so blind?

How could she have been so *naive?*

All those years of fighting and bickering and Luke treating her like a second-class citizen had been a facade to protect himself. He had tortured her for years with his surly attitude and his "not so quiet" disapproval of her. It had all been a lie to cover his tracks!

She didn't know how long she waited impatiently

on the window seat for Luke to return, but it was long enough that her backside was numb.

Finally, *finally* she saw the truck turn up the drive. She sprang into action and headed downstairs.

She poked her head into the kitchen. "They're here."

Startled, Barb turned quickly, her face bright with anticipation. "They're here?"

Sophia nodded as she pulled on her coat. She could barely get the thing buttoned over her bulging belly, but after a minute of struggle and cursing under her breath, the button hooked.

Barb knocked on her husband's study door. "Henry! Come on. They're here!"

Sophia opened the door, ignored the sharp, cold air that blasted in her face, and stood at the edge of the porch stairs. As the truck pulled up, she could see Luke in the front seat. His eyes were on her with that same intense look he always gave her. Armed with her new information, that look made perfect sense. He was looking at the woman he loved: her.

Hank and Barb emerged from the house, and they all walked down the drive together. Tyler, Luke and Jordan piled out of the truck.

"Where's Josephine?" Barb asked.

"Hi, Mom." Jordan threw her arms around her mother.

Barb hugged her daughter tightly. "Hi, my beauty!" Barb kissed her on the cheek and then asked again, "Where's Josephine? Don't tell me she missed her flight!"

Jordan was hugging her father now.

Tyler spoke up. "She isn't coming, Mom."

"What do you mean, she isn't coming? Why not?"

Jordan had her head buried against Hank's chest. She turned her head slightly and said, "She's protesting the war."

"Protesting the war?" Each word was enunciated precisely. "What does that mean exactly?"

Jordan untangled herself from her father and made her way to Sophia. "She's not coming because Luke is a warmongering imperialist and her antiwar, peace-loving convictions won't allow her to stay in the same house with him."

Tyler raised his eyebrow at Jordan. "Is that a direct quote?"

Jordan shrugged nonchalantly. "I may have taken some creative liberties, but you guys got the gist, right?"

Barb was temporarily stunned speechless; Sophia had never actually seen that happen before. Then she snapped out of it. "Tyler, Henry, bring Jordan's bags, will you? I'm going to attend to this."

Without another word, Barb turned and disappeared through the front door. Sophia shook her head as she watched Barb disappear into the house. This was the last thing she would have expected from Josephine. It was the last thing that the Brand family needed at a time like this. What was normally levelheaded Josephine thinking?

"Wow, Soph! You're *huge!*" Jordan threw her arms around her and squeezed her tightly. Jordan leaned back and smiled broadly at her with straight, even, white teeth. "Still gorgeous, but *huge!*"

"Jesus, Jordan… Don't tell her that!" Tyler poked his head around the back of the truck.

"It's okay. I *am* huge." Sophia hugged her sister-in-law. Ever-blunt Jordan. A trait inherited directly from Barb.

Jordan put her hand on Sophia's belly. "So, when do you pop this little guy out?"

"Not soon enough." Sophia laughed. Jordan and she had always gotten along. Jordan was so much like Daniel: quick to smile, quick to laugh and always full of things to say.

Jordan dropped a quick kiss on Sophia's cheek before she headed into the house. "I'm freezing my butt off! Thank God I go to school in California!"

Tyler and Hank started to move toward the house, as well. "You coming?" Tyler asked her over his shoulder.

"Not yet," she said. Luke had headed to the barn soon after they had arrived. She couldn't have planned a more perfect opportunity. The two of them would be alone and the rest of the family would be occupied with Josephine.

Sophia found Luke at the other end of the barn chopping wood. His cane was propped up against the barn and he was hitting the wood in a way that let her know that he wasn't pleased with his sister's decision to stay in California.

Luke stopped his work for a minute and watched as she approached. His expression was neutral; no doubt he was wondering about her sudden appearance back in his life after days of avoiding him. When she looked back, her campaign to avoid him had been a childish thing to do.

"You shouldn't be out in the cold," he said as he wiped the sweat from his brow.

"You shouldn't try to boss me around."

She crossed her arms over her chest and stared him down through slightly narrowed eyes. Could this man really love her? It still didn't seem possible. It didn't seem likely or probable. She wouldn't believe it until she heard it from his lips, and his lips alone.

Luke straightened to his full height and gave her an expression she could describe only as "fed up." "Is there something you want, Sophia? Or did you just come out here to pick another fight with me?"

Sophia closed the distance between them, but stood off to the side as Luke swung the ax down and slammed it into the wood.

"We need to talk," she said bluntly.

Luke swung the ax again. "So talk."

Suddenly all the words that had been throbbing in her brain jammed up behind her lips and she couldn't say a word. She stood there and watched him swing the ax again and again while she tried to figure out how to begin.

Where was her righteous indignation? Where was her moral outrage?

Both had abandoned her, right at the very moment she needed them the most!

Finally, she pulled the letter out of her pocket and held it out to him. "I found this today."

"What is it?" He didn't bother to look at her.

"A letter you wrote to Daniel. About our engagement."

That got his attention. Luke jammed the ax into the wood and took a step toward her. His face was stony. "What did you find again?"

"You heard me," she said firmly as she waved the letter in the air. "This letter says that you love me. Is that true?"

Luke looked around to see who might be within earshot before he walked over to her. He took the letter, glanced at it quickly before he stuffed it into his coat pocket. Then he wrapped his fingers around her wrist and began to walk toward the interior of the barn.

"Where are we going?" she asked and tugged at her arm. It didn't hurt; she just didn't like him leading her around like a pet. He immediately let go and they both stopped.

"It's too cold out here for you. Your lips are blue."

"What does that have to do with whether or not you love me?"

His eyes swept her face, and rested on her trembling lips. "You figure it out."

Luke continued to walk, but she refused to budge.

He stopped and turned. "Are you coming?"

She didn't like the authoritative tone he was using. So she snapped back, "Are you going to answer my question?"

Luke swept his hand toward the office. "Get out of the cold and I'll answer any damn question you have, Soph. Okay?"

"Fine." Grudgingly Sophia followed him to the heated office. In all honesty, although she didn't want to let on to Luke, she was actually grateful to get out of the cold. Boston was cold during the winter, but this was a different kind of cold. This was the type of cold that chilled your bones until they felt as if they were about to crack.

Luke held the door open for her. "You always have to have the last word, don't you?"

Sophia eyed him as she walked through the door. "I could say the *exact* same thing about you, Brand." The warm air from the heater blasted her face and, almost instantly, the winter wear she was bundled up in seemed oppressive. "In fact, I *will* say the same about you!"

Luke shut the door firmly behind him. He yanked off his gloves and tossed them onto the desk. "I don't remember you giving Dan this much of a hard time."

"Daniel didn't spend every single one of his waking moments trying to think up reasons to antagonize me," Sophia snapped. She stood in one spot and didn't remove her outerwear, even though she was starting to sweat profusely under her arms.

"Dan was a saint," Luke said easily.

"Compared to you," she retorted.

Luke shrugged out of his coat and pulled the cap off his head before he closed the short distance between them. As he approached, her heart started to thud in her chest; deeper, harder, longer beats.

"You've got that straight, sweetheart," he said in that

gravelly, suggestive voice of his. "Dan was the good twin."

Her stomach clenched when he reached out and unwrapped the scarf from her neck. It was a possessive move that she should have stopped, and yet...she didn't.

Her scarf joined his gloves on the desk. He reached out and began to unbutton her coat, his eyes locked with hers. He was giving her that hungry, restless, possessive look she had seen in his eyes before; she couldn't look away. She didn't want to look away.

One after another, Luke popped the buttons loose on her coat. When he reached the last one, he circled behind her and slipped it off her shoulders. When he pulled her wool hat off her head, the trance was broken and her temper flared.

"Hey! You don't have the right to manhandle me, Brand!"

Luke dumped the rest of her stuff on the desk. "Jesus, woman! Why are you so dramatic? You haven't seen manhandling."

Sophia cocked a brow at him. She had the distinct feeling that Luke could show her a thing or two about manhandling should she ever ask. A pleasurable kind of manhandling.

She shook her head at him. "You're stalling."

Luke leaned back against the desk and crossed his arms over his chest. The Marine mask was firmly in place. "What is it you want to know?"

A blush of embarrassment and anger stained her neck. She could feel the heat rush into her cheeks as she put her hands on her hips. "Do...you...love...me!"

"Friends love each other, don't they? And that's all we are to each other, right? Just friends?"

"That's not an answer, and you know it!"

"Perhaps it's not the answer you wanted, but it's the answer you got."

"It's not good enough."

"I don't know what to tell you," Luke said with a shrug. "It's the only one you're gonna get."

This time Sophia stepped closer. "Barb said that you're in love with me. She says that you've *always* been in love with me. Is. That. True?"

Luke's jaw clenched. A small crack in the mask. "Mom needs to learn to mind her own damned business."

"Be that as it may. Is it *true?* Is it?" Sophia threw up her hands. "Well? Is it? God, Luke, just *answer* the question! Do you love me?"

Luke looked off to the side for a minute while she waited. She waited to the count of ten rapid heartbeats in her own chest before he looked back at her and simply said, "Yes."

He said it so bluntly, so starkly, without any fanfare or emotion, that it caught her completely off guard. "Yes?" she repeated for no reason at all. Her heart slammed into overdrive and she felt the blood drain from her face.

Luke saw Sophia sway to the left, saw the color drain from her face, and he was immediately at her side. He steadied her with both of his hands on her shoulders. "Take it easy," he said gently.

Truth be told, Sophia wasn't the only one having a physical reaction to the conversation. Luke felt a little sick himself. For the first time in ten years, he didn't have to hide his feelings from Sophia. It was a relief that he never expected to have. But that relief was overshadowed by fear. The idea of her limiting his contact with her son because it was too awkward between them was tearing him up inside. He knew he could never have Sophia; she would always look at him as a runner-up to Dan. But the boy? He couldn't stand the thought of losing him.

Sophia opened her eyes once she felt the dizziness pass. She brushed Luke's hands off her shoulders and moved over to the other side of the small room. Her mind was racing and she didn't know exactly what she wanted to say. There was a tense silence in the room as they both contemplated each other.

Finally, she said, "You love me?"

The mask was back. "That's what I said." Short, clipped, unemotional.

"You've been in love with me for ten years?" she elaborated. "Since college?"

"What is it about the answer 'yes' that's confusing you?"

Sophia's temper flared again. She waved her finger in the air. "Don't you get sarcastic with me, Luke. I'm not the one who sprang all of this on you when you are nearly nine months pregnant! I have a right to ask a few questions."

"Technically, you couldn't spring anything on me when I'm nearly nine months pregnant because I'm not a chick. I don't have a womb. Or ovaries for that matter, so…"

"Zip it, Brand!" Sophia interrupted him. She started to pace. Periodically, she glanced at him as she moved back and forth in the small room. "I'm pregnant, my husband is gone! I'm stuck in Montana, away from my business, my friends and my life." She stopped pacing to emphasize her words; she pointed to her chest. "And now I find out that, although you have acted like you couldn't stand me for the last ten years, you have actually been in love with me for ten years. I believe I've earned the right to ask a few questions!"

"Fine."

"You're damn right it's fine!"

"So ask," Luke said.

"I will!" Sophia started to pace again. When it was time to ask a question, she stopped. "When exactly did all of this 'falling in love' take place?"

She sounded like a prosecuting attorney grilling the defense's star witness. She didn't care.

Luke pushed away from the desk. "Before I answer any questions, I want you to promise me something."

"I'm not promising anything at this point," Sophia said angrily.

"Then this conversation is over." Luke turned around and grabbed her coat.

"Fine!" Sophia snapped. She knew Luke well enough to know that he would clam up in a heartbeat and never answer her questions. And she wanted answers to those questions. She needed answers to those questions. "What do you want?"

Luke kept the coat in his hands. "I want you to promise me that no matter what I say…no matter how you *feel* about what I say…you won't take that baby away from me."

Sophia felt as if Luke had physically slapped her. She was quiet for a split second before she said, "I wouldn't ever do that to you. Is that what you think of me?"

"Just promise," he demanded. She heard pent-up emotion resonating in his voice. It hit her that Luke was truly worried about losing his nephew, and her heart went out to him.

"I promise you, Luke. Of course, I promise. You are the closest thing my son will ever have to his father. I would be crazy to keep the two of you apart," she said firmly. "And I'm not crazy."

Luke accepted her answer and dropped her coat back onto the desk.

Satisfied, Luke answered the question. "I fell in love

with you the minute I saw you." Luke was looking over her shoulder.

"When? The day Daniel introduced you to me?" Sophia tried to recall that moment, tried to remember the look in Luke's eyes. But she could only faintly remember Luke because she had been so wild about Daniel. All of her focus had been on him.

"No." Luke's lip raised in a faint smile. "Not that day." He ran his hands over his cropped hair and sighed. "I fell in love with you weeks before."

Sophia shook her head. "What are you talking about? I'd never met you before that day."

"You hadn't met me. But I had seen you."

"Where?"

"Nordstrom's Department Store."

"Nordstrom's Department..." Her voice trailed off. She had worked at Nordstrom's in the fragrance department all through college and graduate school. She rubbed her temples; her head was throbbing.

There was nothing left to lose as far as Luke was concerned, so he added, "You were talking to a customer. The minute I saw you, I stopped in my tracks. You laughed at something, and I fell in love with you on the spot. I'd never seen anyone in my life as gorgeous as you. I still haven't."

Her legs felt heavy. She sat down in a chair and tried to process what she had just heard. After a minute, she shook her head and said, "But, if that's true, why didn't you come up to me? You never hesitate to go after what you want."

"You were working."

"You could have waited."

"You don't think I haven't been kicking myself about that for ten years? If I had just waited, you would have been mine. Mine. Not Dan's. Mine!" Luke hit himself once on the chest. "But I couldn't wait. I had a meeting with a recruiter, and I couldn't be late."

"You didn't come back for me." There was an accusation in her tone.

Luke's eyes darkened. "Like hell I didn't!"

Sophia had been staring at her wedding ring. She lifted her eyes to meet his. "When?"

"The next morning. You were gone. The lady you worked with told me you had a family emergency, that you wouldn't be back for several weeks. She gave out entirely too much information about you, but that's beside the point."

"That's when Grandpa died...."

"I suppose." Luke sat down in the desk chair so Sophia could look at him without craning her neck.

"I met Daniel when I got back," Sophia said softly, as much to herself as to Luke. "Are you telling me that this was some bizarre cosmic coincidence? You fall in love with me, and then two weeks later I fall in love with your twin brother?"

This wasn't a line of questioning Luke wanted to pursue. There were parts of this story that he'd rather leave unsaid.

Sophia noticed Luke's hesitation and prodded him. "Well?"

Luke took a deep breath in, and let it out in a long, slow, measured breath. "No. It wasn't a bizarre, cosmic coincidence."

"Then, what was it?"

"It was Dan being Dan."

"What's that supposed to mean?"

"Like you said, Dan didn't have a mean bone in his body. But he was a practical joker. And I was his favorite target."

"What does that have to do with me?"

"I told him about you."

"And?" Sophia started to feel queasy. She didn't like where any of this was going, but she couldn't stop herself from going there.

Luke leaned back in his chair and met her eyes head-on. "Dan thought it would be funny to beat me to the punch. Ask you out first."

Luke's words hit her like a swift kick to the gut. Her nausea worsened. She felt tears well up in her eyes, and spill out onto her cheeks. She swiped them away.

"Are you telling me—" rage was thick in her tone "— that I was a *joke* to Daniel?"

Her answer was written all over Luke's face. Enraged, she levered herself up. Once she stood up, she tried to step around Luke to get to the door. Luke sprang into action, grabbed her firmly by the shoulders, spun her around to face him and held on to her arms. "Don't leave here thinking the worst of Dan. He doesn't deserve that."

"He doesn't deserve it? *I* don't deserve *this!* To find out that the last ten years of my life has been based on a joke! My marriage..." She looked down at her belly. "My baby..." She glared up at him. "Why didn't you stop it? If you were so in love with me, why did you let it go on?"

"You're a smart woman. Why do you think?"

"I don't know!" she shouted at him and tried to wiggle away from his grasp. "Let me go!"

"No. I'm not going to let you go. Not *this* time!" Luke held on to her. "Dammit, Sophia! He fell in love with you. Don't you get it? Dan fell in love with you!" Luke's hands left her arms to cup her face. "He took one look at you and he saw everything I saw. You're so damned beautiful. You're smart, funny, kind. You're so *good* to everyone around you. Why wouldn't he fall in love with you? He would have been a fool not to!"

Sophia couldn't speak, but she didn't try to pull away.

Luke's hands moved from her face to her hair, and then down to her neck.

"When he told me he was in love with you, I didn't give a damn. I wanted you for myself. But then I saw you with him. When I saw that you were in love with him…"

"You let Daniel have me."

His hands traveled from the nape of her neck back to her shoulders. The warmth of his hands was replaced by a rush of cold air, which brought with it an undeniable sense of loss.

"Daniel already had you. There wasn't anything I could do about it." Luke dropped his hands to his sides as the silence stretched out between them.

Sophia whispered, "So…I could have been married to you."

Luke said firmly, "I wouldn't have stopped pursuing you until I'd caught you. Until you were mine."

"And this baby could have been yours, not Daniel's."

"That baby is mine." His hand went possessively to her stomach.

"I mean, *really* yours."

Luke's eyes raked over her body; his gaze was undeniably predatory and sensual. "Make no mistake about it, Sophia. If you had been mine, I would have been making love to you every chance I got."

Chapter Thirteen

His hand was still on her stomach, and his lips were so close to hers that she could feel the warmth of his breath on her skin. Every fiber in her being wanted him to engulf her into his arms and kiss her senseless. But her brain wouldn't cooperate.

"I need to get back." She stepped away from him.

Luke stepped back as well and jammed his hands into the pocket of his jeans. He didn't say a word; his eyes were guarded. Silently, Luke helped her into her coat before he put on his. Then he said, "I'll walk you back."

"That's not necessary." This was said quickly.

"I'll walk you back," he repeated quietly, firmly. She could tell by his tone that he wasn't going to take no for an answer.

Sophia nodded. She was being ridiculous. "You're probably right." No sense letting her pride and discomfort put her at risk for slipping on a patch of ice this late in her pregnancy.

As they made their way through the barn, Sophia glanced at Luke from the corner of her eye. Every once in a while, she would see him wince. It was barely perceptible, but she saw it nonetheless.

"Why are you so stubborn about using your cane?"

Luke offered her his arm as they stepped into the snow. "The sooner I can walk without it, the sooner I get back to my men."

She felt sick at the thought of Luke going back to Afghanistan. Why in the world had she ever allowed herself to care about this man, when all he was going to do was put himself right back into harm's way? The last thing she needed was to bury another Brand man she loved.

Sophia stopped walking. The thought of losing Luke, the way she lost Daniel, had halted her in her tracks. She couldn't stand the thought of life without Luke. And in that moment, as that thought pinged through her brain, her muddied emotions began to crystallize. Out of the blue, it struck her like an electric shock. She truly did love Luke. Not as a platonic friend. She loved Luke as a man. And she was scared to death that she was going to lose him.

"What's wrong?" Luke stuck by her, loyal and dependable, just as Daniel had always said.

Sophia shook her head and didn't meet his gaze. She started to walk again, anxious now to get back to her room. She needed time to think; she needed time to figure out what to do. She just needed time....

The family was gathered in the kitchen and everyone was talking at once; the conversation was loud and raucous.

"I sent my daughter to college to get an education. I did *not* send her there to have left-wing liberal professors fill her head with their political agendas! And why, might I ask, isn't your daughter answering that very expensive phone we pay for every month?" Barb was talking while she rearranged the kitchen.

"Honey, will you please stop rearranging the kitchen every time you get upset? None of us can find anything once you're done," Hank asked in a beseeching tone that wasn't his norm.

Barb addressed her husband; she had a spatula in her hand. "This is how I cope. This is how I've *always* coped. In forty-three and three-quarter years of marriage, have I ever let you starve?" She didn't wait for him to answer. "No. I haven't. So, as far as I'm concerned, this is a perfectly acceptable way for me to work through my frustration. *And* until I give you some reason to complain about how I take care of you, I would appreciate it if you would kindly mind your own business when it comes to my kitchen!"

Hank relented easily. "Fair enough." He'd been married to Barb long enough to know when to back away.

"Mom." Jordan drew her mother's attention away from Hank. "I think this is more about Jo wanting to hang out with her boyfriend over the holidays than a war protest."

"Boyfriend?" Barbara and Hank asked in unison.

Tyler let out a long, low whistle. "The plot thickens."

"Not everything's a joke," Barb snapped at Tyler, whose grin only grew wider as he winked at Sophia.

"Why haven't I heard about a boyfriend before now?" Barb zeroed back in on Jordan. "What is going *on* with your sister?"

Jordan held up her hands. "Hey…don't put this on me! Why do I always get the blame for every little thing Jo does? I'm not my sister's keeper…."

"This is payback, if you ask me," Tyler interjected.

"What's that supposed to mean?" Jordan demanded in an indignant tone.

"That means," Tyler explained, "that Jo is usually the one getting the third degree about all of the crap you're normally up to."

Jordan threw up her hands. "You know what? Instead of giving me the third degree about Jo, why don't you guys give me a little credit for being here? I'm the one who's scared to death of flying, and yet I showed up. Shouldn't I get some sort of praise for that?"

Undeterred by Jordan's comment, Barb continued with her line of questioning. "Obviously there's something wrong with this young man, or she wouldn't be hiding him from us. What does this boy do? Is he in school? How old is he?"

Jordan frowned. "Mom, you need to ask *her*. For once, I haven't done anything wrong, and I'm *still* the one on the chopping block. That's totally unfair!"

Barbara swiveled her head and looked at Luke. "What do you think about your sister's behavior?"

"I think that everyone handles grief in their own way, Mom. Dan was Jo's favorite—that's not a big secret. Maybe she just couldn't face Christmas here without him. Either way, it's up to Jo to explain herself."

"Thank you, Luke!" Jordan tipped her head back to look at her older brother. "Finally! The voice of reason!"

While the family was distracted by Josephine, Sophia slipped upstairs. She needed to be off on her own to sort things out. She needed solitude. Later she begged off dinner as well, not ready to leave the darkness and quiet of her room. She found herself retrieving one memory after another of her encounters with Luke. Finally his behavior toward her made perfect sense. But even if she had known about Luke's feelings for her, it wouldn't have changed anything. Her love for Daniel had been absolute. So, in the end, in the calm aftermath of reasonable thought, it made perfect sense for Daniel and Luke to keep this information from her. Still, now that she knew about Luke's feelings for her, what next? How would she act? How would they move on? That's what she needed to figure out, and on that front she didn't have a single answer. For once, she was truly going to live by

Daniel's favorite motto and "go with the flow," see how things panned out.

Sometime later Sophia heard Luke enter his room. Her heart seized at the thought of him being so close, and then it started to thud steadily and strongly in her chest. Almost in an automated movement, she threw back the covers and turned on the bedside lamp. The light hurt her eyes and she covered them for a moment. Everything in her was being pulled to Luke's room. She didn't know what she would say, but she had an undeniable urge to see him. To touch him.

"And there is the truth of it," she said to herself softly. She couldn't deny the magnetic pull she felt whenever Luke was near.

She passed quietly through the bathroom and knocked lightly on the door. Without a word Luke opened the door and let her in. She sat down on the bed next to him, and for several minutes neither one of them spoke.

"Are you okay?" Ever the protector, Luke's concern was for her.

She nodded and reached out for his hand. "Are you?"

His thumb moved over her wedding band before he gave her hand a squeeze. He left her on the bed and moved to a chair across the room from her. He sat down and began to remove his boots. "Honestly? I'm relieved. I've been carrying that around for a long time and I'm glad it's over."

Her stomach flip-flopped when he said "it's over." "You weren't going to tell me, were you?"

His boots made a thud as he dropped them next to the chair. "No."

"Not ever?"

He leaned back. "Not ever."

"Why not?"

"What would it have accomplished, other than make

things more strained between us? I was trying to make things better, not worse. I'd never lay all of this on you when you are grieving and pregnant. Not my style. Honestly, I wish you hadn't found that letter, but what's done is done."

When she didn't say anything, he continued.

"Now that it's out in the open, I feel I can finally move on. I just hope you didn't get too beat up in the process."

"What if I don't want you to move on?" This was blurted out of her mouth before her brain had a chance to stop it.

The room became very still; neither one of them moved. She actually had to remind herself to take a breath while she waited for his response. It never came. He simply sat in the chair without moving an inch, and contemplated her as if she were a code to be deciphered. Humiliated, she finally said, "I don't know why I said that."

"You're all mixed up."

She couldn't argue with him. "Can we forget I said that?"

Luke stood up. "It's already forgotten." He walked over to her and held out his hand. He was being so gentle with her, so kind, that it made her heart break a little for the both of them. She slipped her hand into his, reveled in the strength and warmth of his fingers as they closed over hers.

He seemed so calm now; the tension that she had always sensed in him was released, and now she was left with a man who seemed to accept his fate. They had traded places. Now she was the tense one.

"I'm not going to apologize for loving you, Sophia." He took both of her hands in his and held them. She titled her head up and took in the rugged planes of his face.

"I don't expect you to."

"It never occurred to me that Dan and I would fall for the same woman—we never had before. But it happened, and I suppose the better man won."

She didn't know what to say, so she said nothing at all.

"I can live with loving you and not having you. That's how it's always been. I've become accustomed to it." He lifted his lip in a self-effacing half smile. She returned the smile. "But what I can't tolerate is being cut out of little Danny's life. That's my priority in all of this—it has been ever since I found out you were pregnant...."

"I already told you, Luke, I would never keep you from seeing him as much as you want. Nothing will ever change that, no matter what the future brings for either one of us."

"I know. And I believe you, Soph." Luke released her hands and reached up to brush the hair away from her face. "I just don't want you to feel awkward around me because of all this. Okay? Let's just concentrate on you having a healthy baby."

As his hands dropped away from her face, she found that the feeling of loss was nearly unbearable. She ached to have Luke touch her again. She ached to be in his arms, but she had the distinct feeling that she would never feel his arms around her again. Not like before. He loved her, yes, but he had no intention of pursuing her. And that made her feel ridiculously rejected.

She rubbed her hands over her belly and nodded in agreement. "I was hoping he would arrive for Christmas. You know, like the best Christmas present ever?"

Luke guided her to the door; the meeting was over. "I hope that boy has the good sense not to show up on Christmas."

"Why not?"

"Kids who are born on Christmas always get screwed

in the present department. Let the kid have his own day, at least."

"I hadn't thought of that, but you're right."

Luke held on to the door and leaned toward her slightly. "Are we good now?"

"Yes."

"I'd like for Mom to have the best Christmas she can have, considering..."

"We're good. Really. I wouldn't say it if I didn't mean it."

"I know that's right. Then we're square."

"Square." She smiled as she outlined a square shape with her fingers.

"Good night, Soph."

"Night."

"And keep that baby in there cooking until after the holiday!"

She smiled at him over her shoulder. "Easy for you to say, Brand! You're not the one lugging him around. I'm ready for him to come out on Christmas Day, or any other day for that matter!"

The next week leading up to Christmas raced by for Sophia. The Brand family always made a big deal about holidays, and even without Daniel and Josephine, Barb was determined to make it a merry Christmas. Sophia threw herself into the holiday spirit, doing her best to keep her mind off Luke. But the truth was, it was never far from her mind. Unfortunately, it seemed that his confession had given Luke a sense of ease with the situation, and he didn't seem bothered by her at all. It was as if the release of the secret had washed away the sexual tension that had been emanating from him. In fact, he was acting exactly like her platonic friend, and she should be happy about it. She should be thrilled! But she wasn't. The truth was that she hated it.

And she wanted him to stop it!

She wanted what they had before his family had returned. She wanted her Luke back. And the fact that he could so easily push aside his desire for her made her wonder if he really loved her, or if he had just been infatuated with a fantasy woman who didn't really exist.

In spite of herself, she had become somewhat of a visual stalker. Her eyes would seek Luke out wherever he was. She found that she enjoyed looking at him, enjoyed watching him as he interacted with his family. Of course, she rarely caught him looking back at her, and when he did meet her eyes, he gave her a mild, platonic nod that left her feeling completely dissatisfied.

Her head was saying it was a good thing; after the baby was born, she was going back to Boston. After his leg healed, Luke would go back to active duty. Their lives had intersected briefly at this point in time, but soon their paths would move apart. She had to accept that.

Unfortunately, her heart was having a hard time falling in line with her mind.

She had fallen for Luke; there wasn't any doubt in her mind about that anymore. But she would never be involved with a military man. She couldn't be. And Luke would never leave his career with the Marines. As far as she could see, there wasn't a future for them. Not as a couple. Why was it so hard for her to accept this when it seemed that Luke had already moved on?

Just after midnight New Year's morning, Sophia was alone in the family room watching the lights twinkle on the Christmas tree. The entire family had turned in after the stroke of midnight, even Jordan. She had thought to get up several times to turn in, but she found that she was almost too tired to get up. Nine months pregnant and everything was a chore; she was ready to have the baby and move on. It was a relief to know that if Danny didn't make an appearance of his own in one week, her doctor would induce labor. She was tired of feeling tired, and she hated the fact that she was waddling instead of walking. The thrill of being pregnant was beyond gone.

"I thought I was the only one still awake," Luke said from the doorway.

Sophia caught her breath. "You startled me."

"Want some company?"

"Of course." She patted the seat cushion next to her. "I was just admiring the tree one last time. Your mom is obsessive about packing everything up on New Year's Day."

She had also been feeling sorry for herself, not that she would share this truth with Luke. But this was the first time since college she hadn't received a New Year's kiss. And if she had hoped that Luke would sweep her up into his arms for a New Year's kiss, that little fantasy of hers had been shattered into a thousand pieces. At the stroke of midnight, Luke had crossed the room to her, and he had kissed her cheek in the most annoyingly bland way.

Luke sat down next to her on the couch. "She has her routine, that's for sure."

They both sat in silence for several minutes and then Sophia heard Luke chuckle.

"What?" she asked.

Luke nodded toward the German shepherd sleeping in front of the waning fire. Ranger was draped across the large dog, sound asleep. "Even Elsa has succumbed to his persistence."

Sophia smiled as well. "He's irresistible."

"Yes, he is," Luke agreed, easily.

After a moment of silence Sophia turned her head toward Luke.

"I thought you had already turned in." Sophia admired his strong profile.

"I couldn't sleep."

"I couldn't get out of this couch!"

That got another chuckle out of Luke. After a minute she said, "I want to thank you for my present. I can't imagine how you arranged it."

"The military can be a small world."

She picked up Daniel's dog tags that she now wore around her neck and held them tightly. "These are what I wanted the most. I still can't believe that I have them...."

"I'm glad you like them."

"I love them, Luke. I can't thank you enough. Really."

"No need to thank me. I was happy I could do it for you."

"I didn't have anything for you...."

Luke gave a quick shake of his head. "I have everything I need."

Those words hit her in the gut. After a pause, she asked, "Is that true? There isn't anything else that you need?"

Luke got up and put distance between them. Even in the sparse light, as he straightened after stoking the fire, she could see the tension in his jaw, the stiffness in his shoulders. "I don't need much."

"What about a family?"

Luke leaned against the mantel and crossed his arms over his chest. "I've got family."

"You don't have a wife." Why was she going down this path?

He didn't respond.

"You don't have children," she added belligerently.

Luke pushed away from the mantel. "What's this about, Sophia? What are you driving at?"

"I'm just having a friendly conversation." That was a lie.

"No, you're not." Luke didn't hesitate to call her on that lie. "You're trying to make a point, but I sure as hell don't know what it is."

"No point." She shrugged. "We can change the subject. We could talk about anything you'd like to talk about. Or we can talk about nothing at all."

"Bull," Luke said flatly. He dragged a chair over to the couch and sat facing her. "What's your angle, *friend?* Spit it out. What have I done *now?*"

The word *friend* hit her like a slap in the face; no doubt that was his intention. "Nothing. You haven't done anything." That was the problem. She was feeling neglected by him and she couldn't bring herself to say it. She wasn't going to go chasing after him like a schoolgirl begging for a second of his time.

Luke leaned forward and rested his arms on his thighs. All his attention, every fiber of his energy, was focused on her. "Dammit, Sophia. I can't seem to do anything right with you, can I? No matter how hard I try, I always fall short. I always disappoint you in some way. I always manage to *let you down.*" He blew out a frustrated breath. "Just tell me what I'm doing wrong and I'll fix it. Okay? I'm like goddamned putty in your hands!" Then lower, almost to himself, he said, "That's how damned well pathetic I've become."

"You're not pathetic."

"I'll be the judge of that." He lifted up his head and even in the darkness she was held captive by his striking eyes. "What…have…I…*done?*"

Sophia suddenly felt weary. She felt weary of being pregnant, of dealing with Daniel's loss, of being in Montana, and she was especially weary of her feelings for Luke.

"It's not you, Luke. Honestly, it's not. It's me…."

"Bull."

"I'm being serious. My rotten mood doesn't have anything to do with you. All right? You've been perfect. You've kept your end of the bargain, okay? No complaints. I'm just fed up with feeling like a holiday parade float, and I want to go home. Neither of those things have anything to do with you." She reached out her hand. "Will you help me up, please? I'm ready to go to bed."

"Not a problem."

Luke held on to her hand as she slowly stood. She took a few extra moments to stand upright, and he could tell that she was feeling lousy. He wished he could do something to make her feel better, to ease her pain, but he knew that his hands were tied.

Luke slipped his arm around her shoulder and offered his other arm to Sophia for balance. She held on to Luke's arm gratefully, glad that no matter how irrationally she acted toward him, Luke never failed to offer her support. As Luke walked her to her room, his expression was both guarded and concerned. "Are you certain that I haven't done anything to upset you?"

Her shoulders dropped. She knew that this was all about him not losing touch with his nephew. That's what mattered to him, and she was grateful. But she felt invisible to him now, and that hurt.

"How about this… Ask me when I'm not nine months pregnant, okay? I have no doubt my answer will be a much different one." Her back was against her bedroom door and her hands were resting on her distended belly. "I did have something I wanted to ask you, though. It's something I've been thinking about, but you don't have to do it if you don't want to…."

"What's that?"

"The doctor is inducing me next week. This boy is just getting too big for me."

"Mom told me." Luke took a step closer to her.

"Would you like to be in the room when Danny is born?"

At first Sophia thought that Luke might not have heard her. He stood stock-still, his expression devoid of emotion. She was about to repeat her question when Luke dragged her into his arms for a bear hug that temporarily cut off her breath. He hugged her tightly, then pressed a hard kiss on her cheek before he released her.

"I'd be honored," Luke said finally. In the dim light she could see that Luke's eyes were glassy with emotion.

"I'll be glad to have you there." She reached out and gave his hand one last squeeze.

"Happy New Year," Luke said before he opened his door.

"Happy New Year, Luke."

With that, they parted company, and as Sophia gently closed her door behind her, she felt a deep sadness sweep over her. Luke was still interested in her son; that was apparent. But he had disconnected himself from her. He had unplugged and stepped back; she felt as if she had lost her best friend. Somewhere along the line Luke had gotten under her skin, had become a part of who she was. And then, just as unexpectedly, he had slipped away from her.

Chapter Fourteen

Sophia tried everything she could to sleep, but it was no use. Danny had his foot jammed underneath her rib cage again; he could not be persuaded to move. And, to make matters worse, she couldn't get her earlier conversation with Luke out of her mind. It wasn't like her to play the wounded, wordless female to get out of sticky situations. And yet, that's what she had allowed herself to become. Instead of coming right out and saying what was on her mind when she had the opportunity, she had chickened out. She had lied. She had evaded. And now she couldn't sleep.

"That's it! If I'm awake, he might as well be awake, too." She slipped out of bed, threw on her robe and made her way to Luke's room. She didn't bother to knock. Instead, she gently opened the door and stepped inside. Luke was sprawled out on his back as he slept.

She reached out and shook his arm lightly. Luke's eyes immediately popped open.

"What's the matter? Is it the baby?"

Sophia shook her head. "No."

Luke propped himself up on his elbow. "What's the matter?" He repeated the question.

"You were right earlier. I am upset about something."

Luke took a deep breath in through his nose and looked at his watch on the nightstand. "It's three o'clock in the morning, Soph. Can't it keep?"

"No." She shook her head again. "I can't sleep."

"So I shouldn't sleep either? Is that it?"

"It sounds bad when you put it like that." She frowned.

"It sounds bad because it *is* bad." He stood up and yanked on his jeans. "But you're pregnant and you're a woman, so I guess you have the right."

"That was a real oinky thing to say."

"And your point is?" Luke raised a brow at her. But after a moment of thought he held up his hand. "Wait. Scratch that. Let's stay on track here. I may be a chauvinist…"

"You absolutely *are* a chauvinist…"

"But that's not why you're standing in my room in the middle of the night, correct? Or is it?"

"I don't think I like your tone…."

"You don't like my tone?"

"No. I don't!" Irritation had already crept into her voice.

"Well then, I suppose we're even, sweetheart, because I sure as hell don't like the fact that you just woke me up out of a sound sleep because you're displeased with life in general."

"That's not true. I'm very happy with…"

Luke was at her side. He took her by the shoulders and guided her until she sat down on the bed. He held on to her. "Dammit, Sophia!" he said in a harsh whisper. "You're driving me bloody crazy. Do you understand that? Do you have any concept of it? You are the most annoying, infuriating, disagreeable, frustrating, *complicated* woman I have ever met. And, unfortunately, I love you for it, which makes me a complete nut job! Will you *please* tell me why you woke me up?" By the time he was done, he was no longer whispering.

"Shhhh! Keep your voice down!" she said in a loud whisper. "Someone will hear you."

"I don't give a damn if someone hears me."

"Well, I do! I don't like to have everyone in my business. It's already bad enough that…"

Luke snatched up his watch off the nightstand. "You have ten seconds to start talking."

"Quit bossing me around, Luke! I'm not one of your men. I don't worship the ground you walk on! I'm not mandated to follow every little word you say as if it's the holy gospel, and I'm not just going to jump because you order me to do it.…"

"Eight seconds. Seven. Six." He gave her a questioning look. "Five…"

"All right!" she whispered harshly and waved her hand. "All right! Put that stupid thing down."

"Talk." Luke sat down heavily in the chair and waited.

Sophia muttered, "I still don't like your tone."

"Sophia…"

"Or that you are speaking to me like I'm a toddler. I'm not a child!"

Luke went to stand up. "That's it…"

Sophia made a hand gesture for him to remain sitting. "Will you quit rushing me? You're always rushing me!"

"Pregnant or not, I'm gonna kick your butt right out of my room if you don't start talking. You've worn me out, woman.…"

Sophia clasped her hands together; she knew that her stall tactics weren't working. It was time to come clean with Luke. So she did.

"You were right. I have been upset.…"

"You mentioned that."

She glanced up at him; she had his unwavering attention. "I miss you."

"How can you miss me if I haven't gone anywhere? I'm right here."

She felt emotionally deflated and her body sank lower onto the mattress as her shoulders drooped. "You treat me differently now. I miss how things were between us before your family came back. I miss that."

She waited for him to respond, but he just sat there and stared at her. She added, "Your turn."

"I'm thinking," Luke said in a biting tone. Then, after a moment, he said, "You know, you're really pissing me off right now, and I really need to think about what I'm going to say because I don't want to fight with you."

"I don't want to fight with you either," she interrupted him. "And I wasn't trying to piss you off. Why are you pissed off?"

Luke rubbed his hands several times over his shorn hair and blew out a breath. "Because, Sophia," he said in a slow, measured voice, "I've done everything I can think of to make you happy, to make things right between us, to treat you how you want to be treated. I walk on goddamn eggshells all the frickin' time for you; I'm on pins and needles constantly for you, and yet... It's not enough. You're still not happy. You're still upset! What the *hell* do you want from me? Tell me now. What the hell do you *want* from me!"

"I want you, Luke," she said simply. Honestly. "That's what I want. You."

"You have me. You've always had me. Haven't you been paying attention these last couple of weeks?"

"Ever since the...barn...you've treated me like..." She paused to think of the right word. "Like we've never had anything between us. You avoid me like the plague, and when we do see each other, you do everything you can not to touch me. Don't think I haven't noticed, Luke, because I have."

These words moved Luke to action. He stood up and marched over to her. "I'm sorry. I don't think I heard you correctly. Have you woken me up in the middle of the night to complain about the fact that I don't *touch* you enough?"

"Yes." She felt like a lunatic.

"Unbelievable." Luke's eyes blazed with emotion. "You're unbelievable!"

Luke started to pace; his limp was barely noticeable now. He paused for a moment and addressed her. "Let me get this straight. You've been trying to get me to treat you like we're 'just friends' since the moment I arrived here, and now that I'm finally complying with *your* wishes and demands, you...don't...like...it?" His tone was incredulous. "You have gotten everything *your way,* and you still aren't happy? This is priceless! And you wonder why I'm a chauvinist! Women are nuts!"

She supposed he had a right to be a little caustic at this point. She *was* acting nuts. "I admit that in the beginning, that's what I wanted. But, honestly, I think that I was just trying to push you away because I was afraid of how I was feeling about you...."

"Jesus, woman! Will you lay off the frickin' psycho-babble for one second, please?"

"Understanding the psychological motivation behind our actions is the cornerstone of change," Sophia said with a lift of her chin. "Plus, it's my profession. Analyzing emotions is my stock-in-trade."

Luke looked up at the ceiling, lifted his hands in the air and said, "Shoot me now, Lord. Just shoot me now!"

Not deterred, Sophia continued. "I just want to know why you're treating me like you don't have any feelings for me at all! Why are you pushing me away?"

"Why am I pushing you away?"

"Yes."

"Why am I pushing you away?" he asked again, loudly.

"Shhhh." She lowered her voice to a whisper. "Yes, Luke. Why are you pushing me away?"

"You know what, Sophia? I'm flat-out tired of all of this crap with you. You want to know why I'm pushing you away? Fine! I'll tell you. Why not? What do I have to lose? I'm treating you like a *friend* to keep myself in check, you get it? I treat you like a friend who's off-limits so I don't cross the line. You should be thanking me instead of sitting here busting my balls about it!"

"Cross what line?"

"You're the shrink. You figure it out."

"I want to hear it from you."

Luke crossed the room to her and pulled her gently to a stand. His fingers were in her hair as he tilted her head so they were gazing into each other's eyes. She could see that Luke was warring within himself; he was very close to kissing her, and she was very close to letting him. Instead, he said, "I've wanted you for ten years. *Ten years.* That's a hell of a lot of pent-up desire, woman. I want you all the time, get it? Whenever I see you, I want to put my hands on you. Put my hands all over you. You're just so damn sexy and you think I should be turned off because you're pregnant. But you're sexy as hell like this, too. You drive me nuts, do you get that? I have to fight not to strip you down and put my lips on every damn inch of your body. Do you hear what I'm saying to you, Sophia? I want you so much it hurts. I want you in my bed. Naked. All the time. I want to be able to touch you whenever I damn well please. I want to kiss you whenever I damn well please. This is what you do to me." Luke pressed himself against her, and there was no mistaking that he was aroused. Luke watched as realization dawned in her eyes before he spoke again. "*That*—" and they both knew what *that* was "—is why I have a strict *hands-off* policy with you, Sophia. Are we clear now?" He stepped away from her. "Because if I don't keep a barrier between us, I'll take advantage of your confusion and make love to you every damn chance I get. I'll talk you out of your clothes and into my bed before you know what hit you!" His voice lowered to a lover's caress. "Don't think I can't."

Luke's eyes dropped down to her lips. Speechless, she licked them involuntarily. She cleared her throat and tried to keep herself focused on the conversation. He was making it nearly impossible to think, much less form a coherent sentence. "And then everything would be ruined."

"What?" His eyes drifted back up to hers.

"You're afraid that you'll take advantage of me, we'll make love and then in the morning, I'll regret it and everything will be ruined with Danny."

"That's part of it," he said in a quiet, husky voice.

"What's the other part?"

"You just can't leave well enough alone, can you? You just keep pushing and pushing...."

"This conversation had to happen."

Luke stared at her for several heartbeats; resignation flickered in his eyes just before he spoke. "I'm in love with you, Sophia. What part of that don't you understand? Do you think because I'm a man, that I'm a marine, I don't have any feelings? Do you think I like the fact that the woman I love, the woman I've *always* loved, doesn't love me back? I'm protecting myself from how I feel about you, because for me it's a matter of survival. I didn't know your permission was required."

Sophia put her hand on his arm. "Luke, you don't have to protect yourself from me. I'm not trying to hurt you."

"You can't help yourself." He pulled away from her.

His gesture stung, but it didn't deter her. She continued even though he had his back turned to her. "I don't know when it happened, but somewhere along the way, sometime during the week we spent alone, I fell in love with you, Luke."

If she thought that he was going to take her in his arms and hug her when he heard those words, she was sadly mistaken. Luke slowly spun around and looked at her. That stony mask was back in place, but his eyes were flashing with pent-up rage.

"Get out of my room," Luke bit out through gritted teeth and pointed to the door.

"Didn't you hear what I said? I'm in love with you." She said it more clearly, more decisively.

"I heard you," he snapped. "Now get out!"

"You stand there and tell me that I'm never going to love you back. I'm telling you that I'm in love with you, and now you're kicking me out?"

"Do you think that this is a game? A joke? You're not in love with me. You're in love with Dan! You always have been—no doubt you always will be. And I am not going to be some cheap substitution for my own twin. Do you hear me? I'm not going to be some pathetic second string that's suddenly in the game now because the first string got annihilated! I may be a lot of things, Sophia, but I sure as hell ain't no runner-up to Dan!" Luke's fists were balled up at his sides. "I'm nobody's stand-in."

"Is that what you think? That I want you to be a stand-in for Daniel? That's not it at all, Luke. I love Daniel, but…"

"I'm aware of that," he snapped.

"Will you let me finish, please?"

"Go ahead."

"I'll always love Daniel…."

"Do you think this is news to me or something, sweetheart? 'Cause it ain't," Luke interrupted her again.

"Dammit, Luke! Stop interrupting me. I'm trying to tell you that I'm in love with you. Do you get that, Captain Brand? I'm in love with you! Not Daniel. I love him. I always will, but as your mom put it so eloquently, 'being in love is for the living.' She's right. Being in love *is* for the living, and I'm in love with *you*."

"You're in no condition to know how you feel, Sophia. I look like Dan, you're confused, nothing more. And I'm not about to put myself in a position to have you wake up to that fact one month, two months, one year down the road. I'm not going to put myself out there like that. I'm not going to set myself up for that kind of fall. Do you hear me?"

"First of all, you don't even look that much like Daniel. I can't imagine why I ever thought you did. Your nose has that crooked thing going on, you have that scar on your jaw..." She reached up and traced the jagged white scar. "Probably from a bar fight, knowing you. *And* your eyes are a darker shade of blue with gold flecks around the iris. Second of all, I'd appreciate it if you'd quit throwing my pregnancy in my face! I'm pregnant, not brain-dead. I know my own mind, Luke...."

"Do you?"

"Yes! And I know my own heart. I'm in love with you. If you choose not to believe it, that's your problem. Not mine. The ball's in your court now."

Luke grabbed her left hand and held it up between them. "If you're so in love with me, why do you still have your wedding ring on?"

Sophia waited a minute for Luke to focus in on her finger and see that the wedding ring had been removed. Luke was so accustomed to being right, she truly enjoyed watching as it dawned on him that he was wrong.

Luke sought out her eyes. "When did you take it off?"

"Yesterday." She reached up and rested her hand on his face. "How can I wear Daniel's wedding ring when I'm in love with you? It would be a lie, and I'm not a liar."

Luke spun her around so her back was against the bedroom door. He placed his hands on each side of her, trapped her between his arms. His stormy blue eyes held her captive.

"You're in love with me?" Luke's lips were so close that his breath mingled with hers.

"Yes." Her voice had a soft, sensual quality; her knees felt weak. The scent of his warm skin was making her feel intoxicated.

Suddenly she was engulfed in his arms and his face was buried in her neck. She felt his lips on her skin, and the feel of his mouth on her flesh sent an electrical current racing through her body.

"I play for keeps," he growled as his lips found another spot on her neck. Her knees buckled and her pulse skyrocketed. Luke felt her sway; he held her closer and pressed himself against her possessively.

"So do I."

"I don't believe I gave you a proper New Year's kiss…."

Her heart was thumping in her chest. She licked her lips. "No. I don't believe you did."

Sophia closed her eyes as Luke's lips captured hers. She surrendered into his steely arms as Luke took possession of her mouth with his. Every nerve ending in her body ignited wherever his body touched hers.

"Do you have any idea how long I've waited to make you mine?" Luke abandoned her mouth as he reached for the belt on her robe and tugged it loose. He slowly opened her robe and slipped it off her shoulders. As it fell silently onto the ground at her feet, she felt completely exposed.

Did he mean to make love to her right this minute? She was huge! She couldn't imagine it....

"Beautiful," Luke murmured. His eyes swept her body before they rejoined hers. "My God, you're gorgeous." He buried his nose back into her neck. "You smell so damned good, Soph." He brought his lips back to hers. "You taste so damned good."

"Luke...I don't think that we should..." She pushed lightly on his chest; she felt overwhelmed by his passion for her.

Luke put his finger against her lips. "Shhhh. We aren't going to do anything that you don't want to do. I'm not going to hurt you or the baby." He moved his hand possessively down her body until his hand was on her belly. "But, my God, Sophia. I have to touch you. I have to taste you...."

She reached up for his face, relieved. "Yes. Yes." She said in a silken voice that she hardly recognized. "Yes."

Her last *yes* was cut off as his lips captured hers again. His fingers were in her hair, on her neck, down her back as he claimed her with his strong, unyielding lips. He kissed her again and again until she couldn't tell where his breath ended and hers began. She melted into his arms, felt herself let go of her well-constructed control, and kissed him back as forcefully as he was kissing her. She gave in to him, and claimed him in the very same way he was laying claim to her.

"Get in my bed," he growled against her lips.

His command was so masculine, so sensual, that she found herself complying without putting up her usual fight. She wanted to be in his bed. She wanted to be in his arms. She wanted to be his woman.

Once in his bed, she lay on her back feeling incredibly aroused, insecure and ridiculous. Her body was humming with desire and she was so horny she felt herself writhe on the bed; she needed a release that had been such a long time coming.

Luke's eyes never left her as he stripped out of his jeans. She could see the evidence of his desire for her straining against the thin material of his boxers. It was obvious that he wanted her as much as she wanted him.

He was at her side now; he pressed his body against her. His fingers unbuttoned the buttons at the top of her nightgown. She sucked in her breath as his fingers slipped into her nightgown and cupped her full, warm breast. She arched her back against his hand, helpless to protest.

"Look at me." Luke hovered above her, his lips so close to hers as he spoke. "I want to make love to you, Sophia. Do you want me to love you?"

"Yes," she said without hesitation. "But look at me. I'm in no condition to make love. I'm huge. I feel ridiculous."

Luke's lips found the swell of her breast. "There are many ways for a man to satisfy a woman. All you have to do is let me...."

Sophia closed her eyes and moaned as his mouth moved to her nipple. As he began to suckle, she pressed her hand to the back of his head and moaned louder.

"Let me show you how much I love you..." Luke released her nipple.

She was squirming now, wanting, needing. "I need you, Luke. Please. I *need* you."

"Your wish is my command."

Luke's lips found hers as his hand slipped beneath her nightgown and traveled slowly up her thighs. "Open for me. Let me in," he said against her lips; after a moment she complied, relaxed as his fingers found her.

She reached down between them and slipped her hand into his boxers. Luke moaned her name into her neck as her fingers closed over his rock-hard erection.

He pulled her tightly toward him and grazed the skin

of her neck with his teeth. "I've waited a lifetime for you, Sophia. A *lifetime*."

She couldn't speak. She couldn't respond. All she could do was writhe against the warmth of his hand as he gave her the release that she had been craving.

"Luke." She gasped his name as she climaxed. "Luke."

"I love you, Sophia. God, I love you so damned much." Luke's words were groaned into her neck; his erection stiffened and then pulsated in her hand as he found his own release.

Chapter Fifteen

A week later the entire Brand family was gathered at the hospital to witness Sophia give birth to a healthy seven-pound, two-ounce baby boy. Luke and Barbara had been in the room for the birth while Hank, Tyler and Jordan kept themselves occupied with burned coffee and snacks from the vending machines. Luke held Sophia's hand during the delivery, cut the cord and, once Sophia had drifted off to sleep, made a beeline for the baby. Barbara stood arm in arm with her eldest son as they admired the latest addition to the Brand clan. "Just look at my first grandchild! He looks just like the two of you when you were born!" Barb said with pride. "He's the spitting image of his father *and* his uncle."

"He kind of looks like a raisin, if you ask me. Did Daniel and Luke look like raisins when they were born?" Jordan asked with a playful glint in her eye.

Barbara frowned at her youngest daughter. "Go find your father, Jordy." That was her way of saying "beat it." Jordan took the hint and went off in search of Hank and Tyler.

Barbara squeezed Luke's arm; he shifted his gaze from his nephew to his mom. "It was wonderful for Sophia to let you be in the room. Daniel would have been so happy about that."

Luke covered her hand with his. "She did a good job, didn't she?"

"A fantastic job," Barbara agreed. "He's absolutely perfect."

Luke and his mother stood together and silently admired Daniel's son. Luke hadn't slept, but instead of resting, he watched little Danny; he couldn't seem to get enough. It was going to be tough to leave Sophia and her son when it was time to ship off to rehab. For the first time in his career, it was going to be tough to return to active duty. Luke believed that it was going to be the hardest thing he ever had to do in his life.

"I just wish that she would consider staying at the ranch with us. There are plenty of disturbed individuals in Montana who need counseling," Barb said. "I'm not going to name names, but there are *several* cookoo-noodles within a ten-mile radius of the ranch!"

"Mom... Don't bug her about it. She's been through a tough enough time without you laying a guilt trip on her. She's going back to Boston. Besides, seeing Danny will give you the perfect excuse to get back to the city."

Barb thought for a moment. "They do have very excellent shopping in Boston."

"There you go."

"Wonderful restaurants," Barb added.

"Dad'll hate it, you'll love it."

Barb chuckled. "Your father *will* absolutely hate it. But he'll tag along just to see his grandson. And to make certain I don't melt my credit cards." Barb turned away from the window and faced her son. "Changing the subject, what is going on with Sophia and you? I've tried to keep out of it...."

"You've done amazingly well...."

"But enough is enough. What's going on with you two? Are the two of you going to raise Danny together?"

"We're not there yet, Mom."

"Why not?" Barb demanded. "It's not rocket science."

"Mom…stuff like this takes time. It's new to both of us. There's a lot to work out."

"Have the two of you already…" Barb lifted one suggestive brow. "You know…"

Luke looked down at his mom; a sense of absolute horror rolled around in his gut. "Have the two of us…what?"

"Oh, don't be obtuse, Luke! Have the two of you 'sealed the deal,' I believe your generation calls it…."

For the first time since he was a teenager, Luke felt the tips of his ears turn red with embarrassment. "Mom…"

"What?"

"You've crossed into a restricted area."

"Oh, please! I gave birth to you. I changed your diapers. I bathed you. I took your temperature with an anal thermometer! I don't have any *restricted areas* when it comes to my children."

"Well, you do now!"

Barb waved her hand and ignored his comment. "If you want my advice…"

"I'm not really in the market for it right now, so no…"

Barb's eyes sharpened, and it made Luke back down a bit. "If you want my advice…" She started over again with very pointed, precise speech. "And you're going to get it whether you like it or not, because, no matter how old you are, I'm still your mother and you will always be my business…."

"Yes, ma'am," Luke said respectfully.

Barb pulled out a small box from her purse and handed it to Luke. "I suggest you march right into that hospital room, get down on one knee and ask Sophia to marry you."

Luke cracked open the ring box and looked inside. "This is Grandma's engagement ring."

"Yes." Barb looked lovingly at the ring.

"Dan wanted to give this to Sophia when they were first engaged."

"I know," Barb said with her eyes still on the antique platinum-and-diamond ring. "I know he did. I just couldn't part with it then."

"But you can now?" Luke closed the lid of the box and slipped it into his pocket.

"Yes, I can. Perhaps that ring was always meant for Sophia." Barb's eyes drifted back to her grandson, who was stretching his legs and yawning. Her voice took on a poignant tone. "Don't let her slip away, Lucas. Seize this opportunity. This is *your* moment with Sophia. Don't let her go out of some false loyalty to Daniel. Daniel loved both of you and, as I have told Sophia, he would want the two of you to be together. He would want you to raise his son." Barbara sought out her son's eyes. "You do love her still, don't you, son?"

"More now than ever," Luke said without hesitation.

"Then, marry her, Lucas. Do whatever it takes to make her your wife, to make this boy your son." Barb squeezed her son's arm again and gave it a slight shake. "This is your fork in the road, darling; we all come to them if we live long enough. Think hard and choose wisely, because you will never pass this way again."

Luke knocked lightly on the hospital room door before he opened it. At the sound of the door opening, Sophia opened her eyes and smiled weakly at Luke.

"Hi," she said softly.

Luke sat down in the seat next to the bed and took Sophia's outreached hand. "Hi. How are you feeling?"

"Probably a heck of a lot better than I look," Sophia said with a self-effacing chuckle.

"You look beautiful to me."

Sophia's eyes softened as she looked at him. "Thank you." She squeezed his hand. "Were you with him?"

Luke nodded. "I just came from seeing him. God, Sophia, he's incredible. Perfect."

"He is, isn't he? Barb showed me a baby picture of Daniel and you. Little Danny could be a triplet!"

Luke winked at her. "He's bound to be handsome."

"Bound to be." Sophia laughed before her expression turned more serious. "Listen, there's something I've been thinking about and I'd like to run it by you...."

"Shoot."

"I would like to name him Daniel Lucas Brand. How would you feel about that?"

Stunned temporarily speechless, Luke could only stare at the woman he loved. It never occurred to him that she would want to name her son after him; it was more than he could have ever hoped for. "Soph...you don't have to do that...."

She pushed herself up a bit in the bed. "But I want to. I can't imagine a better name for my son. Unless you'd rather I not..."

Luke pressed his lips hard against the back of her hand before he clasped it in both of his hands. "It's an honor that I never expected to have."

"So, it's okay with you?"

Luke leaned forward, pushed a tendril of hair behind her ear and then kissed her gently on her mouth. "Are you kidding? I'm blown away. I would love nothing more than to have your son carry my name. You're an amazing woman and I love you."

Sophia rested her palm against his stubbly cheek. "I love you, too, Luke."

Luke looked into her eyes as if he were trying to see into her soul. "I'm glad that you do, because there's something…" Luke began to reach into his pocket to pull out the ring box.

Sophia placed her hand on his chest, halting his words. "Oh! Hold that thought!" She had an excited sparkle in her eyes. "I have a Christmas present for you!"

"I told you I have everything I need…."

Sophia hit him on the arm playfully. "Quit spoiling this for me! I have the perfect gift for you!"

"You and Danny are the only gifts I need…."

Sophia made a frustrated noise and pointed. "*Please* go over to my pants and look in the pocket. I brought it with me for good luck."

Luke complied and searched Sophia's pockets. He pulled out a coin and examined it. He looked over to her, his teasing mood temporarily on hold. "This is Dan's Ranger coin."

"Merry Christmas!" Sophia said happily.

Luke came back to her bedside. "I can't accept this."

"Yes, you can. I want you to have it."

"You should hold on to this for Danny."

Sophia saw how Luke held the coin his brother had earned when he became a ranger with reverence. "I have a better idea. Why don't *you* hold on to it for him?"

Luke turned the coin over in his hand. "Are you sure?"

"Of course I am. Why wouldn't I be?"

Luke took one last look at the coin before he put it in his pocket and leaned over to kiss Sophia. "I don't know what to say other than thank you."

"You're welcome." Sophia wrapped her arms around Luke and hugged him tightly. "Thank you for being here with me, Luke. You made everything easier for me."

"This is where I was meant to be."

As Luke hugged Sophia, he thought about what his

mother had said to him in the hospital corridor. This was his moment. This was his woman. He couldn't let her slip away from him a second time. Luke broke the hug, but held on to Sophia's hand. His heart began to pound hard in his chest at the thought of proposing to Sophia. He'd never proposed before, and he felt a wave of nerves and nausea hit him.

No matter what he had faced in combat, nothing compared with asking the woman he loved to be his wife. This was the most fear-producing mission he'd ever faced.

Sophia was eyeing him curiously. "I don't like your pallor, Luke. Have you eaten?"

"I'm not hungry. I'm nervous."

"Nervous!" Sophia said with a laugh. "When has Captain Luke Brand ever been nervous?"

"Right now."

Those words, along with Luke's serious demeanor, made Sophia's expression change from playful to one of concern. Now she felt nervous. "What's going on, Luke? You're scaring me. Are you leaving? Is that it?"

Luke grabbed her hands. "No. I'm not leaving. Not yet, anyway."

Sophia didn't like the "not yet" part, but she wasn't stupid. She knew she would be saying goodbye to Luke sooner or later.

"Then, what's going on?"

Luke pulled the ring box out of his pocket. "You had something in your pocket for me. And, as it turns out, I have something in my pocket for you...."

Sophia's eyes widened and her face drained of color. She couldn't take her eyes off the box in Luke's hand. "Luke..."

"Before you start psychoanalyzing the situation to death, could you just hear me out, please? Let me get through this uninterrupted. Can you do that for me?"

Sophia could only nod. Her tongue felt heavy and her mouth was suddenly dry; when she tried to swallow, her tongue stuck to the roof of her mouth, as if her saliva had turned to glue. She couldn't have gotten two words out if she had tried.

It never occurred to her that Luke might propose marriage; she was stunned. And completely unprepared.

Luke opened the box and held it out for Sophia to see. Sophia immediately recognized the ring and knew that there was only one person who could have given it to Luke: Barb.

"Sophia, I fell in love with you the minute I saw you, and I've loved you every day since. I never thought that I would have a second chance to make you mine, but now that I have it, I can't let you slip away. I have to try to make this work. I love you, Sophia, more than anything or anyone on this planet. I can't imagine my life without you in it; I don't want to imagine my life without you in it. I want you to be my wife, Sophia. I want to be your husband. I want us to live the rest of our lives together watching Danny grow." His eyes swept her body. "I want to watch you grow another child. Our child. I am going to love you until the day I die. I'm asking you to marry me, Sophia. I'm asking you to be my wife. Will you marry me?"

Unshed tears swam in Sophia's eyes as she looked between the ring and the man she loved. She couldn't seem to say a word, because she knew that the words she would say were going to hurt Luke. Luke's eyes were trained on her face; she could tell he was analyzing every flicker of emotion he read in her eyes. After a minute of silence, Luke sat back and snapped the lid of the box shut. Sophia jumped a bit at the noise the box made when it snapped shut. At the same time the box closed, Luke's expression became guarded.

She reached out for him instinctively. "Please, Luke… don't pull away from me, I…"

"You don't have to say anything to me, Sophia," Luke said in that unemotional tone he had picked up in the Marines. "Anything other than a 'yes' doesn't require an explanation."

Sophia felt her temper flare. "You ask me to marry you, and because I don't jump on the offer like some irrational, bubbleheaded teenager, you're going to shut me out? I'll explain myself if I bloody well want to, Brand, and you'll listen!"

Luke stood up, leaned against the windowsill and waited. "So, explain."

"Don't boss me around!" Sophia snapped. Luke could still get her blood boiling quicker than anyone else. After a moment, Sophia composed herself and said in a controlled, irritated tone. "You know, I didn't expect this—" she waved her hand between the two of them "—to happen."

"I didn't say you did."

"Can I please speak without you interrupting me? I didn't interrupt you."

Luke nodded his agreement.

"Thank you," she snapped. "Like I was saying, this thing between us is a complete shock to me. I didn't have any intention of falling in love with you. But I did. I love you, Luke. It's as much a surprise to me as it is to you, but there it is. And I won't regret it now. Loving you seems to be as natural as breathing for me." She clasped her hands together and rested them in her lap. "But let's be realistic, Luke. We're not kids anymore. We both know that it takes a lot more than love and a good romp in bed to make a marriage work."

"I'm aware of this."

"So am I. That's why, as much as I love you Luke,

and I do…I really do, I can't be your wife. I can't stand the thought of marrying you and then losing you." The thought of Luke dying in combat overwhelmed her, and the tears she had been holding back slipped out of her eyes without her consent.

Luke was quick to offer her a tissue box. She pulled a tissue out roughly from the box and blew her nose loudly. "Thank you."

"So, let me get this straight… You won't marry me because of my career? That's the only thing holding you back?"

Sophia blew her nose again. "I just can't do it, Luke. I can't lose another husband like that." She balled the tissue up into her hand and gave him a disgruntled look. "As a matter of fact, it's actually pretty insensitive of you to ask me to marry another military man after what I've just lived through, don't you think?"

"I'd like to say something in own defense now, if you don't mind," Luke said.

Sophia nodded with a loud sniff.

"I made a decision last night. I'm not going to re-up, Soph. When my time is up, I'm leaving the Corps."

Sophia's heart started to flutter in her chest. "Are you serious? I can't let you do that…."

"It's not your choice. It's mine. I'm doing it for me. I'm doing it for us."

"I don't know what to say…."

Luke crossed to her side. He loomed over her, his handsome face tense; his eyes had darkened to a stormy midnight blue. "Say that you love me."

"I *do* love you, Luke. I'm crazy about you…."

Luke clasped her hand in his. "Then, be my wife, Sophia. Put me out of my misery and marry me! Nothing in this world matters to me more than you and Danny. I want us to be a family. Leaving the Marines isn't a big deal if you're the prize waiting for me at the end of that road." He pressed his lips to her hand; his eyes blazed with passion for her. "Say you'll *marry* me, Sophia."

"Yes." The word popped out of her mouth without a second thought.

"Yes?"

Sophia started to laugh. "Yes, Luke. God help me, I will marry you."

"I'd better get this on your finger quick before you change your mind or start to accuse me of being insensitive for proposing to you again." Luke pulled the box out of his pocket and slid the ring onto her finger. "I play for keeps, Sophia. You're never getting rid of me, no matter how angry I make you. No matter how many knockdown, drag-out fights we have, I'm never going to leave your side. Can you handle that?"

She wiggled her finger and watched the fire in the diamond reflect purple and blue and gold. "I can handle anything you throw at me, Captain. But are you really going to give up your career? For me?"

"For you. For me. For all of us."

Sophia reached up and put her hands on each side of his face; the flawless, colorless brilliant cut diamond winked at her as she said, "How could I be so lucky to fall madly in love twice in my life?"

Luke captured her mouth and kissed her breathless. "I'm the lucky one. I'm going to have a beautiful wife and a handsome new son. That's all I need. It's all I ever wanted…." He pressed his lips to the inside of her wrist. "Do you have any idea how much I love you?"

Sophia shook her head as Luke gathered her into his strong arms. She relaxed into his embrace with a contented sigh, just as a shiver of excitement raced up her spine when Luke's lips brushed against her earlobe. He whispered into her ear, "I'm going to show you for the rest of my life how much I love you, my beauty. Every day until I take my last breath."

Sophia smiled as he kissed the line of her jaw; she hugged him until her arms hurt. "You believe me, don't you?" Luke asked as he kissed the corner of her mouth.

"Yes," she said in a breathy voice. "I do."

"You'd better," Luke growled against her lips. Luke pulled her closer to him, molded her body tightly to his, as if he were afraid that she was going to disappear. Sophia pressed her lips to his, and held on to him as tightly as he was holding on to her. For the first time in a long time, Sophia felt safe. She felt secure. She was finally home. Wrapped up in his strong arms, Sophia knew that this loving embrace with Luke was going to last her a lifetime.

* * * * *

Her Christmas Hero

LINDA WARREN

To my hero—Sonny

Two-time Rita® Award-nominated and award-winning author **Linda Warren** loves her job, writing happily-ever-after books for Mills & Boon. Drawing upon her years of growing up on a farm/ranch in Texas, she writes about sexy heroes, feisty heroines and broken families with an emotional punch, all set against the backdrop of Texas. Her favourite pastime is sitting on her patio with her husband watching the wildlife, especially the injured ones that are coming in pairs these days: two Canada geese with broken wings, two does with broken legs and a bobcat ready to pounce on anything tasty. Learn more about Linda and her books at her website, www.lindawarren.net, or on Facebook at www.facebook.com/AuthorLindaWarren.

Chapter One

Stopping her vehicle on the flooded county road, Britt
Davis knew she'd made a big mistake. Sheets of rain
slashed at the windshield like an enraged warrior. Lightning lit up the sky and thunder rumbled with a dire fore-
boding. The wipers swished back and forth in frenetic
motion, trying to ward off the blows—to no avail. The
torrential downpour was winning the battle.

She peered over the steering wheel, searching for the
road through the fury of the storm. All she could see was
water and more water. The worn blacktop was fast becoming a lake. Fear clutched her throat and she flexed
her clammy hands, gripping the wheel. Brushy Creek,
known for flooding out of its banks, wasn't far away, and
she had to be careful.

The shortcut to Taylor, Texas, from Austin seemed
like a good idea thirty minutes ago. She had to get to her
son. That was the only reason she was out in this storm.
It had been four days since she'd held him, hugged him.
Glancing at the papers lying on the passenger seat of her
Camry, she knew she had to reach her baby as soon as
possible. Her ex-husband had filed for temporary custody
of their nine-month-old son, Dillon, on the grounds that
he was the better parent, since her job as an international

flight attendant took her away from their child for long periods of time.

Bastard!

Phil had been looking for a way to get back at her for divorcing him, and he'd found it. The only way to hurt her was through Dillon. She'd been served with the papers as she'd reached her apartment after a flight from Paris. Her mother, who lived in Taylor, kept Dillon while she worked.

Britt clenched her hands into fists. "Damn." Phil would not take her child.

Darkness fell like a heavy cloak as the October storm raged around her. Now her visibility was zilch as the warrior continued his assault. Rain pounded the car with a deafening sound. The headlights showed a watery path in front of her. She'd wait it out. That was all she could do.

Grabbing her purse, she reached for her cell to call her mother. She wanted to hear Dillon's silly giggles. She missed him so much. No signal. Her spirits sank lower. She needed to hear a friendly voice. Her head shot up as she felt the car move. *It couldn't!* She was imagining things. She peered through the swipe of wipers and saw the water on the road was rising. The wind whipped it fiercely against the car. Was she closer to Brushy Creek than she'd thought? Could…?

The thought froze in her mind as the car inched sideways, the wind and the water playing with it like a piece of flotsam. This wasn't her imagination. OhmyGod! No! No! This couldn't be happening. Another gust of wind and the car was swept into the rising waters. She screamed. But nothing stopped the nightmare. Her vehicle kept moving—swiftly. She had to get out. She had to get out of the car! If she didn't, it would be her grave.

Frantically, she undid her seat belt and reached for the window button. It went down with a swoosh. Rain pelted her and water sprayed in. She screamed again, but sanity ruled. She had to keep her wits. As the car filled she fought against the splashing surge and pulled herself through the window, fighting to hold her breath, fighting for her life. The strong current took her slight frame and she struggled to keep her head up, to breathe. She had to stay alive—for Dillon.

Dillon!

The roar of the water filled her ears as its power swept her along. Her head went under and she swallowed putrid water, battling with everything in her to reach precious air. The current tossed her around like driftwood in the cold, dark night.

"Dillon," she called as her strength waned.

Suddenly her body hit an object and her frantic cry stopped. She was pinned against something. Gulping in air, she realized it was a log or part of a fallen tree. She wrapped both arms around the wet wood and tried to inch toward the bank, but the current kept pulling her back into the watery depths. Rain assaulted her eyes, blinding her. Plus it was so dark! How long could she keep up this battle? Terror gnawed at her heart and she shook, choking back a sob. The wind splashed murky slush against her face. As she grew weaker, hope of surviving seemed nil.

Giving in to nature wasn't in her plan, though. She did what she always did in a crisis. She prayed. Then she yelled at the top of her lungs, "Help! Someone please help me! Please!"

Her words mingled with the rain and the wind.

She weakened more and her arms slipped. No! She wouldn't give in. Wrapping herself tighter around the log, even though the bark cut into her skin, she kept yelling.

And praying.

* * *

Quentin Ross was in a hurry to reach Austin. He had a date with Deidre, and she didn't like it when he was late. He'd spent the day with his sister's family in Horseshoe, Texas. It was his nephew's first birthday and no way would he miss that. Peyton was happy with her husband and their two kids. She'd been domesticated, something he thought he'd never see from his pampered, flamboyant sister. These days she was still a little over the top, but that was Peyton, and always would be. But she didn't need pampering anymore, except from her sheriff husband, her soul mate, the right man for her. Watching all that love and family togetherness made Quentin wonder why he was still single at thirty-five.

Because the right woman always seemed to be wrong—wrong for him. Or maybe he chose the wrong women. His law career had been his top priority for years, but now he was feeling a pull for something else. His own family. He always had this feeling when he visited Peyton. Once he was back in the city, it would pass, he knew. There would be another case. Another person needing his help, and his focus would switch back to his career. Then there was Deidre....

She'd sliced and diced his heart so much it was a wonder it was still beating. But once again he'd agreed to go out with her—to talk. They rarely did much talking, though.

The rain was becoming intense and the strong wind tugged at his car. Damn! He should never have taken the shortcut to Texas 79, but he'd driven it many times before. Tonight, though, Mother Nature was bent on a rampage.

He reached Brushy Creek and saw that it was flooded out of its banks, the water swirling like a whirlpool. No way could he cross it. He'd have to turn around and find another way to Austin.

As he was backing up, his headlights flashed across the swollen creek. Something bobbed in the water. What the hell? Was that a car? The driving rain kept him from seeing clearly, but it *looked* like the top of a sedan. Was someone in trouble?

He maneuvered his vehicle so his headlights pointed down the creek. Then he saw it—someone clinging to a log. Someone who needed help. He tried his cell, but the signal was weak. Without another thought, he opened his door and stepped out into the night. He was soaked to the skin in seconds, but didn't have time to think about himself. The person in the water needed help. Having been on the swim team in high school and college, he was a strong swimmer. He kicked off his shoes and dived in.

The cool water hit him like an electric shock, stealing his breath. It took a moment for him to get his bearings. The raging water bubbled around him and he tried floating with the current. But it was fierce, taking him quickly. He struggled to reach the person.

"Help me, please." The voice was faint. It sounded like a woman's.

"Hold on," he shouted, rain filling his mouth. He spit it out.

Finally he reached the log and grabbed on to the end, striving to keep his balance. From the way it wobbled he knew it was about to lose its anchor and drift downstream. "Don't let go," he yelled, inching toward the clinging figure while fighting the current. Coming up behind her, he placed his hands on the log next to hers, keeping her between his arms. At that moment, the log snapped. The flood took it for a ride, and them along with it.

"Don't let go," he said into her left ear, holding her close just in case she did.

"I...I...I..."

"Shh." He tried to calm her. "Just hang on. The log will stop soon."

The rain continued its brutal barrage and the flood-waters churned around them, along with the debris. Just when it seemed they were going to be washed away, the log caught on another fallen tree and stopped. Quinn knew he had to get her out of the creek now. Fighting the force of the wind and the rain, he urged her along the log.

When his feet touched the muddy bottom, he grabbed her around the waist and made for the shore, which was still about forty feet away. The water lapped at them, determined not to let go.

"Try to stand," he suggested.

"Oh, yes, I can touch the bottom," she replied, her voice excited.

"Don't stop. Keep going. We have to make it out of here."

They slogged through the mud and the water, trying to reach safety. At one point a monstrous wave caught her and she went down, flopping wildly. He snagged her and literally dragged her to the bank.

They lay in the mud, exhausted, the rain beating a steady tattoo on their backs. Then Quinn pushed himself up. "Can you stand?"

Without a word she staggered to her feet and followed him to higher ground.

"We have to go farther," he said raggedly. He couldn't see a foot in front of his face and had no idea what was out there. He just knew it was safer than the water.

Leading the way, he guided them into thick woods, into the darkness, into the unknown. Big trees with entwined branches lessened the stinging rain. He fell down beneath one. She huddled beside him as the storm raged on.

"Thank you," Britt said when she could catch her breath. "I don't know what I would have done if you hadn't come along."

"What happened?" he asked, and she liked his voice—strong yet soothing, with a husky undertone.

"I was trying to reach Taylor and I couldn't see for the heavy downpour. I guess I was closer to Brushy Creek than I thought. The water just...just took my car." She couldn't stop the tremor in her voice.

"Are you okay?"

"I don't know. I feel as if I've been used as a punching bag." She wiped at her face. "Is it ever going to stop?"

"Eventually. Try to rest, and we'll walk to safety when it's daylight."

Rest? Was he kidding? She was wet and muddy from head to toe and her nerves were tied into knots. She might never rest again. Might never close her eyes again. But something about his voice, compelling and confident, lulled her into a calmer state. She wondered if he had that effect on all women when they were scared to death.

Taking a long breath, she let the knots ease. She was safe. She would see Dillon soon. But the rain tap-tapping on her head prevented her from sleeping.

"Did your car stall in the water?" she asked.

"No," he replied. "I was on my way to Austin. When I reached Brushy Creek, I could see it was flooded, so I turned around. As I did, I saw your car bobbing in the water and you clinging to the log."

Britt leaned forward, trying to see his face in the darkness. "So you jumped in?"

"Yes," he answered in a matter-of-fact tone.

Without any thought for his own safety? His own life? How many men would do that? She didn't think there were any heroes left, but evidently one had just saved her.

"That was very heroic and dangerous."

"Mmm." He moved restlessly against the tree. "I'm not a hero. I saw you needed help and I didn't think about anything else. Later, when I've had time to think about it, I'll probably question my sanity."

"Well, thank you. My name is Britt."

"Short for Brittany?"

"No. Just Britt."

"Mine's Quinn. Now let's try to rest. Hopefully some-one will be looking for us by morning. My car is parked on the road and someone will spot it. We just have to wait."

She settled beside him once again. "I hate that my mother will be worried."

"Is that where you were going?"

"Yes."

"Maybe she'll think you're waiting out the storm."

"Maybe." Britt closed her eyes and once again forced herself to relax. She was alive and Dillon was safe with her mother. Tomorrow she would set about putting her life back together.

The wind howled and the rain fell. The forest around them was dark, sodden and frightening. But complete exhaustion obliterated any panic. Without conscious thought, she rested her head on Quinn's shoulder and drifted into sleep.

With a perfect stranger.

Britt woke up to a surreal feeling. She was wet, cold and disoriented. She hated nightmares, but this one felt so real. Her hand rested on something solid, hard—and alive, judging by the steady thudding beneath her fin-gertips.

She opened her eyes to an early dawn. A yellow glow bathed the deep woods. The ground was soaked, as was she and the man sitting beside her. Who…? The night came rushing back with vivid clarity.

Dillon.

Her mother must be so worried. Luckily, Dillon was too young to know anything was amiss.

Britt was alive.

And the stranger who'd saved her was sleeping beside her.

She raised her head and stared at him. His drenched hair was slicked back and she guessed when dry it was a shade of blond. His face was all angles, with a jutting chin covered with a growth of dark blond hairs that gave him a sensual look. Long legs stretched out into the leaves. He had to be at least six feet or more, with a whipcord body made for rescuing damsels in distress.

When God was putting together heroes, he'd made this one perfect—brave and strong, with looks and character. The kind of man a woman would want beside her in sickness and in health, in youth and old age, and all the ups and downs in between.

She must have a concussion, Britt thought, touching her soggy, tangled hair. She'd sworn off men a long time ago—the day she'd come home and found her husband of six months doing drugs in their bedroom with a strange woman, naked. That had shattered all Britt's trust in men.

Why was she seeing such good qualities in this one? She didn't even know him. But what did she need to know? He'd risked his life to save hers. That was enough.

And it was good to know there were heroes. Maybe all men weren't scumbag jerks without moral fiber.

He stirred and she moved back on the wet ground, shivering. Not from fear, but the cold. For the first time she realized she was chilled to the bone.

Yawning, he stretched his shoulders and opened his eyes. A wave of warmth shot through her. His eyes were the most beautiful color—sea blue, like she'd seen at the beach on Padre Island. She wanted to dive right in.

"How are you?" he asked.

"Bruised, but happy to be alive." She gestured to the forest. "It's stopped raining."

"Yeah." He swiped a hand over his hair. "I could use a cup of coffee."

Glancing around at the thick woods, she said, "If you find one out here, I'll fight you for it."

A stellar grin turned up the heat like a furnace. Charm, too. The man had it all.

"You'd probably win. You're a fighter. Most women would have let go of that log." He lightly stroked her black-and-blue forearm. "That should heal in no time."

At his gentle touch a tiny jolt of pleasure lurched through her and she lost her voice.

She wasn't a naive teenager. She'd been touched before. What was wrong with her?

He rose to his feet in one lithe movement, his muddy jeans and knit pullover clinging to him like a second skin, emphasizing the taut muscles in his arms, legs and chest. "Are you ready to start walking?"

"Uh...yes." She got to her feet rather slowly, and was unprepared for the weakness in her legs. Her knees buckled.

Quinn quickly caught her before she hit the ground. His arms were solid around her, and a telltale longing in her lower abdomen weakened her even more. She hated herself for that reaction.

To a stranger.

She pushed away. "Please don't touch me. I can stand on my own." Her voice was sharp, something she hadn't intended.

His blue eyes flared. "Excuse me."

Chapter Two

His eyes narrowed on her face and she wanted to take a step backward, but didn't. She'd made a fool of herself, so now she had to take her medicine, which was preferable to explaining how he made her feel.

"I'm not a helpless person. I can take care of myself." She heaved a breath. "I know it doesn't look like it. I made such a stupid decision coming out in the storm. Anyone else would have turned back. I feel like an idiot."

His eyes narrowed even more. "We've been through a harrowing ordeal," he finally said. "Let's push on." He turned and then suddenly swung back. "I was just trying to help you. It was a reflex. That's all."

"I know. I overreacted."

Quinn looked at her, really looked at her for the first time. Her eyes were dark, like the elderberry wine he'd drunk in college that had made him loopy. She probably had the same power to make men crazy. Long, provocative eyelashes framed her eyes. For a moment he thought they were artificial, but nothing about the woman said false. An abundance of dark hair hung in soaked strands around an oval face with defined cheekbones.

Bearing in mind her reaction to his touch, he tried not to stare at her body, but couldn't seem to look anywhere else. The mud on her face and clothes couldn't disguise her appeal. The sludge-coated jeans clung to her curves and the wet knit top left little to the imagination. The force of the water had ripped open three buttons and exposed the soft curve of her breasts.

The words *sex kitten* played through his mind, but were immediately replaced with *sugar and spice and everything nice*. He didn't know anything about her, but somehow sensed the latter fit her to a T.

A clap of thunder diverted his thoughts.

"Oh, no, not more rain," she cried.

"Looks like it. We better find some sort of shelter." As he spoke a fresh onslaught began to fall. "Let's go." He trudged through the deluge, with her a step behind him.

The weather was once again their enemy, and Quinn knew they couldn't continue to try to walk in it. Neither of them had shoes, and the ground was a muddy cesspool. He heard a cry and swung around to see that Britt had fallen headlong into the murky mess.

He rushed back to help, even though she probably didn't want it. Pushing to a sitting position, she wiped mud from her face. He couldn't tell if she was crying, but had a feeling she wasn't.

As he squatted beside her, he noticed some thick bushes around a tree. He pointed. "Shelter," he said above the pounding rain.

She climbed to her feet and he didn't offer assistance. Sloshing through the mud in his bare feet, Quinn reached the bushes and held back their wet branches so she could crawl inside. He quickly joined her. The thick yaupons offered some respite. A damp, musky smell surrounded them.

She shivered.

"Are you cold?"

"A little."

Without thinking, he put his arm around her. She didn't pull away as he expected, but nestled into him, their soaked bodies pressing together. Everything around them was wet, wet, wet, but an infusion of warmth eased through him just from holding her. Most women he knew would have crumpled into weeping hysteria by now.

"I feel like I'm in a nightmare," she murmured, tucking her head beneath his chin.

"Let's talk to get our minds on something else," he suggested. Lightning crackled in the distance, followed by booming thunder. Rain trickled from the branches on to them, but it wasn't bad.

"Men never like to talk."

"My mom says I was born talking."

"Are you close to your mother?"

"Kind of," he hedged, and wondered why. Maybe there were some things he didn't like to talk about.

"What does that mean?"

Before he could stop them, the words came pouring out, much like the rain—without warning. "When my sister and I were growing up, our mother worked for some very influential people in politics. She was gone a lot, running campaigns, doing whatever she needed to get a candidate elected. My dad raised us."

"But it worked for them, right?"

"On the surface."

This time Britt didn't ask what that meant. The rain drummed on, lulling him into a surreal state of mind. Sitting in the downpour holding her seemed natural. It wasn't, but it kept him talking.

"My dad was fifteen years older than my mother. They had a great deal of respect for each other and stayed together for the sake of their children." He paused. "Mom was very discreet about her affairs."

Quinn couldn't believe he'd told Britt that. He'd never

even told Peyton. Maybe he needed to say the words out loud to rid himself of any lingering negative feelings.

"But they hurt you?"

He swallowed, and his throat felt raw. He had told his mother he understood, but he hadn't. Love wasn't supposed to be like that.

When he didn't respond, Britt turned her face to look at him. Her dark eyes were concerned, inviting confidences he somehow knew she'd never tell another soul. Being a defense attorney, he was good at judging people. He sensed she was a woman to be trusted. His instincts never failed him.

"I suppose," he murmured. "But we got through it. My dad died about seven years ago and my mom remarried. Life goes on."

The whirl of a helicopter interrupted him.

Britt sat up as well as she could in the confined area. "Is that…?"

"Hot damn. I believe it is, and it's stopped raining again." Neither had noticed while they were talking.

They scurried out like two squirrels and glanced toward the sky, which was barely visible through the web-like branches.

"They're searching," he said. "We have to find a clearing so they can see us." He took off through the trees and she followed.

The woods were thick and he held low limbs so they wouldn't slap her in the face. He didn't think twice about doing it; that was his nature. If she had a problem, then it was her own. But she didn't say a word and she didn't falter during their flight through the thicket.

When they finally came to a clearing, everything was quiet. The helicopter had moved on.

"Do you think it will come back?" she asked, an edge of desperation in her voice.

"They'll keep searching," he replied, staring at the gray sky.

She didn't panic or cry, and he liked that. She was strong, just as she'd said. But he wondered why she was so sensitive about being touched. The obvious answer was that some man had hurt her. With her pinup looks, he could imagine a lot of men losing their minds over her.

And he was getting into treacherous waters.

He'd had enough of that for one night.

Gulping a breath, he sank onto the damp grass. "We can wait here until it comes back. They'll probably make routine circles along the creek, checking for people in trouble."

"I hope so." She sat beside him. "My mother needs to know I'm okay. She's probably worried sick." Realizing her blouse was open, Britt pulled it together. "I feel like a drowned rat."

As she said the words, the sun poked through the clouds in a burst of warmth.

"Oh, my. Can you believe this?" She held her face up to it like a virgin worshipping the gods. "That feels so-o-o good." Tugging her fingers through her tangled hair, she tossed it about to help it dry.

He could only stare. He'd seen beautiful women before, but this one was different, and he didn't know why. *Real* came to mind. Natural. Fresh. And an aversion to being touched. That was like a rare piece of art never being seen or admired. Sacrilege, to his way of thinking.

Why he was thinking it at all surprised him.

After today, he'd never see the woman again.

He stretched out his legs in the drenched leaves, his bare feet stinging from stepping on sharp sticks. Raising one foot, he rubbed it.

"How are your feet?" he asked.

"They're okay." She stopped fiddling with her hair. "But I don't think I'll ever get this mud out of my hair."

"Sure. Soap and water does the trick every time."

She cocked her head and seemed to relax a little. "So practical."

"That's me."

She twisted her body in discomfort. "I'm caked with mud. I've heard it said that mud wraps are good for the skin. Mine should be glowing."

His eyes traveled over the smooth lines of her face and neck. "It is." The words were in his head and it jolted him to realize he'd said them out loud.

Silence hung between them for a few seconds and a telltale shade of pink crept under her skin. "I get my olive complexion from my mom and grandmother. My grandmother is part Italian and part Polish, and has a fiery temper."

He raised his knees and rested his forearms on them. "Do you have a temper, as well?"

"Not really. I'm more like my father. It takes a lot to make me angry." Her eyes darkened.

"From the look on your face, I'd say someone in particular makes you angry."

"My ex." She picked mud from her jeans with a broken fingernail.

"Ex-boyfriend or ex-husband?" Quinn didn't know why he was inquiring about her personal life. Had to be the lawyer in him, he told himself. He was used to asking questions.

"Husband," she said under her breath.

"Bad split, huh?"

Her mouth tightened. "You could say that."

"You see?" He sat up straight. "That's why I avoid the much-sought-after institution. All my married friends are miserable."

She looked at him, those dark eyes spearing him like a helpless fish. He had the urge to squirm, and he hadn't squirmed in years. "Not all married couples are miserable. Your parents are not the norm. Mine were happily married until my father's death. Mom still misses him and she's never remarried."

Quinn met her glance. "So you still believe in love?"

She gazed off into the distance, not answering for a moment. "Right now I don't trust any man, but I still believe there is such a thing as real, everlasting love. I just chose the wrong man."

"Bargain basement type flashing a Neiman Marcus smile?"

Her mouth curved into a smile and he felt a sucker punch to his heart. "I have no idea what that means, but it fits. He was a phony, a liar, a deceiver, a cheater, a cruel jealous egoistical excuse for a man."

"And the reason you're sensitive about being touched."

Instantly, denial rose in her throat. Answering that question and exposing her weaknesses couldn't happen. Some things were private...and painful. She sat perfectly still, forcing the words down. She wouldn't share intimate details of her life with a stranger. But her ex brought out the worst in her. She just wanted to get out of this place and to her son.

"Wouldn't it be better to start walking?" she asked, to get her mind on something else.

Quinn flung out a hand. "We should head upstream. But rescue teams will be searching along the flooded creek, so we need to stay close."

Two deer emerged from the woods and, startled at the sight of people, leaped across the meadow. They were so graceful, and Britt watched until she couldn't see them anymore. Silence stretched. Crows landed in a tree, their calls echoing. An armadillo lumbered away into the grass. Animals were leaving their shelters after the storm.

She wiggled her toes, trying to dislodge the caked mud. "How about you—have you ever been married?" It seemed natural to question him, as if they'd been talking all their lives.

"A confirmed happy bachelor."

It was hard to believe that someone as handsome and courageous as Quinn was still available. The good ones were supposed to be taken.

"That's hard to believe."

"The lady has doubts," he mocked with a lifted eyebrow.

"You bet. Trusting men is not my strong suit."

He leaned back on his elbows. "I've had this off-and-on relationship with someone. It suits us both and neither one of us has been eager to tie the knot. I had a date with her last night and she's going to be royally pissed at my no-show."

"I'm sorry." Britt felt responsible.

"Don't be. There have been plenty of times when Deidre hasn't shown up."

Britt frowned. "Sounds as if you don't have much respect for one another."

"Mmm." He sat up. "I'm consumed with my work and she's consumed with spending her father's money. We're aware of each other's faults, but we still get together when the need arises. Bottom line, we're comfortable together."

"That's very candid," Britt said. And routine. And safe. He didn't seem the type of man to choose safe.

"My sister tells me that all the time." He glanced at her, a gleam in his eyes.

That lazy, infectious gaze made her stomach wobble. She cleared her throat. "Are you close to your sister?"

"Yes. I'm five years older and her protector. When she

was in her teens I was the one to get her out of trouble before our parents could find out. It became a major job while she was in college. She loved to party and have fun."

"What happened to her?"

"She got arrested."

"What?" That gleam in his eyes intensified. "You're joking."

"Absolutely not. She was arrested for attempting to bribe a sheriff."

"Is she in jail?"

"No. She married the sheriff."

Britt stared at him, not sure whether to believe him or not.

Leaning toward her, Quinn said, "It's true. Peyton was tired of being a party girl, and when she had to look at herself through the sheriff's eyes, she didn't like what she saw. She changed her life. Not for him, but for herself, so she could feel good about her life."

Britt started to speak and he held up a hand, stopping her. "In case you're going to remind me, yes, I know someone who is happily married."

"There's hope for you then."

"Afraid not. I'll be a crusty old bachelor at sixty, yelling at kids who dare to walk on my lawn."

She ran her fingers through the grass. "You don't like kids?"

He shrugged. "I have a niece and a nephew and I'm crazy about them, but I can't see myself as a father."

"Why not?"

The whirl of helicopter blades prevented his answer. Britt jumped to her feet and ran toward the sound. "Here! Please! Stop!" But she only saw the tail of the aircraft as it moved farther south. "No. No. No!" She sank to her knees, frustrated and out of patience.

Quinn stopped beside her. "They must have just picked up someone, or they would have come in this direction."

"We're never going to get out of here."

"We just have to wait." He held out a hand to her. She stared at it for a second and then placed hers in his bigger one. His fingers were strong, capable, and with one tug he pulled her to her feet.

"Thank you," she said, her voice raspy to her own ears.

"That wasn't so hard, was it?" The gleam was back in his eyes, and she sensed he was a man who teased and laughed a lot.

"No," she replied, feeling warm all over. And it wasn't from the sun. After the horrendous night, she felt strong enough to face whatever came next.

Because she'd met a hero.

Carin Davis opened the front door to a deputy sheriff. "Have you found my daughter?" she asked without waiting for an introduction.

"No, ma'am," he answered, removing his hat.

"What's taking so long? It's been hours."

The man took a breath. "The weather's been a hindrance, but they found her car. That's what I came to tell you."

"Oh!" Carin felt the blood drain from her face.

"It was in Brushy Creek." The officer took another breath. "We think the car was swept away into the flooding waters." Carin's knees buckled and the deputy caught her. "Are you okay?"

"Where's...where's my daughter?"

"Rescue teams are out searching, and we've got helicopters. We should know something soon."

But from the young man's voice Carin knew what he was thinking. Britt had drowned in the raging waters.

No!

She refused to believe that.

"Who's at the door?" Ona called.

"A deputy sheriff." Carin stood ramrod straight, not wanting her mother to see her anguish.

Ona hurried to the door, carrying Dillon. He immediately reached for Carin, and she cradled him close. *Mommy will come home, my angel.*

"Where's my granddaughter?" Ona demanded in her usual flame-throwing voice.

"We don't know, ma'am."

"Now listen…"

"They found her car in Brushy Creek, Mama," Carin told her before she could chastise the officer and his department.

"Hail, Mary…" Ona made the sign of the cross and went to the sofa to sit and pray.

"Please let us know the moment you hear anything," Carin said.

"Yes, ma'am. I'm sorry I don't have better news."

"Me, too."

She closed the door and sat by her mother. Ona was the strongest person she knew. She'd lived through the depression, the death of her son and then her husband. Carin never saw fear in her eyes. But she saw it now.

"What are we going to do?" Ona rocked back and forth, her arms wrapped around her ample waist. "Not my Britt… Without her…"

"Don't say it," Carin snapped. She couldn't hear those words. Britt was her only child, the light of her life, her world. Her young and beautiful daughter had to be alive. Carin couldn't, wouldn't believe anything else.

Sensing the fear in the adults, Dillon began to cry. Loud wails filled the room.

"Shh. Shh, my angel." Carin cuddled him, kissing his

fat cheek. "Mommy's coming." He immediately stopped crying, his dark eyes, so like his mother's, opened wide.

"Ma-ma-ma-ma," Dillon chanted, once again happy.

Carin placed him in the Pack 'n Play and gave him a truck to play with.

"You know if that bastard finds out something has happened to Britt he'll be here for the baby."

Carin could process only so much, and didn't want to think about her mother's words. But she had to be prepared.

Ona got to her feet. "I'm looking for Enzo's gun. I'll shoot that bastard before I let him take that child."

"You're not shooting anyone." Carin ran both hands though her short salt-and-pepper hair. "Mama, please, I can't take much more."

"Don't you worry, my pretty." She touched Carin's face. "Mama will take care of everything."

"Mama…" Her cry fell on deaf ears. Ona was already rummaging in her room. Carin sank onto the sofa and buried her face in her hands.

Please, please, bring my baby home, she prayed.

Chapter Three

Britt sat in the wet grass, trying to remain positive, trying not to lose her grip. Quinn lounged beside her, staring at the sky. They both were listening. Waiting.

The sun had chased away the chill and Britt reveled in its warmth. Home. She yearned for home, her baby, mother and grandmother. She couldn't wait to kiss Dillon's fat cheeks, to see his dimples when he smiled. Oh, she missed him. Being away from him for long periods of time was getting harder and harder. But her job paid extremely well and she had benefits. In the lousy economy she couldn't find anything else that would even come close to supporting them.

Of course, Phil paid child support, and he made sure it was always late. Upsetting her was his main objective. He had Dillon every other weekend and a week in the summer, but he never kept to the schedule. She cringed every time he walked out her door with Dillon, but there was nothing she could do to stop him. He had rights, the judge had said. And her drug allegations were unsubstantiated. Being a lawyer, Phil was an expert at fooling people.

Every time he picked up Dillon, the baby cried and clung to her, not wanting to go with a man he rarely saw. Phil always smiled and said, "You know how to stop this.

Come back." Those times when Dillon was so upset, she thought about it for a nanosecond, but knew it would be detrimental for her and Dillon. The man had no morals. He couldn't understand why she was so upset. He had told her his drug use and the other women had nothing to do with their marriage.

Britt couldn't believe she'd ever loved the man. Looking back, she saw her first mistake—trusting every word that came out of his mouth. It had been a whirlwind courtship. After two weeks of dating, Phil had asked her to marry him. There wasn't much to think about. He'd wined and dined her until she was head-over-heels for him.

His family was wealthy, his father a senior partner with a lot of clout in a big law firm in Austin. His dad had retired to their home in Colorado, and Phil became a partner in the firm. It was ideal. Britt wouldn't have to work again, Phil had said, but she'd held on to her job, anyway. Now she was glad she had.

Six weeks later they were married, and the fairy tale began. Phil bought her gifts for no reason, hired a maid for the condo and treated Britt as if she were a queen. Then the complaints started. He wanted her to quit her job. He bought sexy clothes, low-cut, short and tight, for her to wear, but she'd refused to look like a hooker. He didn't understand why she had to visit her mother and grandmother so often. At times she wondered if there was anything about her he liked.

On that fatal morning they'd had another argument about her job. When her flight was canceled, she'd decided to quit. Maybe they could get their marriage back on track. She'd just found out she was pregnant, and staying home and being a mother appealed to her.

Hurrying home, she'd stopped for groceries and candles, planning to prepare a special dinner to surprise him. They had been arguing so much she hadn't told him about the baby. But she was the one who'd been surprised. The moment she saw him curled up with the blonde, drug paraphernalia on the nightstand, the fairy tale had ended. Abruptly.

And forever.

He'd begged and pleaded, told her it meant nothing, that it was something he did for stress. She was shocked and sickened at his cavalier attitude. The diseases he had exposed her to were too much to contemplate. She'd walked out there and then, and had never looked back.

After that the threats began. He said she would rue the day she'd left him. Funny, she never had. She just regretted the day she'd met him.

Allowing him access to Dillon was the hardest thing she'd ever had to do. One of his high-priced attorneys made sure it happened. Now she had to deal with Phil for the rest of her life.

She worried about all the bad influences Dillon was exposed to while in Phil's care. That's why she had to make sure this custody attempt was shut down quickly. But for now, she was stuck.

Waiting.

"Do you live with your mother?"

That voice. She was beginning to really like Quinn's smooth, confident voice. The kind that made a woman forget she had morals. Made her forget her distrust of men. And made her forget her dire situation. She'd never met anyone who was so easy to talk to.

"No. I live in Austin. My grandmother lives with my mom, and she's a handful."

"Your grandmother is?" His eyes twinkled.

"She's had a lot of sadness in her life and it's hardened her. She doesn't take crap from anyone."

"So she's an angry old woman?" He ran a hand around the collar of his shirt to loosen the drying mud.

"She's hard-nosed about a lot of things. It's not easy to explain." Britt gazed into the distance. "One October her neighbors made a Halloween scene on their lawn with hay, pumpkins and ghosts. My grandmother said part of it was on her property, and she asked them to remove it. They didn't, so she set fire to it."

He laughed. "You're kidding."

"No." Britt shook her head. "The neighbors called the cops and they contacted my mother. To keep my grandmother out of jail, my mom paid for the damages, but never told Onnie. That's what I call my grandmother."

"Does she do things like that often?"

"Yes, and it's very frustrating for my mom. The last episode was the straw that broke the camel's back, so to speak. Onnie always has a big garden in her backyard, and she does a lot of canning. Two years ago she said her neighbor, not the same one, was stealing her tomatoes. My mom told her she just forgets she's picked them, but Onnie wouldn't believe that for a second."

"What did she do?"

Britt didn't miss the laughter in Quinn's voice. That was not the usual effect Onnie had on people.

Britt shifted into a more comfortable position. "Her uncle Enzo is ninety-two, and he gave her an old World War II pistol for protection after my grandfather died. I'm not sure it even has bullets, but Onnie took it over to the neighbors and told them if she caught them in her garden she was going to shoot them. Of course, they called the police about the crazy lady with a gun. My mom thought it was time for Onnie to move, since she wasn't welcome in the neighborhood anymore."

"So she moved in with your mother?"

"Yes, and it hasn't been easy. Onnie is stubborn, but they're managing to get along. At least Mom is keeping her out of trouble."

The drying mud was becoming uncomfortable. Britt shifted again to ease the tightness of her jeans. "These pants are drying like paint, and I'm never going to be able to remove them."

"Call me and I'll come help you."

She glanced at him, expecting laughter on his face, but there wasn't any. "I never know when you're teasing."

His eyes held hers. "I'm not teasing."

Tiny pinpoints of heat dotted her body, and she was sure her clothes were melting off under his warm gaze. In his eyes she saw the one thing she'd been avoiding for a very long time—desire. She was surprised she could still recognize it. But she was about to drown in pure, pure waves of blue.

His hand gently moved tangles of hair from her face. Everything faded away. They were two people, a man and a woman, stranded in the woods and discovering a whole new realm of emotions. And Britt wasn't uncomfortable with the discovery.

"I'm not sensitive about being touched," she blurted out.

He lifted an eyebrow. "Really? It seemed that way to me."

She glanced down at her hands and saw the dirt and grime. "Since you saved my life, I have to be honest with you." She wiped her palms down her jeans. "I haven't been with anyone since my marriage ended." She hadn't meant to get this personal, but she couldn't seem to stop herself. "When you touched me, I was feeling emotions I hadn't felt in a long time, and it made me angry. I was fighting for my life and you're a stranger. I shouldn't feel attracted to you."

"Are you thinking your senses were just heightened?"

She raised her head to look at him. "Has to be."

"Want to put it to the test?" His voice was seductive,

lulling her into a relaxed state. There was only one answer in her head. Yes!

He lifted the heavy hair from her neck and she had no qualms about meeting his kiss. Her heart hammered in expectation and...

They both heard it.

The helicopter.

Britt jumped up, running with her arms in the air. "Here! Here! We're here!"

She tripped and fell headlong in the grass. Quinn fell down beside her, laughing. "You fall more than any woman I know."

"I do not," she stated, laughter bubbling inside her. She sat up and without thinking hugged and kissed him lightly. "Thank you."

"Britt..."

The loud sound of the copter drowned out his words. In less than a minute the aircraft landed. Two men jumped out.

"Are you okay?" one called.

"Yes," Quinn shouted back, helping Britt to her feet.

They were assisted aboard, then were headed for Austin. After a paramedic checked her vitals, Britt asked, "May I please call my mother?"

"Yes, ma'am."

She talked for a moment, just to let her mom know she was fine. She also told her where the aircraft was taking her. It wasn't long before they landed at Breckenridge Hospital in Austin.

These were Britt's last moments with Quinn. Why she was feeling nostalgic she wasn't sure. She looked up to find him staring at her.

"I hope you find that real love. Don't settle for anything less," he murmured.

She swallowed and wondered if there was such a thing

as finding love with a stranger. Pushing the thought aside, she said, "Good luck with Deidre. I hope she's not too upset with you."

He leaned over and kissed her forehead. "Goodbye, Britt."

"Goodbye," she whispered with a lump in her throat.

Stretchers were rolled out to the helicopter, and Britt and Quinn were whisked away for a thorough examination.

She got a glimpse of the sky and saw it was darkening once again. They'd been rescued just in time. Turning her head, she noticed Quinn being pushed into an E.R. room down the hall. A pretty blonde ran to hug him. A man in khakis, a white shirt and boots, with a badge on his chest, followed. It had to be Quinn's sister and the sheriff. Quinn had his family. Britt was happy about that.

Together for less than twenty-four hours, and now they'd be separated for a lifetime.

Goodbye, Quinn.

My hero.

"Britt, my baby." Carin rushed into the E.R. room, cradling Dillon on her hip. Onnie was right behind them. It was the most beautiful sight Britt had ever seen.

Carin took a startled look at her, no doubt surprised at how bedraggled she was, and hugged her. "Are you okay?"

"I'm fine now."

Dillon wiggled from his grandmother to his mother. "No…" Carin started, but Britt grabbed her baby and held him.

She soaked up his sweet scent, kissing his cheek. His heart beat rapidly against her. "Ma-ma-ma," he cooed.

A nurse came in. "Everyone will have to leave. I have to check the patient and get her cleaned up."

"Now listen here, missy." Onnie stepped up to the plate, fire in her eyes. "This is my granddaughter and I ain't leaving her."

"Mama," Carin said in a sharp voice that usually got Onnie's attention. "We'll go to the waiting room until they've checked Britt. We need to know she's okay."

"How long is it going to take?" The question was directed at the nurse.

"Not long. I'll come and get you when the doctor has completed his exam."

"Yeah. Like I believe that." Onnie snorted. "I wasn't born yesterday, missy."

"Onnie, please," Britt begged, nuzzling Dillon.

Her grandmother patted her hand. "I'll be just down the hall. If you need anything, just holler. I still got good ears." Onnie looked her over. "My, you're a mess. Looks like someone used you as a mop."

Carin reached for Dillon. He clung to Britt. "It's okay, sweetie. Mommy's right here. Go with Nana."

Reluctantly, he let go, his bottom lip trembling. Britt felt herself wobble as they walked out. "Please hurry," she told the nurse. She wanted to hold her son until her arms couldn't hold him any longer.

Within minutes the nurse had cut off Britt's clothes, and a doctor came in to examine her. She had scratches and bruises, but he wanted some tests run, mostly a Cat scan of her head and an X-ray of her lungs.

She begged for a shower first and the doctor allowed it. The nurse took her down the hall to a bathroom and stayed with her just in case she passed out. Britt scrubbed her hair twice before she'd removed all the mud and grime. Quinn was right—soap and water did the trick. Stepping out, she wondered if he was also taking a shower.

She had to stop thinking about him.

A few minutes later she was back in her room. The nurse said they'd take her for tests soon. Britt felt one hundred percent better. Almost. The custody hearing was still hanging over her head. What was Phil up to? Caring for their son wasn't on his list of priorities.

Her mother slipped into the room.

"Mom. Where's Dillon?" Britt sat up.

Carin tucked her hair behind her ears in a nervous gesture. "Don't worry. He's with Onnie. I just wanted to make sure you were okay."

"I'm fine." A tear trailed from her eye, belying her words.

Her mother gathered her into her arms. "Oh, my baby, I've been so worried."

Britt clutched her. "I was so stupid going out in the storm, but I had to see my son."

Carin sat down on the bed. "What happened?"

"It was awful." Britt scrubbed at her eyes, telling her mother the whole story.

"What a courageous young man," Carin said.

"I couldn't have held on to the log much longer, Mom. I…"

"Shh, my baby." Carin wiped away Britt's tears. "You're alive and we have to thank this man."

"I have…several times." Britt sat up straighter. "Have you seen any reporters in the hospital?"

"There was one talking to a nurse, trying to get information, but she said she couldn't help him."

"Good. I don't want any of this to get back to Phil."

Carin frowned. "I'm sure it will be on the news."

"Not if we don't give them any information." Britt tugged at her hospital gown. "Would you mind going to my apartment and getting me a change of clothes? By then I should be through with the tests and able to leave."

"You got it." Her mother kissed her forehead. "Try not to worry. There's no way Phil can take Dillon."

Britt sincerely hoped that was true.

For the next hour she underwent tests, but they didn't find anything and the doctor finally released her, telling her to check with her own doctor if she had any problems. Her mother came back with her clothes and Britt quickly dressed. Determined to avoid reporters, she told her mother to pull the car to the front entrance instead of the E.R. That way she could dodge the press. The last thing she wanted was having her picture in the papers.

"Here's your wheelchair," the nurse said.

"No, that's fine."

The woman scowled. "I'm sorry. It's policy and—"

"I really can walk. I don't want to face any newspeople and I don't want any media attention."

Something in her voice must have gotten to the nurse. She chewed on her lip. "I'll take you out a back way." She held up a finger. "But in a wheelchair."

Britt nodded, grateful for her help.

The ride was short. The nurse stopped at a door. "This will take you to the front entrance."

"Thank you. I appreciate it."

"Just stay out of rising waters," the woman replied with a smile.

Britt nodded and opened the door. She stopped as she saw a group down the hall. Quinn was dressed in dark slacks and a white shirt, and a different tall blonde was hugging him. Had to be Deidre. Evidently she'd forgiven him. Quinn's sister and her sheriff stood to the side.

Britt's eyes were glued to Quinn's tall lean frame. Her heart pounded against her ribs as she said another silent goodbye to the man who had risked his life to save hers.

Why were the good ones always taken?

Chapter Four

During the next couple of days Britt spent a lot of time filling out papers for her insurance company, getting a new driver's license and reporting lost credit cards. The company rented her a car until all the paperwork was finalized and approved.

Every morning she seemed to find a new ache or pain. Her body had taken a beating in the water, but each day she felt better and stronger. Strong enough to face Phil in court.

She met with her lawyer, Mona Tibbs, and Mona assured her they had nothing to worry about. It was just another attempt of Phil's to scare her into returning to him. After talking to Mona, Britt felt optimistic. Returning to Phil wasn't an option.

All through the busyness and worry, Britt thought often of Quinn. He lived in Austin, but she didn't even know his last name. She'd like to send him a thank-you, a gift of some sort. And she had to admit she'd like to see him again. Maybe Phil hadn't destroyed all her trust in men.

The temperature hovered in the forties on the day of the hearing. Her mother was coming into Austin to sit with Dillon while Britt was at the hearing. When her doorbell rang, Britt knew who it was, so she ran to let her mother in. She was surprised to see her grandmother, too.

"I've decided to go with you," her mother informed her. "Mama will stay with Dillon."

"There's no need." Britt tried to reassure her. "Mona says it will take only a few minutes. Phil doesn't have a leg to stand on. A judge hardly ever takes a child away from a loving mother."

"Still, I'd feel better if you weren't alone."

"Mom…" Britt didn't get to voice her complaint as Onnie pushed passed her to the small kitchenette.

"Do you have any beer?" her grandmother asked, opening the refrigerator.

"What? Beer?" Britt's thoughts zipped in a completely different direction.

"Mama, you're not drinking beer this early in the day," Carin snapped.

"It's not for me. It's for Enzo." Onnie stopped snooping in the refrigerator and faced her daughter.

"Enzo!" Carin's voice rose a notch.

Britt closed the front door with a sigh. She didn't need this today.

"Yeah. His assisted living facility is not far away. I told him he can catch the bus and come visit."

"No, no." Carin shook her head. "Not today."

Onnie placed her hands on her hips. "You may be my daughter but you can't boss me around."

"Please, could we not argue?" Britt asked. "I'm nervous enough."

Onnie hugged her. "Don't worry. That sleazebag is not taking sweet Dillon." She shot a glance at her daughter. "But we're visiting Enzo before we go home."

"Fine," Carin replied through tight lips.

Britt picked up her purse. "I really have to run. The hearing is at two."

"I'm ready," her mother said, and Britt knew there was no way to dissuade her.

She turned to her grandmother. "Dillon is down for his nap. When he wakes up…"

"I know the drill, my pretty." Onnie pinched her cheek and reached for the TV remote control. "We'll be just dandy. Go stick it to the bastard."

The ride to family court was done mostly in silence. Britt was nervous and she couldn't shake it. Mona met them outside the courtroom. In her forties, with a blond bob, the lawyer was impeccably dressed in a dark suit and heels. Britt liked her confident attitude.

"This shouldn't take long," Mona said. "Your ex has to show just cause to remove Dillon from your care, and he simply doesn't have any grounds." She touched Britt's forearm. "Relax."

"I'm trying to," she replied, feeling her face muscles stretch into tight lines of worry. But she knew Phil well enough to know he was up to something. She wouldn't relax until this was over.

Footsteps echoed on the tiled floor. Britt looked up to see Phil strolling toward her, a tall man blocked by Phil's frame behind him. Blond and green-eyed, Phil was suave, handsome, a man who had once turned her head with his charm and words of love. His attraction and phony words had been exposed for what they really were, and now he just turned her stomach.

"Good afternoon, Roslyn," he said in a voice that slid across her nerves with the sharpness of a nail. He always called her by her first name. At first it had been charming. Now it was insulting.

"There is nothing good about any meeting with you," she managed to say.

"Tut-tut. You need to keep that temper in check."

Temper? What was he talking about?

"Phil, I don't think…"

That voice! It resonated in Britt's head with sweet memories as she gaped at the man who stepped forward. *No. It couldn't be.*

But it was.

Her hero from the creek stood staring at her with the same look of shock she was sure was on her face.

"Roslyn, this is my lawyer, Quentin Ross."

Quentin Ross.

In the stunned silence no one spoke. The sturdy, efficient clock on the wall ticked away seconds like a time bomb. Voices echoed down the hall. A faint scent of aftershave filled her nostrils. Behind Britt a door opened, the turning of the door handle sounding like cymbals in her ears.

"The judge will see you now," a lady said.

Mona nudged her. "Let's go inside."

"Are you okay?" her mother asked. "You're as white as a sheet."

"I'm fine," she muttered, but somewhere deep inside her she knew she was never going to be the same again.

They took seats on the right of the judge's desk. Britt was glad of the chair for support. Her legs were trembling. She drew a long breath, forcing herself to breathe in and out in a normal rhythm. But there was nothing normal about the fear gripping her throat.

He was Phil's lawyer kept running through her mind like a 9-1-1 call. Her hero, the man she'd put on a pedestal, was now supporting Phil to take Dillon from her. How could that be? He had to know Phil in some way. What had she revealed to him in the woods? Had she inadvertently hurt her case?

She was searching for answers, but didn't find any. Gripping her hands together until they were bloodless, she looked around the room. The Texan and American flags hung in one corner. Polished dark wood and brass were all around her. Dark and forbidding—much like the feeling in her heart. She shivered.

It took a full minute for her shock to dissipate and her strength to kick in. She didn't care who Phil's attorney was. Quentin Ross didn't matter. Keeping her son did. She focused on that, but had to resist looking Quinn's way. She couldn't believe how hard that was.

The judge entered from a side door and took her seat at the big desk. "Good afternoon," she said, folding her hands on the file folders in front of her. "I'm Judge Evelyn Norcutt and we're here today at the request of Phil Rutherford to modify custody of minor child Dillon Allan Rutherford." She fingered a piece of paper on the desk. "I received this memo yesterday. Ms. Tibbs, I assume you've received it, too."

"Yes, Your Honor."

"Do you have any objections?"

"No, Your Honor."

"What is it?" Britt whispered.

"Mr. Rutherford's original attorney is ill and Mr. Ross is taking over."

"Why didn't you tell me this?" she hissed.

"I didn't think it mattered."

"It matters when—"

"Mr. Ross!" The judge's strong voice broke through her words. "You're taking a step down by visiting us in family court."

Quinn stood, and against her will Britt looked at him. In a dark blue suit, white shirt and a blue-striped tie he looked all-business. No mud, no grime, no mischievous grin, just business behind a brooding expression. She noticed his hair was a medium blond streaked with an even lighter shade. Her guess would be that he spent a lot of time in the sun.

With Deidre.

Britt gritted her teeth. Quinn Ross meant nothing to her.

"Your Honor, I'm helping out a friend. I spent a year in family law before switching to defense. I'm more than qualified to handle this case."

His deep, confident voice sliced through her as memories of lightning and thunder rumbled in her head.

"I have no doubt."

Friend. She picked up on that one word. He was friends with Phil. She'd been married to Phil for six months and she'd never heard of him.

The judge pushed her glasses up the bridge of her nose. "I've gone over the petition Mr. Wallis filed with the court." She glanced over the top of her glasses at Quinn. "I assume you're up-to-date."

"Yes, Your Honor. I spoke with Herb over the phone about every detail of the case."

"Good." The judge opened a folder and pulled out papers. "Seems Mr. Rutherford is concerned about the amount of time Ms. Rutherford—"

"It's Davis," Britt corrected, before she could stop herself. "I took back my maiden name."

The judge looked up with a frown. "Davis, then. Mr. Rutherford is concerned about the amount of time Ms. Davis spends away from their son."

"Your Honor." Mona was on her feet. "I've seen the petition and it's completely misleading, a blatant attempt to discredit Ms. Davis's abilities as a mother. Ms. Davis is an international flight attendant. It requires her to be gone for long periods."

"I'm aware of that, and I'm also aware she has a nine-month-old son."

"Ms. Davis's mother takes very good care of him while Ms. Davis is away."

"But Dillon is not being cared for by either of his parents." The judge flipped through the papers. "A six-month work log of Ms. Davis has also been filed by Mr. Wallis. In June and July she was home only one week each month. That concerns me."

"Your Honor." Britt had to speak. She could feel this spiraling in the wrong direction. "I took the summer flights to make extra money to support my child. It's not something I do on a regular basis. And when I'm away, I speak with him every morning, and every night before he goes to bed. I love my son and I'm trying to make a better life for him."

"But you're not there for him physically."

The truth of that hit her in the chest like a sledgehammer, and she had no words to defend herself.

"Mr. Ross." The judge turned her attention to Quinn. "Do you have anything to add?"

"Yes, Your Honor." He stood and buttoned his jacket. "With Ms. Davis's…busy schedule, Mr. Rutherford is concerned about his son being raised…by a grandmother. He's offering…to be there for the boy full time…morning, night and he'll come home for lunch. Mr. Rutherford will hire a nanny for when he's at work. I submit… that at this time Philip Rutherford…is the better parent to raise Dillon Allan."

The judge frowned. "Mr. Ross, is there something wrong with your voice?"

Quinn raised a hand to his neck. "I have a bit of a sore throat."

"Thought so. Your usual stellar voice is a little off, but nonetheless effective."

"Do something," Britt whispered to Mona. "Don't let them take my son." The fear in her became very real.

She felt it with every beat of her heart. Phil's father was very powerful in Austin, and somehow they had gotten to the judge. That was the only explanation. And they'd hired Quentin Ross to deliver the blow that would rip out Britt's heart.

Mona was on her feet once again. "Your Honor, they're using Ms. Davis's job as a weapon to take her son. A baby needs to be with his mother."

The judge folded her hands on the papers. "I agree, Ms. Tibbs, a baby needs to be with his mother. But Ms. Davis isn't there. She's a drop-in mother. A nine-month-old boy needs more. He needs a full-time mother. A full-time parent."

"A lot of mothers work."

"But they're there in the morning and at night. As the situation stands I see no recourse but—"

"No." Britt jumped to her feet. "You can't take my son. He's my life. I'm his *mother*."

"Ms. Davis, I rarely take a child from the mother, but as I said, and Mr. Rutherford's lawyer has stated, you're not there for your baby. Until your situation changes I'm granting temporary custody to the father, Phil Rutherford."

"No, no, don't do this. Can't you see what they're doing? Don't, please." Tears rolled from her eyes and she quickly brushed them away. She felt her mother's arm around her waist and she leaned on her for support.

"I said temporary, Ms. Davis. I'll review this case in four months. That will give you time to sort out your life." She turned to the laptop on her left and typed in information. "You are to hand over the boy to Mr. Rutherford at ten in the morning and—"

"No," Britt said with force. "I refuse to hand over my child to a drug addict. You're endangering his life. What kind of judge are you?"

"Sit down, Ms. Davis."

Britt stared at the judge, anger in every bone of her body. If the judge thought she would back down, she was in for a shock. Britt had nothing left to lose. "Isn't this supposed to be about the best interest of the child? Well, you've just blown that to hell with your bigoted attitude."

"Ms. Tibbs, get your client under control or I will hold her in contempt."

"Let me handle this, Britt," Mona whispered. "You don't need to go to jail. Sit down, please."

Her mother tugged her back into her chair.

"Thank you," the judge said. "As I was saying, all child support will stop. Sundays, from eight in the morning until five in the afternoon, will be Ms. Davis's time to see Dillon, and every Tuesday and Thursday afternoon from one to six, if her schedule permits. Mr. Rutherford, I expressly do not want you there during those times, and order no contact between you and Ms. Davis. Mr. Ross's office will oversee the visits."

"My client will not be allowed any time alone with her child?" Mona asked rather tartly.

"With her connection to the airlines, she's a flight risk. For now, someone will always be with her."

Britt gritted her teeth at the injustice.

"I object to this, Your Honor. Ms. Davis is a loving mother and I resent you using her job as a means to remove her child from her. I resent it as a woman and as a lawyer."

"Resent away. You have that right."

"I'll file an appeal."

"Go ahead, but my ruling stands. This court is adjourned."

Just like that they had taken her child. Her precious baby.

Britt was numb and empty and couldn't focus on what

to do next. There *was* no next. Phil would raise Dillon for the next four months. He'd won.

They had taken her child. It was her worst nightmare come true.

Her mother hugged her. "Baby, I'm so sorry, but we'll get through this."

"I don't know how," she murmured, looking down at her broken nails from her time in the creek. A choked sob left her throat and she raised her head. Her eyes collided with Quinn's. His blue eyes were somber, almost apologetic. She immediately looked away and grabbed her coat. She would not let him see her cry.

Picking up her purse, she walked from the room, her mother beside her.

Phil waited at the door, a smirk on his face. "I'll be at your apartment at ten in the morning for Dillon."

She couldn't speak; pain and anger locked her vocal cords. Without a word, she pushed by him. He grabbed her arm and she jerked away.

"Don't touch me."

"Leave my daughter alone," Carin said. "Haven't you hurt her enough?"

Ignoring her mother, Phil looked straight at Britt. "You know how to stop this."

Yes, she did, but she'd rather die first. And that's what she was doing, dying inside. She walked away without giving him any satisfaction.

And she refused to even spare Quentin Ross a glance.

Quinn watched this exchange with a knot in his gut. He felt as if he had been sucker punched by the heavyweight champion of the world. Or maybe by a devious, cunning, so-called friend.

"What did you mean by that?"

Instead of answering, Phil slapped Quinn on the back. "You did great today, old friend."

He wasn't Phil's friend. They'd been classmates in law school. Through that connection, Quinn had gotten an internship in Philip Sr.'s prestigious law firm. He was deeply grateful, but he didn't want to continue to pay that debt for the rest of his life.

Quinn placed papers in his briefcase and snapped it shut. "Why did you call me to handle this case at the last minute?"

"Because you're the best. And since Herb was indisposed, I knew you were the one who could stick it to Roslyn in a big way. Dad's going to be so excited to hear Dillon will be living with me."

"I didn't accept as a favor to your father." Who was he kidding? It was the only reason. Quinn's law career was his life, and Philip Sr. could ruin it with just a couple of calls. It wasn't easy admitting that, and Quinn felt lower than the dust lingering beneath the rug on the floor. "I did it because I thought your ex was a lousy mother and a tramp, like you and Herb painted her."

Phil punched him on the arm as if they were teenagers. "She got to you with that sweet demeanor and gorgeous looks, not to mention totally awesome body."

Phil didn't know the half of it. "I don't like taking a child from his mother."

"Don't worry, she'll be back in my bed by the end of the week."

Quinn frowned. "Is that what this hearing was about?"

"You bet. I know how to push her buttons, and now she knows I have the upper hand."

Quinn picked up his briefcase. "Don't call me for any more help. My specialty is defense law and that's where I'm staying."

"Now, ol' buddy, Herb is out of commission, so you're

the lawyer of record for this case. You wouldn't want me to tell Dad that you bailed."

Quinn kept a tight rein on his temper. "You really are a jerk."

Phil's face darkened. "Don't push your luck."

"I'm only just starting." He walked away without another word, but he left his dignity, his ethics and his self-respect behind.

What had he done?

Chapter Five

Quinn sat in his paneled study surrounded by bookshelves holding his father's ancient-history tomes. Taking a sip of wine, he gazed at the leather-bound relics neatly lined up on the shelves. Books were also haphazardly stacked on the hardwood floor. He'd been meaning to donate some to a library, but so far hadn't gotten round to it. Sometime soon he needed to call Professor Withers, a colleague of his dad's, and offer him some volumes.

Peyton had taken the ones she'd wanted, but the room was still full of the books his father loved. As a history professor, Malcolm Ross's focus was the past. Though he'd been a quiet, gentle man, his voice would rise in excitement as he spoke of ancient civilizations. Egypt, Greece and China were his favorite places, and in the summers Quinn and Peyton would travel with their father to explore the fascinating ruins of those countries.

Quinn never found an interest in the past. He was more like his mother, who was also a lawyer. But he respected his father more than anyone he'd ever known. The man never complained or judged.

Quinn poured another glass of wine, wishing he could talk to his dad, who had a way of solving problems with logic and reason.

And Quinn had one big problem.

Britt.

She was Phil's ex.

Quinn was supposed to be smart, but he couldn't wrap his brain around that. Rarely was his composure shaken. He'd mastered the appearance of calm over the years in the courtroom. But today, when he saw Britt and realized she was Phil's ex, he'd almost lost his grip on himself.

The woman he'd saved in the creek was Phil's ex-wife. Phil had cheated, lied and deceived her, and he was the reason she had an aversion to being touched. Quinn believed everything Britt had told him. She had no reason to lie. And Quinn had stood in open court and followed the plan Phil and Herb had laid out to take her child. Because he owed Philip Sr.

The thought left a bitter taste in his mouth.

He took a gulp of wine. He'd been planning to call her to see how she was, but his busy schedule had prevented him from following through. Now she would probably never speak to him again. He didn't blame her.

He yanked off his tie and took his wine to the large living area with the floor-to-ceiling windows overlooking the pool. Since it was winter, the pool was covered, but he rarely used it, anyway. He sank onto the sofa and propped his feet on the hundred-year-old coffee table that had belonged to his ancestors on his father's side. He took another big swallow of wine. His father had been raised in the colonial revival style house, as had Peyton and Quinn. Quinn had bought out Peyton's share, and now the sprawling house was his—one man and more rooms than he'd ever use. The quiet of those empty rooms seemed to gnaw at him, reminding him he was alone.

And he'd never felt lonelier.

He stared at a family photo on the limestone fireplace. The four people in it were smiling and looked happy. In retrospect, Quinn knew they hadn't been. His mother had found happiness with other men. His father had buried himself in the past. When Quinn was older he'd spent a lot of time away from home, and Peyton had rebelled in every way she could. Not a happy family, but they'd survived, because despite all that they still loved each other.

He ran his hands through his hair, knowing he was avoiding what was really bothering him.

Britt.

He'd thought she was beautiful, all bedraggled in the creek, but today she'd eclipsed that. She'd been eye-catching in a silky print dress that hugged her curvy body. Her dark hair had hung loose around her shoulders, making her eyes look that much darker. Her skin had glowed and her eyes had sparkled—until she'd spotted him. Then it was like someone turned off a light. That expression on her face had cut right through him.

What had he done?

He prided himself on the one thing he did well—being a lawyer. For the first time he felt tainted by his profession. He placed his empty glass on the table.

Something wasn't quite right with what had happened today. The last-minute call. The documents all being filed. Did Phil know Quinn had a connection to Britt? Quinn hadn't given out any interviews, and he hadn't seen anything about the incident in the paper. But he felt as if every detail had been staged—for Britt's benefit— to humiliate her.

He hurried toward his study, retrieved his cell phone and punched in Herb's number.

"Herb, it's Quinn," he said as the lawyer clicked on.

"Thanks for filling in today. I heard it went well."

"From who?"

There was a long pause. "Phil, of course."

"All the damaging info on Roslyn Davis was just a little too convenient. Luckily, I didn't have to use it." Britt's many affairs were listed in a file with the men's names and dates. Her vicious, jealous temper was documented, along with dates of when she had trashed Phil's condo. Photos were attached in a folder, but Quinn hadn't had a chance to look at them. Now he wished he had taken the time.

"Are you questioning my research and my investigators?" Herb's voice grew angry.

So did Quinn's. "You're goddamn right I am."

Another long pause. "Stay out of it, Quinn."

"I'd love to do that, Herb, but for some reason I've been cast smack-dab in the middle."

"If you value your law career, you'll leave it alone."

That was the crux of the whole situation. Everyone knew what his law career meant to him, especially Phil and Philip Sr.

"A mother lost her child today. I can't leave that alone."

"Everything will work out."

You know how to stop this. Phil's words came back to him, and Quinn wondered how long it would be before Britt caved to her ex's demands. How long could she live without her child? Phil gave her a week, but Quinn knew she was much stronger than that.

"To whose advantage?"

"I can't answer that. I just did my job."

"Or what you were told to do. That folder on Roslyn Davis was very inflammatory, and I suspect very little of it was true. And it's strange that you don't sound the least bit sick now, not like yesterday, when you were wheezing to catch a breath."

"This conversation is over."

"You're damn right it is." Quinn slammed his phone onto the desk.

He paced in his study. His first instinct was to resign from the case, but then sleazy attorneys willing to do anything for money would take over, and Britt's fate would be sealed.

Philip would blackball him and no one would win except the Rutherfords. Quinn had to stick this out one way or another.

That night in his bedroom he went through the folder of photos that Herb had sent him. There were several pictures of Britt with pilots and businessmen, and dates and names were written on the back. None of the photos showed any signs of intimacy between Britt and the men, but they were damaging because it looked as if she was partying while away from her son. Evidently, Phil had her watched all the time.

Watched!

Was the detective tailing her the night of the storm? Had he seen them being rescued? Was that the reason Phil had called him to handle the case—to make Britt aware that Phil knew her every move? If so, the man was a sick son of a bitch.

There were photos that showed his trashed condo. Apparently, she'd lost control of her temper more than once. Even though he could see the photos, something about them didn't ring true. He'd spent twenty-four hours with the woman and he knew beyond a shadow of a doubt that this was not the real Roslyn Britt Davis.

How he wished he had looked at these photos earlier. If he had, he would never have stepped foot in that courtroom. *Right?* He fervently believed he wouldn't have, but the truth taunted his conscience.

Would he jeopardize everything he'd worked for over the years? Would he tarnish his law career?

He put the folder back in his briefcase, took a shower and went to bed. Closing his eyes, he recalled her face when she'd spotted him in the courtroom. Her expression had held blatant fear. It wasn't the same fear he'd seen in her at the creek. This was basic, primal, and it reinforced the horror that she'd just lost everything she loved. Then anger had quickly replaced the fear.

And it had been directed at him.

Turning over, he groaned. After rescuing her from the creek, he somehow knew their lives would irrevocably be woven together. Thrown together by tragedy and bound by its aftereffects.

But not like this.

She now hated him.

The thought lingered in his mind as he fell asleep.

Britt slept with Dillon in her arms. She knew it wasn't good for him, but she couldn't help herself. She had to hold him, to feel him. The darkness of the night closed around them, keeping them together for now. His soft breathing tickled her chin, and she held on because it would be a long time before she'd hold him like this again.

She wanted to explain to him what would happen tomorrow, but he wouldn't understand. She didn't understand herself. How could the judge give custody to Phil? How could her job be a factor? How could Quinn be involved in this?

The questions kept beating at her and the answers continued to elude her. She forced herself not to think about Quinn. He'd saved her life, and she'd always be grateful for that. But he'd saved it just to take it. She pushed the thought away because it only upset her more.

Her mother had wanted to spend the night, but Britt insisted she go home. Now Britt desperately wanted someone to talk to.

She closed her eyes, but didn't sleep. The pain was

too deep for any rest. At six she got up and carried Dillon to his crib. The apartment had only one bedroom, so they shared the space. When she had enough money saved, she was going to look for a bigger place. That's why she'd taken the extra flights this summer—for the money. She'd never dreamed her decision would come back to haunt her.

Gently, she laid Dillon down and covered him, staring at his precious face. The night-light was just bright enough for her to see his chubby cheeks and dark hair. A choked sob left her throat and she tore herself away from him to go take a shower. In fifteen minutes she was dressed for this horrible day.

All during the night thoughts of running had plagued her. She could be out of the country in no time, but she knew deep down that being on the run was no life for Dillon or her. She would stay and fight.

There was only one way to do that—to make a secure, happy home for Dillon with his mother there at all times. Somewhere during the night Britt realized she had to quit her job. Being with the airlines eight years, she'd built up seniority. But that security meant nothing without her son. Once that decision was made she felt better.

Phil would not keep her son.

She pulled a suitcase from the closet and began to pack Dillon's clothes. Then she made lists: of Dillon's schedule, his nap times, medication for his sniffles or colds, foods she was now feeding him, what he liked at bedtime and so on. The list was for the nanny; Phil would have little to do with his son.

She gave Phil lists all the time when he picked up Dillon, but she suspected he just threw them away. This time she tucked them in with Dillon's clothes, so the nanny would find the lists and use them.

As she packed Dillon's toys, she vowed she wouldn't

cry. This was only temporary, but it didn't keep that crippling pain at bay. She would be strong—and it would take every ounce of courage she had.

After the suitcase was packed, she carried it to the front door. She couldn't bear a long goodbye. Back in the bedroom, she brushed her hair and clipped it back. As she did, she heard, "Ma-ma-i-ah-o-ma."

Dillon's chatter warmed her cold heart. He stood holding on to the rail of his crib. The first time he'd done that it had shocked her. He was too young to stand, but she had a feeling her son was going to do everything early. He moved his feet as if he were standing in hot ashes. He crawled the same way—fast. Soon he would be walking everywhere. Oh, she hoped she didn't miss that. She swallowed, telling herself not to cry.

She changed his diaper and dressed him. As she slipped a long-sleeved T-shirt over his head, he started to whine. He wanted his bottle. She knew that sound.

"Just a minute, precious." She kissed his cheek and carried him to the kitchen, placing him in his high chair. He slapped his hands on the tray while she prepared his milk. When he saw the bottle, he bounced up and down and grabbed for it eagerly. She had a hard time getting his bib on.

After she fed him his cereal and part of a banana, she washed his face and again changed his diaper. She wanted Dillon clean when Phil took him.

She sat with him on the sofa. His big brown eyes stared at her.

"Mommy loves you."

"Ma-oh-ah-ma-ma," he cooed, his two new bottom teeth gleaming.

How did she tell him?

"You'll be staying with Daddy for a while." Her throat

closed up. She had to swallow. "Mommy will see you on Sunday. I love you, love you, love you, my Dilly bear."

"Ma-ma-ma-ma." He bounced in her arms.

"Give me a kiss."

He placed his wet mouth against her cheek and she held him as tightly as she could. Maybe too tight, for he wiggled to get free. It was play time and he wanted down. Just as she was about to place him on the floor, the doorbell rang. Her heart rate skyrocketed into overdrive.

She glanced at the clock on the oven and saw it was exactly ten—time to have the courage to let go. She gritted her teeth, wishing she could hold back the seconds. The inevitable. Cradling Dillon close, she walked to the door. The only thing that gave her the strength to do so was that she knew Phil would not hurt his own son. He might be uncaring and unfeeling, but he would pay someone to look after Dillon. That was the irony of the whole ordeal. Phil didn't want Dillon. He just wanted Britt's attention and eventual surrender.

Never.

Breathing in the sweet scent of her baby, she felt a stub of temptation. But only for a second.

She took a deep breath and opened the door. Phil stood there with his usual smirk, the nanny, who she had met before, behind him. Quinn stood to the side, briefcase in hand. She ignored him.

"Is the boy ready?" Phil asked.

"Yes," she murmured, keeping her features set in a mask of pain.

As soon as Dillon saw Phil, he buried his face in her neck and clung to her like he always did. And that made it so hard. She rubbed his back, trying to soothe him.

"His clothes are packed," she said, glancing at the case at her feet.

"No lists?" Phil asked with a lifted brow.

"Would it do any good?"

"Let's go," Quinn intervened. "The judge advises as little contact as possible." He just wanted to get the transfer over with, and he could see that Phil wanted to linger, to keep needling Britt.

Phil shot him a cold stare, but Quinn didn't back down.

"Get the case." Phil spoke to the nanny and reached for his son. The boy tried to wiggle as far away as possible. Britt's features tightened in pain and Quinn felt a jolt in his heart. How had he gotten involved in this?

Phil gripped the boy around his waist and tried to pull him away from Britt. In doing so he made sure his hands touched her breasts. A look of disgust spread over her face, a look she couldn't disguise.

As Phil pulled Dillon away, the boy began to cry loudly, hands outstretched toward his mother. Britt clasped trembling hands to her face, and Quinn had to look away. *This is wrong,* he kept thinking, but there was nothing he could do. For now.

"You know how to stop this," Phil said to Britt, and the sadness in her eyes turned to anger. In that instance, Quinn knew Britt Davis was never going to bend.

When she didn't respond, Phil walked away with Dillon, who was now screaming at the top of his lungs, holding his arms toward his mother. She stood as if turned to stone.

"Britt," Quinn murmured in a low voice, wanting to say something, anything, to take that look from her face.

She leveled that angry gaze on him and slammed the door in his face.

Chapter Six

How dare he!

Britt would never speak to Quinn again. He was of no concern to her now.

Her emotions overtook her and she slid down to collapse on the floor. The tears she'd been holding in check burst forth like water from a broken pipe. Her stomach cramped with nausea and she drew up her knees to stop the pain. Loud, heart-wrenching sobs echoed around the room, but not even her anguish could block out Dillon's pitiful wails.

I'm sorry, baby. Mommy didn't protect you. Mommy screwed up.

She wasn't sure how long she sat there in her agony. It could have been a few minutes or an hour. Finally, she raised her head and wiped away tears with the back of her hand. She had to get her son back and would start her quest this instant. Pushing herself to her feet, she headed for her phone. It rang before she reached it.

Her mother, Britt knew without a doubt.

"Hi, Mom," she said into the receiver, trying to sound as cheerful as possible.

"Are you okay?"

"Emotionally I'm a little ragged, but I'll be fine."

"Oh, baby."

"I've decided to quit my job," she blurted.

"Oh. That's rather sudden."

"It's the only way I can get Dillon back. I'll find somethin' else."

"Whatever you feel is best."

She could always count on her mom for support.

"Why don't you come home and stay for a few days until you get used—"

"Thanks, Mom, but I have a lot to do. I'm calling my supervisor as soon as I get off the phone with you, and I'll probably fly to New York tomorrow to turn in my ID and manuals. I'm sure I'll have papers to sign."

"It just breaks my heart what that man has done to you."

Britt bit her lip. "He fooled me, but another man will never get that chance. If anything, I'm tougher and wiser."

"Oh, sweetie, would you like for me to come over?" Britt could hear the worry in her mother's voice. It hurt that she'd caused her so much anguish. Carin had wanted her to stay in college and get her degree, but Britt had had a friend who was leaving college to attend an airline attendant program. Seeing the world was a dream come true, and when the semester ended, Britt had joined her friend. She'd never regretted her decision. Until now.

That's how she'd met Phil—on a flight to London with a lady friend. He'd flirted shamelessly in front of the woman, and had called Britt when they were back in the States. He'd never told her how he got her number. By devious means, she was sure. She was so gullible. She'd never seen the warning signs, and she should have.

"Britt, are you there?"

It took her a moment to gather her thoughts. "Mom, I'm fine. I'll call you later."

"Okay. Oh, have you heard from Mama today?"

"No, why?"

"She wasn't here this morning when I got up. I thought she was working in that ridiculous winter garden, but when I checked she wasn't. She was on the phone with Enzo a long time last night, and I have a suspicion that she caught a bus to go see him."

"Didn't y'all stop by yesterday?"

"No, I was too upset."

"Just call Uncle Enzo."

"I did, but he doesn't answer. Sometimes he doesn't hear the phone. I better start looking. I swear she's worse than a child."

"If she shows up, I'll call you."

"Phone me anyway. I want to hear from you."

Britt's doorbell rang. "Gotta go. Someone's here."

"Call if it's Mama."

Britt walked to the door, hoping it was Onnie. Her grandmother being out on her own could not be good for anyone.

"Britt, I'd like to talk to you," a voice said loudly.

She stopped in her tracks. *Quinn.*

"I have nothing to say to you—ever."

"Just five minutes."

"If you don't leave, I'm calling the police."

She pressed her ear against the door. *Silence.* He was gone.

Resting her head against the wood, she allowed herself to think about him. She had really liked him—his humor, his bravery—and had felt an attraction, a connection she'd never experienced before. She'd trusted him.

But her hero was one of the bad guys.

When would she ever learn?

Curling her hands into fists, she marched back to the phone to call her lawyer. Mona needed to hear her decision, and then Britt would call her supervisor. She had a full day ahead of her.

And maybe somewhere in the busyness she wouldn't hear Dillon crying.

Or see Quinn's face. Or hear his voice.

Quinn hurried into his office, his stomach tied into a tight reef knot. He had only wanted to talk, but Britt wasn't willing to listen to any explanations. He had crossed a line by going back without his client. But he'd crossed lines before.

He just wanted to make sure she was okay, even though he knew she wasn't. There was nothing left to say and he had to accept that.

His secretary, Denise, handed him some messages and walked out. Levi Coyote, his P.I., lounged in a chair, his long legs stretched out, his cowboy boots crossed at the ankles. A Stetson, pulled low, hid his expression, but Quinn knew he wasn't asleep. Levi was part Indian and he didn't know what else, but the man had better tracking and hunting skills than anyone he'd ever met.

They'd attended the same high school, two young lads as different as night and day. Quinn was a city boy, Levi country, but somewhere they'd made a connection. Quinn helped Levi with his homework, and Levi taught him how to be tough. After graduation, they went their separate ways. Levi attended the academy and became a police officer. Quinn went to law school. When Quinn became a defense attorney he'd needed a good P.I. He'd heard that Levi had left the department and was doing investigative work. One phone call was all it took for them to connect again. Levi had worked for him ever since.

As Quinn laid his briefcase on the desk, Levi sat up straight, his dark eyes alert. "What's up? Your secretary called."

Quinn opened his briefcase, pulled out the folder with the photos of Britt and placed them on the desk in front of his friend. "I want you to verify these."

Levi flipped through the pictures. He didn't ask questions or comment. Quinn liked that about Levi. He was very straightforward. "Just so we're clear, explain 'verify.'"

"I want to know Ms. Davis's involvement with the men in the pictures and when, where and how that condo was trashed."

Levi stood. "Consider it done."

"I need the info as soon as possible."

"You always do." His friend headed for the door.

"This is important."

Levi looked back with his hand on the doorknob, one eyebrow lifted slightly beneath the brim of his hat. "Aren't they all?"

Quinn shrugged. "This one more than most."

He nodded and walked through the door just before Quinn's assistant, Steve Archer, walked in.

"The Bailey case is on the docket at the end of November."

"Good." Quinn opened his laptop. "I have a meeting with the D.A. next week and I'm hoping to get a plea bargain. Jerry Bailey doesn't need to be in prison. He needs help."

"Good luck with that. He did kill his stepfather." Steve was a skeptic about most things.

Quinn leaned back. "Lloyd Dixon was an abusive drunk who repeatedly beat his wife and her two kids. Jerry shot him trying to stop him from beating and raping his sister. I think he deserves a medal."

"If I know you, you'll make sure he gets it."

Steve was fresh out of law school and tended to cast Quinn as a hero, whereas many people vilified defense attorneys. But Quinn only took cases where he felt the defendant was innocent or being railroaded by the D.A.'s office. It was well known that if Quinn took a case, he'd done his homework, and the D.A. had a fight on his hands. These days the D.A.'s office usually listened to him. Not that he always got his way, but he was in there fighting.

Denise popped her head around the corner. "Deidre has called three times. Those messages are from her."

"Are you saying I should call her back?" Quinn asked in a teasing tone.

"Please." She placed her hands on her hips. "Or I'll just answer the phone all day."

He winked. "I'll do it right away. And I'll need someone to oversee the Rutherford case."

"We're babysitting now?" Steve asked with a touch of cynicism.

"Anything the judge orders." Quinn dropped his voice. "Got it?"

"Yes, sir. I was—"

Quinn held up a hand. "Never mind. If I need you at the Rutherford condo, you'll be there."

"Yes, sir."

"This might be a good job for Bea or Gail," Denise ventured. "They like babies."

"Set it up. Whoever it is has to be there at eight on Sunday morning, and, of course, she'll be off on Monday."

"Will do." Denise headed back to her office.

And Quinn's day went on, chaotic and stressful. Through it all he was haunted by Britt's sad, dark eyes.

Britt met with Mona after lunch. Her firm was located in an old house off Congress Avenue that had been converted into offices. It was pleasant, with lots of green plants and homey touches like candles and fluffy pillows.

Britt sat in a comfy chair gripping a pillow printed with bright red flowers.

"Are you sure you want to quit your job?" Mona was seated at her white French provincial desk.

"I've been dissatisfied for months with being away from Dillon. I should have quit long ago, and today might not have happened."

Mona pushed back her blond hair with a weary hand. "I don't think so. I got the feeling Mr. Wallis and Mr. Ross had all sorts of ammunition to fire at us. The judge had already made up her mind, though, which is a little suspicious to me." She touched legal papers on her desk. "I'm drafting an appeal and thinking about filing a complaint against Judge Norcutt. A woman's job shouldn't matter. Her mothering capabilities should. The judge didn't want to hear anything I had to say."

Mona was a fighter and Britt liked that about her. "How long will an appeal take?"

"Too long, so I suppose quitting your job is the best solution. But it bugs the crap out of me that we have to cave in to the judge's antiquated ideas."

"I just want my baby." Britt stood. "I'm flying to New York in the morning to do the necessary paperwork. I'll start job hunting when I get back. You have my cell number if you need to contact me."

"Hang in there, Britt."

"I'm trying."

As Britt was leaving the office, her mother called.

"I finally found Mama," Carin said.

"Where was she?" Britt walked out the door to her car.

"At Enzo's. Evidently, he called early this morning and said he was sick. Strange I didn't hear the phone.

Anyway, she took him chicken soup and said she might stay the night."

"Why didn't she tell you?"

"She insisted she left a note, but I can't find it."

"Mom, this sounds strange." Britt slid into her car.

"I know. I promised Vera I'd sit with her mother today so she could have a day off, but I plan to pick up Mama later. She can't spend the night. It's not allowed."

Britt's mom was always there for everyone. Vera was a neighbor whose mother had had a stroke, and Carin helped out when she could. When Britt was growing up, Carin had been a stay-at-home mom and a homemaker, and she still was. Her husband's death had shaken them all, and Britt thought getting a job might help Carin. Instead, she continued to help others. And she didn't need to work. Ten years ago her husband's car had been hit by an eighteen wheeler whose brakes had malfunctioned. The company made a large financial settlement, enabling Britt to go to college and Carin to take care of Onnie and anyone else who needed it. Her mother was very frugal, making the money last. How Britt wished she had been more like her mom—being there for her child. She pushed the thought away, resolving to be there from now on.

Backing out of the parking lot, she asked, "Do you want me to check on them?"

"No, you have enough to deal with."

"I have an early flight so I'll talk to you when I get back."

"Okay, baby, and try not to worry."

That was almost impossible, Britt decided as she drove home. Inside the apartment she picked up a few of Dillon's toys, holding them to her chest for a moment before putting them away. Her heart ached and tears weren't far off. And it was only the first day. How was she going to survive four months without her baby?

After losing a lot of the morning dealing with the Rutherford case, Quinn was working late. Deidre wanted to spend the weekend on her dad's houseboat on Lake Austin. He wanted to make sure Sunday went smoothly for Britt, so he refused to join Deidre, using work as an excuse, even though it ticked her off. But it wasn't really an excuse. He had to get all his ducks in a row for his meeting with the D.A. in the Bailey case. For every argument he wanted to have a counterargument.

A shuffling sound interrupted his thoughts. All his employees had gone for the day and it was too early for the cleaning crew. He heard muffled voices. Clearly, someone was in the outer office. Getting up, he walked around his desk to the door. He paused as he saw two elderly people, a man and a woman. Evidently they were lost.

"Are you sure this is it, Ona?" the man asked. He was tall, thin, stooped over and was completely bald. The woman was just the opposite, short and round with gray permed hair, support hose and a large purse on one arm. Their backs were to him.

Quinn stepped forward. "May I help you?"

The woman swung around, the man more slowly. Quinn froze. In the man's hand was a gun. And it was pointed at Quinn.

"What the…"

"Are you Quentin Ross?" the woman asked in a direct, no-nonsense voice.

Quinn stared at the gun. It looked big, old and heavy, and he could swear it had rust on it.

"What are you doing in here and what are you doing with that gun?"

"Now listen here, mister." The woman moved closer, her brown eyes narrowed on him. "I'll ask the questions, and if you know what's good for you, you'll answer them."

Had they escaped from a home or something? An asylum maybe? This was bizarre.

"Are you Quentin Ross?" the woman asked again, her voice angry now.

Despite the gun, the two looked fairly harmless. Maybe they just needed a lawyer. "Yes. I'm Quentin Ross."

"Figured you'd be some slick sonobitch." She flicked a glance over his suit, white shirt and tie as if she was looking at dog poop.

"What?" He was taken aback by the vicious words.

"Listen up. You're gonna do exactly what we tell you or Enzo's gonna shoot you."

Quinn's body tightened. He wasn't afraid, just getting more annoyed by the minute. "What would that be?"

"Give Britt back her baby—tonight."

Britt.

Then it dawned on him. The infamous grandmother. "I don't have Britt's baby. He's with his father."

"But you made it happen. Now make it unhappen."

"Ma'am..." He took a step toward her, hoping to make her understand.

She moved back. "Don't come a step closer or Enzo will shoot."

At that precise moment they heard a snore, and both of them glanced at Enzo. Standing there, he'd fallen asleep, his chin on his chest, the gun still in his hand.

"Enzo!" the woman shouted.

He blinked and looked around. "Did we find him?"

"You idiot." She jerked the ancient gun from his hand. "I thought I could depend on you."

"You can, Ona, but I'm tired after walking up all those stairs."

"Why didn't you take the elevator?" Quinn asked.

"Because we didn't want anyone to see us, that's why, hotshot." The woman waved the gun at him. "Now are you going to do what we want?"

Enzo appeared shaky, and Quinn grabbed his arm before he collapsed. "Here." He pulled out a chair. "Have a seat."

"Bless you, son. That's mighty nice."

"He's not nice, Enzo," Ona yelled. "He's the lawyer who took Britt's baby."

"You sonobitch. You shouldn't have done that. Now we're gonna have to hurt you," her companion stated.

The man couldn't hurt a cockroach. But Quinn wasn't so sure about Ona.

"Enzo, you're looking a little pale." Britt's grandmother tucked the gun under her arm and opened her suitcase of a purse. "Probably low blood sugar. Here." She handed him a candy bar. "Eat this."

Quinn knew he could overpower them at any time, but he decided to let this play out. Just to humor them. And that was the most insane thing he'd ever done, except for jumping into a swollen creek to save her granddaughter.

Enzo took a bite and glanced at him. "Got any beer?"

Quinn had liquor in his office, but he wasn't offering it to Enzo. That was the last thing the man needed. "No. But I have water. Just a minute." He went into the small kitchen off Denise's office and found a bottle of water. He glanced at the phone, knowing he could call the police. But he wasn't sure what that would accomplish. And he didn't relish the thought of putting Britt's grandmother in jail, even if she was off her rocker.

When he returned, Ona had pulled up a chair next to Enzo, the gun and purse in her lap. He removed the cap and handed Enzo the water, and then carefully reached over for the gun.

But Ona was too quick. She jerked it away. "Not so fast, hotshot." She pointed the weapon at his chest.

"I don't think that rusty gun will fire," he told her, not batting an eye.

"Wanna find out?" A gleam entered her eyes similar to one he'd seen in Britt's.

"Fired in 1945," Enzo said, munching on the candy bar.

"Go ahead then, shoot me." Quinn held out his arms, thinking the only way to deal with insanity was with more insanity.

Chapter Seven

Quinn and Ona stared at each other.

Her eyes squinted down the barrel of the gun. "You don't think I will, do you?"

"No, ma'am." He lowered his arms. "You wouldn't shoot a man in cold blood."

"Don't be too sure about that, hotshot. My Britt's heart is broken and I aim to change that."

Enzo choked, gasping for air. Ona laid the gun on her purse and slapped him on the back.

"Goddamn nuts," Enzo choked out, his eyes watery. "You know I can't eat nuts with my false teeth."

"Good heavens, they're just little bitty things."

"But you know—"

"Give it a rest, Enzo."

While they were arguing, Quinn reached down and slowly removed the gun, slipping it into Denise's desk drawer without either of them noticing.

Enzo took a big swallow of water and handed him the bottle. "I'd rather have beer."

Ona looked around and then directly at him. "Did you take my gun?"

"Yes, I did, and you're not getting it back."

"Listen here…" She started to rise, but Enzo caught her arm.

"Leave it alone, Ona. We can't kill nobody. I tried to tell you that." The old man stared at Quinn through his thick bifocals. "But I have mob connections and I can get someone to take him out."

Quinn crossed his arms over his chest. "You have mob connections?"

"As a boy in Chicago I ran errands for the mob, and I still have connections."

"So you see, you better give Britt her baby." Ona was big on threats.

Quinn's patience was wearing thin. "Okay, now listen. This is only a separation. Britt will have her baby back soon. And you don't need to hurt anyone to accomplish that."

"But not quick enough," Ona wailed, a tear sparkling in her eye. Quinn would have sworn that this tougher-than-nails woman never cried.

"I'm Phil Rutherford's lawyer, so I can't say anything else. Just rest assured things will change." Quinn wasn't making empty promises. He planned to get to the bottom of the custody hearing.

"See, I told you he's a nice man," Enzo said.

"You're so gullible." Ona pursed her lips, not convinced.

Enzo leaned forward. "Do you know if a bus runs by here at this hour? I'm ready for bed."

Quinn sighed. "I'll see if I can get you a ride home."

"We don't need your help," Ona retorted.

"Yes, we do." Enzo overruled her. "It's past my bedtime."

"You sleep all the damn time."

"I'm ninety-two and I can damn well sleep anytime I want to, missy."

"Mob connection, ha!" Quinn heard Ona say as he walked into his office, letting them argue.

He sat at his desk and opened the Rutherford file. Britt's number was in there, and he had to call her. If she didn't answer, or hung up on him, he'd have to take Bonnie and Clyde home. Leaving them to their own devices at this time of night would be dangerous.

Punching in Britt's number, he waited. And waited. Evidently she had caller ID and wasn't taking his calls. Damn it! She was one stubborn woman, and he knew exactly where she got if from—the fireball in his reception area.

"If you'd have bought me beer like I asked, this would have gone better." The argument was still going on.

"You'd have been drunk on your ass," Ona retorted.

"You're becoming one bitchy old woman, Ona."

"Old? I'm nine years younger than you!"

"That ain't saying much."

Quinn slipped into his black coat and noticed that neither Bonnie nor Clyde had a jacket. It had been fifty degrees earlier, and the temperature was dropping.

"Where are your coats?"

"Don't need one," Ona replied.

"Forgot them at my place," Enzo replied. "Ona has a head like a rock."

"Shut up, Enzo."

Slowly, they made their way to the elevator. Quinn decided that Enzo really needed a cane, and he wondered if they'd forgotten that, too. He made them wait in front of the building while he went to the parking area to get his car. Enzo couldn't walk any farther, and Quinn wanted to get them out of the weather as soon as possible.

When he pulled up to the curb, both of them were shivering. He just shook his head and helped them into his Mercedes, which was nice and warm. Before he drove two blocks, Enzo was asleep, snoring.

Quinn had to wake him at his assisted living facility.

With his and Ona's help, Enzo made it to his room. The place had a distinct smell and it wasn't pleasant. A sad fact of life. At least Enzo was able to get around and go on crazy missions with Ona. Dim lights lit the hallway and the sound of coughing could be heard, but otherwise everything was quiet.

Inside, Enzo said, "I missed my supper."

"I'll fix you something," Ona offered, and hurried to the compact refrigerator in a corner. Enzo sank onto the twin bed and was instantly asleep again.

"He's out," Quinn said to Ona.

She closed the refrigerator and came over to Enzo. Lifting his feet onto the bed, she removed his worn tennis shoes, jerked a quilt from a recliner and covered him. She kissed his forehead. "'Night, Enzo. I'll call you tomorrow. Don't worry, we'll think of something else."

Back in the car, Quinn asked Ona, "You didn't mean that, did you?"

"What?"

"About somethin' else."

She pulled the wool coat she'd retrieved from Enzo's room tighter around her. "I'm not going to rest until Dillon is with his mother again."

"Give the court some time to work."

"Harrumph."

"I'm not trying to hurt your granddaughter."

"Coulda fooled me."

"Try having a little faith and trust."

She turned slightly in the darkness of the car and he felt those razor sharp eyes slicing into him. "I stopped believing and trusting the day my son was killed in Vietnam."

"I'm sorry." Quinn remembered Britt saying something about her grandmother's losses in life. It certainly had hardened her.

"Don't be. If the gun had worked, you'd be a dead dirtbag."

"You never pulled the trigger."

"Minor technicality." Ona looked out at the traffic and at the buildings they were passing. "Are you taking me to the warden?"

"Who's that?"

"My daughter."

"I'm taking you to Britt's."

"Good. The lecture won't be as severe. Carin can ramble on for days."

He pulled up to Britt's apartment complex. It was a newer brick building in a good area of Austin. A small children's playground was to the left. That must have been one of its selling features for Britt. Another pang of regret hit him at his involvement in the case.

Turning off the engine, he asked, "Ready to face the music?"

There was a long pause. "A baby should be with his mother." The words came out low and hoarse.

"Yes, ma'am. God willing, that will happen soon."

"It never would have happened if you hadn't represented that low-life sleazebag." She opened her door. "I hope you can live with yourself."

He sighed. That was becoming harder and harder.

Britt packed what she needed in a carryall. She'd didn't plan to spend the night. The sooner she was back in Austin the better.

Her doorbell rang and she went to answer it, looking through the peephole first. Her mother. Britt quickly opened the door.

"I can't find Mama anywhere," Carin said, walking in and removing her coat.

Britt closed the door. "She's not at Enzo's?"

"No." Carin sank onto the sofa, placing her purse beside her. "Uncle Enzo's not there, either. The lady at the home said he was there earlier and Mama was visiting him, but they don't know where they are now." Carin gripped her hands together in her lap. "Where are they, Britt? And what are they up to? I keep waiting for a call."

She sat by her mother and hugged her. "Is the home looking for them?"

"Mrs. Gaston said they would, but—"

The doorbell rang.

"I'll get it, and please stay calm. We'll find them even if I have to cancel my flight."

"You have enough to worry about."

"It's no worry. I love Onnie."

Britt hurried to the door and once again looked through the peephole. Him again!

"Go away. I'm not talking to you."

Carin got to her feet. "Who is it?"

"No one who matters."

"This is not a social call. Your grandmother is with me."

What? Britt yanked open the door. "Onnie, where have you been?"

"Mama." Carin hurried to confront her mother. "I've been worried out of my mind."

"You're always worried." Ona shrugged out of her coat.

"Where have you been?" Carin demanded.

"Somethin' had to be done, so Enzo and I decided to kill Quentin Ross."

Carin fainted.

"Mom!" Britt screamed, and knelt beside her. "Mom. Mom!"

Quinn bent to help. "Don't touch my mother," she growled in a low voice.

They eyed each other over her prone body for a second. Britt was angry and wanted him out of her apartment. His eyes flashed a blue warning. Looking away, he lifted Carin's head. "Mrs. Davis."

"Oo-o-o-h." She reached for her forehead.

"Are you okay?" Britt helped her sit up. Quinn held on to her, too. Britt shot him a go-to-hell glance.

"Did Mama say...?"

"It's okay, Mrs. Davis," Quinn murmured. "As you can see, I'm alive."

"He wouldn't be if I had my way." Onnie sat with her arms crossed over her chest, a stubborn expression Britt knew well firmly in place.

"Have you lost your mind? What were you thinking?" Carin was recovering, going into full rant.

"I was thinking of helping my granddaughter. That bastard took her baby." Onnie pointed at Quinn, unmoved by Carin's anger. "Somebody had to do somethin'. Dillon needs to be here, with his mother. With us." Her voice wavered on the last word and Britt went to her.

Sitting beside her, she gave her a hug. "You know, I thought about killing him myself—with my bare hands." Her eyes held Quinn's as she said the words.

The blue eyes darkened and she knew she'd hit a nerve.

"Hot damn. Now we're talking."

"Britt!" Carin gasped.

"But I don't want to go to prison. I just want Dillon home."

"Me, too," Onnie said under her breath, and Britt hugged her again.

"Tell me what happened," Britt suggested, rubbing her arm.

"Let the hotshot attorney tell you."

Britt glanced at Quinn. For a moment she didn't think he was going to say anything, but then he began to speak.

"Enzo and Ona showed up at my office earlier with a gun, threatening to shoot me if I didn't get Dillon back. I explained it was the judge's decision, not mine and—"

"Oh, but you had a big hand in it, didn't you." Britt got to her feet, unable to stop the words she'd kept locked inside and sworn she would never say to him. Not one word. But...

"I didn't know you were Roslyn Davis." He got that in before she could finish her tirade.

"It didn't stop you, though, did it? You stood there and took my child even after all the bad things I told you about Phil. You put my baby in his care. How could you do that? How could you do that to Dillon? To me?"

"I was honor bound—"

"Shove your honor," she shouted, and her mother touched her arm.

"Sweetie, do you know Mr. Ross?"

Britt gulped a breath. "Regrettably, yes. He's the man who pulled me from the flooded creek."

"Oh, my goodness." Carin placed a hand on her chest.

"And I almost shot him," Ona quipped.

"You couldn't pull the trigger, Ona," Quinn told her. "The gun is still at my office. I'd appreciate it if someone could pick it up tomorrow."

"Throw it away," Carin instructed. "I never want to see that thing again."

"Now wait a minute." Onnie was on her feet.

"Throw it away," Carin said again. "It's time for us to go home. It's getting late."

Carin and Ona slipped into their coats. "I'm going to put an alarm on the front and back doors so I know when you're leaving," Carin informed her mother.

"Why don't you put bars on the windows, too?"

"I might." Carin kissed Britt. "I'll talk to you tomorrow." She looked at Quinn. "I don't know what to say to you, Mr. Ross, so I'll say nothing. Let's go, Mama."

Britt kissed her grandmother and the door closed, leaving her and Quinn alone. She walked back into the living area, which suddenly seemed smaller than usual due to Quinn's overpowering presence.

"You can leave," she murmured.

"Not until I've said my piece."

"Oh, please." She wrapped her arms around her waist as if to ward off any attraction she might feel.

"Family law is not my field. It was when I first started, but then I switched to defense. Phil and I were in law school together. We weren't close, just acquaintances with the same classes and same friends. Philip Sr. gave me my start, and I worked for his law firm for several years. I've always been grateful for that. When Phil called me to take over for his ailing attorney, I agreed. The file on Roslyn Davis was very clear—she was a bad mother leaving her child for long periods of time."

"How dare you!"

"I'm telling you what was in the file. That's not my opinion."

Their eyes locked and she saw the concern, the empathy in his eyes. No! She would not weaken.

But she found herself asking, "What's your opinion?"

"I believe what you told me in the woods."

Unbelievable relief flooded her, surprising her. Why should she care? But she couldn't deny that she did.

"It doesn't change anything, though. I am now Phil's lawyer of record for this case."

She stiffened. "Then we have nothing else to say to each other."

"I'm breaking the rules by even talking to you."

"Then leave."

But he didn't. He kept staring at her with those blue,

blue eyes. "I find that hard to do," he admitted in a hoarse voice.

Could her life get any crazier? They were pulled together by emotions and torn apart by circumstances out of their control.

She swallowed. "Thank you for not calling the police on my grandmother and Enzo."

"It's kind of hard to have Bonnie and Clyde arrested." A twinkle was back in his eyes.

"Bonnie and Clyde?"

"That's my name for them. Kind of fits, don't you think?"

"Mmm."

"I really thought you were exaggerating about your grandmother."

"No, Onnie's in a class all her own."

"Yeah." He slipped his hands into the pockets of his slacks, drawing her attention to his long, lean body, and from out of nowhere she remembered the feel of his lips on hers, that hard form pressed into hers. Her breath caught in her throat.

"I think it's wise if we don't see each other outside of the courtroom."

"That's probably best." But he didn't move or make an attempt to leave. They kept staring at each other as if their eyes could say what they couldn't. He cleared his throat. "Someone from my office will meet with you at eight on Sunday morning at Phil's condo."

"I'll be there."

"Britt…"

The entreaty in his voice sent her nerves spinning, but she maintained her dignity. And that was about all she had left. "Please, we've said enough."

He nodded and headed for the door, stopping at her side. "I'm sorry things turned out this way."

A tangy, manly scent reached her nostrils. She resisted the temptation to fill her system with the taste of him. If she turned, their faces would be inches apart. So close. So tempting.

She couldn't. Wouldn't. She bit her lip as he walked out the door.

Chapter Eight

Quinn was back in his office early the next morning. He retrieved the gun from Denise's desk and placed it in the safe until he figured out what to do with it. The thing was as rusty as a nail left out in the rain. The chamber wouldn't even move. Bonnie and Clyde couldn't even see that the gun was no longer usable. But it had worked for their purpose—getting his attention.

Last night, he'd thought of telling them they were trying to shoot the wrong man—that Phil should be their target. But then they might actually try to kill him. Quinn hoped it never occurred to them to go after Phil because he would most definitely have them arrested.

Quinn's own grandparents had been quite sane, so he'd never met anyone like Ona. Britt's life must have been entertaining, at best.

Britt.

Last night he'd wanted to touch her, to take the pain from her eyes and to explore all those feelings he'd experienced in the woods. No woman had ever made him feel like that—an all-conquering male who could move mountains. The gulf was so wide between them now that any relationship was out of the question. That's why he'd left, when he'd wanted to linger.

And then there was Deidre.

He sighed, wondering why he hadn't heard from her. Anytime he'd canceled on her, she'd usually pout for a few days and then call as if everything was fine. Soon he'd have to decide about his relationship with her. If they even had one.

His cell buzzed. He looked at the caller ID. His sister. He clicked on.

"Hey, sis, what are you doing up so early?"

"Remember? I have a one-year-old."

"Oh, yeah. How is J.W.?"

"He's awake and helping Jody get dressed for school."

"Mommy!" Quinn could hear Jody shouting in the background.

"I guess he's helping a little too much. I have to go, but I wanted to see if you can come for dinner on Sunday."

"Sorry, sis, I have plans."

"Please tell me you've met someone."

"No, just business plans." But Britt's face was right there at the front of his mind.

"Mommy!" This time Jody was screaming.

"Bye," Peyton said, and hung up.

Quinn laid his phone on the desk, feeling a pang of envy. His sister was happy. He was glad one of them had found happiness. Home and family. The older he got the more important those two things became. But as he'd told Britt, he'd probably wind up a crusty old bachelor.

His career always came first and he'd worked hard to get where he was. The Rutherfords were now jeopardizing that success. As long as they could pull his strings everything was fine, but how long could he allow that? Philip Sr. had deep pockets and long arms when it came to the Texas Bar Association. At the first sign of an ethical violation, he would have Quinn disbarred in the blink of an eye.

Quinn shifted uneasily in his chair. He didn't like anyone having that much power over his career. Over *him*.

A tap at the door brought him out of his thoughts.

"Yes," he called.

Levi walked in with a folder in his hand. It wasn't unusual for the investigator to be here early. If he was working a case, he was sometimes in the office before Quinn.

Levi slapped the folder on the desk. "That was a piece of cake."

"What do you mean?"

He sank into a chair and crossed one booted foot over his knee. "The men were easy to locate and willing to talk."

"And?"

In one swift movement Levi was on his feet and had opened the folder. It always surprised Quinn how fast he could move.

"This man—" Levi poked one photo "—is a New York businessman with dealings in the Middle East. He has two boys, ages two and four. He and Ms. Davis had dinner during a layover and talked about their children. Same with the pilot from Atlanta and the race car driver from Italy. They talked about their kids—that's it. And they were not happy that photos had been taken of them. But none of them were worried, since they all have secure, happy marriages. All three had told their wives about Ms. Davis and how she made their time away from their families so much easier."

Just as Quinn had suspected. "And the trashed condo?"

"No police report. Nothing. That was a dead end. But I used a computer program to blow up the photos, and if you'll look closely—" he pulled out two large photos "—you'll see there's a lamp knocked over and women's clothes thrown on the floor. Nothing else is disturbed." He pointed to the other photo. "This is in a bedroom.

The bedding is all tumbled up and grocery items are strewn around. You can see a busted bag, a box of long candles, unopened, French bread, a salad mix, a piece of meat—looks like prime rib—and two potatoes. Nothing else is disturbed. If you ask me, it appears as if someone dropped the bag. I wouldn't call that trashing a condo."

"Thanks, Levi. This helps a lot." Everything was just as he suspected. Britt was being railroaded, and Quinn knew without a doubt that the Rutherfords were not planning to give Dillon back to his mother. And they would use Quinn as long as he allowed it. He had to bide his time and gather more evidence. When Philip Sr. made his move, Quinn had to be prepared.

"One more thing," he said as Levi made to leave. "Ms. Davis is being tailed. I want to know who, and who hired him."

"Sure." Levi rubbed his chin. "Is this personal?"

"Yes." Quinn surprised himself with the answer. It felt good to admit that out loud.

Levi hesitated, which was unlike him. He was a man who did his job and didn't ask questions. "Ms. Davis is very beautiful."

Quinn looked up. "It's more than that."

Levi raised his hands. "I'm not prying or giving advice, but you're Phil Rutherford's attorney."

"Yeah." Quinn leaned back in his leather chair. "That does present a problem."

"You wouldn't be the first man to lose his head over a woman."

"Have you?" Quinn lifted an eyebrow.

"Hell, no. I have more sense than that."

The quick denial told Quinn that he had.

"Just be careful," Levi added. "The Rutherfords have a lot of power in this town. In this state."

Quinn nodded; he knew that better than anyone. He

leaned forward. "Damn, Levi, this is the first time we've had a personal conversation."

"And let's keep it that way," his colleague replied with a half grin. "Just know I have your back...and your ass."

"Thanks. Oh, don't you want Ms. Davis's address?"

"I wouldn't be much of a detective if I didn't already have it." With that, Levi sauntered out the door.

Britt flew to New York and did what she had to. Her friends, Wendy and Donna, were getting ready for a flight, and she was glad for the chance to say goodbye. They hated to see her go, but understood. She didn't linger in the city she loved. She didn't see a Broadway show, shop, stroll through Times Square or visit Central Park. Her focus wasn't in New York anymore. It was in Austin—with Dillon.

When she arrived back, she quickly packed a bag and drove to Taylor to spend the weekend with her mother and Onnie. Britt couldn't stay in the apartment without Dillon, even though she knew she would eventually have to. But not this weekend.

The main purpose of the visit was to talk to her grandmother. Onnie had to understand how wrong she had been to try to hurt Quinn. But talking to Onnie was sometimes like talking to a wall. Britt didn't need any more aggravation, and neither did her mother, so for all their sakes, she hoped Onnie would listen to her.

She planned to stay Friday night and soothe ruffled feathers, and come home on Saturday to get ready for her day with her son. She hoped he was settling in and not missing her. Her focus was on this Sunday, when she'd be able to see and hold her baby. That was all Britt could think about. She would make the most of her time with Dillon. Until the next time. Until he was with her again.

* * *

Quinn had the conversation with Deidre, but it wasn't fun. She'd called from the lake to tell him that since he was so busy, she'd invited another man. Quinn hated when she tried to make him jealous. He told her to have a good time, and she became angrier, telling him this was it. They were over. He agreed and she hung up on him.

Staring at the phone, he wondered why some women had to manipulate, to control. He was so tired of the endless tug-of-war between them. It was time for it to end. And, oddly, he wasn't upset.

Denise walked in and handed him a letter. "This just came by courier."

"Thanks." He ripped open the envelope and a check fell out. For twenty thousand dollars. His stomach clenched and he glanced at the attached letter: *Quinn, I appreciate your help in securing my grandson's future. Your loyalty will not go unnoticed. Enjoy the bonus.* It was signed by Philip Sr.

"Son of a bitch!"

Quinn grabbed a page of letterhead stationery and scribbled a note that read thanks but no thanks. Slipping the check inside, he sealed the envelope and shouted for Denise.

She ran in, her eyes huge. "What? What?"

Handing her the letter, he said, "Get this back to Philip Rutherford Sr. as soon as possible."

"Oh, okay. I thought there was a fire in here."

"Take care of the letter," Quinn snapped.

She hurried away and he sucked in a deep breath, the air burning his lungs. Damn! He hit the desk with his fist, the sound echoing in his ears. The Rutherfords were setting him up to take Britt's baby—forever. He knew that without any doubt. It was time to pay the piper.

Standing, he stretched the tight muscles in his shoulders. When Quinn's interest had turned to defense, Philip had supported his decision. After courtroom training and several more law classes, he'd joined the Rutherford defense team, but it wasn't quite his niche. Quinn disliked the expensive retainers and the total lack of respect for the victims. He'd wanted his own firm, to do things his way. Philip had again supported him, sending him clients when his own team was backlogged. Without that help, Quinn wouldn't be where he was today.

How much was that support worth?

His soul?

Guilt scraped across his conscience and he couldn't breathe. He needed air, freedom. Grabbing his coat, he headed for the door. "Cancel my appointments for the afternoon," he said to Denise. "Reschedule for Monday."

"What?"

But he wasn't listening. He hit the stairwell, slipping into his coat. In a matter of minutes he was in his car, driving out of Austin toward Horseshoe, Texas. And his sister.

It was ironic that as an adult he turned to her for advice. In their youth, Peyton had always been running to him.

Right now, Quinn had to face his options and make the right decision for himself.

And for Britt.

An hour and a half later he sat in the living room of the large Victorian house Peyton and Wyatt had renovated. J.W. sat on his lap, holding a worn teddy bear, listening to a story Quinn was reading. Peyton and Wyatt were curled up on the sofa side by side, watching them.

Jody ran in in her pajamas and fuzzy slippers, followed by her yellow Lab, Doolittle. "I'm ready for bed," she announced.

Wyatt stood and lifted a sleeping J.W. out of his arms. Quinn never realized how good it felt to hold a child. He could only imagine Britt's torment at not having her son with her.

"Time for bed, kiddos," his brother-in-law said. "Daddy will put you to bed."

"What about Mommy?" Jody asked.

"Mommy is visiting with Uncle Quinn."

"Oh." The little girl ran to Peyton and kissed her. "'Night, Mommy, and don't forget Erin's coming for a sleepover tomorrow. Love you."

"How could I forget?" Peyton kissed her daughter. "I love you, too. I'll check on you later."

Jody hugged Quinn. "I'm glad you surprised us."

"'Night, Jody." He hugged her back.

Wyatt, the kids and Doolittle walked up the stairs. Quinn watched them go and then concentrated on the crackling fire. He rarely lit the fireplace at his house, and tonight he found looking at the flames warm and soothing. Calming.

Peyton got up and sat cross-legged in front of the fire, facing him. The flames behind her highlighted her blonde hair, and she gazed at him in concern.

"What's going on, Quinn? You said you were busy and now you're here."

And just like that he told her everything that had happened since the flood.

When he'd finished, she stood, and he knew that look on her face. He'd seen it may times when she was younger. She was angry.

"That stupid judge took her child?"

"Yes."

"And you let it happen?"

He swallowed. "Yes."

"Quentin Ross, I can't believe you'd do such a thing."

"Haven't you listened to anything I've said? They're setting me up and they're framing Britt."

"You're the best lawyer I know. You can change things."

"I'm the Rutherfords' attorney. If I do anything to thwart their plans, I'll lose my license. And Philip Sr. will make sure I never practice law again—anywhere."

"So it comes down to what you value more—your career or your conscience. Can you live with yourself if you take that baby from his mother?"

Quinn looked down at his hands, clasped between his legs. Peyton had a way of getting to the point, and the truth dug into him.

"I think this has a lot to do with Daddy," she added thoughtfully.

His head shot up. "What?"

"He said you didn't have what it takes to be a cutthroat defense attorney. He said you were too soft, and you've been trying to prove him wrong ever since."

Was he? Why did Peyton have to dredge up something Quinn didn't want to face—his father's disappointment in his choices? Malcolm Ross had said that he should consider political law, like his mother. Or teaching. That was Quinn's forte—winning people over with his charm and rhetoric. But the thought of politics and teaching bored him. So he'd gone against his father's wishes and pursued his own goals. With the help of Philip Rutherford Sr. Oh, God! Had his dad been right?

Was Peyton right?

"I like my job and I'm damn good at it," he said in his defense.

"Until now," his sister murmured.

"Yeah."

"You obviously feel something for this woman or you wouldn't be in such turmoil."

He stared at Peyton, his eyebrows knotted together.

"When you share a life-and-death situation with someone, you form a connection. Wyatt and I did." She looked at Quinn soberly. "Although it was more his death than mine. How dare he arrest me? I wanted to poke his eyes out with my fingernails. Now…" her voice grew dreamy "…I just want to love him for the rest of my life."

"How did you know it was love?" Quinn found himself asking.

"I couldn't stop thinking about him," she replied. "I didn't want him to think bad things about me. Up until then, I didn't care what people thought, as you well know. Whenever I was with him, I was out of my mind with happiness. The world didn't seem so hopeless and…"

Quinn held up a hand. "I get it."

"Do you?" She lifted an eyebrow.

He stood and flexed his shoulders. "I'm not sure I'll have those feelings for any woman."

"You certainly don't have them for Deidre. If you did, you'd be having this conversation with her instead of me."

Quinn never analyzed it much, but he had to admit he didn't have those feelings for Deidre.

"You'll be happy to know she and I are over," he announced.

"Oh, please." Peyton rolled her eyes. "How many times have I heard that?"

"My life's a mess at the moment, but I feel certain that's the last time you'll hear those words from me." He walked over and kissed her forehead. "I've got to go."

"Get that baby back to his mother as fast as you can."

"It's not that simple."

"If someone ever took J.W. from me, you would fight tooth and nail to get him back."

"I'm not Britt's attorney and I can't fight for her."

Peyton touched his face. "Oh, but I think you are fighting for her, and that's why you're feeling so torn."

On his way back to Austin, Quinn found his mind was in a tailspin. He had few options, but he planned to make the best decisions so he could live with himself. How he'd do that he wasn't sure. He would play this out to the bitter end and hope he had learned something from his father—to stand up for what he believed in. Quinn believed in justice. Britt losing her baby was not justice.

He might lose everything he'd worked for, but his conscience would be clear. And Britt would not view him as a bad person.

Somehow that was important to him.

Chapter Nine

Quinn fell into a restless sleep, but he woke up refreshed, and was in the office by eight. It was Saturday and, he had to admit, he worked a lot of Saturdays. He'd been told the Rutherford case was just a court appearance, a favor to a friend—simple, easy, no time drain on his own cases. To his surprise, more had been going on behind the scenes than he'd ever imagined. He didn't plan on getting caught in that trap again.

That's why he'd called Levi.

Quinn had to be prepared for whatever was thrown at him.

Levi breezed in, a coffee in each hand. He placed one in front of Quinn.

"Thanks." Quinn picked it up. "I was just fixing to make a cup."

"No problem." His colleague took a seat. "My engine doesn't run without coffee. And this is pure knock-your-socks-off black coffee. Nothing fancy in it."

"Didn't think so." Quinn took a sip.

"What's up?" Levi asked.

After several more sips, he placed the paper cup on his desk. "Just want to cross our t's and dot our i's on the Rutherford case."

"Like what?"

"I have a gut feeling the situation is going to get nasty."

"Figured that by the smear tactics."

"I want to be very sure what the men in the photos will say in four months."

Levi rested his elbows on his knees, staring at his coffee. "Mmm. You think with a little extra cash they might have something else to say?"

He nodded. "That's my fear."

Levi looked up. "Didn't I tell you I have your ass covered?"

Quinn frowned.

"I asked if they objected to being recorded, and all three said no. I have it all on tape—their praise of Ms. Davis and exactly what they were doing."

"Hot damn, Levi. It was my lucky day when you came to work for me."

The investigator twisted his cup. "I'm a little concerned, and keep in mind I'm with you one hundred percent…but who exactly are we working for?"

"That's where it gets a little sticky." Quinn picked up a pen and twirled it between his fingers. "I guess I should be honest with you."

"Aren't you always?"

"Lately, the line is getting blurred." But it was good to know his friend had this much faith in him. Quinn told him everything, from the creek flooding to the hearing, to everything he suspected.

"You feel Mr. Rutherford brought you in for the big showdown in four months?"

"I'm almost certain of it."

"Resign from the case."

"Then they'll bring in someone to really do a hatchet job on Ms. Davis."

"And that's got you?"

"Yes," Quinn admitted.

Levi stood and threw his cup in the trash can by the desk. "What do you want me to do?"

"Get those phone calls transcribed. I want every word on paper."

"You got it."

Quinn leaned back, tapping his pen on the desk. "Did you find out who's tailing Ms. Davis?"

Levi lifted an eyebrow. "Chester Bates. P.I. for the Rutherford firm, but I'm betting you already knew that."

"Just a suspicion. But I thought Phil would hire someone outside the firm."

"Why? Let Daddy-Big-Bucks pay for it." His friend stared at him. "I have a feeling you have something up your sleeve."

"I don't like being manipulated. Philip Sr. thinks I'll do anything he asks. But I draw the line at taking a baby from his mother."

"The baby is already with his father."

"Only briefly. I don't intend for it to stay that way."

"Crossing the Rutherfords will cost you—big. Are you prepared for that?"

Quinn ran a hand through his hair. "Yes."

Levi shook his head. "Never thought I'd see this day. The man with his focus on his career is risking it all for a woman he barely knows."

Throwing his pen on the desk, Quinn clasped his hands behind his head. "Are you with me?"

"Hell, yeah," Levi replied without pausing. "I love taking down a man like Rutherford."

"What if my plan backfires and I'm the one who's taken down?" Quinn had to think about that possibility.

"I'll give you a job on my ranch, minimum wage. Can you cowboy?"

Quinn laughed, a robust sound that released the tension inside him. He leaned forward. "I can wear boots and a Stetson as well as any man."

Levi's lips twitched. "That's not what I had in mind."

"Didn't think so."

"Like I said, I have your back. Just let me know what you need, and consider it done. I'll get the calls transcribed." Levi headed for the door and then stopped. "Need anything else on the Bailey or Morris cases?"

"No. Thanks for all your work."

"Call if you need anything." With that, Levi was gone.

Quinn settled in for the day. As he worked, the Rutherford case lingered at the back of his mind like an itch that needed scratching. Yes, he was risking it all for a woman he barely knew.

But he'd saved her life.

He knew her.

He knew Britt.

Steve arrived and they worked on the Bailey and Morris cases, which were coming up at the end of November. Quinn was meeting with the D.A. on Wednesday and he had the first one hammered out to his liking. He just had to hone his argument a little more.

The Morris case worried him. Kathy Morris was a twenty-four-year-old mother of three who'd shot her husband in the back while he was eating supper. The D.A. was going for premeditated murder, and Quinn had his work cut out disproving that.

He let Steve go midafternoon. Since Steve had a girlfriend, Quinn knew he probably had a date. He'd almost forgotten that feeling of being young and full of energy. But it came in clearly when he thought of Britt.

Looking out his window, he could glimpse the capitol building, and in the distance and over the treetops loomed the University of Texas, his alma mater. He'd wanted to

go to Harvard, Yale or Princeton, but his father had persuaded him to stick to his roots, his home state. Quinn
had, and he'd never regretted that. But somewhere in a
corner of his mind shadowed by the exuberance of youth,
he wondered if his father had influenced his decision.

Did Peyton know him better than he knew himself?

Sighing, he reached for his briefcase and went home.

The buzz of Quinn's phone woke him at seven-thirty
Sunday morning. He reached for it on his nightstand.

"Quinn, it's Gail. I have a problem."

He sat up straight. He'd talked to her last night to
make sure she would arrive at the condo early, to give
Phil time to leave.

"What is it?"

"I'm here and Mr. Rutherford is refusing to leave. He
told me to get my ass out of his house."

Son of a bitch! Quinn should have known Phil was
going to pull something. "I'll be right there."

"Do you want me to stay?"

"No. I'll handle it from here, and you still have tomorrow off."

"Oh, thanks."

Quinn grabbed jeans and a T-shirt and quickly yanked
them on, his anger boiling over. If Phil thought he could
manipulate him again, he had another thought coming.
Quinn could also play this game. And ethics be damned.

Slipping on his loafers, he hurried downstairs to his
study and found Mona's number. She answered on the
sixth ring.

"Mona, it's Quentin Ross."

"What? It's Sunday." Her voice was sleepy.

"I know, but there's a situation. I wanted you to be
aware of what's happening, and to know that I have everything under control."

"What are you talking about?"

"Phil is refusing to leave the condo, but I'm on my way to sort it out."

"Like hell. I'll meet you there."

Quinn hung up, a grin on his face. If he knew Mona Tibbs, she'd more than show up. And he was counting on that.

His first step over the line.

Since it was Sunday, the traffic was light. He made it to Phil's place in fifteen minutes. Britt's ex lived in an exclusive area not far from downtown. The condos were two-story, with private driveways and garages, all beautifully landscaped.

As Quinn got out of his car, Mona drove up with a police car behind her. She came with fire in her eyes, just as he'd planned. Thank God Britt wasn't here yet.

Quinn met her at the door. Mona wore a coat over her nightgown, he suspected. Her hair was pulled back into a short ponytail and her face was free of makeup. She'd left in a rush.

"What are you trying to pull, Ross?" she asked, poking the doorbell.

"I didn't know he was going to do this."

"Yeah, right." She held up some papers. "I have the judge's order in my hand and an officer here to make sure Phil Rutherford obeys it."

The door swung open and Phil stood there in his pajama bottoms. "What the…"

"May I speak to my client first?" Quinn asked.

"You have five minutes. I want him out before Britt arrives."

Quinn stepped inside and slammed the door. "What the hell do you think you're doing?"

"Whatever the hell I please. I'm not leaving my house on a Sunday."

"The judge says otherwise, so get your things and get out."

Phil's eyes darkened. "I'm ordering you to get rid of those people outside. I want them gone before Roslyn gets here. You got it?"

Quinn moved closer to him, his voice low and threatening. "I may be your lawyer, but I'm not breaking the law for you. You get dressed and get out, or that cop in the yard will take you away. Legally."

"You bastard. I should fire you."

"Go ahead."

The two men faced each other. They were the same height, and basically the same build. One was blatantly obnoxious. The other was pissed off.

"You'd like that, wouldn't you?" Phil sneered.

"Yes. I don't appreciate being dragged into this mess—your mess. If you feel anything for Roslyn Davis, you'll give her back her child and let her see you're a better man than she ever thought you were."

"Feel anything for Roslyn?" Phil laughed, a sound that was jarring. "I just want her to beg, and she will the day I take Dillon for good."

For good. That was the first time those words had been spoken, and Quinn wondered if Phil even realized what he'd said. For now he let it pass. He was more focused on the man's need for revenge.

He studied Phil's sinister expression. "Then why do you want her back? Why are you here waiting to see her?"

"Because this time—" he poked a finger into his chest "—I'll be the one walking away with everything she loves. I want her to know who's in control."

"Phil, I advise you to get some counseling, because you desperately need it. This is not normal behavior."

"She's trash, Quinn. That's all she is, and not worth your concern."

Quinn drew a long breath and curled his hands into fists to keep from striking the man.

"I've changed my mind," Phil said suddenly. "I'd rather not see the bitch."

Quinn nodded. "Wise decision. Get dressed as fast as you can and go out through the garage."

Phil walked away without responding.

Quinn went to the front door and opened it. "He's getting dressed. It'll take a few minutes."

"Then everything's okay here, sir?" the officer asked.

"Yes," Quinn replied, and noticed Britt was standing to Mona's right, looking worried. He forced himself to glance away.

"I'd rather you stay until Mr. Rutherford is off the premises," Mona told the officer.

A screech of tires burning against the pavement echoed through the quiet morning. Phil's Maserati whizzed by.

"He's gone," Quinn said, and opened the door wider. Dillon's cries filled the air.

Britt charged forward and ran toward the stairs. "Mommy's coming," she called.

Mona folded her arms across her breasts. "I take it, Mr. Ross, this won't happen again?"

"I'll do my best."

"I'll be going," the officer interjected.

"Thank you so much." Mona smiled at him. As the officer walked away, she turned to Quinn. "I don't know what your agenda is, Mr. Ross, but…"

"My agenda is justice."

She eyed him strangely. "I've heard that about you. I'm still trying to figure out why you called me."

"Justice, Ms. Tibbs."

"Yeah, right." Clearly, she didn't believe him. "I'm going home to my husband and kids. Britt knows to call me if anything goes wrong."

Quinn closed the door and went inside, shrugging out of his leather jacket. He laid it over a chair and looked around. The condo was very contemporary—muted walls with accent pieces in black, silver and glass. He wondered if Britt had decorated the place. It didn't seem likely. He pictured her taste as something more homey and comfortable.

Her voice came from upstairs and he headed there, finding her in the nursery. Leaning over a crib, she was talking to the baby as she changed his diaper.

"How's Mommy's Dilly bear?" she said soothingly.

The boy waved his arms and kicked his feet in excitement, obviously glad to see her. Britt removed his sleeper and slipped knit pants over the diaper, then pulled a T-shirt with a duck in front over his head. Dillon held up his hands, wanting her to take him.

"In a minute." She leaned down and kissed his cheek. "I have to put your socks on. It's cold."

He twisted and turned, but she managed to get them on his feet, and then she lifted him out of the crib. "Ready for breakfast?" The boy bounced on her hip. "I know you want your bottle." She walked out, not sparing Quinn a glance.

He went to his car to get his laptop and briefcase, and settled on the sofa. He was here for the day and he had to keep busy. But his attention kept drifting to Britt's voice as she chatted to her son in the kitchen. This was her time and he didn't intrude.

Engrossed in his work, he was taken aback when the baby shot around the sofa. The kid was fast on all fours. At the coffee table, he pulled himself up, slapping his hands on the glass and bouncing on his feet. Innocent big brown eyes stared at Quinn. Dillon looked just like his mother, and Quinn felt a catch in his throat.

The toddler spied Quinn's papers on the table and sidestepped toward them.

"Oh, no, you don't." Britt swung him into her arms, and childish giggles echoed through the room.

She sank into a chair, cuddling her son. "I was cleaning the kitchen and he got away from me. He crawls so fast."

"I noticed." And Quinn noticed her. He'd thought she was beautiful before, but with her baby in her arms she was stunning. Her dark hair was in disarray around her shoulders, and with that sparkle in her eyes and the glow of her skin, he found it hard to breathe.

"Why are you here?" she asked.

Chapter Ten

Quinn was so absorbed in watching Dillon, it took him a moment to realize she was talking to him. He cleared his throat. "The judge ordered it."

"But why you, specifically? I'm sure you have employees who can handle this." Britt bounced Dillon up and down as she spoke.

"I do, but she got a little flustered when Phil refused to leave, so she called me. I'm staying in case he gets it in his head to come back. Sorry that's not to your liking."

"I'd prefer if we had very little contact." Britt had to for her own peace of mind. Quentin Ross was a temptation she didn't need. He looked so different today, more like the man who'd rescued her. He wore faded jeans, a long-sleeved T-shirt that molded his broad chest, and a glint in his eyes that made her very aware of every feminine need in her. His disheveled hair looked as if he'd just gotten out of bed.

"Phil made that impossible." He waved a hand toward his laptop. "I'll work. Just pretend I'm not here."

As if that was humanly possible. Her attention was drawn to him every other second—to his hands, which seemed too big for the laptop as he typed. To his blond hair, which fell across his forehead. And to the thrust of his jaw, covered with a growth of beard. He oozed testosterone and every vibe found a mark inside her, making her very aware of what was missing in her life.

Dillon rubbed his face against hers and her heart swelled. She had everything she needed in her arms. But she only had him for the day. If she thought about it, she'd become upset, so she didn't.

"Playtime." She carried Dillon to his room to gather toys and books, and went back to the living room. They sat together on the floor, and she placed his blocks in front of him. He loved to stack them. After Dillon grew tired, she read to him. He slapped at the pages if there was a dog or a horse, his favorite animals.

"Do you mind if I make a cup of coffee?" Quinn asked.

She looked up. "Of course not." He probably hadn't even had breakfast.

Dillon grew sleepy and Britt knew it was his lunchtime. As Quinn walked back with a cup in hand, she said, "I brought Dillon's lunch. I'm going to the car to get it." She placed blocks in front of Dillon. "Mommy will be right back."

"I'll watch him," Quinn offered.

"Thanks." She fished her keys out of her purse and hurried to the door. As soon as Dillon realized she was leaving, he fell to his hands and knees and shot after her, crying loudly. She swung him into her arms, trying to soothe him. "It's okay. Mommy's here." She couldn't say the words she wanted to—that she would never leave him. Her temper boiled but she banked it down.

"I'll get it," Quinn said.

"Thank you." She handed him her keys and rubbed Dillon's back. "It's a small ice chest on the passenger side."

In a few minutes Quinn was back and handed her the

chest. "Why did you bring his food? Isn't there something here for him to eat?"

"I like for him to have something fresh and not out of a jar. I made him mashed potatoes, finely chopped up chicken and green peas. He loves it."

She placed Dillon in his high chair and tied a bib around his neck. He slapped a hand on the tray, knowing what was coming. After she heated the food in the microwave, she fed it to him. He gobbled it up. Growing sleepy, he rubbed his eyes.

She looked up to see Quinn watching them. He held up his cup. "I was just getting a refill."

"It's time for his nap." She lifted Dillon out of the chair and washed his face and hands. "I'm going to change his diaper and give him a bottle. The kitchen's all yours."

With Dillon asleep, she went back into the living room. Quinn was working at his laptop, a coffee cup beside him. Onnie had made her a sandwich for lunch out of leftover roast beef from their Saturday lunch. Britt hated to eat in front of him, or alone in the kitchen.

It didn't take her long to make up her mind. She grabbed the chest, two forks and two napkins, and carried them to the coffee table. Sitting on the floor, she pulled out food from the ice chest. "How about lunch?"

He glanced at her. "I'm good. Thanks."

"Did you have breakfast?"

"No. I left in rather a hurry."

She unwrapped the sandwich and laid it on a napkin. "This sandwich is huge. Onnie doesn't know how to make anything small."

Glancing over at the sandwich, he asked, "What kind is it?"

"Roast beef on Onnie's homemade bread." Britt pointed. "Just look at that. It's enormous. I'll never eat it all. You have to help." She dropped her voice to a cajoling tone.

He closed his laptop and slid to the floor. "Okay. You've convinced me."

"And we have coconut pie, fruit and water. How's that?"

"Sounds delicious." He picked up half of the cut sandwich.

They ate in silence, and Britt couldn't help thinking the same thing she'd thought before: why did he have to be one of the bad guys?

"This is delicious," he said around a mouthful of roast beef.

"Onnie's a great cook. You should taste her spaghetti and meatballs."

He picked up a slice of apple. "I don't think I'll ever get that chance."

"Probably not," she muttered. They were on opposite sides and there was no way they could ever be together.

Except in her mind.

And she hated herself for even thinking it.

They shared the coconut pie and she pushed the biggest piece to him, licking her lips. "You have to eat the rest. I can feel my hips spreading."

He studied her mouth, and his eyes darkened. A sizzle of awareness coiled through her.

"There's nothing wrong with your hips," he remarked.

She gathered the remains and carried them to the trash in the kitchen, needing to do something to ease the tension in her stomach. "I wasn't looking for a compliment," she called over her shoulder.

"It wasn't one," he called back. "It's the truth."

She put the lid on the ice chest and placed it by her purse, then resumed her seat on the floor. Neither said anything else. Quinn leaned against the sofa, his eyes on her.

"I am sorry for the way things turned out."

She brushed a crumb from her jeans. "Somehow I believe that."

"I had no idea you were the Britt I knew."

"It makes no difference now."

"I suppose not." His eyes held hers. "I'm really not a bad person."

"You just work for people who are."

"I owe a lot to Philip Sr. That's not an excuse. It's just how I got caught in this situation."

"Were you and Phil good friends?" She drew up her knees and watched his face. His wide brow was slightly furrowed as he thought before he spoke, which she imagined he also did in court.

"Just law students together. That's how I met his dad."

She frowned. "I'm not sure what Philip has to do with my son. He never showed any interest in him."

Quinn shrugged and she knew he wasn't going to tell her anything else. Looking around the apartment, he asked, "Did you decorate the condo?"

"No. It was decorated when I moved in." Unable to stop herself, she ran her hands up her arms. "I hate this place. There are so many bad memories here."

"There had to have been some good ones."

"Phil's cruelty obliterated them all."

"I'm sorry."

"Then make him give me back my son." She held his blue eyes, mentally willing him to agree.

A loud wail erupted and Britt jumped to her feet. Her baby was awake.

The rest of the afternoon went quickly, too quickly. She didn't know how she was going to leave Dillon. She held and kissed him, and he picked up on her distress and became fussy.

"This is hard," she said to Quinn.

A look crossed his face, an expression she hadn't seen before. This was hard for him, too. That had never crossed her mind and it threw her for a second.

"It's ten to five," he said, glancing at his watch. "You better go before Phil arrives."

A tear rolled from her eye as she pulled a package of Goldfish crackers from her purse. Handing them to Quinn, she said, "Give him some of these and it will keep him occupied for a while." She held Dillon tight and kissed him. "Mommy loves you, Dilly bear."

Quinn sat on the floor and fed Dillon crackers. "I'll take very good care of him," he promised.

Holding back tears, she quietly picked up her things and slipped out, running to her car.

The moment Dillon realized his mother wasn't in the room he crawled to the kitchen looking for her. Quinn followed. Dillon's bottom lip dropped and he started to cry.

Picking up the boy, Quinn tried to comfort him. "It's okay, buddy. You'll see her again real soon." Dillon cried that much louder.

Through the wails, Quinn heard the front door open. He carried the baby into the living room. A middle-aged woman with graying brown hair was removing her coat. When she saw them she immediately came and took Dillon. He went to her, but his dark, watery eyes kept searching the room.

"I'm Debi Carr, the nanny. I'll take care of this little one."

Quinn reached for his jacket. "Isn't Phil coming home?"

"He said he'd be out late tonight, but don't worry, Dillon will be fine. I have a room next to his."

Dillon seemed comfortable with the nanny, so Quinn gathered his laptop and briefcase, his anger once again getting the best of him. The whole point of the hearing was so Dillon would be with one of his parents, but that was just a blind for what was really going on. To take Dillon from the person who loved him. To make Britt pay. To hurt her.

Walking out the door, Quinn knew every risk he took was worth it. If it was the last thing he did as a lawyer, Britt would get her son back.

Britt cried herself to sleep, but was up early to start job hunting. Through the night she'd made a decision. She'd been dealt a crippling blow and it had sidetracked her, but not anymore. She was fighting back. Phil and Quentin Ross were not going to get the best of her. After showering and dressing, she called Mona.

When Mona answered, Britt got right to the point. "I'm not happy with what happened yesterday. Do something to get this changed. I should be able to see my son in my own home—his home."

"I completely agree with you and I'm already on it. I plan to call the judge as soon as I'm in the office."

"Thank you, Mona. I just don't feel comfortable with Phil able to pop in anytime he pleases. Make sure the judge understands that."

"I'll make that very clear. I'll call when I hear something."

Britt spoke with her mother and grandmother, and then hit the streets looking for a job. Carin wanted to loan her money until Britt was back on her feet. Britt refused. She had to make it on her own.

Every place she went, from department stores to dress shops to secretarial agencies, she was told the same thing—they weren't hiring. Finally she tried the employment office. She'd take anything. She had to have an income to keep Dillon and to pay the rent.

Midmorning, Quinn got a call from Judge Norcutt's office. She wanted to see him at one. He had a full schedule, but it was about the Rutherford case, so he made time. Getting in touch with Phil was impossible. The man didn't answer his phone or return Quinn's calls.

Quinn was running late and arrived a little after one. Mona was already there. They didn't have time to talk before they were shown into the judge's chamber.

Evidently Judge Norcutt didn't have much time, either. She was at her desk going through some papers. She waved a hand. "Please have a seat. As I don't have a lot of time, I'll get right to it."

She glanced at Quinn. "I understand there was an incident at the Rutherford house yesterday."

He stood. "Yes, Your honor."

"Can you guarantee it won't happen again?"

Quinn didn't have to weigh his answer. He had to be honest. "No. I can't."

"Due to Mr. Rutherford's disregard of the law—" she scribbled her signature on a document "—I'm changing the order. Ms. Davis will be allowed to visit with her son in her home. Mr. Ross, your office will continue to oversee the visits. The nanny will deliver the boy and pick him up at the designated times." The judge looked at him again. "Mr. Rutherford is to follow the order, Mr. Ross, and I trust you will see that he does."

"I'll do my best."

Out in the hall, he said to Mona, "I'm impressed."

"Thanks, and thanks for not throwing a wrench into the works. But I have to tell you this whole case stinks to high heaven." She turned and frowned at him. "And what the hell are you doing in family court, anyway,

Ross?" She didn't give him a chance to answer. "It really ticks me off that the Rutherfords are using a high profile lawyer with a reputation for winning. That stinks, too."

"I'm glad you recognized that." He suppressed a grin.

She gave him a skeptical look before walking off down the hall, her heels clicking on the tiled floor.

Yes. He was very glad she'd recognized that. And he was glad Britt had a lawyer who was fighting for her. She needed one. But Britt had her own strength. She wasn't falling apart, just as she hadn't in the storm. From the start Quinn knew Britt was strong, and she'd need all that strength in the days ahead.

But in the words of Levi, Quinn had her back.

By the end of the day Britt realized that finding a job was going to be almost impossible. But she wasn't giving up. The next morning she hit more businesses, looking for work. She stopped at noon, had lunch and waited for Dillon.

She was ecstatic that Mona had gotten the ruling overturned. Dillon would now be home for a while. And he seemed to recognize that, smiling and crawling everywhere.

When a lady named Gail showed up, Britt was surprised at her reaction. She'd been expecting Quinn and was disappointed. How big a fool could she be? She had a knack for falling for the wrong men. Quentin Ross wasn't the man for her. He wasn't her hero.

But, oh, her heart wanted him to be.

Quinn wasn't there on Thursday, either.

Britt knew it was for the best, but she couldn't stop thinking about him or looking for him on Sunday. Gail arrived as usual.

It irked Britt that someone had to watch her while Dillon was with her. But Gail was very respectful of Britt's time with Dillon. She stayed out of the way, reading the paper, doing crossword puzzles or working on her laptop.

Britt had invited her mother and grandmother for lunch, because they wanted to see Dillon so desperately. Carin and Onnie cooked in her kitchen, and Dillon was happy, chattering and playing. It came to an end too soon. Dillon gave hugs and kisses as the two women left. Britt held on to him, bracing herself for when, once again, she'd have to let him go.

She was playing patty-cake with Dillon when her doorbell rang. It was too early for the nanny. Could it be Phil? A chill crawled across her skin.

Taking a deep breath, she walked toward the door.

Chapter Eleven

Holding Dillon, she glanced through the peephole and smiled.

Quinn.

Her heart fluttered with excitement. *Fool* rang through her head with vivid clarity, but she ignored that annoying little voice for now.

She opened the door. "Quinn, what are you doing here?"

In jeans and a leather jacket, he looked rugged, handsome and bad. Bad for her.

"I came so Gail could leave early." He walked inside. "I meant to get here earlier but I got sidetracked at my sister's."

"Oh, thank you, Mr. Ross." Gail gathered her things and was gone.

Quinn followed Britt into the living room. She sat on the carpet with Dillon and Quinn took a seat on the sofa.

"It's really annoying to have someone here to watch me," she told him.

"Sorry, it's the judge's ruling," he replied, removing his jacket. "Other than that how's it going?"

"Okay. Mom and Onnie came today and Dillon was so glad to see them." Dillon crawled to his toys on the floor and picked up a small NERF ball and threw it to her. It landed at her feet. She threw it back to him.

"How are you?" Quinn's eyes held hers and she found it hard to look away. How did he do that—trigger all her feminine emotions with just a glance?

"I'm better. I'm not so angry."

"Does that mean you're not so angry at me anymore?"

Instead of answering, she replied, "Mona said you didn't throw up any roadblocks at the meeting with the judge. I'm grateful for that—grateful to have Dillon home."

"That's where he should be."

She stared at him. "You're an enigma, Quentin Ross. I never know when you're serious."

Dillon threw the ball again and it landed on the coffee table in front of Quinn. He picked it up and held it out to the toddler. "You want it? Come get it."

Dillon glanced at Britt and then at Quinn. Clearly, he was undecided whether to trust this strange man. *Yes, you can* soared through Britt's mind like words from a well-loved hymn. After all that had happened, she still trusted Quinn.

And she trusted him with Dillon.

She was either the biggest fool who had ever lived or she was a romantic to the core who believed in love. As she let the thought simmer in her head she had to admit a hard truth. She had feelings for Quinn.

But they could never go anywhere.

Dillon shot across the floor and reached with one hand to get the ball. Sitting back on his butt, he chewed on it, his eyes on Quinn. Then he crawled over and handed Quinn the ball. In a second he took it back. They did this over and over, and Britt was amazed at Quinn's patience. Finally, Quinn threw it across the room. Dillon squealed and crawled after it, retrieving the ball and carrying it back to Quinn. It was plain to see that Quinn had a rapport with kids.

The doorbell interrupted them.

Britt rose to her feet. "Oh, my. I forgot the time. It has to be the nanny."

"I'll get the door," Quinn offered, "while you get Dillon ready."

Britt changed Dillon's diaper and bundled him in his coat. "Debi's here," she said to him, trying to prepare him for what was going to happen. "You like Debi." In the living room she kissed him. "Mommy will see you on Tuesday."

"I'll take very good care of him," Debi said as she took him. Dillon's bottom lip trembled and he whined.

Britt kissed him again. "Mommy loves you, Dilly bear."

Debi quickly left and Britt wrapped her arms around her waist. This didn't get any easier. She felt as if her heart were being ripped out each time. She brushed away an errant tear.

"Are you okay?"

She swung toward the voice, having forgotten that Quinn was still in the room. "You should go, too," she said instead of answering, and the tension was back. The tension that reminded her Quinn was Phil's lawyer.

Quinn noted the sadness on her face and his gut twisted. "I'd like to talk to you."

"About what?" She wiped away another tear.

"Your marriage to Phil."

"Why?" Her eyes narrowed. "So you can use it against me in court?"

"No. I'd just like to hear your side of the story."

"Why?" she asked again.

"Just trust me." For a moment he thought she was

going to tell him to go to hell, but the leeriness left her eyes and she walked into the living room and sat down.

Great. He wanted her to trust him again.

He resumed his seat on the sofa and looked around the apartment. This was Britt, from the comfy sofa and chair to the serene landscapes on the wall to the toys strewn around the room. It was comfortable. It was home.

Clearing his throat, he asked, "How long were you married to Phil?"

She curled up in the chair. "Barely six months."

"What happened?"

She tucked her dark hair behind her ears, her eyes troubled. "We argued a lot about my job. After we were married, he assumed I would quit. But I didn't. I couldn't see myself sitting in that big condo all day waiting for him to come home. The arguments escalated. We had a really bad one before I was scheduled to leave for four days. On the way to the airport my supervisor called. The flight had been canceled. At that moment I decided I couldn't keep up the constant arguing. I told my supervisor about my situation and quit my job. I felt better after I made that decision. I had to make my marriage work. I stopped for groceries, planning a special dinner for Phil."

She had a pained look on her face, as if she was reliving that time. "I'd just found out I was pregnant, and I was going to tell Phil that morning, but we'd argued instead. So I planned this big happy evening."

She stopped talking.

"What happened?" he coaxed.

"When I walked into the condo, I could hear music. Puzzled, I didn't even put the groceries down. I went straight up to the bedroom." She took a long breath. "Phil was there with a blonde in our bed. They were naked and wrapped around each other. Drug paraphernalia was on the nightstand. I was so shocked I dropped the groceries on the hardwood floor. The sound alerted them and Phil saw me. I ran, but he caught me at the door and said it was nothing, just something he did for stress."

The anguish in her voice weakened Quinn's defenses and he wanted to go to her, hold her and tell her all men weren't like that. He had to keep his distance, though. But he knew without a doubt the groceries on the floor were the ones in the photo—the picture Phil used to say Britt had trashed the condo.

"What happened next?"

"I left and filed for divorce the next day."

"Did you ever go back?"

"I went back to get my things when I knew Phil wasn't there, but he came home with the blonde as I was leaving. He wanted to talk and I said no way. He became angry and asked for my key, saying I couldn't take anything out of the apartment without his permission. I threw my clothes at him and left, and I haven't been back until last Sunday."

The clothes on the floor. The supposed second trashing. Phil was making up evidence, and if he thought Quinn would go into a courtroom with that kind of bogus proof he was highly mistaken. And so was Philip Sr.

Quinn cleared his throat. "And Phil let the divorce go through?"

"Not without a lot of threats. Then he found out about the baby and he repeatedly said he would make me pay." She sighed. "I guess he is."

"Do you have any feelings for Phil?" Somehow Quinn had to ask that question.

Her eyes flew to his. "Hatred. Disgust. Do those count?"

"I meant love."

She swung her feet to the floor. "I had my head in

the clouds and I believed that he really loved me. How naive could I be?"

"It's called trusting."

Her dark eyes flared. "I'm good at trusting the wrong men."

"Oh, that stings." Quinn held a hand to his chest.

"It should." A grin played on her lips and that light in her eyes was mesmerizing.

He cleared his throat again. "I better go." As he stood, he reached down and picked up the ball and handed it to her. His eyes holding hers, he added, "Trust me, Britt. Do you think you can do that?"

She stood, her eyes never leaving his. "You're Phil's attorney."

"Yes, I am."

"You're asking the impossible."

Unable to stop himself, he cupped her face and took her lips gently, tasting, cajoling. The scent of baby powder lingered on her skin and she tasted like the banana she'd fed Dillon. Quinn was drowning in the sweetness of her. Drawing circles on her cheeks with his thumbs, he traced her bottom lip with his tongue and she moaned, igniting a flame deep inside him. She opened her mouth and a new discovery, new emotions took over—powerful, explosive feelings that bound them closer than a flooding creek.

She drew back, her lips red and her eyes bright. "That might be an ethical violation."

"Yeah." He ran both hands through his hair. "I've been wanting to do that for a long time."

"You shouldn't. We shouldn't."

He reached for his jacket, just to do something with his hands besides touch her. "That's the trouble with emotions. They don't have a schedule. They just happen."

"Quinn…"

He touched her lips with his finger, not wanting to hear what she had to say because he knew it wasn't going to be in his favor. "Trust me, Britt. That's all I'm asking." Saying that, he made himself leave.

Trust me.

Britt stood with her fingers touching her mouth, remembering the feel of those male lips on hers—firm, yet soft and tantalizing, awakening feelings in her that she'd kept dormant. After being hurt so badly she had to be on guard, but Quinn demolished her well-established guard with just one knee-wobbling, heart-thumping kiss.

Trust me.

How could she do that?

In her heart she knew she already had.

The next morning Phil stormed into Quinn's office before Quinn had finished his first cup of coffee.

"What the hell's going on?" Phil demanded.

Quinn waved Denise out the door. Evidently Phil had rushed past her. "What are you talking about?"

"The nanny now has to deliver the kid to Roslyn. How the hell did that happen?"

Quinn leaned back. "I called. My secretary phoned, but you never answered or returned the calls. How am I supposed to get in touch with you?"

Some of the anger oozed out of Phil. "I was busy. I figured you could handle whatever came up."

"I did. After your rude behavior, Ms. Tibbs asked the judge to reconsider her decision about where Ms. Davis could see her son. The judge asked if I could guarantee that you wouldn't do it again and I had to be honest, so she changed the ruling."

"You bastard."

Quinn's eyes zeroed in on Phil's red face. "Haven't you been home since Sunday before last?"

"Of course I have," Phil snapped.

But he paused, and that bothered Quinn. Was the man out doing drugs? Was Dillon in any danger?

"Then why the outrage now?"

"I've been working on a case and this is my first chance to get here. It just pisses me off that I have to pay a nanny to carry my son to his mother and pick him up."

Quinn leaned forward, his forearms on the desk. "Well, it pisses me off that one of my staff has to work on Sunday. That means I'm a person short on Monday and a half a day on Tuesdays and Thursdays. This whole thing is ridiculous and needs to be changed. Don't you agree?"

"Yeah, but that's the judge's ruling."

Quinn had Phil's attention and he was going to milk it for all it was worth. "I was thinking of a tracking device for Ms. Davis so we'll know where she is at all times. That would free up my people."

Phil's eyes lit up. "I like that. If she's tracked at all times, she won't be able to flee the States with Dillon, and I can pull my P.I. off her."

"Why do you have a P.I. watching her?"

"I want to know who she's seeing, when and where. But it's proved to be throwing money down the drain."

"Then get rid of him."

Phil pointed a finger at him. "You make sure she doesn't leave Austin."

Quinn nodded. "You'll still have to pay for the nanny."

"It'll be worth it. In three months Roslyn will fold like a greenhorn poker player and everything will go my way."

You sorry bastard.

Phil pointed his finger again and Quinn wanted to slap him in the face. "Daddy's not going to be pleased at this turn of events."

"Daddy knows where to find me."

"Don't push him, Quinn," Phil threatened. "You'll regret it."

Quinn watched him leave with a steely eyed gaze. *It's only beginning, old friend.*

He touched a button on his phone. "Denise, tell Levi I want to see him as soon as possible."

A lot of things were going to change, and the action started now.

On Tuesday morning Quinn met Mona in the judge's chamber once again.

"What's this about?" Mona asked. "I just got a call to be here."

Judge Norcutt came in, preventing him from answering. Not that he planned to, anyway.

The judge sat down and adjusted her glasses. "I'm getting tired of rescheduling my day to suit you two. What is it, Mr. Ross?" She clearly was irritated.

He opened his briefcase, pulled out the item Levi had given him and placed it on the desk in front of her. "This is a tracking device, Your Honor."

"Why are you showing me this?" Her voice dropped from irritated to sub-zero infuriated.

"Your Honor, having a member of my staff off a whole day and two half days is putting a strain on my office. I need my staff at work, not babysitting."

"You're skating on thin ice, Mr. Ross."

"Hear me out, please. The device is a bracelet that will be locked on Ms. Davis's wrist. My P.I., Levi Coyote—you know Levi, don't you, Judge?"

"Yes. A fine cop and detective."

"Levi will have the control, and monitor Ms. Davis's whereabouts at all times. That should put your mind at ease about her fleeing with the boy."

The judge picked up the object. "It just looks like a nice bracelet."

"Trust me, it's more than that." And those words could ruin his whole career, yet he didn't retract them.

Judge Norcutt shot him a glance. "Is Mr. Rutherford on board with this?"

"Yes, Your Honor."

"Ms. Tibbs, how do you feel about this device?"

"I'll have to talk to my client."

"Fine. If Ms. Davis agrees, get it done, Mr. Ross. Otherwise the dictates of this court stand. And please stop bothering me."

"Thank you, Your Honor."

"Your Honor..." Ms. Tibbs spoke up. "I'd like the court to know that Ms. Davis has quit her job and is now searching for work in Austin to support her son."

Quinn was taken aback. Britt had quit her job. Why hadn't she said something? But then, why would she?

"I'll take that into consideration at the hearing," the judge replied.

"Pompous twit," Mona said out in the hall.

"Now, Ms. Tibbs..."

She turned on him. "What are you up to, Ross?"

"Don't look a gift horse in the mouth."

"Oh, I'm looking at a whole lot more and seeing things I'm not believing."

Quinn smiled. "Let me know what Ms. Davis says."

He strolled away, feeling victorious as he never had before. The line between right and wrong was so blurred now that he couldn't distinguish the difference if he tried. His whole career wobbled on that line.

He never strayed from his ethic of doing the right thing. It was his mantra. His goal. And he still believed he was doing so.

* * *

In his car he called Levi.

"How did it go?" the P.I. asked.

"Like a charm. The judge bought it. We just have to wait and see how Ms. Davis takes it."

"You just put both our asses on the line."

"Have you ever been in jail, Levi?"

"Just booking people. But I'm not worried. I have a crackerjack lawyer."

Quinn laughed. "You might give me his number. I'll probably need him, too."

"Look in the mirror."

"Oh, him."

"Yeah."

Quinn negotiated a turn on to Congress Avenue. "I'm worried that Phil is still using. See what you can find out and hire someone else to watch his condo. I want to make sure the nanny is there at all times. Dillon's safety is the most important thing."

"I'm on it."

Quinn clicked off and wondered what Britt would say if she knew the bracelet was just that—a bracelet.

Chapter Twelve

"What? They want me to wear a tracking device?" Britt's blood pressure shot through the roof and all she could see was a red haze. "I'm not a criminal and they can't do that. I refuse to be treated this way."

"Calm down, Britt," Mona suggested, placing her briefcase on the sofa in Britt's apartment. "This was Quentin Ross's idea."

"What?" The raging blood drained from her face.

"I'm not sure what's going on, but it sounds like a good idea."

"How can you say that? I'm not wearing some bulky device like a hardened criminal."

"It's a bracelet. A very nice bracelet, as the judge said. To tell you the truth, I've never seen a tracking device like it."

She frowned. "A bracelet?"

"It's like jewelry, so no one will ever know the difference. And look at it this way—you'll have Dillon all to yourself. No one has to watch you."

"Oh." The situation was sounding better.

"So what do you say?"

"Mr. Ross did this?" That still puzzled her.

"Yes. Seems it's putting a strain on his office staff

having to stop their work and come here. He says it's ridiculous and I have to agree."

"Is Phil going along with this?"

Mona nodded. "That's what Mr. Ross said."

Britt sat down, forcing her nerves to calm down so she could think. *Trust me.* Those two words kept running through her mind. After everything that had happened, trust didn't come easy. She weighed the pros and cons. The only thing that mattered was that she'd have Dillon to herself without someone watching over her shoulder. But wearing a tracking device still rankled her.

Trust me.

"What's your answer?" Mona asked.

She touched her lips. "Yes."

The lawyer picked up her briefcase. "I feel it's a good decision. I'll let Mr. Ross know."

"Thank you, Mona."

Britt sat there for a long time, hoping she'd done the right thing. And hoping she hadn't let her heart sway her, once again.

The next morning she was about to leave the apartment for another day of job hunting when her phone rang. She picked up.

"Britt, it's Quinn." Her heart soared at the familiar voice and she wanted to smack herself.

"Good morning."

"Are you going to be there awhile?"

"I was just leaving."

"It will only take a few minutes."

"What will?"

"My P.I., Levi Coyote, will put the bracelet on this morning. That is, if you have time."

"Okay."

"You sound hesitant."

"I don't understand why I can't be trusted not to leave the country with my child."

"Work with me here, not against me."

She gripped the receiver. "I never know what the hell you're talking about or whose side you're on half the time."

"Ah, Britt, just be patient." She could almost see the grin on his face.

"Okay." She gave in reluctantly. "I hope it's not going to take long. I have to find a job to support myself and my kid."

"Yeah. I heard you quit your job."

"I've been thinking about it for a while. Dillon needs me and I'll be here from now on. I just hate that it happened this way. And I hate that you're Phil's attorney."

There was a pause on the line. "It's a cruel twist of fate for sure."

"Mmm."

There was another pause, as if he was gauging his words. "Levi will be there in five minutes and it won't take long."

"Fine."

"Good luck job hunting."

"Yeah, right," she murmured, hanging up.

She took two steps and her doorbell rang. That was quick. The man must have been outside the whole time. She opened the door to a tall cowboy type in boots and a Stetson. He held a small box in his hand.

"Levi Coyote, ma'am." He tipped his hat, and she stepped aside, feeling as if the man was a leftover from an old Western.

"Come in." She closed the door behind him.

"This'll only take a minute," he said, opening the box and pulling out a small silver bracelet. Undoing the clasp, he snapped it onto her left wrist.

She stared at it. The silver had an intricate pattern of x's and o's carved into it. When she twisted her wrist, the silver caught the light and glistened.

"This is it?"

"Yes, ma'am. You won't be able to undo it or to slip it off."

"How will you remove it?" She wasn't wearing it longer than necessary, even though it was rather nice, as Mona had said.

"I'll have to cut that tiny chain dangling from the clasp."

"Oh."

He pulled a cell phone from his jeans and punched in some numbers. Turning the screen so she could see it, he said, "This is how I'll keep track of you." He pointed to a red dot visible on the map displayed on the screen. "That's you. I can check your whereabouts at any time. Easy and simple."

"And annoying."

He shrugged. "You'll have to take that up with your attorney."

"Like that will move mountains."

He gave a lopsided grin, slipped the phone into his pocket and left.

Britt rotated her wrist, getting a feel for the bracelet. *Not bad,* she thought. She could handle this.

The next week Britt's insurance company approved her claim for a new Camry. She was happy to have her own vehicle, but she began to despair of ever finding a job. Her savings were dwindling fast and she had to take whatever was offered. But there was nothing out there. The economy had caused many businesses to cut costs.

She thought stores would be hiring for the upcoming holidays, but they weren't. Just when she was weighing her options and thinking of moving back in with her mother, she got a call from a local McDonald's. She had no problem accepting. After all, beggars couldn't be choosers. It paid minimum wage but it was a job. The hours were six to one. Being just hired, she hated to make demands, so she explained about her days with her son. She wouldn't give those up. The manager, who looked as if he was still in high school, seemed sympathetic, and agreed to let her go at twelve forty-five on Tuesdays and Thursdays. Sunday was her day off.

She was just settling in at McDonald's, working with teenagers who made her feel old, and getting used to asking, "Do you want that supersized?" when the lady at the unemployment office called. She had an opening for a waitress at Threadgill's. Did Britt want the job?

She jumped at it, but again she had to explain about Dillon. They hired her to work six-hour shifts on Fridays, Saturdays, Mondays and Wednesdays.

It worked for Britt. She had two jobs, but she soon found that going on a few hours' sleep was getting to her. She could handle it, she told herself. The highlight of her existence was her time with Dillon.

She now took him out and about as she used to. They went to the park, which Dillon loved, and on Sundays they usually visited her mother and grandmother. It was almost normal. But it wasn't. Dillon wasn't with her at night. Debi put him to bed and got him up in the mornings. Dillon didn't have his mother. Britt worked tirelessly to make sure that when the hearing came, she would be able to take Dillon home.

She hadn't heard from Quinn since his P.I. had put the bracelet on her wrist. That was just as well. But she found she couldn't stop thinking about him. She'd gotten used to him checking on her.

She was probably always going to have a soft spot for Quentin Ross.

Some heroes were hard to resist.

Quinn was busy. He'd plea-bargained in the Bailey case and was pleased with the result. Jerry would spend two years in a psychiatric ward and then be reevaluated. It was a good arrangement. Jerry would get the help he needed to deal with what had happened, and he had a chance at a life.

The Morris case was different. The D.A. refused to plea-bargain it out. The case was going to trial after Thanksgiving and Quinn had to be ready. Kathy Morris had three kids under the age of five. Quinn had gotten her out of jail, but he didn't know how long he could keep her with her kids. And the holidays were close—a hell of a time to go to jail and leave them.

He thought of Britt, as he so often did. How was she coping? Had she found work? He had to force himself not to go to her apartment, but his strength didn't last long. He wanted to see her. Grabbing his coat, he headed for his car.

As he passed the large Rutherford building on Congress Avenue, he thought of Phil. He hadn't heard from him or Philip Sr. But he knew it was only a lull before the storm.

Tailing Phil had been fruitless. Levi hadn't been able to find any evidence that Phil was still doing drugs. Levi was a damn good detective, and if Phil was, he would soon find the evidence. The good news was that Phil was home at nights where he should be.

As Quinn drove toward Britt's apartment, his cell rang. Pulling it out of his coat pocket, he glanced at the caller ID. Deidre.

He clicked on.

"Hi, Quinn. Are you still mad at me?" Sugary words wafted through the phone.

"I was never mad at you."

"Good. Let's do something tonight. I've missed you."

This was the part where he would usually say something about the new boyfriend. But he really didn't care anymore.

"Sorry. I'm busy."

"With what?"

He gripped the steering wheel. "I'm going to check on someone and then I'm heading home for a relaxing evening."

"That sounds boring."

"It doesn't to me. I've had a long day."

"Come on, Quinn. Let's go to the club and—"

"Deidre." He cut her off. "You said it was over and it really is over."

"You don't mean that."

"Yes, I do. Our merry-go-round relationship is truly over."

"You're being an ass."

"Goodbye, Deidre." He clicked off and drove on, knowing he'd let the relationship go on too long. He didn't worry about Deidre. She'd find someone else. She always did.

Ten minutes later he rang Britt's doorbell. And waited. He saw her car in the parking area, so she had to be here. Was she avoiding him?

Finally, he heard, "Who's there?"

"Quinn," he called.

She opened the door, tying a white terry-cloth bathrobe around her waist. Her dark hair was wet and disheveled. She'd just gotten out of the shower, he guessed.

Staring into her dark eyes, Quinn felt a tightness

grip his abdomen, and the tiredness of the day seem to ebb away.

"How are you doing?" he asked, his voice husky to his own ears.

She opened the door wider and he stepped into the apartment. "You came all the way over here to ask me that?"

"It's on my way home, and since I left the office early tonight I thought I'd check."

She lifted an eyebrow. "You work this late?"

He removed his coat and sat on the sofa. "I have an important case coming up and it requires all my attention."

Her eyebrow lifted higher. "That wouldn't be…?"

"No," he assured her.

She tilted her head. "Why aren't you on a date with, hmm, what's her name?"

"Deidre," he told her. "We broke up."

"Really? I hope…"

"It had nothing to do with my being late for our date."

"Oh." Was that a pleased note in Britt's voice?

"How's the bracelet working?" he asked, to change the subject.

She sat in the chair and curled her bare feet beneath her. Raising her wrist, she said, "Fine. I hardly know it's there and I've gotten a couple of compliments on it."

"Really?"

"Yeah. The girls at McDonald's think it's oh so cool." She made a silly face as she said it.

"You're hanging out at McDonald's these days?"

She shrugged. "I kind of have to, since I work there."

"What?"

"There's nothing else out there and I have to work."

He'd had no idea, but she seemed fine with it.

"I work from six to one at McDonald's, and six-hour shifts at Threadgill's on the days I don't have Dillon, so

I'm a little deprived of sleep. I was just going to bed when you rang the bell."

"I'm sorry." Quinn started to rise.

She waved him back down. "It's okay. I can pay my rent now." Her lips curved into a smile and he felt a jolt to his heart. Her hair was damp from the shower, her face bare of makeup, and yet she still managed to look gorgeous. She had a natural beauty that was hard to ignore.

"So…you're able to keep your days with Dillon?"

"You bet. I wouldn't take the jobs otherwise." She yawned, resting her head against the chair.

"I should go." Her tired face was about to do him in. He just wanted to gather her into his arms, hold her close and reassure her that her life would be back to normal soon. But he couldn't do that.

"Tell me about your case," she murmured, half-asleep.

He told her about Kathy Morris and the abuse she'd suffered. It wasn't long before Britt was sound asleep. Without thinking about it, he scooped her into his arms and carried her into the bedroom. The ecru sheet and peach comforter were pulled back. He laid her down and covered her.

"Quinn?" she whispered.

"Hmm?"

"Will the lady get to raise her kids?"

"I'm doing my best to see that she does." Gently, he tucked Britt's hair behind her ear and kissed her cheek.

And you, too. I'm doing everything I can so you can keep Dillon.

He watched her sleep for a moment, the classic lines of her face at peace. She made a wispy sound as she slept, her mouth slightly open. The urge to kiss those pink lips overtook him but he turned away. Reaching for the light switch, he paused. Dillon's empty crib was against one wall by a changing table and a toy box. They shared the room.

Every morning she saw that empty crib, and how that must hurt her. He hated his part in this whole custody debacle. His stomach churned with distaste and he glanced at her face. Yet she didn't seem to hate him.

He flipped off the light, quietly closed the door and let himself out.

All the way home he thought about how tired she was. How long could she continue going on so little sleep? He had to do something.

Pulling into his driveway, he saw the old Lincoln parked to the side. Harmon Withers, a colleague of his dad's, was walking from the front door. Quinn parked and went to meet him. Quinn had called him about the books, so assumed that was the reason for the visit.

They shook hands. Quinn's father had been Harmon's mentor. Even though there was a large age gap the men had been close.

"Forgive my rudeness in not calling," Harmon said in his soft-spoken voice, "but I was returning home after a late evening at the university and thought about the books of Malcolm's that you mentioned. On the off chance you might be home, I stopped. I do hope it's not an inconvenience."

"No, no. Come on in." Quinn unlocked the door and they went through the large foyer into the library. Quinn pointed to two boxes on the hardwood floor. "Those are the books I was talking about. Some are in foreign languages. I know Dad would want them to go to good use."

Harmon knelt near the boxes, as eager as a child, and gently opened a couple of the books. "Oh, yes. These are rare. I will gladly give them a home." Harmon pushed himself to his feet, using the desk for stability.

In his sixties, he was neatly dressed as usual in a three-piece suit, tie and a matching pocket square in his breast pocket. His gray hair was cut short, and his glasses were perched on his nose.

"I'll carry these to your car," Quinn offered.

"Thank you, Quinn."

After the boxes were in the car, Harmon asked, "Were you working late, too?"

"Yes. I have a difficult case coming up."

Harmon patted Quinn's shoulder. "Even though Malcolm was proud of everything you did, he always said you didn't have the heart to be a defense attorney. My boy, you have proved him wrong. You've helped a lot of people." Harmon tapped his glasses. "You see, I follow your trials in the paper."

"Thank you," Quinn said, and to get off the subject he asked, "And what is a professor doing working so late?"

"Oh, don't ask." He waved a hand as he slid into his car. "My assistant is on maternity leave and isn't planning on returning. I can't find anything in that office, can't even locate some of my research papers. Plus, I have papers to grade, which she puts into the computer. Now I have to do it. I don't have enough time." He shook his head in frustration. "Thanks again, Quinn." The door closed and Quinn waved goodbye.

Then it hit him. He knocked on the window before the professor could back out. The window slid down and Harmon squinted at him.

"Are you looking for someone else?"

"Yes, but I'm picky."

"I might know someone."

Harmon frowned. "She's not a ditzy blonde, is she?"

Did Quinn have a reputation for dating ditzy blondes? That stung a little, but he brushed it off.

"She actually has dark hair and is very pleasant. She's going through a bitter divorce and needs a job."

"Oh." The frown reappeared. "I don't want to get involved."

"I'll vouch for her."

"Well…" Harmon reached into his pocket. "Give her my card and I'll interview her, but I'm not promising anything."

"Thank you, Harmon."

The man drove away with his treasures and Quinn went to his car and retrieved his briefcase. Walking into his study, he remembered Harmon's words: *Your father didn't believe you had the heart to be a defense attorney.* He sighed, sinking into his chair.

"You were right," he said to the room that permeated Malcolm Ross. The abuse and the violence were getting to him. It was hard to find a measure of happiness for himself when he dealt with it every day. Maybe his career choice all those years ago had been wrong. Was he better suited to teaching law, as his father had believed, instead of practicing it?

Quinn removed his coat and felt the loneliness of the house. At Britt's he'd felt at home. But it wasn't the apartment that made him feel that way. It was her.

She made him feel at home.

Chapter Thirteen

"Quinn."

Britt woke up calling his name. She stirred, and a warm feeling suffused her whole body. Touching her cheek, she sighed, and then sat bolt upright.

The room was in darkness, but she felt Quinn's presence for some reason. Then she remembered last night and them talking about his case. However, she didn't remember him leaving.

The alarm shrilled through the apartment. Five-fifteen. Time to get ready for work.

She crawled from beneath the covers and flipped on the light, realizing for the first time that she was still in her robe. How? She tried to remember and couldn't. She had no recollection of going to bed. Had Quinn put her there?

Her hand went to her cheek again, which seemed to be extra sensitive this morning. Oh! His touch. His kiss. Her body remembered. And she'd slept through it. Damn! She must have been really tired.

The alarm buzzed again. She didn't have time to daydream. Slapping the off button, she gazed at the empty crib. That familiar ache inside her blossomed and she hurried to the bathroom. Dillon would be back in his bed soon, she promised herself.

She was rushing to the door when the bell rang. She paused. Who was at her apartment this early? Tentatively, she checked—and realized she was spending a lot of her time looking at Quentin Ross through a peephole.

Slowly, she opened the door. He leaned on the door-jamb with a lazy grin, and every feminine sensory receptor she had came to full attention. He was so handsome in a dark, two-piece suit and long winter coat. His blond hair curled into the collar. His blue eyes twinkled.

"Morning, ma'am." His voice was low, infectious and any thought of resisting his charm went south.

"I—I'm on my way to work."

He handed her a business card. "This guy is a history professor at the university. He's looking for an assistant. Decent hours, good wages and benefits. If you're interested, give him a call."

Feeling like poor helpless Britt who couldn't find a decent job got to her. Even Quinn's charm couldn't wipe away that feeling.

"I can find my own job, thank you."

His eyebrow shot up. "A little touchy, aren't you?"

"And you are Phil's attorney, so stop being nice to me. Stop…"

"Stop what?"

Stop making me love you. But she didn't say that. Her pride wouldn't let her. "Stop helping me."

"That might be impossible." He reached for her left hand and fingered the silver bracelet, then tucked the card into her palm. "Just think about it."

Warm sensations shot up her arm. She raised her eyes to his and wished she hadn't. Those same sensuous emotions were in his. She melted like butter under a heat lamp.

"Did you get a good night's rest?" he asked in a low voice.

"Yes." Her reply was barely audible.

He bent his head and kissed her lips lightly, briefly, blowing whatever defense she had against him out of the water.

"Think about the job." After one last glance, he strolled to his car.

She let out the breath she was holding, turned off the lights, locked the door and ran to her car with the card still in her hand. Tucking it into her purse, she smiled. She had no idea where she and Quinn were headed. Every time she put up her guard, he found a way to break through it. Mostly with just his voice, his kindness.

A man like that couldn't be all bad.

She wanted to believe that with all her heart.

When Britt fell into bed at eleven o'clock that night she was exhausted. Threadgill's had had a small band playing, and the place was packed with college students and families, as well as singles looking for dates. She'd been hit on more times than a Vegas stripper and was getting good at the smiling brush-off.

The music was loud, the patrons louder. But everyone came for a good time and good food. Threadgill's had been an Austin tradition for over seventy-five years. Kenneth Threadgill was the first person to have a liquor license in the county. Back then musicians were paid with beer. Things had changed since the olden days, but Threadgill's was still a favorite musical venue. She worked in the south Austin restaurant, which was next door to the old great Armadillo World Headquarters. The walls were covered with memorabilia of famed musicians, from Count Basie to Willie Nelson and Waylon

Jennings, who had played the 'Dillo in Austin's musical heyday.

Britt served so many chicken fried steaks with Threadgill's Texas margaritas that she lost track. But the tips were good and she loved the friendly environment.

The next morning she was back at McDonald's, and wondered how long she could keep up the pace. She revived for her afternoon with Dillon. That made it all worthwhile. At times, though, she found it hard to stay awake. After the nanny picked up Dillon, Britt fished the professor's business card out of her purse.

Decent hours. Oh, God, she'd love decent hours.

Before she could stop herself, she called Harmon Withers, and she made an appointment for Friday at two. That was her rest time between jobs, but that was the only way she could work it. Hopefully, it was a step in the right direction.

Britt liked Professor Withers. He was a soft-spoken man who made her feel at ease. He didn't ask a lot of questions and that surprised her. His main concern was that she could use a computer, file and do research. Another concern was he wanted her to work quietly and not burden him with endless chatter.

She promised she could do that, and he hired her on the spot. That was strange to her. She'd expected a thorough interview. Red flags went up. Did Quinn have something to do with this? *Of course,* was the immediate answer. Now her options were to accept or just walk out.

She would be beholden to Quinn. But she already was—he'd saved her life. She had to look at this realistically, though. With a better job she had the added ammunition she needed to fight Phil in court.

"The position is eight to five, Monday through Friday," the professor was saying.

It gave her the opportunity to explain about Dillon.

He looked up from the papers on his desk. "Mr. Ross your attorney?"

She swallowed. "No. He's my ex's attorney."

The professor blinked, clearly thrown. "Interesting and totally confusing."

"Does it make a difference?" she asked.

"Not to me, my dear. You start on Monday if you want the job."

"I do, and thank you." The decision was easy, after all.

"Just do the work—that's all I ask—and you can have Tuesday and Thursday afternoons off. But you might have to take work home."

"No problem. I'll see you on Monday."

Britt left, thinking there were a lot of nice people in the world and she was grateful for their help. She wouldn't let Professor Withers down. Just as she'd never let her son down again.

Her life took a turn for the better. She quit her job at McDonald's, but still helped out at Threadgill's at night. She was saving every dime she could so she'd be able to rent a bigger place. Dillon needed his own room.

She and the professor worked well together. He was a quaint, eccentric man who liked his privacy, and Britt made sure he had that, fielding calls and dealing with students who just had to talk to him. She didn't know a lot about ancient civilization but she was learning.

Going to work at the university was a little different than McDonald's. She enjoyed wearing nice clothes, and the campus was beautiful with its gnarled oaks and historic buildings, which were overshadowed by the 307 foot UT tower. If the weather wasn't bad, she loved to sit under one of the big oaks and watch the students with their backpacks, laptops and cells phones, full of life and energy, with their whole lives ahead of them. She'd once been like that.

Then she'd met Phil Rutherford.

And she felt old and used up.

Until she thought about Quinn.

He made her feel young and alive again. She wanted to call and tell him about the job and thank him. But she hesitated. She had to do this on her own without any more favors from him. Every time he saw her she knew he was putting his job on the line. And she couldn't get involved with a man who was working for Phil.

But she couldn't change the fact that she already was. How were they going to fix their messed up lives?

Quinn was working late again. It was the Wednesday before Thanksgiving. Jury selection for the Morris case started on Monday, so he was going to have a short weekend. Peyton had already informed him that he was expected for dinner on Thursday. His mother and her husband would be there, too. A family Thanksgiving, Peyton had said.

He eased back in his chair, thinking of Britt. She'd have Dillon for part of the day and he knew she was happy about that. Staring at his cell phone on his desk, he thought of calling her. She'd taken the job with Harmon and he wondered how she was doing. As he reached for his cell, Steve walked in.

"I can't find any precedent you can use in the Morris case. Damn! Why did she have to shoot him in the back?"

"When you're that afraid, logic is not a strong suit. I have to hope we get an understanding jury."

"It sucks, having her trial right before Christmas. If she's convicted, those kids will go into foster care."

"Well, thanks for the vote of confidence."

"Sorry." Steve's face turned a slight pink. "You know what I mean, though. This case is a bitch. But if anyone can get her off, you can."

Quinn waved a hand toward the door. "Go spend the holiday with your family."

"I'm staying to watch the UT and Aggie game with my brothers, but I'll be back in town on Saturday. If you need anything, just call."

"I will. And happy Thanksgiving."

"You, too." Steve frowned. "You're not going to work through the holiday, are you?"

"No. I have orders to be at my sister's."

Steve nodded and walked out.

Quinn would love to spend Thanksgiving with Britt and Dillon, but he knew that was impossible. He wasn't a member of her family. He was the man who'd taken her child from her. That still burned like raw acid in his gut.

Suddenly a shuffling noise came from the outer office and then he heard low voices. It wasn't Steve. *It couldn't be....* He hurried around his desk and through the door, and there they were, Bonnie and Clyde. What were they up to now?

"Are you sure this is it, Ona?" Enzo asked. "It doesn't look the same."

"You don't remember anything, Enzo. Of course this is it. Now let's find Mr. Hotshot."

"Are you two vampires who only come out at night?" Quinn asked, walking into the reception area.

"What he say?" Enzo asked with a giant-size frown.

"He said you're a vampire," Ona replied.

"What's that?"

"Think Dracula," Ona told him.

Enzo's frown welded into his wrinkled forehead. Clearly, he didn't get it. Tonight he wore a baseball cap with the University of Texas logo on it, a heavy coat and pants two sizes too big for him. And he leaned heavily on a cane.

Ona wore a bright red knitted hat, a long gray coat and support shoes. In her hand was a large brown paper bag.

"Aren't you two grounded?" he asked.

"We've come to get my gun," Enzo said. "I had it since the war and I want it back."

"Sorry. Mrs. Davis told me to throw it away." It was still in Quinn's safe, but no way was he giving it to Enzo.

"What? She had no right. That's my gun." Enzo sank into a chair in front of Denise's desk. "Did you get any beer?"

Ona grunted. "He has the attention span of a child. I brought you something." She held up the paper bag.

Quinn eyed it warily. "Is that a bomb?"

Ona laughed, a real laugh, and Quinn knew underneath her hellfire and fury she had a sense of humor. "Hear that, Enzo? We never thought of a bomb."

"Yeah. Could have blown up the whole place, except I don't know how to make a bomb."

"Me, neither, but it's a hell of an idea."

"You know they lock people up for saying things like that." Quinn knew they were harmless, and he wondered if they even realized the consequences of their actions.

"Yeah. Go figure." She raised the bag again. "I made you a chocolate pie for saving my granddaughter's life."

"Ona makes good pies." Enzo bobbed his head.

Quinn took the bag. "So I'm forgiven?"

"Hell, no," Ona was quick to say. "But one good deed deserves another."

Quinn didn't think he was, but he thought he'd ask.

"Did you get any beer?" Enzo asked again. Loudly.

Quinn looked at the old man. "Are you even allowed to have beer?"

Enzo bristled. "Damn right. I can have anything I want. I'm ninety-two and not on any medication. What do you think about that, hotshot?"

"I think it's great and I'm wondering why you don't buy your own beer."

"Because that sour-faced daughter of his won't give him any money," Ona said.

Enzo pointed his cane at her, his wrinkly face scrunched in anger. "Don't talk about Frances."

"I'll talk about that whiney, lazy, no good cheap-skate—"

"Time out," Quinn shouted, knowing this was turning into a full-blown argument. "How did you get here? And does Mrs. Davis know?"

"We came on the bus," Ona answered tartly. "Carin doesn't have a clue where we are. She's sitting with a neighbor's sick mother while they're out for the evening. It's their anniversary or something. Carin's always a sucker for someone in need. She brought me in earlier so I could spend the night with my Britt, and get up early to cook dinner tomorrow. Enzo wanted to get his gun and I wanted to bring you that pie." She pointed to the bag. "So here we are. Does that answer your nosy questions?"

He ignored the snarky attitude. "Does Britt know you're here?"

Ona shook her head. "Nope. We're over twenty-one and do whatever we please."

"I figured that one out on my own." He turned toward his office. "I'll get my coat and take you home."

"Did you get any beer?" Enzo asked again.

Quinn stopped in his tracks. "Enzo, I'll buy you beer on the way home. How does that sound?"

The wrinkles on the old man's face weaved into a smile. "Like the pearly gates are opening."

"Hallelujah," Ona said. "I drink beer, too."

Great, Quinn thought as he slipped into his coat. He was getting two old people drunk. Well, then maybe they would stop trying to kill him.

* * *

Thirty minutes later they were in Enzo's room, the elderly man stretched back in his recliner, sucking on a Budweiser. Ona sat beside him in a chair, doing the same thing, her feet propped on a small coffee table. The TV blared full blast.

Quinn was about to leave when there was a knock at the door and Britt walked in. She stared at him, shock in her dark eyes, before her gaze swung to her grandmother, to Enzo and then back to him.

"Quinn, what are you doing here?"

"Your grandmother and Enzo paid me another visit and I brought them home."

"What did they do?"

"We didn't do nothing, my pretty." Ona took a big swallow of beer. "Enzo wanted his gun back and I baked Mr. Hotshot a pie for saving your life."

"You didn't…" Britt whispered to him.

"No. I didn't give him the gun," he whispered back.

"She baked you a pie?"

He nodded. "It's in my car. I wonder if it has strychnine in it?"

A smile curved her lips and his heart zoomed as if he'd stepped on a gas pedal.

"You look great," he said, his eyes lingering on her face.

She wrinkled her nose. "I smell like margaritas. I've been serving them all evening."

He leaned in closer and breathed deeply. "I love margaritas."

"Hey, hotshot, we need two more beers," Ona called.

Quinn groaned, but went to the compact refrigerator for the beer. Popping the tops, he handed the cans to them.

"See, Ona?" Enzo said, taking his. "He's not a bad man."

"Onnie, where did you get the beer?" Britt asked before he could say anything.

Ona thrust a thumb toward Quinn.

Britt gaped at him. "You bought my grandmother and my uncle beer?"

By the tone of her voice he surmised that wasn't a good thing.

"Yes," he replied. "Is there something wrong with that?"

"He's ninety-two. She's eighty-three. You figure it out."

"Just because they're older doesn't mean they can't still enjoy life."

She placed her hands on her hips. "Really? Enzo pees on himself if he has more than one beer and Onnie gets crazier than she already is."

"Oh, sorry." Quinn reached for his coat. "On that, I think I'll leave."

"Hey, hotshot," Ona shouted. "Why don't you come for dinner tomorrow? I always cook plenty."

"Thank you, Ona. I appreciate the invitation, but I'm visiting my family."

"Just as well," Ona muttered. "I'd probably try to poison you, anyway."

"Hell, no, Ona," Enzo yelled. "He buys us beer."

Quinn shrugged into his coat and his eyes caught Britt's. "I really am sorry."

She tucked a tendril of hair behind her ear. "It's okay. You're the only person I know who puts up with them, even after they tried to shoot you."

"I think they're all bark and no bite."

"Don't always count on that."

"I won't, believe me." He stared into her eyes. "Have a wonderful Thanksgiving."

She wrapped her arms around her waist. "I will. Dillon will be home for the afternoon."

"Good night," Quinn said to her alone, his voice low. Then he called to Ona and Enzo, "'Night."

"We need more beer," Enzo shouted.

Oh, God, what had he done? Quinn hurried to the fridge and removed the last two beers, stuffing them into his coat pocket.

"Hey…" Ona protested.

"Party's over."

At the door he paused, staring into Britt's eyes one more time. He needed the warmth he saw there to last him the rest of the weekend.

"Happy Thanksgiving," she murmured.

"You, too," he replied, walking out the door and wondering how happy it would be without her.

For the first time he realized how deep his feelings were for Britt and how much they'd grown since he'd rescued her from the flood. He didn't have to ask his sister how it felt to be in love.

He knew.

Chapter Fourteen

Peyton had outdone herself. The table was tastefully decorated with china, silver and crystal on a linen table-cloth that had been in their family for years. His sister couldn't boil water before she'd married Wyatt, so the turkey, dressing and all the trimmings were like a mir-acle in his eyes. And the fact that it made Peyton happy was an even bigger miracle.

Wyatt occupied the head of the table, while Garland, Quinn and Peyton's stepfather, took the chair at the other end. Maureen, their mother, and Mae, Wyatt's mother, sat on one side, along with Jody, and he and Peyton were seated across from them. J.W. was tethered in his high chair between Wyatt and Peyton.

Jody said the blessing and ended it with, "God bless Elvis." No one batted an eye because they knew Jody's Gramma Mae loved Elvis and it was always part of the prayer in the Carson household.

Mae was as eccentric as Ona. They could even be friends. Quinn shook his head, knowing he was getting ahead of himself. He had no idea what the future held for him and Britt. The next four weeks would be crucial. Philip Sr. would make a move soon, and Quinn would have to make the biggest decision of his life.

Peyton was puzzled by the chocolate pie he'd brought, but everyone loved it, and he had to admit it was the best he'd ever eaten. Of course, he didn't tell Peyton, but her pumpkin pie didn't hold a candle to it. It was clear Ona was in a class all by herself in the cooking department. And a few other departments.

The conversation was lively, but Quinn's mind kept wandering to Britt. He kept glancing at his watch. Had Dillon arrived at Britt's? Was she happy?

"You're very distant today," his mother said. "Are you okay?"

"Sure." He wiped his mouth with a napkin. "I just have an important case coming up." He wasn't talking about the Morris case.

Peyton shook a finger at him. "No work today, big brother."

He made a face at her.

Maureen straightened her napkin in her lap. "I want all of you to come to Dallas for Christmas."

"Sorry, Mom," Peyton said. "We want the kids home for Christmas."

"Yeah," Jody added. "Santa won't be able to find us."

"Oh, sweetie," Maureen hastened to reassure her. "Santa will find you wherever you are."

Jody glanced at her mother and Peyton was quick to say, "Sorry, Mom, but you and Garland are welcome to come here and watch the kids open their gifts."

When Peyton was younger, she'd never stood up to their formidable mother. It did Quinn's heart good to see her now guarding her happiness like a lioness. He admired that.

And just like that, he realized he loved his family, but this wasn't where he wanted to be today. He laid his napkin beside his plate. "I hate to eat and run, but I have to get back to Austin."

"What?" The protest echoed from his sister and his mother.

He stood and kissed Peyton's cheek. "I really have to go," he whispered in her ear.

"Oh. Okay." She looked puzzled but didn't try to stop him.

He said his goodbyes, kissed Jody and J.W., and headed for the entry to get his coat. His mother followed him, as he knew she would. She was tenacious, one of the reasons she was so good in politics.

"Quinn, honey, do you have to go?"

"Yes." He slipped on his coat and looked into her concerned blue eyes. "I'm fine, really," he added. In that moment he knew his mother loved him and worried about him. She had done the best she could with her marriage to Quinn's father, and Quinn had no reason to harbor any resentment from his childhood. It only embittered him and he didn't want that. But he had to say something before he could completely let go of the resentment. He hadn't even known it was there until Britt had brought it up when they were waiting to be rescued.

He hugged his mother tightly and she hugged him back. "I forgive you," he murmured.

She went completely still, but didn't ask what he was forgiving her for. She knew. "I loved your father, but we grew so far apart we could never find our way back to what we once had."

"I know. Dad was hard to live with."

"I tried."

"I know," he said again. "And you don't have to explain anything to me."

She drew back and looked into his face. "What brought this on?"

"I'm finding out what real love is, and I don't want to hold any animosity in my heart that will tarnish it."

She held a hand to her breast. "Oh, Quinn."

He kissed her forehead. "I love you, Mom."

"Thank you, son." She paused, eyeing him. "Who...?"

Smiling, he opened the door and ran to his car. He wasn't answering that question.

Driving toward Austin, he could think of only one person.

Britt.

Britt was having a late lunch. Since Dillon didn't get there until one, she wanted him to play for a while before he ate. He was fussy today, wanting to be held. The separation was taking its toll on both of them.

She told her mother the whole story about what had happened last night, and Carin was aghast.

"What am I going to do with Mama?" she asked while Onnie was in the bathroom.

"Quinn said something about letting her enjoy life."

"But she tries to destroy more than enjoy, and what was Quinn thinking, buying them beer?"

"You know how Uncle Enzo is." Britt sliced an apple for fruit salad. "He's always asking for beer."

"But it's not allowed in the home." Carin shoved the sweet potatoes in the oven. "I'll probably be getting a call from Frances." She cocked her head. "Yeah. I hope Frances does call me. I'd like to know why she can't ever have her father for the holidays."

"He's happier with us," Britt commented. "He and Onnie grew up like sister and brother and they're kindred spirits."

Her mother groaned and Britt laughed.

Two hours later they sat at the kitchen table replenished from a meal mostly prepared by Onnie. Dillon had eaten and then started whining to get out of his chair. He fell asleep against Britt and she worried he was coming down with something. He wasn't his usual happy self.

"Every time I think about this custody thing I just get angry," Carin said, watching Dillon.

"We should have killed that bastard Phil instead of the hotshot attorney," Ona replied.

"Mama, I do not want to hear that kind of talk." Carin got up and carried dishes to the sink, her shoulders stiff.

Britt was about to go to her when the doorbell rang. She glanced at the clock. Three-thirty. It couldn't be the nanny. She walked to the door with Dillon cradled against her.

Looking through the peephole, she smiled and opened the door.

"Come in," she said to Quinn, taking in his lean physique, his dark slacks, white shirt and dress coat. A manly, fresh scent reached her and her stomach quivered. He was so tempting.

"Ona invited me and I thought I'd—"

"What are you doing here, Mr. Ross?" her mother asked over Britt's shoulder. Her angry Onnie-type voice was so unlike her.

"Mom…"

"I'd prefer if he wasn't here."

"Hey, Mr. Hotshot!" Onnie called from the kitchen. "Come on in. I'll make you a plate."

"Did you bring any beer?" Enzo asked.

"No, Enzo," Quinn answered, gingerly walking into the kitchen. "I'm not buying you any more beer. That got me in trouble."

"Sucker. The women got to you."

"See what he causes…"

Britt took her mother's arm and pulled her aside, still cradling Dillon in the other. "What's wrong with you? You're being rude."

"I'm just so afraid we're going to lose…" Her mother's voice cracked and she stopped.

Britt hugged her with her free arm. "Mom, let me handle this. Please."

"But he's…" Carin glanced at Quinn.

Dillon stirred against Britt and she thought it was time to get her mother's mind on something else. "Look. Dilly bear's awake."

Carin reached for her grandson and carried him into the living room. Dillon looked back at Britt, but didn't cry. She saw that Onnie was stuffing Quinn with pumpkin pie and whipped cream. Like her mother, Britt wondered what Quinn was doing here. But unlike Carin, she was happy to see him. She couldn't seem to get it through her head that she should hate him.

"They're fattening me up for something," Quinn said when he saw her. His voice was soothing and affable, washing away her doubts. "And I don't think it's for something good."

"You'll never know, hotshot." Onnie piled more whipped cream on the pie.

Her mother settled down and Dillon started playing with his toys, carrying the NERF ball to Quinn, as if he remembered. Football was on the TV and Britt sat on the floor with Dillon, and Quinn joined them. The toddler climbed all over him, slobbering on his clothes, and he didn't seem to mind. Her mother watched them closely. That didn't escape Britt.

Uncle Enzo fell asleep in a chair and Onnie snoozed on the sofa. The afternoon passed quickly. Soon Debi arrived, and Dillon clung to Britt. It made letting go that much harder. She told Debi to be sure to watch him because she felt he was coming down with something.

Her mother and grandmother packed up their things to go home. Quinn was in the living room with Enzo.

"Please come home with us," Carin begged Britt. "I hate for you to be here by yourself."

"I have to work at the restaurant tomorrow. I'll be fine."

Carin glanced toward the living room. "Why is he still here?"

"Give it a rest," Ona said, placing dishes in a bag. "There's more than one way to trap a weasel."

Carin blinked. "We're not trapping weasels."

"Oh, but we are, sweet daughter." Ona grabbed her purse. "Let's go. We have to take Enzo to the home."

"I'll take Enzo. It's on my way," Quinn said, and Britt wondered how long he'd been standing there and how much he'd heard.

"There's no need, Mr. Ross." Her mother's voice was as cold as she'd ever heard it.

"I'm going with Mr. Hotshot." Enzo fitted his baseball cap on his head and reached for his cane. "He might buy me beer."

Carin whirled toward Quinn. "Do not buy him any more beer."

Quinn nodded and glanced at Britt. She gave a tentative smile and suddenly knew why he had come today. He wanted to be with her as much as she wanted to be with him. And God help her, that just made their situation worse.

"Are we going by any strip clubs?" Enzo asked Quinn as they walked toward the door.

Her mother gasped.

"Sorry, Enzo," Quinn said. "No beer, no strip clubs."

"You're still more fun than Carin."

"Boy, he said a mouthful," Ona remarked.

"Don't start with me, Mama."

"Goodbye, my pretty." Onnie hugged Britt. "Let's go,

Carin. Maybe we can stop for a beer so you can loosen up a bit."

The words hit a nerve. Her mother's face became pinched and Britt thought she was going to cry. Britt immediately went to her.

"Mom…it's okay. Onnie is teasing."

"I'm just so worried about you."

"Listen to me." Britt hugged her mother. "I'll be fine. I'll get through this, but I need you to be strong."

"Okay." Carin sniffed. "I love you, baby."

"I love you, too, Mom. I'll call tomorrow." She playfully shook a finger in her face. "And do not stop at any beer joints."

Carin laughed and the sound made Britt feel better. They would get through this—as a family.

The apartment was very quiet after everyone had gone. She checked the kitchen, but Onnie had made sure it was spotless. Britt picked up Dillon's toys and took a shower. It was too early to go to bed, so she decided to watch TV. It had been a while since she'd had any time to relax. She flipped through the channels and found nothing she liked. Curling up on the sofa, she promptly fell asleep.

The doorbell woke her.

She turned off the TV and stumbled toward the door, tying her robe tighter. Looking through the peephole, she was surprised to see Quinn again. Had something happened to Uncle Enzo? She quickly opened the door.

"What happened? What's wrong?"

Quinn stepped in and closed the door. "I forgot to do something."

"What?" she asked, completely baffled.

"This." He slipped his arms around her waist and pulled her to him. His eyes twinkled into hers as he took her lips. With a moan she leaned into him, soaking up the scent of the outdoors, the cold and him. It enveloped her, and thoughts of stopping never entered her mind.

As the kiss deepened, her arms slid up the sleeves of his coat to his neck. Her mouth opened, inviting him in to new discoveries, new heights of passion. The kiss went on until he trailed kisses from her mouth to her cheek, to her chin and to the warmth of her throat.

She arched her neck as every need in her came alive. At that moment the cold hard truth hit her and she pushed away. *He was Phil's lawyer.*

She flipped back her tangled hair. "We shouldn't do this."

"I know." Quinn took a long breath and she saw the desire in his hooded eyes, just as she'd seen before. She closed hers and blocked it out. *Tell him to go. Tell him to go.* But not one word left her mouth.

Nor did he make a move to leave.

"I can't get you out of my head," he said with a ragged sigh.

"Me neither," she admitted in a voice she didn't recognize.

He cupped her face with one hand and made circles on her cheek with his thumb. Coherent thoughts were impossible when he was touching her. Besides, she didn't want to think. She just wanted to feel.

She leaned her face into his palm, giving in to something stronger than herself. In that moment she knew she'd made a decision. He knew it, too.

He swung her up in his arms and strolled into her bedroom, his warm, seductive lips taking hers in a slow, burning kiss that obliterated any lingering doubts. She slid from his embrace and pushed his coat from his shoulders.

"Are you sure?" he asked, his eyes a sleepy dark blue.

Nodding her head, she unbuttoned his shirt. When she

touched his chest, he groaned, and in a matter of frenzied seconds their clothes were on the floor. He paused for a moment to stare at her, his eyes cloudy with need.

"God, you're so beautiful," he said in a husky voice as he pulled her naked body to him. His hands were gentle, coaxing, as they touched her back, her bottom. Every hard muscle of his magnificent frame pressed into her. She gasped at the sheer gratification. Turning, they fell backward onto the bed. He kissed her deeply and then his lips explored her breasts, her stomach and below.

Wispy sighs of pleasure left her throat and she reached for him, her hands massaging his strong shoulders and traveling through the swirls of blond chest hairs arrowing down to his groin. When she touched his hardness, he let out a long breath and pulled her to him, pressing every muscle into her once again.

Her senses throbbed, and they both knew they'd reached a point of no return. He took her lips and rolled her to her back. The kiss went on and on, and she opened her legs, needing more. With one sure thrust he was inside her. Her body accepted him gladly, willingly, as they joined in a primitive dance as old as time that bound them together closer than they had ever been.

She cried his name as waves of pleasure convulsed through her. A moment later he gasped and shuddered against her in release. They lay still as their sweat-bathed bodies enjoyed the aftermath.

Britt had made love before, but never like this, never with all her heart and all her body. Finally, Quinn rolled to the side and gathered her against him. She drifted into sleep with her head on his chest, feeling at peace for the first time in a long time.

Quinn watched her sleep, brushing her dark hair from her face. He felt rejuvenated, alive. He now knew the difference between having sex and making love. The heart had to be involved totally and completely. From the moment he'd looked into her dark eyes he had probably known this day was coming. But he'd never dreamed it would be with this much intensity, this much emotion.

He didn't question the right or wrong of what had happened. Even though love words hadn't been spoken, they were there in every kiss, every touch.

Pulling her closer, he whispered, "I love you." And knew the days ahead would be a test of that love.

Chapter Fifteen

Quinn worried how Britt was going to feel when she woke up, but he needn't have. In the middle of the night she woke him with sweet kisses and they explored a new realm of lovemaking. Afterward they made turkey sandwiches. They were hungry from all the exercise.

Later, they sat on the sofa in the darkened living room, completely naked, sipping wine and talking about her job with Harmon, and other, inane things. He'd never felt a connection to any other person like he did with Britt. It had been that way from the start.

In the morning he reached for Britt, but she wasn't there. Fear shot through him and he sat up, glancing around. He relaxed as he saw her in the bathroom, putting up her hair.

Glancing at the clock on the nightstand, he saw it was after ten. What? He never slept this late, not even when working long hours on a trial.

"Where are you going?" he asked.

She applied lipstick. "To work."

"Oh." He wanted to ask her to skip work, but he didn't. Making her own way was important to her and he wouldn't interfere with that. "What time do you get off?"

She came out of the bathroom in tight jeans and a

T-shirt that had Threadgill's written on it, her dark hair neatly pinned back. Her skin glowed and a need uncurled inside him.

"At six," she replied, putting her lipstick in her purse. Glancing at him, she asked, "Will you be here when I get back?"

"Do you want me to be?"

Her eyes held his. "Yes."

He grinned. "Then I'll be here."

She leaned over and kissed him. Holding her face, he deepened the kiss.

"You're not playing fair," she whispered against his lips.

He let her go with a disgruntled sound and she laughed. "You're insatiable."

"For you."

They stared at each for a long moment, both knowing they'd crossed a line last night that neither could undo. And they were comfortable with that.

Britt lived in a fairy tale for three days. She rushed to work and then hurried home to be with Quinn. They made love and talked about their lives, sharing tidbits they hadn't revealed before. It felt right, natural, for them to be together. Spending time with him eased the ache inside her and she didn't miss Dillon so much.

Quinn worked on the Morris case while she was at the restaurant, and she thought about her own case, but didn't bring it up. Saturday night, though, after passionate, heated sex, Britt lay awake cradled in Quinn's arms. Her eyes caught the crib—the empty crib. And tonight she couldn't ignore it. When Quinn went to sleep, she slipped out and curled up in a chair.

She was in love with a man who had taken her child. And he was still Phil's attorney. Reality hit her. What was she doing? Once again she'd followed her heart without thinking. It could cost her more than she'd ever dreamed.

Quinn stirred and reached for her in the bed. Realizing she wasn't there, he sat up, brushing his hair from his forehead. The moon was bright, so he could see her sitting in the chair.

"What's wrong?" he asked.

"I saw the empty crib and…"

"Britt…" He made to come to her, but she held out her hands to stop him.

"No. I want to talk."

"Okay." He eased back on the bed.

She swallowed hard, saying the words she had to. "Please resign from the Rutherford case."

The silence in the room became deafening.

"I can't do that."

She felt a blow to her chest and had trouble breathing.

"Britt, trust me."

"You keep saying that, but I don't have my baby. He won't be home for Christmas or his birthday. I'm all out of trust."

"Britt." Quinn came toward her then, naked, the moonlight glistening off his long, lean body. But she held tight to her control. "I have other clients who depend on me, so I have to be careful how I handle the Rutherford situation. Trust me not to hurt you."

At the softness of his voice, she weakened. Her heart pulled her in one direction, her mind in the other. But Dillon had to be her top priority. She couldn't think about herself. "No." She got out of the chair and moved as far away from Quinn as she could. "I'm asking you again. If you feel anything for me, please resign from this case."

Their future hung between them. And it was all up to him.

He ran his hands through his tousled hair. "I can't. Just—"

"Get out," she shouted.

"Let me explain," he pleaded.

"Not unless it ends with you quitting the Rutherford case."

Grabbing his jeans, he slipped into them. Within a minute he was dressed, and strolled from the room.

When she heard the click of the front door, she curled up in the bed, her arms around Quinn's pillow, and cried loudly, the sobs coming from deep in her heart. She had gambled and lost. He didn't love her enough to give up his career. And she was aware that's what it came down to. The Rutherfords would ruin Quinn if he resigned. Just like they had ruined her life. Now she had to wonder how far they would go to take her child permanently.

And if Quinn would do their bidding.

Quinn stood outside Britt's door, feeling pain like he'd never felt before. He'd hurt her and that was the last thing he'd wanted to do. Time was all he needed. Why couldn't she give him time?

Because her child's future was involved. He understood that. But he wanted her to trust him—trust him not to hurt her or Dillon. He could go back in there and force her to listen to him, but what would that accomplish? He couldn't give her any guarantees, and that's what she wanted. A guarantee for a future with her son.

And with him.

"Goodbye." He lightly touched her door before walking away.

Quinn threw himself into the Morris case and tried to keep memories of Britt at bay. The jury was seated on the first day and they went to trial. He portrayed Kathy Morris as a woman who lived in fear. She'd suffered physical and mental abuse from her husband for years, but when he started beating the kids she'd snapped. She'd feared for her children's lives.

Through three days of grueling testimonies and cross-examinations, Quinn hung in there, trying to convince the jury that Kathy Morris did not belong in jail. The jury was finally sequestered, and Quinn waited. On Friday the verdict came in.

The jury was deadlocked.

The judge asked them to go back and see if they could reach a verdict. The foreman said it was useless. None of them were budging on their decision. Quinn was relieved. The state would now plea-bargain with him to avoid another trial. Kathy Morris would get the help she needed and she'd be home for Christmas with her kids.

Quinn had fought hard for the Morris case, with Britt and Dillon at the back of his mind. Why couldn't Britt trust him to do the same for her?

He returned to his office amid congratulations from his staff. Denise, however, kept rolling her eyes and nodding toward his door.

Shaking off her strange behavior, he strolled toward his office. The door was slightly ajar. He pushed it opened and stopped short.

Philip Sr. was sitting in a leather chair across from Quinn's desk.

Showdown!

Quinn shook the man's hand. Of medium height, Philip was dressed in a tailored suit, with his styled silver hair perfectly in place, as always. He was slick, suave and cunning. Quinn had to be on his toes.

"Congratulations," Philip said. "I believe you could get a cold-blooded murderer off."

"I wouldn't represent a cold-blooded murderer," Quinn replied, sliding into his chair.

"High ethics." Philip resumed his seat. "I admire that."

Quinn didn't feel that required an answer, so he waited for the proverbial shoe to drop. And felt it was coming with the force of a Peterbilt truck.

"I'm in town catching up on some details at my firm." Philip formed a steeple with his fingers. "And I wanted to touch base with you on Phil's case."

"What about it?" he asked in his best courtroom voice.

Philip glanced at Quinn over the tips of his fingers. "I want you to go after Ms. Davis. I want that child to stay with Phil—permanently."

Quinn leaned back, his hands resting on the arms of his chair. "On what grounds?"

"Wallis sent you plenty of grounds."

Quinn reached for the Rutherford folder on his desk and pulled out the photos Levi had blown up. "Are you talking about these?"

"Yes. She trashed his condo. She has a bad temper. Not to mention that she sleeps around. She's not fit to be a mother."

Quinn's jaw clenched. "I don't use evidence that other people have collected. I do my own investigation." He pointed to one photo. "In this one, food items are strewn on the floor. Nothing else is disturbed. I investigated further and found the groceries were what Ms. Davis bought to celebrate with Phil on the news of her pregnancy, and to tell him she was quitting her job. She dropped the bag when she found Phil in bed with another woman, doing drugs."

Philip rose to his feet in a slow, sure movement. "My son does not do drugs. If that bitch told you that, she's lying."

"Are you positive?" Quinn asked, his eyes never wavering from the older man's lethal gaze.

"How dare you question me."

Quinn stood, the tension in the room a tangible thing he could feel down to his bones. This was where he was supposed to fold like a frightened intern. He did just the opposite, and it wasn't as hard as he'd thought it would be. "I'm not arguing a case on fabricated evidence, and that's all Wallis has. No temper. No affairs. It's all false."

Philip's eyes narrowed. "I don't think you know who you're talking to."

Quinn stared straight at the man he had once thought could walk on water. "Yes, sir, I do, and my advice is to leave that child with his mother."

Philip slipped his hands into the pockets of his slacks with a sly grin. "That wouldn't be because you have a connection to Ms. Davis?"

Quinn tensed, but made certain nothing showed on his face.

"You see, I know you and Ms. Davis were rescued together from the Brushy Creek flooding."

"Is that why Wallis suddenly became ill and I got the call?"

"Thought it would be a nice touch for Ms. Davis." The chill in Philip's eyes got a few degrees colder as he pulled some snapshots from his pocket and laid them on the desk. Photos of Quinn and Britt kissing at her front door….

Son of a bitch!

"I'm always in control. Remember that."

Quinn raised his eyes to the older man's. "I never forget it."

"Good. We're clear then. File for permanent custody on new grounds."

Quinn took a sharp breath. "I told you I'm not arguing a case on fabricated evidence."

"Excuse me?" Philip bristled at his audacity.

"You heard me."

"You just signed your death warrant as a lawyer. I'll have you disbarred, and you'll never work again in this state or in this country. I hope she's worth it." He walked to the door. With his hand on the knob, Philip looked back. "I'll send a courier for all the files and anything else you have on the case. You're no longer the lawyer of record."

Quinn sank into his chair and let out an agonized sigh. Luckily, he'd gotten through his caseload before the holidays. No one was depending on him except clients scheduled for the New Year. To keep his license he now had to fight fire with fire.

He pushed a button on the phone. "Get Levi over here as soon as possible."

Britt had to stay busy to keep from thinking about Quinn. He had to make a choice, and she knew it wasn't easy for him. It wasn't for her, either. Her broken heart was evidence of that. Some relationships weren't meant to happen, and she and Quinn would never be together. They were on opposites sides. He wasn't her hero. She'd accepted that.

Professor Withers made work a joy. When he learned she had two years of college, he encouraged her to continue her education. He said she could take a couple of classes and still keep her job. The more she thought about it the more she liked the idea. Elementary education had been her choice of major years ago, and it still was. She could work in the school system when Dillon was enrolled.

But first she had to make sure her son was returned

to her. She had several meetings with Mona and told her she wanted Dillon either on Christmas Eve or Christmas Day. Mona made the request and it was denied. That was a devastating blow. She wouldn't see her son until after Christmas, but was determined not to let it get her down. Dillon wouldn't know the difference. Only she would.

She put up a tree in the living room just for Dillon, and bought his presents. Even the judge couldn't diminish the love in her heart. As she hung each ornament, she wished Quinn was here, just to hold her, to make the pain go away.

There was nothing so lonely as spending Christmas alone. She had her mother and Onnie, but she didn't have Dillon.

And she didn't have Quinn.

All she had to do was call him, but that would change nothing. He would still be Phil's attorney.

Quinn paced in his office and swung around as Levi entered. "Have you got anything?"

The P.I. shook his head. "Not a lot. Phil was gone from his condo three nights in the last two weeks. He's spending time with a woman named Jenna Lawson. She works in his office and she's stayed four nights at the condo."

"Nothing else?"

Levi shook his head.

"Come on, Levi. You're a better detective than that." Quinn sank into his chair. "The only way to get out of this mess and to get Dillon out of that house is to prove Phil is doing drugs. I know he is. Britt wouldn't lie."

"Maybe he's just a social user."

"Doesn't matter. Either way we need evidence." Quinn tapped his fingers on the desk. "Where does he go with this Jenna woman?"

"Her apartment or his condo. That's it."

"Strange," Quinn mumbled, mostly to himself. "You'd think she'd want to go out and party or something."

"I thought the same thing."

Quinn tapped his fingers louder as he thought. "Do they take Dillon out?"

"No. He's always with the nanny."

Quinn touched the files on his desk. "I've been doing a lot of checking on Phil, but Philip has called in a lot of favors. No one's willing to talk or risk being blackballed in this town."

"Must be nice to have that much power."

"Yeah." Quinn stood. "I have a meeting with Judge Norcutt."

Levi pushed back his hat. "Is that necessary?"

"Yes. I want her to know what's going on."

"Don't burn all your bridges."

"I think I already have." Quinn reached for his coat. "Keep digging for something I can use. My office is closed until after the holidays, so I'll be able to help you. Between us we have to find the evidence we need."

Levi faced him. "Or you'll lose it all."

"That's about it." Quinn walked out, knowing none of it mattered except losing the woman who'd stolen his heart. She might not trust him, but he was risking everything to return Dillon to her.

Judge Norcutt was waiting for him in her office. "Make this short, Mr. Ross. I don't have a lot of time, since I'm clearing my schedule for the holidays."

"It's about the Rutherford case."

"It's the only case you have in my court, so that's a given."

Quinn looked right at her. "You made the wrong decision in that case. The boy should have stayed with his mother."

"Excuse me?" Her eyes flared behind her glasses. "You're skating very close to the edge, Mr. Ross. You're Rutherford's attorney, and you either retract those words or I'll file a complaint against you for breach of ethics."

"I'm no longer the Rutherfords' attorney, but that doesn't make a lot of difference to me. I came here to say something and I'm saying it. Phil Rutherford is a drug user and you put Dillon Rutherford in danger every moment he's been living with his father."

"What? Do you have proof?"

Quinn had to swallow his pride. "No."

The judge's face relaxed and she picked up a pen on her desk. "So this is an assumption on your part, because you're ticked off at Mr. Rutherford for firing you?"

"This has nothing to do with that."

She pointed the pen at him. "I think it does, Mr. Ross. Your conduct is out of line and I have no choice but to file a complaint. I can't believe you'd risk your career, your reputation over this."

Quinn rubbed his jaw, not moved by the criticism. "It's a little strange to me that a judge would award custody to a father because of the mother's job."

Judge Norcutt rose to her feet, her body stiff with rage. "Get out, Mr. Ross."

Quinn ignored her outrage. "How long have you been on the bench, Judge? Fifteen? Twenty years? A long while, and time enough to cross paths with the mighty Philip Rutherford Sr."

"What are you saying?"

"I'm saying that complaint thing goes both ways. I'm going to check into your background, and if I find the tiniest connection to Philip Rutherford Sr., I'm coming after you like a pit bull. And if my license is pulled I know a lot of good lawyers, like Mona Tibbs, who will happily take up the cause." Pivoting, he strolled toward the door.

"Mr. Ross."

He stopped and turned back.

"I don't respond well to threats," the judge said.

"Neither do I."

"Well then, let's agree to disagree," she suggested in a stiff tone. "And if you find any evidence Phil Rutherford is doing drugs, bring it to me and I'll reverse my decision immediately."

Quinn inclined his head. The good judge was guilty as hell and covering her ass six ways from Sunday, but Quinn took the forced olive branch. Now he had to uncover the evidence as quickly as possible.

So Dillon could be home with his mother for Christmas.

Chapter Sixteen

A week before Christmas Quinn feared he was running out of time. Levi was the best detective in the state and he still couldn't turn up anything on Phil. If the man was doing drugs, he was very good at covering his tracks.

Every day Quinn waited for disciplinary action to be taken against him, but so far he hadn't heard from the Texas Bar Association. Philip hadn't changed his mind, Quinn was sure of that. Judicial action took time, and it gave him the time he needed to end the custody battle over Dillon once and for all.

Lenny Skokel had been hired by the Rutherfords. A courier had picked up the files, but Quinn saved copies. Lenny was a trial lawyer without ethics, morals or character, who, for a big fee, would slice and dice Britt's life to shreds. After Lenny was finished, a judge wouldn't grant her custody of a puppy. Quinn couldn't let that happen. Time was now his enemy.

Grabbing his cell, he punched in Levi's number to find out if he was making any progress. Without warning, his door opened and Britt's ex walked in.

Quinn slowly placed his phone on the desk. "I don't believe you have an appointment, Phil," he said in his best don't-mess-with-me tone.

The man thumbed toward the front door. "The sign says you're closed until January 3."

"Yes, and that means I'm not seeing anyone."

Phil reared back on his heels, a smug expression on his face. "Instead of the third you should put forever. Dad's not going to let you practice law much longer."

"Philip is powerful but he doesn't run the Texas Bar."

"Don't be too sure about that."

Quinn clenched his jaw. "Is there a purpose for this visit?"

"Yeah. My new attorney says I have to inform Roslyn that I'm taking Dillon away for the holidays, and I thought you'd be the best person to deliver that information." A thread of accusation ran through each word.

Quinn ignored the finger-pointing tactics. "Has the judge signed off on this?"

"Of course. I wouldn't do anything illegal."

Yeah, right. How did Phil get that by Judge Norcutt? Quinn didn't have to think long about the answer. Philip Sr. Damn!

"Why don't *you* tell Ms. Davis?"

"Her lawyer filed a restraining order against me, and as I said, I'm not doing anything illegal."

Thank God Mona was a step ahead of the bastard. Quinn was seething at this turn of events and he had to get all the information he could. "What about Ms. Davis's visitation days?"

"She can have a few days with the boy when I return."

"When is that?"

"Whenever I please." A sly grin spread across Phil's face.

Quinn stood, his body coiled in anger, and he had to restrain himself from physically attacking Phil. "How many people did your dad pay off for that?"

"Go to hell." Phil's face suddenly darkened.

Quinn tried to reach a softer side of the man, if he had one. "Think about your son for a change. He'll miss his mother. You can't be that coldhearted."

"See that Roslyn gets the message." Phil paused for a second. "And tell her if she wants to spend Christmas with her son, she knows how to make that happen."

"You can't be serious."

The sly grin was back in place before Phil turned and walked to the door.

"Phil."

He glanced back.

"Does your father know your plans concerning Ms. Davis?"

"He doesn't need to know everything."

Sorry bastard. "This isn't over."

"Oh, yeah, it's over, and you lose big time, old friend." Phil sauntered out with a chilling laugh.

Quinn plopped into his chair and ran his hands over his face. How was he going to tell Britt she wasn't going to see her son for Christmas? Or...

He slammed his fist onto the desk, the blunt sound echoing within him. How had he let this happen? He'd thought he had things under control, but now everything was spiraling into a vortex of pain. How did he stop it? It was going to take a miracle.

After Quinn calmed down, he called Mona to make sure she was aware of what was going on, and then he had to call Britt. He thought of going to her apartment, but there were too many good and happy memories there. And he wasn't sure he was welcome.

The university was closed for the holidays, so Britt worked as much as she could at the restaurant and planned her time around her visits with Dillon. From the university to the restaurant to the stores and streets, everything was decorated and lit up with the spirit of Christmas. People with shopping bags hurried everywhere. Christmas was almost here. Dillon's eyes grew big at the decorations and lights, but he wasn't crazy about Santa Claus. It was exciting showing him everything and watching his reaction.

She had come to grips with the fact that she would have to wait until the day after Christmas to celebrate the holiday with her son. It was just a day, and she would enjoy it no matter when it was. She wrapped one more present and placed it under the tree. Dillon was going to love the soft stuffed bear she'd found.

She was putting the wrapping paper away when her phone rang. She saw the caller ID and quickly picked up, her heart racing.

"Could you please come to my office?" Quinn asked, and his voice filled her with so much love, so much regret. It hit her how lonely she'd been without him.

"Yes," she replied, without even thinking about it. They had to talk. He gave her the address and she quickly changed into black slacks, a white turtleneck and heels. Her hand trembled as she applied lipstick. Oh, God, she had missed him so much, and she couldn't contain her excitement.

But she tried, for her own sanity.

Forty minutes later she found his office. She'd never been here before. It was on the fifth floor of a professional building on Congress Avenue that catered primarily to lawyers. The decor was very contemporary: glass, stainless steel and strategically placed potted plants. There was a notice on Quinn's office that said it was closed, but she pushed open the heavy oak door and went in. Inside, warm wood greeted her, from the floor to the desks, and the walls were a muted gold with eye-catching Texas landscapes taking pride of place. It was a soothing and relaxing atmosphere.

She heard Quinn talking on the phone, and followed his voice. The door was ajar so she walked in. He was sitting at his desk, his white shirtsleeves rolled up to his elbows. The shirt was opened at the neck and she glimpsed swirls of blond hairs—hair she'd run her fingers through…. Her stomach tightened with need and her eyes went to his face. His hair was longer, curling into his collar, as if he hadn't had time to get it cut. The angular lines of his face were tight with worry.

Still talking, he waved her to a chair. She had no idea what he was saying. She was too busy soaking up his presence. Easing into a leather chair, she slipped off her wool coat and placed her purse on the floor. She waited with her breath wedged in her throat like a cotton ball.

"Sorry," Quinn said as he laid his cell down, his eyes on her. At his warm gaze, a ripple of awareness flowed through her. "How are you?"

She swallowed a portion of the cotton. "Fine. Whawhat's this about?"

"I had a visit from Phil."

"And?" She braced herself.

He leaned back. "First, I have to tell you I'm no longer Phil's attorney."

Her pulse leaped. She hadn't expected this. "What happened?"

He seemed to be measuring his words like he always did. "They wanted me to file for permanent custody of Dillon and I refused."

Her heart sank to the pit of her stomach. "Can they do that?" she asked tentatively. "They don't have any grounds to do something like that." Her eyes flew to his. "Do they?"

He pushed a folder on the desk toward her.

She jumped up and flipped through it, her temper rising at the contents. "What is this?"

"Fabricated evidence that you have a temper and sleep around."

She stumbled back into the chair, feeling a paralyzing fear grip her. But she fought it. She wasn't going to break over this. She'd fight with her last breath.

"Phil brought you this so-called evidence?"

"No. I've had it from the start."

That took what little air she had left in her lungs.

"I had a feeling Phil and his dad would try something like this. That's why I asked for you to trust me."

And she hadn't. Her pride took a big hit and words eluded her.

"I was chosen for this case because they knew you and I were rescued together from the flooding. They also have photos of us kissing at your door. Phil wants revenge and he's stopping at nothing."

It took a moment for her to process everything Quinn was saying. "They used your connection to the Rutherfords to get to me."

"Exactly."

"And...and our relationship has..."

"Given them more grounds to take your child and have me disbarred."

She tried to speak and couldn't. Finally, she managed to murmur, "I'm sorry."

"Doesn't matter." He brushed it off with a wave of his hand. "We have to think about Dillon now."

"What have they planned?"

"They hired Lenny Skokel, a high-powered trial lawyer, to file for permanent custody of Dillon."

"No, no, no!" She didn't even realize she was screaming until she heard her voice echoing through the room.

He came around the desk and squatted in front of her. "You remember how strong you were in the creek?"

She nodded.

"You need to find that strength now."

"C-can they take him?" Her voice cracked.

He reached for her hand and entwined his fingers with hers. "I'm asking you again to trust me. Can you do that?"

She nodded, knowing she trusted him more than anyone on earth.

"Good." He squeezed her hand. "There's more."

"What?"

"Phil is taking Dillon away for the holidays."

"He can't do that. It's not in the ruling."

"The judge signed off on it."

"What?" Britt was being hit so many times she felt as if she was in the creek again, fighting for her life. And her hero was right in front of her. Why hadn't she trusted him all along? Fear. Plain old fear. Just like she was feeling now.

She gathered herself quickly, and only one thing made sense. "If he takes Dillon, I'll never see him again." She held out her left hand. "Please have Levi remove this."

Quinn seemed taken aback. "What for?"

"I don't have many options. I'll have to take Dillon and run."

His eyes widened. "What about trusting me?"

She closed her own eyes as a pain shot through her. "I can't lose my baby."

He reached out, undid the clasp and removed the bracelet.

"How did you do that?" she gasped. "I thought it needed to be cut or something."

He shook his head. "No. It's just a bracelet."

"What?"

"A trick I played on the judge and the Rutherfords so you could have time alone with Dillon."

"But—but Levi had a map and..."

"GPS gadget to make it look real. You were free to run at any time, but you didn't. Now you can." He pushed himself to his feet. "Once you do that, you'll seal your fate. If they catch you, you'll never see your son again and you'll go to jail. That would devastate Carin and Ona. But it's your choice."

Her emotions were waffling and precariously close to snapping. But through the turmoil in her mind she heard the hurt in his voice, and that got to her. He'd risked his life to save hers in the creek, and now she had to repay the favor. She had to risk her very life to believe in him. To trust him.

"This isn't easy," she whispered. "I'm so afraid...."

"I know you are. I am, too." He leaned back against the desk and folded his arms across his chest. "Phil wanted me to tell you something else that might make this easier for you."

"What?" The cotton swelled in her throat.

"He said to tell Roslyn if she wants to spend Christmas with her son, she knows how to make that happen. Going back to Phil would solve your problem."

Her eyes shot to his. "Are you serious?"

He shrugged.

She stood on shaky legs, her strength returning full force. "I would never ever go back to that bastard."

"Then is it so hard to trust me?"

Without having to think about it she whispered, "No." They'd been on opposite sides for so long, but fear couldn't block what she felt for him. Fear couldn't block that she needed him. Fear couldn't block that once again he'd risked everything for her. "You might have a problem keeping me sane, though." She tilted her head. "You see, I have some of Ona's genes."

To keep from touching her, Quinn walked back around the desk. It would be so easy to take her into his arms and forget the giant elephant in the room—the Rutherfords. Quinn's and Britt's future, if they had one, had to wait. He had to focus all his attention on Phil.

He pulled a legal pad out of a drawer. "The only way to stop all this is to prove Phil is a user."

"What can I do?"

That's what he wanted—her full cooperation.

He sat down. "In the six months you were married to him, did you see any signs?"

"No." She resumed her seat. "That's why it was such a shock. But he did have a lot of mood swings that sometimes frightened me."

Quinn twisted the pen between his fingers. "Could he have just been experimenting that day because he was upset with you?"

"I don't think so. The woman said something like 'Get rid of your wife or I'm not coming back again.' It sounded as if she'd been in my bed before."

"Did you get a name?"

"Phil kept saying 'Shut up, Candy.'"

"Had you seen her before?"

Britt shook her head.

"Think, Britt. I need something. Did you notice anything about the room that was different?"

"I was only there a minute." She closed her eyes. "The bed was in disarray and on the nightstand were a couple of plastic packets of brownish stuff. A syringe was there, too. And a little square of purple that looked like matches from a bar."

"Was there any wording on it?"

"Black lines weaved through the purple and there was *e s* something. I didn't stick around to read the rest."

Quinn scribbled that on the pad. "Do you know of any bars Phil liked to frequent?"

"I thought he liked the country club where he plays golf. But I really never knew him."

Quinn watched the expression on her face and it twisted his gut. He wanted to give her some reassurance, but again he had no guarantees.

"This should help some." He tapped the pen on the pad. "Levi's good at taking one clue and uncovering evidence."

"How much time do we have?"

Quinn lifted his shoulders. "I have someone watching the condo. If he leaves with Dillon, I'll know." He stared at the pen. "But I don't look for him to make a move until next Friday. He's waiting to see how badly you want to keep your son." Quinn looked at her when he said the last.

She visibly trembled, her eyes holding his. "I trust you. I wish I had from the start."

His heart wobbled. "Thank you. This has been a difficult situation. I wanted to tell you about the file, but I was still hanging on to my ethics. Now it doesn't even matter. Philip Sr. has threatened to have me disbarred."

"Can he do that?"

"Oh, yeah. I left ethics behind the moment I looked into your dark eyes."

She bit her lip. "I…"

"You don't have to say anything. Let's concentrate on Dillon."

She picked up the bracelet, which he'd placed on the desk. "I believe this belongs to me."

He lifted an eyebrow at that. Why did she want it? He hoped it was for the reason he thought.

She reached for her coat. "Now I'm going to go visit Mona and—"

"I've already apprised her of the situation."

"Oh, good, then I'll just touch base with her." She picked up her purse and walked from the room with smooth elegant strides, her courage firmly in place. At the door, she said, "I'll wait to hear from you."

As she left, Quinn ran his hands over his face. He couldn't let her down. That miracle was within his reach. He just had to find it. And that might prove the biggest challenge of his law career.

Chapter Seventeen

Quinn knew he had a few days, and each hour counted. His sister called about Christmas, and with everything going on it had completely slipped his mind. He had to give Peyton some details to make her understand. She was outraged at the Rutherfords, but he assured her he was doing his best to rectify the situation. Why he might miss the family Christmas took a lot more explaining.

Finally, he told her he would try to make it. That was the best he could do. When he got off the phone, he went online and ordered gifts for the family, paying the extra postage to have them delivered to Peyton's house fully wrapped by Christmas Eve.

Levi was working on the lead Britt had given them. They finally concluded *e s* stood for an escort service, one that Phil probably frequented often. Levi was working overtime trying to locate the service Phil used.

Quinn spent his time staking out Phil's condo. Levi's sidekick, Butch, relieved him so he could catch a few hours sleep, shower and change. Quinn wanted someone watching the place at all times. The moment Phil left with Dillon, he had to know. He wasn't sure about the plan if that happened, but Phil wasn't getting on a plane with Dillon. That Quinn knew for sure.

Levi finally located the escort service with a girl named Candy. He was having a meeting with her now— as a client. If Quinn was in a laughing mood, he'd find that funny. But Levi would take it as far as he had to to get the information they needed.

It was early in the morning on Christmas Eve and the neighborhood was quiet. All the houses and condos were decorated for the big day, but a lot of people had gone out of town for the holiday. Mostly retired people lived in the exclusive condos, so no children were out in the street playing.

To remain inconspicuous, Quinn had rented a vacant condo across the street. He had to sign a six-month lease to get the place, but the money was a minor issue and it had a perfect view of Phil's. Quinn rented a car so Phil wouldn't recognize his Mercedes parked in the garage. From the master bedroom he could see Phil's driveway. No one seemed to notice him or Butch coming or going. He sat in a straight-backed chair and watched.

A white Corvette drove into Phil's driveway. Jenna Lawson slid out and ran inside, carrying a small suitcase. She didn't knock or use a key, so obviously the door was open. Something was about to happen. Quinn didn't take his eyes off the place. In his peripheral vision he saw a large city bus stop at the end of the street. He hadn't realized the buses ran in this area. Stretching his shoulders, he eased the tired muscles and kept waiting. And waiting for Levi to call.

Sometimes it was hard staying awake, but Quinn forced himself to. The thermos of black coffee helped. He was taking a swig when something caught his eye. He blinked, not believing what he was seeing. Bonnie and Clyde were walking down the sidewalk, straight to Phil's door. Damn it! What were they up to?

He reached for his cell and punched in Britt's number. "Get over to Phil's right away. Ona's here," he said, before she could get in a word.

"Damn it!" he cursed, leaping out of the chair and running down the stairs. Ona and Enzo had just blown everything to hell. He didn't know how he was going to explain his presence, but he had no choice but to get them out of there.

He went out the back way, crossed the street farther down and ran like hell toward Phil's. When he was about twenty feet away, Phil opened the door.

"What the hell do you want?"

"I brought my great-grandson a gift for Christmas," Ona replied.

"And you think I'm going to let you give it to him?"

"Why not? You got somethin' to hide?"

"Go away," Phil shouted, and moved to close the door. But Ona was ready for him. She pushed past him, using her big purse as a shield. Enzo was on her heels.

"Get out of my house," Phil shouted. "Or I'm calling the cops."

Quinn rushed in and all eyes turned to him.

"Lookie, Enzo, Mr. Hotshot has arrived."

"Get them out of here," Phil growled. Quinn noticed he had on a robe and pajamas.

"I'm not going anywhere until I see my great-grand-son," Ona threatened, clutching a bag in one hand and her purse in the other.

"You know," Enzo said to Phil, "I have connections to the mob, and with one phone call I can have you taken out like yesterday's rotten garbage."

"You're a senile old man with one foot in the grave," Phil told him.

Enzo swung his cane and hit him on his kneecap, wood hitting bone with a sharp crack. Phil grabbed his leg, screaming, "You son of a bitch. You son of a bitch!"

Quinn felt as if he was in a comedy skit, especially when Jenna came running in wearing a short, silky, black negligee. "What's going on in here?" She glanced around. "Phil, who are these people?"

"Call the cops," Phil moaned, holding his leg.

"I don't think you want to do that," Quinn said, trying to calm things down.

Undeterred by Phil's threat, Ona gave Jenna the once-over and said, "Lookie, Enzo, here's a stripper for you."

"I'm not a stripper," Jenna declared hotly, trying to cover her breasts, which were spilling out of her gown.

"Sure look like one, honey."

"Nah, Ona, she's too skinny," Enzo piped.

"I'm not skinny!" Jenna turned on him.

Phil straightened, his face dark. "Quinn, you better get them out of here now."

Before Quinn could move or speak, Britt appeared in the doorway, out of breath. Phil's eyes swung to her and his face cleared. This was what he was waiting for, Quinn thought.

As well as jeans and dress boots, she wore a red knit top covered with a brown corduroy jacket. Her hair was down, framing her beautiful face. Her dark eyes flashed with irritation. She took in the situation with one glance. "Let's go, Onnie, Enzo."

"Sorry, my pretty, I'm not going anywhere until I see Dillon. I have his Christmas gift." Ona held up the bag.

Quinn could see Britt was calculating her next move. He could almost read her mind. She had nothing to lose. "Well, then. Let's give it to him."

"I don't think so," Phil said in a threatening voice.

Jenna moved closer to him, linking her arm through his. "For heaven sakes, Phil, it's Christmas."

That put Phil in a difficult situation—look bad in front of his girlfriend or let Britt and Ona see Dillon? But Britt didn't give him time to make up his mind. She took her grandmother's arm and headed for the stairs.

And Phil did nothing.

Silence enveloped the four people standing in the entry. Finally, Enzo looked at Phil. "You got any beer?"

"Go to hell," Phil snapped, and walked into the living area.

"Guess that means no," Enzo remarked.

Quinn frowned at the old man, and then wanted to laugh. But it wasn't a day for laughing.

Britt hugged, kissed and touched her little boy. His bubbles of delight melted her heart. "Mommy loves you, Dilly bear." Britt was grateful for this moment on Christmas Eve with her son.

Onnie pulled a big bag from her purse. "Enough of that. Let's put Dillon in here and get the hell out."

"What?" Britt stopped bouncing her baby.

"That's what Enzo and me planned. We'd put the baby in here—it's not plastic if that's what you're worried about. We'll go out the back way. That bastard will never know and Dillon will be with us for Christmas."

Britt gave Dillon a long kiss and placed him in his bed. "We're not putting Dillon in anything. We're not stealing him. That makes us criminals. I'm getting him back the legal way." Quinn was right. She had to trust him. Running away with Dillon was not an option. She could clearly see that. "Give Dillon your gift."

"I didn't bring a gift." Onnie scrunched up her face. "Aren't you listening? We plan to take him."

Britt groaned. "What were you going to do about the nanny?"

"That skinny thing? She wouldn't be a problem."

"Let's go, Onnie." Britt turned her grandmother toward the door. "This little stunt is over."

"You're getting more and more like your mother," Onnie grumbled.

"Thank you." She stopped at the door and blew Dillon a kiss. He whined and she steeled herself to go. "Mommy will see you soon," she called, closing the door and trying very hard not to cry.

Debi was in the hall and went back in.

Britt forced herself to walk away, though all she could think was this might be the last time she'd see her son.

Her stomach cramped, but she was trusting Quinn with everything in her.

When they reached the bottom of the stairs, Quinn and Enzo were still in the foyer. Phil and his girlfriend were sitting in the living room. When Phil saw her, he got up and came forward. Britt had to force herself to face him.

"I hope you enjoyed your visit, Roslyn, because it will be your last for a while."

Something in the tone of his voice, or maybe something about her kick-butt grandmother's attitude, had her stepping closer to him. She'd had it. She wasn't going to cry or beg. She was going to fight.

"I thought I really loved you once, but you shattered every illusion I had about love. What type of man would take a child from his mother? Only the very worst kind, and you've proved it over and over again."

His face blanched and she knew she'd hit a nerve. She could feel Quinn's presence to her right and it gave her the courage to say what she had to. "How you can listen to your own son cry so heartbreakingly for his mother, and do nothing, is beyond me. I guess it shows where your priorities are. They've never been with Dillon or me. You're only concerned about yourself."

She drew a quick breath. "And to use your own son as bait to lure me back is beyond contempt."

"What?" Phil's girlfriend cried, but Britt ignored her.

"I will never come back to you, so do your evil best with threats of keeping Dillon from me. Bribe all the judges you need to, but wherever you go I will find you. I'll call newspapers, TV stations, radio stations, and give interviews exposing you as the bastard you are. You will never keep my son. That's a promise." She turned and walked from the condo with her dignity intact.

Outside, she clung to her grandmother. "You told him, my pretty." Onnie stroked her hair.

Britt caught Quinn's concerned gaze and she went to him. "Do you have anything?"

"Not yet," he told her, still blown away by her courage. Phil had looked like a battered fighter brought down by a surprise opponent. "Levi has located the hooker Phil was with the day you found him. I'm hoping to hear something shortly."

"Call me when you do." She leaned in close. "Now I have to take Bonnie and Clyde home and once again try to explain this to my mother."

He wanted to wrap his arms around her and never let her go. Instead, he reached for her hand, twisting the bracelet she'd put back on. When he felt her cold fingers, he realized just how afraid she was. "You were awesome. Don't lose that strength."

"It's Christmas Eve," she murmured in a small voice, and leaned against him. His heart lurched at her sadness. *I love you.* But he couldn't say the words. Not now. The cool December breeze blew against them and he kissed the top of her head. She sighed and then went to help Ona and Enzo into her car.

He lifted a hand in goodbye and strolled down the walk with a heart as heavy as a bowling ball. Getting to his rented condo proved to be tricky. Several people passing by gave him odd glances, so he hurried around the back, slipping in without Phil noticing or anyone calling the cops. Not that Rutherford was looking. Quinn suspected the man had his hands full trying to explain Britt's remark about luring her back. Jenna had not been pleased.

The condo was empty, but Quinn kept food in the refrigerator. He grabbed a soft drink and a bag of nuts and went back to his post. Again everything was quiet.

Quinn pulled out his phone and sent a text message to Levi. It was one word: *hurry*. He didn't understand what was taking so damn long. He stretched and walked around the room, keeping his eyes on Phil's.

The day dragged. The sky grew cloudy and the wind rattled through the large oak outside the window. Quinn could hear a limb brushing against the roof. The swishing sound helped count away the time.

Sitting down again, he thought this was a hell of a way to spend Christmas Eve. And his sister was probably so pissed she was never going to speak to him again. His mother…well, he'd just as soon not think about that.

His cell buzzed and he yanked it out of his pocket. He cursed when he saw the name. Deidre.

He clicked on, knowing she'd keep trying if he didn't. "Hello."

"Hi, Quinn. Are you busy?"

"Yes."

"I'm at my dad's and I'm bored out of my mind. Let's go to a nightclub or something."

She didn't even hear what he'd said. He took a long, hard breath. "Deidre, please don't call me again. It's over, and you might think about spending some time with your father. It's Christmas Eve."

There was a long pause. "Are you kidding?"

"No."

Another long pause, as if she was trying to figure out why he'd made such a suggestion. "Have you found someone else?"

"Yes. Have a Merry Christmas." He clicked off and slipped the phone into his shirt pocket. He'd found the most wonderful woman, one he'd give his life for. That's why he was sitting in an empty condo staring out a window when he should be celebrating with his family.

Suddenly his whole world was Britt and Dillon.

They were his family.

For the first time he wondered if Britt felt the same way.

By midafternoon Quinn grew weary of waiting for something to happen. There was no activity at Phil's. If they were leaving for the holiday, there were no signs.

Where in the hell was Levi? He sent another text, wanting to throw the phone out the window. Instead, he stood and stretched again, hating the waiting. Suddenly the front door was flung open and Jenna ran to her car, buttoning her blouse, tears streaming down her face. The Corvette revved up and spun out of the driveway, tires squealing.

What was that about? Obviously, they'd had a big argument. Quinn resumed his seat, his eyes glued to Phil's. About thirty minutes later, the garage door went up and he put luggage into the backseat of the car. The nanny came out and placed baby things inside, and then the door went down.

Phil was getting ready to leave, so why didn't he leave the door up? That puzzled Quinn. He was ready to sprint downstairs as soon as Phil got into his car with Dillon. But it didn't happen. Quinn kept waiting.

He was so engrossed with the scene that he didn't hear Levi come in. He jumped straight up when the P.I. spoke.

"Where in the hell have you been? I've sent a dozen messages." Quinn's voice was sharp with frustration.

Levi pulled up the extra chair. "Calm down. This wasn't easy."

Quinn blew out a breath and plopped back into his seat. "What happened?"

"I didn't want to spook 'em so I had to appear as a normal customer."

"You didn't...?" Quinn lifted an eyebrow.

"Hell, no. I'm not sleeping with a hooker, not even for you." Levi stretched out his legs. "Seems Candy is very busy, and I had to wait. And the whole time the madam was shoving all these other women at me. I couldn't call or text because they were watching me like a hawk. The business is exclusive, very private, very confidential. I only got in by using Phil's name."

"And?"

"When I finally got to see her, I told her I wanted what Phil got because he always bragged about her. She was leery at first and had to go talk to the madam. What it comes down to is sex and drugs. Phil's preference is heroin at a whopping cost of five grand. I told her no way and got the hell out of there."

Suddenly, Quinn's chest felt lighter. "You have this on tape, right?"

"Damn straight. I had to hide the mic in my hat but I got every word she said."

Quinn reached for his jacket on the back of his chair. "I'm going to call Judge Norcutt. You keep an eye on the place. Phil put luggage in his car a little while..." His voice trailed off as he saw the nanny come out, get in her car and drive away.

"What the hell?" Quinn ran a hand through his hair. "Why is she leaving?"

"There are two nannies," Levi replied. "Maybe the other one is on the way."

Quinn shook his head. "Something's not right. I don't like Dillon being in the house without the nanny."

"Relax," Levi advised. "Let's see what happens."

Quinn eased back into his chair, knowing Phil wouldn't physically harm his own son. In the meantime Quinn tried the judge's number and was told she wasn't taking calls until after the holidays. Damn it! He'd have to find a way around that.

Darkness crawled in like a lazy cat settling over the neighborhood. A light was on downstairs and one upstairs. Otherwise there was no activity at Phil's. No other nanny arrived and Phil didn't get in his car and leave.

Quinn stood. "I'm going over there. Something's wrong." He could feel it in his gut.

"I'm right behind you," Levi said. "But first I'm calling the police so we do everything legally."

When they reached the front door, a police car drove up. Quinn rang the bell. No response. He called on his cell. No one answered.

"A baby's inside and no one's responding," Quinn told the officers.

"Let me call my supervisor." One officer stepped away to talk on his phone. The other one searched around outside, looking for a way in.

"We have permission to kick in the door." The officer put away his phone. And the two uniformed men gave it their best shot, but the door was strong and heavy. Quinn and Levi gave them a hand and it took the strength of all four men to bring the door down.

Quinn was the first inside. He stopped short in the living room. Phil lay on the sofa, a needle stuck in his arm.

"Oh, my God!" Quinn didn't know if he was dead or alive.

Chapter Eighteen

"Dillon!"

Quinn shot up the stairs as an officer called for an ambulance. When he reached the landing, he heard loud wails, and bolted through the nursery door. Dillon stood up in his crib, holding on to the railing, crying his little heart out.

"Hey, buddy." Quinn lifted him out and Dillon quieted down, rubbing his wet eyes. Quinn realized that wasn't the only thing wet. Dillon needed a diaper change. Grabbing a clean one from a bag on the end of the crib, he laid Dillon in the bed and removed the soiled diaper and his all-in-one pajamas.

"Ma-ma-ma-ma," Dillon cooed as Quinn scooted the fresh diaper beneath him.

"Bear with me, buddy. I'm new at this." Oh, the diaper had tabs. How efficient. All the time he dressed Dillon he tried not to think about the situation downstairs. How could Phil do that? And why would he?

"Ma-ma-ma-ma." Dillon waved his arms around.

"I'm taking you to her just as soon as I can." He gathered Dillon, freshly dressed, into his arms just as a middle-aged woman with a large bag entered.

"I'm Gina Hardy with Child Protective Service. I'm here to take the boy."

"No," Quinn said, wondering where in the hell she'd come from so quickly. But then he remembered CPS was always notified when a child was involved. "He has a mother who's waiting for him."

"Sorry." She shook her head. "Phil Rutherford has custody, and until I get a court order saying otherwise the baby goes with me."

"Listen, this child needs to be with his mother. It's Christmas."

"You think I want to be working on Christmas?" She lifted an eyebrow. "If I don't follow the rules, I could lose my job."

Quinn knew about the rules. He was a lawyer. Reluctantly, he handed over Dillon. "Where can I reach you? I'll be picking him up as soon as possible."

While juggling Dillon, she pulled out a card from her coat pocket. "It's Christmas Eve. You're not going to get a judge tonight or tomorrow."

"Don't bet on it, Ms. Hardy." He kissed Dillon's head. "Hang tight, little one, you're going home for Christmas."

Placing Dillon in his bed, she said, "Consider yourself a miracle worker, huh?"

"No. Just a damn good lawyer."

"Heaven help us." She started to collect Dillon's things.

Quinn let that slide and looked at the card. "You can be reached at this number at all times?"

"Yes," she replied, taking the card and turning it over. "That's my address. He'll have to stay with me until after Christmas. Then I'll find a foster home for him."

"Don't bother." Quinn swung toward the door. "I'll see you later."

"Yeah, right…" Her words followed him out the door.

Downstairs, Phil was being wheeled out of the condo on a stretcher. "Is he alive?" Quinn asked Levi.

"The paramedic found a pulse and they're getting him to an E.R."

Quinn ran both hands through his hair. "Why did he do something like that with Dillon right upstairs?"

"You can never tell with a drug user," Levi said. "They're unpredictable."

"Mr. Ross."

Quinn turned to an officer, who had a lot of questions. Quinn told him everything he knew about Jenna and the nanny leaving, and what Levi had uncovered about Candy. The officer wrote everything down and they moved out of the way for the crime unit to gather evidence.

"If that's it for the night—" Levi straightened his hat "—I'm going home. Someone told me it was Christmas."

"Yep. It's slipping right by us," Quinn remarked.

"Call if you need anything."

"I'm going to break down a judge's door on Christmas Eve. Want to come with me?"

"I'll pass," Levi replied as they walked outside into the cool night air. "But call if you need me to get you out of jail."

Quinn forced a smile. "Thanks for all your help."

"Anytime." Levi strolled across the street to his truck, parked in the garage of the condo.

Quinn drew a hard breath. The wind now rustled through the oaks with a distant, chilling sound that went right through him. What a hell of a way to spend Christmas. He wanted to call Britt, just to hear her voice, but he had to tell her this kind of news in person. And he couldn't tell her CPS had Dillon. That would be too painful. He wouldn't call until he had good news.

Pulling out his cell, he punched in Philip's number. He

had no idea if the man was in Austin or Colorado, but he had to know about his son.

"What do you want, Quinn?" The gruff voice came in clearly. "You're not getting any favors from me."

Quinn ignored the tone. "It's about Phil."

"What about him? Is he with you? He was supposed to have been here three hours ago."

"Where are you?"

"At my house in Rob Roy in Austin. My wife's kids are here for Christmas and we're waiting on Phil. He won't answer his damn phone. You better not have pulled anything."

So Phil wasn't going out of town, just to his father's. It was all a ruse to get Britt to capitulate.

"Phil's had an accident." Quinn didn't know how else to say it. "He's in the E.R. at Saint David's. You need to get there as soon as you can."

"What kind of accident?"

"Just get there." Quinn clicked off, not willing to say anything else. Philip wouldn't believe him, anyway. He had to find out for himself.

Quinn ran across the street and grabbed his briefcase out of his car. Standing at the large island in the kitchen at the condo, he withdrew papers and went over them, writing in dates. He'd had the papers drawn up for days and now he was going to use them.

When he'd finished, he called the judge again, but got the same annoying message. He then called Denise. She knew everything about the lawyers and judges in Austin. Within minutes he had the good judge's home address.

He closed his briefcase, locked the condo and headed for his car. Backing out, he took a last look at Phil's house. A sadness pulsed inside him and he wondered whether, if he had gone over sooner, he would have been able to stop him. Probably not. Quinn had a feeling Phil was lost the day he'd started using heroin. Still, it wasn't an easy thing to deal with. Quinn hoped he'd make it.

As he drove, Quinn couldn't stop thinking about Phil, and he found himself heading to the hospital. An antiseptic smell greeted him as he walked though the sliding doors. Nurses and doctors hurried here and there, and Quinn moved out of their way.

He spotted Philip and several family members he didn't recognize waiting in a secluded area. When Philip spotted him, he hurried over.

"How's Phil?"

"He died a little while ago," Philip said without emotion, without one ounce of sadness.

"I'm sorry." Quinn felt a tightness in his chest.

"You tried to tell me and I wouldn't listen."

"You had no idea?"

"He had some problems in college, but I thought that was all behind him." The man's voice cracked, the first sign he was holding everything inside like the strong man he was supposed to be. "The girlfriend, whatever her name is, said they started doing drugs in the early afternoon, but Phil wouldn't stop. He said he wanted to take the edge off. He was meeting my new wife and her two kids for the first time. The son works in the U.S. Attorney General's office and the daughter is a special prosecutor for the FBI. Both Harvard graduates. Both outstanding young people. I told Phil he'd better get his act together. I guess I pushed too hard." Philip blinked as if he had something in his eye. "The girlfriend said she tried to get him to stop, and he hit her. She left. The nanny said they packed everything in the car, ready to leave, and then Phil changed his mind. When she asked questions, he ordered her out. I guess he was bent on a night of destruction."

"With his son upstairs."

"Yeah." Philip wiped a hand across his face. "I'm sorry about that."

The man didn't ask about Dillon or where he was. That irked Quinn. "A CPS worker took Dillon. I'm on my way to Judge Norcutt to get a court order to return the boy to his mother."

Philip only nodded.

"Please don't throw up any roadblocks, because you don't want to meet me in court on this one. I might get a reprimand or have my license revoked by the Texas Bar, but—"

Philip held up a hand. "I'm not doing anything about you or the boy. I don't have any strength left." He glanced back at the waiting group. "Now I have to try and explain this horrendous night to my new family."

That seemed to be the man's top priority, but Quinn wanted to be clear. "Dillon stays with his mother…permanently."

"Yes…yes."

Quinn watched a man he'd once idolized, and thought how money and power could destroy character, morals and families. Philip had aged ten years in the last few minutes. His face was haggard, his vision dull, and he would spend the rest of his life wondering what he could have done differently to save his son.

"I am sorry about Phil," was all Quinn could say.

"Thank you. I know you mean that."

"Yes, sir." Quinn walked away, hoping that Philip's new family could help him find a measure of peace.

Twenty minutes later he knocked on the judge's door. A young woman in her thirties opened it.

"Quentin Ross to see Judge Norcutt," he said without preamble.

"I'm sorry. She's not seeing anyone but family to-night."

Quinn stepped into the foyer without an invitation. Voices and laughter could be heard in another room. "Tell her or I'm interrupting the party."

The woman scowled at him, but turned and went into a room on the left. In a minute the judge came out, dressed in a white gown and heels. She looked different than the stern official he was used to.

"What is this, Mr. Ross? I resent you interrupting my evening."

"Phil Rutherford died of a heroin overdose tonight." He didn't feel the need to sugarcoat it.

"What?" She sank into a high-back chair next to a small entry table.

He laid the custody papers on the table next to her. "CPS took Dillon Rutherford. All I need from you is your signature on this order returning full custody of Dillon to his mother."

"Of course. I'm so sorry."

He handed her a pen, not willing to be lenient. "You should be. You took a baby away from a loving mother and put him in the hands of a drug addict."

She scribbled her name in the appropriate places and stood. "I made the best call I could with the evidence I had. And you, Mr. Ross, were the Rutherfords' attorney."

He picked up the papers. "Not by choice. But yes, ma'am, there's enough blame to go around." He turned toward the door. "Have a nice Christmas."

In his car, he glanced at his watch. Eleven o'clock. He hoped Ms. Hardy was still up.

Britt sat on the sofa in the dark with only the Christmas tree lights on, her cell clutched in her hand. Why hadn't Quinn called? What had happened? The questions went round and round in her brain like naughty children on a merry-go-round.

She stretched out and rested her head on a cushion. Dillon's toys were under the tree waiting for him. But would he ever open them? A sob wedged in her throat and she swallowed.

Quinn, please call.

No news was good news, she kept telling herself.

Flipping onto her side, she forced herself to think about something else. Her mother had wanted to spend the night, but Britt made her and Onnie go home. She planned to leave early in the morning to spend Christmas with them. Tonight she had to stay in Austin so she'd know if Phil had taken Dillon out of the state.

Quinn would call.

She just had to wait.

Strangely, her mother wasn't angry with Onnie for pulling another stunt. Mainly because it had given Britt a chance to see Dillon on Christmas Eve. Carin had said that if she had known what Onnie was going to do, she would have helped her. They laughed about that. Britt and Carin agreed that they were going to be more lenient with Onnie, and maybe, just maybe, she wouldn't feel the need to pull such stunts. Knowing Onnie, though, she would always keep their lives interesting.

Britt went into the bedroom and grabbed Quinn's pillow. She still hadn't washed the pillowcase. It reminded her of him. Taking it back to the sofa, she curled up with it. She breathed in his manly scent and drifted off to sleep.

The faint ringing of a doorbell woke her. She sat up, pushing her hair out of her eyes. *Was that...?* The doorbell rang again. *It was.* She shot to the entry and glanced through the peephole, and her heart hammered loudly in her ears. "Oh, my. Oh, my." She couldn't get the door opened fast enough.

Quinn, looking a little ragged and tired, but gorgeous, stood there holding the most beautiful sight in the world. Her baby—Dillon—was asleep on his shoulder.

"Oh, my baby." She scooped him out of Quinn's arms and they walked into the apartment. Britt sat on the sofa, smoothing Dillon's hair and loving the feel of him.

"What happened?" she asked.

Quinn took a long breath and told her a story that sent chills up her spine.

"He's…he's dead?" She could hardly say the words.

"Yes. You were right all along. He's been doing drugs for a long time. The judge awarded you full custody of Dillon, so you don't have to worry anymore."

Britt's eyes met Quinn's in the light from the tree. "Thank you for being there for Dillon. And for me."

Quinn glanced at the tree. "Dillon is where he should be, home with you and ready for Christmas."

"I'll never be able to thank you enough."

"Just be happy."

She kissed Dillon's cheek. "When you rescued me from the flooding creek, I thought of you as my hero." Her gaze caught his. "You're always going to be my hero. My Christmas hero."

He bent down and touched her lips with his. "Merry Christmas," he whispered.

Before she could respond, Dillon stirred and rubbed his eyes, whining.

"Time to put Dilly bear to bed." She stood, rubbing her son's back. "It's going to feel so good to see him back in his crib. Thank you." She smiled at Quinn and walked into the bedroom.

She changed Dillon's diaper and tucked him in, staring at her Christmas miracle. All because of Quinn. Now she just wanted him to hold her forever. She hurried back into the living room and stopped short. Quinn wasn't there. He wasn't in the kitchen. He was gone.

Her heart sank. Why had he left? He was tired, she knew. He'd been watching Phil's condo for days. Wrapping her arms around her waist, she sat on the sofa again. What a horrendous night, and Quinn had been there to see it all. That had to have been mentally and physically draining. And he had done it all for her.

Phil was dead. That took some getting used to. Although she had grown to despise him, she had also loved him once, and felt a deep sadness for the life he'd thrown away. She would remember the Phil who'd been fun, generous and full of dreams when she'd first met him. That would be the man she'd tell Dillon about.

The nightmare was over. But there was still an emptiness inside her. She had her son. She had her life back.

But she didn't have Quinn.

The Christmas lights blinked at her. Quinn had been working around the clock on her case. He probably hadn't had time to put up a tree.

Without thinking about it, and going with her heart, she went into the utility room for a plastic container and began to take down her tree.

Quinn was dog tired when he let himself into his house. He didn't bother turning on any lights as he made his way to his study. Sinking into his leather chair, he ran his hands over his face. What a night. What a horrible, horrible night. The only light shining through was that Britt and Dillon were back together. Their Christmas would be complete.

He'd wanted to stay at her place tonight, but too much had happened for him to take that leap. They had to adjust to the sadness of the situation and learn to live with it. He'd call her after the holiday, if he lasted that long.

He wanted to offer her the world. She deserved no less after what she'd been through with Phil. Quinn knew he was at the crossroads of his life. His work wasn't exciting or exhilarating anymore. The violence and abuse had taken its toll.

Glancing around the study, he could feel his father's presence. That gentle, soothing nature of his was all around Quinn. As a young man he'd wanted his father to be forceful, dynamic, a take-charge type of person, but he wasn't, so Quinn had emulated men like Philip Rutherford who fit that bill. How wrong he had been! He'd traded gold for fool's gold. And that was never more apparent than tonight.

He picked up a stone from Egypt his dad used as a paperweight. Rubbing his thumb over it, he said, "I'm not cut out to be a cutthroat defense attorney. I'm good at it, but it puts a strain on my heart. You knew it would get to me, didn't you?"

He stood and flexed his stiff shoulders, knowing he had already made a decision about his future. A future that included happiness. And a family.

Heading for the stairs, he decided to shower and catch a few hours sleep before going to Peyton's for Christmas.

As he laid his weary body on the mattress ten minutes later, the doorbell rang. "What the...?"

He grabbed a robe and some warm slippers and made his way to the foyer. Glancing through the glass, he frowned but quickly opened the door. Britt stood there, holding a sleeping Dillon.

"What's wrong?" he asked, pulling them inside out of the cold.

"You left. That's what's wrong," she replied, her eyes

sparkling like stars in a pitch-black sky. "And heroes don't leave."

"What?" He was thrown for a second.

"Heroes don't leave," she repeated.

"They don't?" He felt a grin spreading across his face like butter on a hot biscuit. He was still her hero. That said everything he wanted to hear.

"No," she said huskily. "They ride off into the sunset and live happily ever after."

He stroked her cheek with the back of his hand and loved the way her eyes darkened when he did that. Cupping her face, he kissed her with all the fire and love inside him. "I love you, Britt Davis," he said against her trembling lips. "I just thought it was too soon, with everything that had happened."

"I love you, too," she whispered back, and the words had never sounded so heartfelt, so everlasting. "I can't get through this night without you." She rested her forehead against his chin, clutching Dillon in her arms. "Would you please get Dillon's Pack 'n Play out of the car so I can kiss you like there's no tomorrow?"

"Yes, ma'am. Hold that thought...."

It took him a few minutes to get the thing out of the trunk, and he hurried back to her. Setting it up by the gas fireplace, he said, "There's a tree and presents jammed into the backseat of your car."

She kissed Dillon and laid him in the bed, tucking a blanket around him. The baby never moved or made a sound. "Of course, we can't have Christmas without a tree and gifts for Dillon."

"Did you take down your tree?" He turned on the fire and it roared to life.

She straightened, her eyes twinkling. "Crazy, huh?"

He locked his hands behind her back and whirled her onto the sofa. "Crazy and wonderful. Just like you."

He took her lips once again and she wrapped her arms around him, and he lost himself in her sweetness, her love and the heated emotions they'd shared. Her fingers slipped inside his robe to his chest, and his body tightened with uncontrollable need. He caressed her hand. "I was feeling so down, but now I'm on top of the world."

She kissed his knuckles. "Me, too. Hold me, please."

He gathered her against his chest and stroked her hair.

"I'm going to trust you forever, my hero," she whispered sleepily.

The flickering fire cast a glow over them, and he looked into her eyes and knew he'd found exactly what he'd been searching for—the woman to fill his heart, his life, with love.

"I'm going to love you every day like there's no tomorrow."

She laughed, and the old house seemed to sigh as a new era of Rosses began.

Epilogue

One year later...

Britt straightened an ornament on the eight-foot Douglas fir that stood in front of the French windows looking out into the backyard. Brightly wrapped packages rested beneath the tree. The house was fully decorated, with garlands on the staircase and mantel. Poinsettias added color and the lights sparkled invitingly. They were ready for Christmas.

This year was different.

They were happy, and together.

Last Christmas was a painful memory that time and love had managed to diminish. The past year had been a time of change. A year of healing, discovering new goals and dreams, and living life to the fullest.

She and Quinn had married a month after she'd come to his lovely home in the middle of the night to give him her heart. She never went back to her apartment to live. Their life together had started that moment.

They'd talked about their future, slept in each other's arms and awoke in time to put up the tree before Dillon stirred. They'd embraced change together. Quinn was back in school to get his doctorate so he could teach on the university level. She was in school, too. She was now a mother and a student, and she loved it. Quinn would eventually phase out his law practice and teach full time. But for now he was still helping people who needed him.

She glanced at her watch. He had a meeting with the dean, but he should have been home by now. Where was he? It was Christmas Eve.

Dillon, dressed in his new slacks and white shirt, knelt on the hardwood floor, playing with a train set Quinn had bought him. Quinn had taken him to get his hair cut, and she'd combed it neatly, but knew it wouldn't stay that way long. Dillon was a typical little boy.

He watched the train go round and round, and then stopped it and started it again, over and over. Content. Happy. That's what she wanted for her son.

The first couple of months after Phil's death had been hard on Dillon. He'd cried if Britt was out of his sight. He was fussy and threw temper tantrums. Young as he was, he knew something was wrong in his world.

Quinn made the difference. The two bonded immediately, and Dillon didn't cry if she left him with Quinn. Gradually, Dillon became more and more secure, and today he was a completely different child. She would probably always blame herself that her baby had to go through such trauma. But she vowed from here on his life would be as idyllic as she could make it.

A car engine purred in the driveway. Dillon's head shot up. "Dad-dy," he shouted, and was off and running for the back door.

Britt followed more slowly. Quinn had adopted Dillon. They kept waiting for Philip to throw a wrench in the works, but they never heard a word from him. He'd sold the Rutherford firm to his partners, and he'd also sold Phil's condo and the house in Rob Roy, moving to

Colorado with his new family. Quinn said that he didn't think the man would ever return to Austin.

Dillon would grow up with a father who loved him and who Dillon adored. Britt would tell him about his real father only if he asked. Now he was Dillon Ross to the world. She was grateful for that.

She stopped short in the kitchen. Quinn squatted with Dillon in one arm and a dog that looked like a Jack Russell terrier in the other.

"Mommy, doggie," Dillon said, pointing to the dog.

"I see."

"Let me explain." Quinn's eyes twinkled as she'd seen them do so many times, and her heart melted. He stood, and his gorgeous blue eyes roamed over her red dress and heels, igniting the flame that always flared between them. "Whoa, are we going somewhere?"

"Don't change the subject."

He wrapped an arm around her waist and tugged her to him. Her body welded to every strong masculine line of his. "This feels good," he murmured against her face.

"Mmm. So good." She moved against him and loved his instant response. "But first things first. Why did the dean want to see you?"

"A professor was taken unexpectedly ill, and that's why the dean was in his office on Christmas Eve. He asked me to monitor one of the professor's classes until he returns, sort of an intern thing. I start when the semester begins again, and balance the class with my studies."

She kissed him. "Wonderful."

He rested his forehead against hers. "I'm changing my whole life all because of you, and it feels right. You made me realize that change isn't so bad, especially when it makes me a better person, a better husband and father. You made me want everything out of my reach—home, family and love. With you everything is possible."

"Oh, Quinn." She looked into his eyes. "I love you and I'm so glad I found the perfect hero."

He kissed the tip of her nose.

Dillon giggled, rolling around with the dog on the tiled floor, his shirttail untucked from his pants and his shoes untied. And she'd just dressed him.

"Now about the dog, Mr. Hero."

"Well, the dean had him in his office. He'd bought him for his grandson for Christmas, but the son reminded him that his wife has allergies, so they couldn't accept him. Luckily, the grandson didn't know. The dean was trying to find the dog a good home. We were talking about getting Dillon a puppy, so I offered to take him."

Dillon squealed with delight as the dog licked his face.

"See? They're already friends."

Britt stroked Quinn's face. "You're such a good father."

His eyes darkened. "You keep doing that and we won't get out of the kitchen."

"Mom and Onnie are on the way to spend the night, so they'll be here when Dillon opens his presents in the morning. And they're bringing food."

"Ah, food or passion?" He leaned his head back and pretended to consider it. She laughed.

Quinn loved her musical laugh, and he loved her. She filled all the empty places in his heart and in his life. She made the old house come alive again. She made him feel alive. And loneliness was nowhere in sight.

He kissed her again. "What's the plan with Peyton?"

"We're having a late dinner tomorrow at her house with your mother. It's all arranged." Britt's sexy mouth curved playfully. "I'm a good wife."

"How did I get so lucky?"

"You jumped into a raging creek to save my life. Now you're stuck with me and my dysfunctional family."

He grinned. "I wouldn't have it any other way."

The doorbell rang.

"Nana, Onnie," Dillon cried, and ran for the front door with the dog on his heels.

Quinn cupped Britt's face and kissed her deeply. "Merry Christmas, Mrs. Ross, and may we never come unstuck."

She smiled, and Quinn took her hand and fingered the bracelet that she never took off. They'd weathered the storm. Even though life wouldn't always be smooth, they would continue to find shelter in each other's arms.

* * * * *